"There is no greater tyranny than that which is perpetrated under the shield of the law and in the name of justice."
Montesquieu

BLAINE L. PARDOE

NO GREATER
TYRANNY

BOOK FOUR IN THE
BLUE DAWN SERIES

ISBN-13: 978-1-959677-51-2 (Paperback)
ISBN-13: 978-1-959677-50-5 (eBook)

Published by Defiance Press and Publishing, LLC

Bulk orders of this book may be obtained by contacting Defiance Press and Publishing, LLC at: www.defiancepress.com.

Public Relations Dept. – Defiance Press & Publishing, LLC
281-581-9300
pr@defiancepress.com

Defiance Press & Publishing, LLC
281-581-9300
info@defiancepress.com

ACKNOWLEDGEMENTS

For fans of the Blue Dawn series, thank you for your continued support. There is a grand story arc in play with these novels. I can't tell you how many books it will take to reach the end, but there is, indeed an end. Events like civil wars are not about plots; they are about powerful characters and their exciting and intriguing interactions.

No Greater Tyranny is a book about civil war, foreign enemies, and the depravity of big government. It is designed to make you think, to get a little frustrated, even angry. A good novel should engage and fire up its readers. Fiction is supposed to tap passions and engage a reader. Hopefully you will ask, "What freedoms do I cherish most? What would be my tipping point if those rights were to be taken from me?"

DEDICATION

To my wife Cyndi who keeps asking, "Where are you going with this next?" Hold my beer babe, I've got this.

This book is also dedicated to the Mihaleks, Chad, Claire, Gavin and Bennett. Chad is a real life Oklahoma National Guard warrior who has fought for our nation and continues to do so. Also to the Hickey's—Jack (the real-life Jack), Tracy, Gary, and Murphy.

THE KEY CHARACTERS

Alex. Short for Alexandria (no last name given). Former Congresswoman from New York, she sits on the Ruling Council and commands the National Security Force (NSF) as its Secretary. She removed her opposition and folded the Social Enforcers into the NSF. She is the Newmerica Vice President-Elect.

Randy Birdsell. Leader of the Sons of Liberty (SOL) in New Hampshire.

Trudy Ford. Member of the Sons of Liberty (SOL) from the Upper Peninsula of Michigan.

Andy Forest. Andy's father was a member of the Sons of Liberty (SOL), and Andy was instrumental in recovering the original copy of the Constitution and Declaration of Independence.

Arthur Forrest. Andy's father and a persecuted professor at the University of Mary Washington. His actions saved the Constitution and Declaration of Independence.

Frank Campbell. Private investigator in Virginia.

Rebecca (Becky) Clarke. The Director of the Truth Reconciliation Committee (TRC) and member of the Ruling Council. Was instrumental in seizing control of Congress during the Liberation.

Travis Cullen. Former Navy SEAL, now a covert operative supporting the American administration.

Jack Desmond. Former Director of the Secret Service and now the American President's Chief of Staff. Jack was instrumental in bringing the former American Vice President to power and for years was the clandestine leader of the Sons of Liberty (SOL).

Lieutenant Duwe. Intelligence officer, New Hampshire National Guard.

Herb Fletcher. The leader of a cell of the Sons of Liberty.

General Hank Griffiths. Commanding General of
the New Hampshire National Guard.

Booker Hickox. Self-proclaimed General of the Free Texas movement.

Miley Hines. Supporter of Free Texas and a musician.

Deja Jordan. A Social Enforcer from Minneapolis.

Charli Kazinski. Current Director of the American Secret Service.
For years she lived as an NSF officer named Angel Frisosky to
avoid detection. She was with the last President when he died.

Caylee Leatrom. Former NSF Operative, she has flipped
sides and now offers her skills to the Americans.
She killed Alex's mother and brother.

Senator Earl Taft Lewis. One of the few surviving
Senators after the Liberation.

Dr. Weber Liu. A deep-planted Chinese agent operating under the
guise of being a professor at the University of Michigan.

Maria Lopez. Sister of Raul Lopez.

Raul Lopez. Former member of the Youth Corps; his murder of a
man led to riots in Detroit. As a member of the Sons of Liberty
(SOL), he liberated the Social Enforcement Camp at Valley Forge.

Aiguo Lung. Chinese spymaster in North America.

Salem Marshall. Self-proclaimed President of Free Texas.

Captain Judy Mercury. Officer in the Texas
National Guard and the American Army.

Tate Palmer. New Hampshire patriot.

Daniel Porter. Former Chairman of the Ruling Council and
the President-Elect of Newmerica. Daniel orchestrated the
overthrow of the government during the Liberation/Fall.

John Quang. Chinese agent.

General Trip Reager. Renowned and scorned for his actions in San Antonio several years back, Reager is a Texan who is loyal to the American cause and is the Commanding General of the American Army.

Kiffin "Kiff" Renner. A government cyber-security specialist and friend of Jack Desmond.

Colonel Dan "The Dancer" Ricketts. Officer in the American Army.

General Hollings Rinehart. Commanding General, Newmerican military forces.

David Steele. Maddie's younger brother.

Grayson Steele. Former conservative member of the Virginia House of Delegates and father of Maddie and David.

Ted (no last name given). Former Texas Senator held prisoner by Newmerica.

Valerie Turner. Former New York City police commissioner, leader of a Sons of Liberty (SOL) cell from New York.

Rita Zhang. NSF Operative.

Hachi Zhou. Wife of Su-Hui, she is an active member in the Sons of Liberty (SOL).

Su-Hui Zhou. Refugee from Taiwan. He is a leader in the Sons of Liberty (SOL).

Ya-ting Zhou. Daughter of Hachi and Su-Hui.

Acronyms:

ADMAX—Administrative Maximum Facility—the Supermax Prison's official designation.

ANTIFA—Acronym for Anti-Fascists. These radicals violently rioted during the summer of 2020 in an effort to influence the presidential election. They evolve into the roles of Social Enforcers in the Newmerican nation.

ATF—Bureau of Alcohol, Tobacco, and Firearms. With the formation of the NSF, this agency is now part of that new organization.

CAP—Combat Air Patrol.

CHOP—Capitol Hill Occupied Protest. The occupation
of Seattle by protesters in 2020.

Fedgov—The Newmerican rebranding of the federal government.

FOIA—Freedom of Information Act.

HE—High Explosives

IED—Improvised Explosive Device.

IWB—The Immigrant Welcoming Bureau formerly Immigration
and Customs Enforcement prior to the Fall.

JCS—The military Joint Chiefs of Staff.

MRE—Meal Ready to Eat

NSF—National Security Force. This is a combination of
all federal and local law enforcement agencies.

SAC—Special Agent in Charge.

SE—Social Enforcement. Groups supporting the
Newmerican government that operate beyond the law,
inflicting their own 'social justice' as they see fit.

SOL—Sons of Liberty. These groups of patriot partisans
fight for the restoration of America.

TOW—A missile type. Tube-Launched, Optically
Tracked, Wireless-Guided.

TRC—Truth Reconciliation Committee. Working with Big Tech and
the mainstream media, the TRC determines what truth is and
what is misinformation. It clears all official stories and either
censors or blocks those that would be considered dangerous.

UP—Upper Peninsula of Michigan.

UVA—the University of Virginia.

PROLOGUE

*"If it is not for the betterment of all, it is
not for the betterment of one."*

Five Years Earlier ...
Ann Arbor, Michigan

D r. Weber Liu watched the television in his modest home and could not help but smile. The White House was ablaze as rioters swarmed over the security fence, looting the icon of America. The camera cut to protesters swarming inside the Capitol as well, tearing down portraits, toppling busts of former presidents. The images of raw violence on the television couldn't be more satisfying to him.

He had known that these 'peaceful protests' were going to be different than those just a week earlier. One ANTIFA leader, Daniel Porter, was coordinating the ANTIFA groups and students—something that had not been done up to that point. Also the students that left from the University of Michigan where he was an adjunct professor, were taking real weapons—homemade mortars and rockets, implements of death and carnage.

He felt a swell of pride at watching the American capital city descend into utter chaos.

For ten years he had been a professor at the University of Michigan. While he technically taught social equity classes, the reality was that he was energizing the students for violence. When he taught, he wove a narrative of the corruption of the United States, how it was built on the exploitation of many minority people. It was a story and the students were more than open to hearing. Their high school teachers had done their job well, convincing their impressionable minds that America was decadent and needed to be 'reset.' All Weber Liu did was confirm what they had already been taught.

Liu loved his own artificial backstory so much that he almost believed it himself. A refugee from Chinese oppression, he claimed to come to America with nothing—his parents having smuggled him out at the age of eighteen. Despite the prevalent racism of the US, he had saved enough money to go to college and eventually earn his doctorate in philosophy, securing himself a teaching position at a prestigious university. Liu told the tale of being oppressed at every turn, yet somehow prevailing. He could speak freely about the horrors of America's systemic racism because he claimed he endured and overcame it. It gave him an aura of credibility that he knew resonated with the students.

As he leaned back in his easy chair, watching the flames lap up into the smoke-filled skies over Washington DC, Liu knew that the nation was at a tipping point. Many would claim that they saw it coming, but few could claim, as he did, that they had influenced it. It wasn't just the instruction of the students ... it was far more. Weber Liu led a network of Chinese agents, who, like himself, worked for the Ministry of State Security.

During the last two elections, their activities had been simply to ramp up tensions between the various factions in the United States. They had done it by planting thousands of memes that twisted facts and were aimed at escalating tensions and hate. Liu had been an advocate of backing the more progressive elements of the American government, so he attacked them most, infuriating them more and making them appear to be victims.

Race had been easy to prey upon. Police shootings, whether warranted or not, were twisted by his network of agents into being racially motivated. The defunding-the-police movement had been supported by his tiny army of social media posters, using thousands of accounts to make sure that certain hot topics trended on Twitter.

Painting the sitting U.S. President as a tool of the Russians had been easy as well. His cyber team had planted bogus reports, fake emails, and even played with the back account transfers to make it appear that the Russians were indeed corrupting the President. For Liu and his Chinese handlers, it was a win-win, smearing the other two superpowers and pitting them against each other.

Liu had provided the students going to the riots in DC with money for their personal riot gear. He contributed to their funds for banners, signs, baseball bats, Kevlar, whatever they needed. Discreet cash inducements to other local universities helped students transition from peaceful protesters to armed rioters. No one questioned where the money came from; the students didn't care. And because it was cash, there was no paper trail that could link it to him. *It is pitiful that these students are so easily manipulated. Their wanton ignorance is a useful tool. We have been able to convince them that capitalism, which enabled them to go to college, is evil. We have enabled them to go to their capital and destroy it. The west is as weak as we have always believed. They are so ignorant, they believe this is all their doing—that it was their idea. They have played into our hands perfectly.*

He had long argued that the way to take America down was to do it from the inside out. After his successes in the 2016 election, the Ministry of State Security gave him additional resources, a cyber-attack team, additional social media response personnel, etc. He assumed that his efforts were not isolated. Liu assumed that his nation was a driving factor of the social equality initiatives in the military and in business. The push for businesses to create Diversity and Inclusiveness officers and teams was something that his government backed. *They will only sow more seeds of division, further dividing America into furious little factions.*

Tonight was the apogee of a political arc. *From this point forward, things will never be the same for the United States.* There was no way that the President of the United States would come through this uprising alive. This was a *coup d'etat* of the highest order, plastered on television and the Internet. America would be replaced by something else, something new, something that he and his people could manipulate and control. *It will be impossible to go back from this. Those responsible will only go further.*

His phone chirped and he saw the number. The professor had been expecting this call on his encrypted private call phone, and seeing the number only made his grin wider. "Hello," he said picking it up.

"You are no doubt watching the television," the female voice of his handler, Chun Koh, stated. She was a professor at Berkley and only spoke to him when necessary to preserve their security.

"I am."

"Things have escalated faster than most anticipated."

"Not me," he said, doing what he could to avoid saying, "I told you so."

"No, not you. You saw this before most. It appears you were correct about their military."

Liu had sent up a detailed report saying that if a coup had occurred, the American military would sideline itself rather than take sides. "I only applied logic to the situation."

"You have mapped this out quite well. As such, you recognize that this is a rare opportunity, one we must exploit."

"Agreed," Liu replied. "There will be a few weeks of chaos before the new order settles in."

"Our friends will want to know the best way for us to take advantage of this situation."

"I have several thoughts on the matter," he said politely. *More than a few.* "There will be a push for unity. This is only a greater opportunity to keep these people divided. A divided America is a crippled America."

"On this, we are agreed," Koh replied. "Assemble your ideas. I will arrange a secured conference call to review them. In the meantime, I offer you the appreciation of a grateful nation." She hung up before he could even respond.

On the television, he caught a glimpse of a group of young people setting fire to the American flag. He thought for a moment of the old proverb, "May you live in interesting times." *The interesting times are upon us right now ...*

Fairfax, Virginia

Kiffin "Kiff" Renner watched the television in amazement and shock. The White House was under assault, live, on the air. Explosions rocked the pristine structure as people swarmed over the security fence. He saw ladders go up to assist with the rush of people. Gunfire cracked, popped and sputtered in the darkness. *This is insanity! This can't be happening. Where is the military?* The ABC7 commentator actually seemed to be happy that it was happening. "The people are finally showing they are fed up with the President and his policies. Tonight is the night when he will pay the price for his betrayal of the American people." *This is third world craziness.*

Each of those words felt like a blow to his stomach. Kiff worked at the Department of Homeland Security in their Cyber Security Division. He was part of the massive Federal government, though it was more out of necessity than by desire. Kiff had been arrested for hacking PNC Bank at the ripe age of seventeen. For Kiff, it had been a challenge, something that he did on a lark. He played with the balances of a few accounts, moving money to causes he supported. The irony of having Democratic Congressmen donating money to the Republican Party was more funny than harmful in his mind.

It had taken a team of investigators nearly a year to finally pin him down. Even when he was arrested, the evidence was thin enough for the government to offer a bargain. A Director in the Secret Service, Jack Desmond, took a special interest in him—recognizing his unique set of talents. He said they could use someone with his expertise ... that sending him to jail would be wasting a good resource. Rather than face a costly trial and the risk of jail, he accepted a plea bargain probation and a position within the Department of Homeland Security.

Seeing the flames of various DC landmarks lighting up the night sky on his television, his heart sank. He had friends and coworkers who were likely to be down there, on both sides of the chaos. Kiff knew he stood out at work, not just for his brilliance, but for his values. He wasn't ashamed of his political beliefs, but did what most conservatives did: He kept them to himself unlike so many others he worked with. Still, there were moments when he let it slip, when he spoke his mind. Plenty of his coworkers would be cheering the destruction of the White House, and that frustrated him.

Some mainstream media latched onto the concept of Washington DC being a swamp. Kiff learned after he started work at DHS that there was a true deep state in the federal government. They saw the President as a true threat—a man swearing to cut the size of the government's workforce. Kiff called them 'seasoned staff,' older federal workers who actively worked against the current administration. He had even gone into leadership when he was able to prove that several senior staffers had leaked material to the press. Then he got his own hand slapped for digging without authorization. It was then that he learned just how corrupt the government really was. *Tonight those same people were either downtown orchestrating this madness or celebrating.*

His phone rang and he glanced down, seeing it was Cairo, one of the few people at work that shared his same values. "Yo, Cairo," he said, his eyes returning to the battle raging only a few miles away.

"Dude, tell me that you're watching this shit."

"Of course I am." *Fuck—the whole world is watching.* "I can't believe it," Kiff said. "This was planned. It is organized. They had mortars, rockets, fucking ladders."

"I know! Where in the hell is the Army?" Cairo asked.

Kiff rolled his eyes. "If they were going to help, they'd be there."

"They're in on it?"

Kiff nodded, changing channels to NBC 4 for a different camera angle on the pandemonium. "They certainly are hanging the President out to dry."

"Do you think he'll get out?"

"The President? I don't know. Hell, he may not even be in the White House. Then again, this has the earmarks of an inside job. The Secret Service is being overwhelmed." Kiff's mind went to his friend, Jack Desmond. Jack had transferred back to the Presidential Detail as Director just recently. *I hope to hell he gets out!*

"CNN is saying that Congress has been taken hostage," Cairo sputtered anxiously. That was Cairo ... his mouth couldn't keep up with his brilliant mind. "If they are hostages, then the whole system has fallen."

"Funny how the media knows where to be," Kiff said.

"Yeah. Like they are part of it all," he quipped. *Of course the media is involved with this. They hated the President before he ever won his first term.* When he lost the second term, they had not relented on him. When the President-Elect died and the VP Elect were assassinated, they crafted conspiracy theories that the President had arranged their deaths—that he was a tyrant that refused to give up power even after he lost. Despite the fact they called for a new election; they claimed he was stealing it.

Amazingly people consumed the lies like fat people swarming a Golden Corral buffet. The media trotted out 'experts' that portrayed the 'Traitor President' as a despot determined to hold onto power. *They set the stage for all of this, even if they aren't involved with this ... this coup d'etat.* "Things are out of control. If they kill him, they will never let the VP take office."

"The government has fallen," Cairo said.

"No. It imploded. It is the dirty players on the inside that brought this down. We've both seen it."

"You don't think they'll come for us, do you Kiff?" Genuine concern rang in the words that Cairo spoke.

"Why would they come for us?"

"They know we aren't part of their little party. You ratted out some of them for leaking information. I gotta wonder—will they come for us?"

It was something that Kiff had not thought about until that moment. "If they would do this to the President and Congress, there is nothing they won't stoop to," he said more to himself than to Cairo.

"What do we do?"

We never thought this was possible, the overthrow of the government on live TV. It would be stupid to not take steps to protect themselves. "We prepare. Get some money set aside so that it is fluid, not something they can track. We'll go into work like always, if they even allow us downtown after all of this. We don't do or say anything that might trigger suspicion."

"I can spin up some fake IDs," Cairo said.

Will it come to that? "Okay. Let's hope we don't need them."

"You have a gun?"

Kiff paused. He had inherited his grandfather's pistol years ago. It was in his bedroom closet in a shoebox, along with some old ammunition. The thought that he might need it was chilling ... and frightened him in ways he had not expected. "Yeah. You?"

"My dad has some. I'm getting one."

"Good idea," he said. "No more phones, Cairo. We talk via encrypted comms only. If this is bigger than just a peaceful protest out of control, we can't give them anything to latch onto."

"Right," Cairo replied slowly. "Dude ... this is out of control."

"No, it's not," Kiff said. "We just don't know who is in control."

As they hung up, he changed the channel again, to MSNBC, which showed ANTIFA flags being waved on the steps of the US Capitol.

Kiff never called himself a patriot. ... He always felt that was a declaration of a pompous person. He was patriotic. Yes, the government had arrested him, but now he was part of the government. It felt dirty to him to be part of something that might be behind what he was witnessing on television.

I need to call my mother. She's going to be upset by all of this. His mother understood both his intelligence and how he had chosen to use his talents. Kiff was an only child; his father had died when he was ten leaving Kiff with only his mother as family. When he had been offered a deal on his prison term to join the DHS, he had initially hesitated. His mother had convinced him to go straight.

Kiff thought *This is a tipping point. History will swing on this hinge. This will change things in ways we can't expect. The best I can do is be prepared and aware.*

Abilene, Texas

Judy Mercury sat at the bar of the Abilene VFW hall, cradling her Shiner Ruby Redbird beer and watching the television in amazement. It was a dingy place, dark with an aroma of long-ago spilled beer, sweat, and based on the guy sitting two seats down—Aqua Velva. Judy felt oddly comfortable in the place, not for its lack of ambiance, but for the people there. She had served several tours in the Middle East and being with other veterans helped ease some of her bad memories. She had been awarded a Silver Star and Purple Heart for fending off an attack on a convoy. Judy had more than earned her seat at the bar, and the locals all knew it.

The attack was something that always gnawed at the corners of her mind. The IEDs going off had been jarring; she had almost gotten a concussion from hitting the door of the Humvee she was riding in. Standard doctrine was to hold your ground, call in for support for the crippled vehicles, form a DP, defensive perimeter. Judy didn't play that way. Her aggression was only tempered by her creativity when it came to combat situations. She had ordered the driver to head off in a long sweeping circle around the attacking Iraqi's, coming in from their flank. It was the exact wrong thing to do, but it had caught the bad guys off guard.

Her gunner had been wounded right off the bat, catching some shrapnel from the IED that had taken out the lead vehicle in the convoy. Judy had climbed on top of the Humvee, gotten the gunner inside, and taken his position. Ordering the driver to swing around the surging attackers, she sprayed them with fast bursts of machine gun fire. To some it would have seemed like suicide, with rocket propelled grenades streaking at them as they made the arc around the enemy. To Judy, it was not playing by the book, which the insurgents seemed to have already mastered. Besides, she had been pissed off by the attack and when she was angry, she got aggressive. It had been a "Front to rear, disappear" moment for her. Worse yet, it had come with only five days and a wake-up before she was to return to the states. *Asshats were trying to kill me before I got home!* Memories of that made her take a drink of her beer.

She flanked the flankers; at least that was how she described it during the after action report. When the smoke had cleared, enemy dead bodies were everywhere. She and the other convoy defenders had slaughtered their attackers, and much of the credit was hers.

Credit ... for killing other human beings. It never felt right to her. She wanted to turn down the commendation, but the Army insisted ... she was a rarity, a female who was thrust into a combat position and had performed heroically. Her CO at the time, Trip Reager, had told her she had an obligation to be an example for others. *Damn him for being right!* Reager was like that though; he had a way of putting things in perspective.

As much as Mercury tried to shake the memories of that day, they came at her at weird times and strange ways. At least in the VFW hall, she was with people who might understand. She couldn't talk over the ambush with her parents; they simply didn't have the frame of reference.

She came there for calm, but tonight that was impossible as the images on the TV demonstrated. There had been threats of massive riots since the death of Joe Biden and the assassination of Kamala Harris. She expected that. After COVID-summer, where 'peaceful protests' had been a smokescreen for violence and looting, she knew that the President's enemies used rioting as one of their primary weapons against his administration. As she watched the events unfold on TV, with the White House being swarmed by angry protesters, she was stunned.

I wonder if Betty is watching this? She'll be angry about this too. Betty was her girlfriend, another member of her National Guard unit. Betty was far more wrapped up in politics than she was. *She will want to book a flight to DC and take out those snot-nosed kids.* Judy understood that sentiment. *Dad was right all along. They were always planning a stunt like this—waiting for the right opportunity. They are far worse than foreign communists…they should know better as Americans.*

The bartender, a portly Vietnam vet named Adolphus Kerry shook his head. "Do you believe this bullshit?"

"I do," she said glumly, taking a sip of her beer. "I think there's a lot of Americans out there that want this kind of violence. They don't care how it looks to the rest of our country. Hell, to the rest of the world. The people behind these riots are just filled with hate and feel justified in what they are doing."

"At least in the '60s the cause was peace," Adolphus said. "This is pure crazy."

"Do you think they got the President out of there?" she said as flames started to ignite inside the White House.

"Oh, I'm sure they did," Adolphus replied, putting down the glass he had been cleaning and starting on another one. His voice didn't ring with confidence as he watched the chaos on the streets of Washington DC.

"It didn't have to come to this," she said. "The President told them he supported a new election."

The bartender finished with his glass, moved in front of her, took her glass and filled it with more beer. "It doesn't matter what he says. They are so full of their 'resist!' bullshit, this was bound to happen. They impeached him for something he didn't do; they smeared his name and those of his family. They were running out of options."

Judy took another sip of the now much cooler drink. "Our enemies aboard are going to see this and be happy—and that pisses me off."

"Damned straight they will be happy," the bartender said bitterly. "It makes me want to punch a wall. Fucking libtards!"

Her iPhone chirped and she pulled it out, reading the text message. "Fuck me."

"Bad news?" Adolphus asked.

"Our Guard unit is being activated," she said, stuffing the phone into her front blue jeans pocket and taking a long swig of her beer.

"They must be expecting this trouble to spread," the bartender said.

She put a ten dollar bill on the table. "I've gotta go—you know—make the world safe for Democracy," she snarkily replied. For a second, she paused. While she had intended it as a wise crack, suddenly she realized that it was incredibly accurate—and that was chilling.

"Kick their asses Judy," Adolphus said.

As she reached the door and was greeted by the early evening air, she cringed. *They have lit the fuse on a bomb and have no idea what kind of damage this shit is going to cause down the road.* She wasn't sure how she was going to tell Wanda about it. Wanda hated that Judy was still in the National Guard. As much as she and Judy tried to avoid politics, it was not easy with the two of them living together. Judy knew enough to change the news from Fox every time Wanda came into the room. Where Judy kept her tongue in check, her lover did not and would often go off about the role of the military or the man she called the Traitor President.

She's going to hate this, ... that I'm being called up. A part of her dreaded the conversation that was about to come.

CHAPTER 1

"Denial of racism is the worst kind of racism."

Berlin, New Hampshire

Su-Hui Zhou assembled the Sons of Liberty groups he was in charge of in Saint Anne Roman Catholic Church in the quaint town of Berlin. Today was a special day, and since their arrival, he had not pulled them all together. Most needed rest; some needed time to grieve for their losses. The priest, father Ron McKinney, had insisted that they use his church as their shelter and home. Su-Hui was in awe of the splendor of the inside of the red brick church. There was a majesty to it that was beyond impressive to him.

Father Ron, as he insisted he be called, told him that the attendance at his church had fallen off since the Fall. Churches, especially the Catholic Church, had been targeted by the Ruling Council as 'insensitive and insulting' in terms of their beliefs about transgenders and gays. Most people knew the truth, which was that the government didn't like the church preaching morals that conflicted with their political agendas. Conservative Catholics had been high on the targeting lists for the Newmerica government when they opened the Social Quarantine camps.

The citizens of Berlin brought in food and clothing, and opened their homes for Su-Hui's people to use. Many stayed at the church. After the destruction of Lisbon and the loss of a number of their people, a strange unspoken feeling kept them close to each other. *Safety comes from us being with each other.*

Su-Hui had been voted in as a leader of the group after the bombing of

Lisbon. It was not a role that he had desired or sought. In some respects, he believed he had been chosen because he was not autocratic in nature … because he was able to work well with others. Some of the more bombastic voices, like that of Herb Fletcher of the small volunteer SOL group from Kentucky, constantly questioned every decision that Su-Hui put on the table. According to what he had been told, Herb had tried to assume leadership after the death of Randy Birdsell in the attack. His pushy attitude and ego had worked against him. *They chose me because I am the opposite of him. Where he is mouthy, I am quiet. Where Herb uses harsh language, I am controlled in what I say.* To Su-Hui, Herb was his own worst problem.

They had needed a home after the loss of Lisbon. One of the locals from Berlin had suggested going there. They had sneaked there, some of the time going cross-country to avoid the military patrols from the Newmerican occupation troops. One snowmobile broke down and had to be abandoned entirely when its engine seized up. The trek had taken three days before they arrived, weary and exhausted.

The killing of General Donaldson was all over the TRC-sponsored news for days. It brought a bit of satisfaction for his ordering the destruction of Lisbon. His wife, Hachi, didn't like the praise she got from the others for shooting the General. The attention was embarrassing, and Su-Hui understood. *She had no idea who it was; she was simply protecting us all.*

He hoped that today would energize his people. It was the day that the American President would be sworn in. Picking up a news channel that would cover it was tricky, but Father Ron assured him he had it set up. The members of the parish had brought in a large screen TV and put it on the steps of the altar for everyone to watch.

There had been one election for the Presidency since the Fall. The former Vice President of the United States, who had been filling the role since he returned to the public scene months ago, had won the hotly contested election. His counterpart, the Chairman of the Ruling Council, had declared himself the winner—claiming that his American counterpart had suppressed votes and cheated. The United States had a long history of cheating in elections and contesting outcomes. This was different however. The Newmerican nation refused to acknowledge the results in those states that had voted for the American leader. The United States was split—mostly by states, but in some cases, large cities—self-proclaimed Newmerican autonomous zones. Civil War was underway, and New Hampshire was one of those battleground states. *This has gone beyond election shenanigans to outright war.*

The remaining Sons of Liberty gathered in the forward pews so as to see the television better. The new Fox News channel, NeoFox, came on with an image of the steps of a stately, old plantation home outside of Nashville. The President took the oath of office from an older female judge. It was quick, almost as if it were a formality, though Su-Hui knew it was far more.

The small audience applauded; then the white-haired President moved to a podium. He held both sides of the stand with his hands, not as if to prop himself up, but to hold his arms wide.

"I take this oath as a solemn obligation, not just to the people of our great nation, but to God. I do so in a time of civil war. Over five years ago, a cabal of armed insurgents seized control of our nation. They killed my predecessor and believed they had killed me as well. For the last half-decade, they reshaped the United States of America into an abomination called Newmerica."

He paused, clearly for dramatic effect. "Innocent people were sent to unlawful Social Quarantine Camps simply out of fear of the values they held dear. Citizens turned on other citizens for rewards. Armed gangs of thugs took to the street, operating outside of the law, inflicting what they called justice with no due process, no oversight, and no authority. They used fear, first of a virus, then of their vile government, to intimidate and rule. They pitted citizens against each other, turning our country into a police state.

"When presented with conducting fair elections, they refused. They claimed a victory that is not theirs. Rather than accept the will of the people, they stand in arrogant defiance. Rather than allow democracy rule, they refuse and stand in rebellion.

"I took this oath a few moments ago to be President of the *United* States. It is clear by their actions that they seek to further divide an already fractured people. As such, I will do what is necessary to bring these states that renounce the legitimate election results back into our great union.

"Where our enemies have entrenched, we must walk. We took back Atlanta from the defiant people that refused to acknowledge what the people wanted. The good hard people of New Hampshire valiantly fight on, despite hardships and the horrific slaughter of Lisbon. It is up to us to ensure that their sacrifice was not in vain. America stands with Georgia. America stands with New Hampshire. America stands with the good people of Iowa who have been attacked by their neighboring states for no reason. America stands with Texas ... *all* of Texas.

"The crimes of the Ruling Council are dark and eat away at the foundation of our country. As some of my first actions, I am ordering the immediate dismantling of all Social Quarantine Camps. I am, via executive order, defining all Social Enforcement organizations as terrorist organizations. I will ask the new Attorney General to work with state prosecutors to seek charges against Social Enforcers for the crimes they have committed, including but limited to kidnapping, wrongful imprisonment, suppression of civil rights, and hate crimes. The era of Americans living in fear of gangs using intimidation and brutality to impose their interpretation of social norms is over.

"Where our enemies act with tyranny and hate, we offer liberty and hope. In the end, that is what separates us ... what is in our hearts. They know we will hold them accountable for their actions; and there is a great deal they must atone for when this is done.

"I cannot do this alone. This has never been about me. The Presidency position is filled by good and lesser people. The Presidency is not what defines us. *You* are what makes America, not the person holding my office. As such, I ask for your help. We need volunteers in almost every aspect of our government. This war needs people, regardless of race, sex, age, or background. If you believe as I do, in the hope for a greater future for the American people, we need your help.

"This will not be an easy road for us to walk, but it is a journey that we must take together. We will face hardships, but we will face them, together, like family. You need to know that we will eventually emerge from this long ordeal stronger than before. When we do, we will witness, as President Lincoln called it, *a rebirth of freedom.*" With those words, he stood and embraced the applause from the bleachers that flanked him. People in the church joined those on the television, their clapping echoing in the vastness of the building. Father Rob shut off the television.

All eyes shifted to Su-Hui. They looked to him for what they should do next. He understood their feelings. The losses of cherished friends and comrades in Lisbon had shaken the Sons of Liberty. *They look to me for miracles ... but I am just a man like them.*

Gathering his resolve, he took the first three steps of the altar and faced the crowd. "I know you are all looking to me to tell you of a daring plan that will cripple our enemy. This is war; the Newmericans made that painfully clear to us. You do not win wars in a single battle, but in the culmination of battles."

"He's right," said a gravelly voice from the rear of the church. It had a tone to it, a commanding presence in the words. All eyes shifted as General Hank Griffiths and a small security detail entered the church.

"I'm General Griffiths of the New Hampshire National Guard. I wanted to make sure you fine folks got here safely. My people have set up a perimeter around Berlin, just to ensure that the Newmericans don't pull another Lisbon." His words seemed to make everyone in the room feel a bit more relaxed.

The General moved up next to Su-Hui; shaking his hand, they surveyed the rest of the gathered Sons of Liberty. "What you people have done is damned remarkable. You people have the Governor of Vermont pissing his pants after that last raid. He's recalled a number of his guard units, which has caused some angst with the folks in the District. I find a little political turmoil with your enemies to be a good thing. He's promising to send in Social Enforcers to take their place, which is like swapping out Tom Brady with Pee Wee Herman." His comment brought a murmur and chuckles from the crowd.

"The TRC calls us an insurgency. Frankly, I don't give a damn what they call us. You know what the Southern White House calls us? They call us *The Defiance*. I don't know about you, but I like the sound of that. We are a thorn in their side, a pain in their ass. As long as all of you are in the fight, there is hope for New Hampshire." Su-Hui liked the sound of that. *The Defiance—that is something we can rally behind.*

"You've done a remarkable job. I know it has cost us, dearly, but I'm counting on you being up for the challenges that are in front of us."

Su-Hui cleared his throat, his eyes moving slowly around the room, contacting each person with his gaze. "They believe they have crippled us, possibly forever. Lisbon was our home, the people there our friends. They expect us to fight and we will. We will not let the destruction of Lisbon define this war. We need to hurt them where they will not expect it."

Griffiths nodded. "You've got the right idea. Vermont is one of several states that have sent troops to New Hampshire. Your strategy was sound, but focused on one of the invaders. While we will continue our IED and ambush attacks, I propose we expand what we have already started."

"What do you have in mind?" Herb Fletcher asked. The inquiry sounded like a demand.

Griffiths stared at Fletcher as he responded. "Albany, the capital of New York is just across the border—as is Boston. Both of their Governors have sent troops here as well. What I propose is simple—let's make these states feel the pain of the war they are bringing to us here. I think we should start with Boston."

Those words brought grins, and then, a few at a time, applause.

Su-Hui nodded. "The Sons of Liberty stand ready General."

"As they always have …" the General added.

The District

Even her nickname, Alex, told the people around her about her commitment to their cause. While she had a female name, Alexandria—she made people refer to her as if she were a male. It was something she enjoyed; it made her part of the male patriarchy with a simple word.

The Vice President of Newmerica stood in the small circle of officials and guests that surrounded Daniel Porter as he was sworn in by one of the ten Supreme Court Justices he had named after the Ruling Council came to power. He had chosen her, less for her legal background than for her demographics. Her Asian background, the fact that she was a transgender—they checked off important boxes. The original nine Justices had claimed that the Ruling Council's actions were illegal. Adding the right people to the court nullified such unwanted dissent. *Of course now that we are legitimately in power, I can arrange for some of these old justices to be permanently silenced.*

When seeing him take the oath, she would be the Vice President of Newmerica. That was an excitement that she could barely contain. *My mom would be so proud. I started with almost nothing and have risen to be a heartbeat away from governing the country.*

Alex already controlled the Truth Reconciliation Committee and the National Security Force—which was the real power behind Newmerica. Daniel had suggested that she hand off her duties, but she had brushed aside his concerns. "The role of the Vice President doesn't take up much time. It is a placeholder that hopefully we will never need. I'll keep my jobs for now." He didn't raise the topic again with her, which was smart on her part. *He knows enough to keep me in his good graces, especially after the assassination attempt.*

Since the night of the Liberation, Alex had been the real power behind the Ruling Council, though few people knew to what extent. Her policies had transformed the corrupt nation into a progressive utopia. Despite the advances, there was still plenty of work to do. The fact that half of the nation had voted for the Pretender President was disturbing. For her, it was proof that the racism and oppression that America stood for still had deep roots in those places. *Once we have brought them back into the fold, we will dig those roots out. This time we will do it right. No more reeducation. This time we need to kill the problems once and for all.*

She longed for her mother and brother to see her, but that had been denied her. Caylee Leatrom, a rogue operative, had killed them as some twisted plot to hurt her. She hated to admit it had been successful, but deep down knew that their murders had cut her deeply. *She is a coward. Rather than try and come for me, she went for my family instead. She will pay for all of the things she has done.*

Daniel took the podium, glancing at the teleprompter. Alex took a sidestep so as to stand in the frame of the cameras that were focusing on him. *It is important for people to see me at his side, partners.* "I accept the responsibilities that the office of President of our nation means. I don't do this lightly, given the nature of our enemies and former country-people.

"My so-called counterpart in the south will no doubt talk about the future, or at least his twisted version of it. In reality, he wants to take us backwards—back to a time before the equity and equality we brought to the country. Even the use of the word America evokes a step back to an era of systemic racism, hate, and suppression.

"They have attempted to steal this election, all of you know it. They relied on the antiquated and outdated and clearly corrupt Electoral College to seize power. We won the popular vote, and in the end that is all that matters. That is true democracy. The Electoral College is a throwback, created when we were thirteen imperialist colonies, slave-states.

"This election has pointed to a greater problem. We are no longer the states of old. We have evolved, grown, changed into an equity-based democracy built on a foundation of innovative and daring progressive ideals. The laws of old that, that some backwards-thinking states cling to, are not a stable foundation for us to move forward. Having so many dissenting and differing voices, some counterproductive to what is best for our nation, is unproductive and dangerous.

"As your President, I believe that our path to the future is to throw out the old ways of thinking and the corrupt laws the supported them. As such, I call for a new Constitutional Convention to be convened. We will draft a new Bill of Rights, and new rules of law to govern Newmerica. While our military forces restore order in the traitorous states, we will create a new Constitution and a set of laws for the nation we desire, one built to meet our ideals.

"We will no longer be bound by outdated and confusing laws like the Second Amendment. We will ensure that everyone in our nation, regardless of their status, has to the right to vote from the age of sixteen on. Everyone, regardless of their status, will have an equal voice. The corrupt barrier of citizenship will no longer have meaning. We have learned painful lessons of state and local governments having too much authority and the inclination to resist policies that are in the national best interest. I promise you, the people of Newmerica, that we will resolve these deficiencies. We will cement the equality and equity we have worked so hard to create for future generations.

"This isn't going to be easy," Daniel cautioned. "We have seen how vicious our enemy can be. The sacrifices of men like General Donaldson help us continue forward. His struggle for control of rebellious New Hampshire is something that inspires us all.

He paused, sweeping the crowd that was assembled in front of the newly repaired Capitol; the bomb damage was still visible in a few areas. It had been deliberate, for the cameras to soak in and put in front of the viewers of the inauguration ceremony. Her own TRC had suggested it as a reminder of American's viciousness. Of course the assassination had been a false-flag attack, one she had the NSF fabricate. The Vice President beamed at the thought of that day and the fallout that had followed. Many of her detractors in the government had been swept up in the arrests that followed. Their actual involvement in the attack was fabricated ... a small lie to cement her legacy. *We make our own history.*

Daniel continued. "We must avenge the cruel siege of Atlanta and the capture of that city's brave defenders. To achieve this, we will need people who will fight for our cause. One of my first actions as President of Newmerica is to impose a limited draft. We will start with those people incarcerated in our prisons who will be offered freedom for their service to our cause. We will use Social Enforcement to identify individuals with the skills and dedication to take the fight to our enemy. Veterans will be asked to once more stand and fight with us. Loyal student groups will be armed and given a chance to turn their words into action for our nation. We will raise more troops to finish the job that General Donaldson and people like him have started. We will take back the rebel states and once and for all put an end to this myth of the United States of America."

Applause rose from the crowd, and the Vice President led the clapping. *The military has straddled the fence in terms of supporting us and the American President. These steps are necessary, and the people need to understand that. We will raise our own army, one that reflects our value, and take the war right to their doorsteps.*

There were other things she knew were in play as well. Three counties in Texas had declared themselves a Texas Republic, aided militarily by Newmerica. With some luck and skill, that movement might grow. *If Texas becomes its own nation, we will recognize it for the short term. It will strip America of vital oil and gas resources and leave a big hole in the middle of their maps.*

The nation needs this war. It will kill off the last bits of poisoned thinking in the south and west. When the dust settles from the fighting, Newmerica will be all that is left. The dream of an American nation will be buried once and for all.

Ann Arbor, Michigan

Dr. Liu stood at his podium in the lecture room in the Social Sciences Building on the University of Michigan campus. The dueling swearing in speeches by the men claiming to the title of President had been earlier in the day. They were fertile ground for the sophomores of his class to pick apart.

When he played the American President's speech, there was actual booing and a few outbursts of, "Pretender!" in the hall mixed with catcalls of 'Traitor!" The TRC had blocked most media coverage of his swearing in, but the Internet had played the video faster than the Big Tech companies could take down all of the copies. His own team of hackers, some of them operating within the Big Tech companies, contributed to that chaos, right under the noses of their managers. Years ago he would have silenced such verbal disruptions. Now it was expected. *They hate an America that few of them really remember. They were still in junior high, or they were freshmen in High School when the Liberation took place.* He took the catcalls as a compliment, validation that he had contributed to their disdain for what had come before.

Their reaction to the Newmerican President's speech was intense staring and interest. He could appreciate what they were experiencing. In his own youth, he had been in China. When the state said something, you had your doubts, but they were kept quiet. Over time, you were conditioned to simply accept the state's version of events and not question them at all. *Freedom breeds confrontation and debate. It is hard for a people to truly prosper when they are arguing with each other.*

As he finished the videos, he turned to his class. "Your thoughts?" he asked his students.

A young lady in the second row shot her hand up, and he called on her. "Go ahead Doris."

"The Pretender was sworn in at the Hermitage, Andrew Jackson's home. That's racial signaling right there. It's just like the media said—he's wanting to turn back to the days of racism." Her comments brought numerous nods.

Liu called on an Indian student near the rear. "Mahesh, your thoughts?"

"There were mostly white men on stage with the Pretender. You look at President Porter, and you can see women of color, transgenders ... a number of different races in the background. The Pretender doesn't even try and mask his hatred of the full spectrum of people."

"And this war he started," another female spoke up. "He acts like New Hampshire is a good thing. Those people all deserve to be sent to Social Quarantine for supporting terrorists. His people are no better than al-Qaeda or ISIS-J."

Dr. Liu nodded. "These are all good observations. What do you make of the call for a draft on the part of President Porter?"

"I'm going to volunteer," another student said. "Killing these enemies of the state would be an honor."

"I think it's a good idea," one large student named Francis spoke up. "I don't think the damned SOL would be fighting if a bunch of us got into the mix."

Another male student weighed in, "Francis, the closest thing you have seen to combat is Call of Duty." That brought a ripple of chuckles to the class. Francis was undeterred. "I'm still more of a match against the Sons of Fucking Liberty."

"We have to fight," a non-binary student named D said. "These terrorists have to be taken down, or more people will side with them."

It was amazing to hear people in the country he lived in saying they thought that war was good and not resisting a draft. *They would be a disappointment to the students of the 1960s who resisted the Vietnam War.* Dr. Liu knew that his students had no idea what real war was like. Most of his students were like Francis; they somehow equate hours in front of their game systems with real fighting. Both sides in the conflict were clearly geared for war—the Battle of Stone Mountain demonstrated that. *The progressives have numbers on their side, but will that be enough?*

"Are they really terrorists?" he posed hypothetically.

"Only when they lose," one student, a rigid-voiced female named Vicki said. "If they win, they are patriots." Weber made note of her. Such independent thought could be dangerous. *She will need a visit from one of the campus social enforcement groups.*

"We'll win," another student said with bold confidence.

"What makes you so sure?" Dr. Liu asked coyly.

"Because if we don't, we'll be forced to change," he said flatly in response.

Weber Liu smiled at the response. America was divided before the election. *My people were able to twist that to our advantage. Matters are even riper for unrest now. We have outright civil war. It makes this nation weaker than it has ever been. All I have to do is have my people seed the right inflammatory content onto the net, leak the right rumors, spread the right lies.*

One thing was for sure—it was going to be a long night, something he relished. *My teams need to press harder. We have fed money to the revolt in Texas. ... Perhaps we can inflict similar pain on Newmerica somewhere.*

CHAPTER 2

"The freedoms of a society trump personal freedoms."

The Southern White House
Nashville, Tennessee

General Trip Reager was ushered into what served as the Oval Office. It was a remarkably plain office; it could have belonged to any government employee. Small portraits of Abraham Lincoln and George Washington hung on the wall. On the credenza behind the President was a smaller image of his predecessor who had been killed during the Fall. A diagonally black ribbon hung across that photograph. The President was reading some documents on his desk as Jack Desmond ushered the General in.

Trip thoughtfully eyed the photograph of the previous President. *They called him Traitor so much that few people even use his name anymore. They told us he died the night of the Liberation—but that was all a lie. The Ruling Council is so embedded with their lies; they no longer can fathom what is the truth. Was that their plan all along?* The President raised his head and stood, extending his hand. "General Reager," the President said.

Trip saluted, then shook his hand. "Mr. President."

The Commander in Chief gestured to the chair opposite his desk and Trip took it, with Jack Desmond seating himself at his side. As the President sat down, he opened the conversation. "I want to congratulate you for bringing Atlanta back into our union."

"Thank you, sir. The congratulations go to the people serving under me."

"Jack said you were modest," the President said, casting a quick glance at his chief of staff. "In my experience, that is a rarity among generals."

"I never planned on this being my career," Trip candidly replied. "Circumstances forced this on me."

"Me too," the President said candidly. "Fate seems to have an agenda of its own ... for both of us." He paused for a moment, then pressed the conversation forward. "We are facing problems on multiple fronts it seems."

"That we are."

"What are your thoughts on dealing with these challenges?"

Trip shifted in his seat as he started. "St. Louis's autonomous zone has been extended to secure their water supply. Enemy forces are flying in more food than troops, which is a blessing. They have learned from what we did with Atlanta. That simply means we don't use the same strategy there. We will have to fight a more traditional siege, one that is going to drag out much longer."

"I hate that people suffer during such operations," the President said glumly.

"As do I sir. If the civilians choose to stay, they are bringing the suffering on themselves," Trip countered. "If you are agreeable, I intend to send our advance forces in next week toward St. Louis to begin our encirclement. The Missouri National Guard units loyal to us are already staged in Columbia."

The President nodded. "How are we on this incursion in Iowa?"

"As you know, the Illinois National Guard made a thrust at Davenport, Iowa. The Iowa National Guard has been reinforced with units from South Dakota and have bogged the enemy down, with half of the city in their possession."

"What was their intent in launching that attack?" Jack Desmond asked.

"On the surface, it doesn't make a lot of sense," Trip conceded. "The only thing of real value is the Rock Island Arsenal in the middle of the Mississippi River. This is a hell of a lot of effort for just that lone target, which makes me believe that this is politically motivated. We have bogged them down in New Hampshire and defeated them in Atlanta.

They needed a victory, even a pointless one. They are trying to throw us off with this, it's a strategic diversion … bloody, but a diversion."

"From what?" the President asked.

"Unknown," Trip replied.

Jack Desmond's turn to shift in his seat came up. "Our intelligence framework isn't what we used to have back in the day, but we are getting indications of a troop buildup in southern Virginia. It might indicate some sort of thrust into North Carolina."

Trip's jaw slid forward as he thought. "I saw those reports and that makes sense. Fort Bragg is there. The base commander turned it over to us without a shot, evacuating the personnel except for those that stayed who wanted to fight for us. It could be they want to try to take it back."

"Can they?" the President queried.

"They can try," Trip said. "Now that I know this, we can prepare a defense in-depth—make it costly as hell for them to attempt it."

"Make it happen General," the President said firmly. "That still leaves us with them taking Davenport."

"It is a thorny proposition," Trip said. "But I think we should take a page out of the New Hampshire's playbook. What I propose is a deep raiding task force, old-school cavalry type of thing. They are committed to Davenport and expect us to do the same. We will not. We will plunge deep into Illinois and drive on Springfield. They will be forced to break off in Davenport or lose their own capital."

"The best defense is an offense," the President said, cracking a smile.

Trip nodded. "It's better to fight them where they are not expecting it. Frankly, after Chicago, I'd like to take Illinois out of the war if we can—or at least prevent them from causing more trouble."

"And New Hampshire?" the President asked.

"I spoke with General Griffiths and agreed with the strategy they started with Vermont. Next up is New York and Massachusetts. We will give them good reasons to reconsider keeping their troops in New Hampshire."

"How will that play out?" Jack asked.

"Honestly?"

"I demand it," the President added.

Trip appreciated that. "Very well. One thing we know about these people is that they double-down; they escalate. The destruction of Lisbon was as much a test as a message. They will do worse before this is over. They don't care if it works or not. It's the old adage, "The whole world looks like a nail when all you have is a hammer." Until spring comes, we are fighting to frustrate the hell out of them, whittle them down, get their politicians involved to muck things up.

"Then, when spring comes, the New Hampshire National Guard is not going to be easy to hide. We will hit them with a more conventional fight. By then, they won't be expecting it."

"How do we support them in the meantime?" the President poised.

"We encourage the Sons of Liberty cells in the neighboring states to make life uncomfortable for the enemy. We use them to smuggle in explosives and munitions. Slowly, the SOL units already in New Hampshire will become army irregulars, highly experienced militia units. By spring, when the shit hits the fan, the Newmericans will be facing a battle-hewn force. In the meantime, we help them with supplies, and do not interfere with them."

There was a pause. Trip knew that the last might raise some ire with the American leader. *The Newmerican politicians are getting involved, starting to push the military around. That rarely adds up to anything good. He needs to know that the best thing he can do is let us do our job.*

"Agreed," the President replied. "I would like to have you weigh in on this nasty business with Texas."

Trip sighed. Three counties had declared themselves The Republic of Texas. They called for the rest of the state to secede from America and be their own nation. He understood that feeling as a native Texan himself. *Still, this doesn't feel right. We aren't voting on it; they are simply proclaiming independence and backing it up with guns and violence.* "We Texans have never forgotten that we were our own nation sir. It is taught to us in grade school on up. That doesn't justify what they have done. The fact that this started during our siege of Atlanta makes me wonder who's behind this."

Jack spoke next. "General Reager voiced his concerns and has suggested that we check where these rebels got their funding. I'm pulling in one of our best cyber security people to dig deeper into this."

"What makes you think they have outside help?"

Trip responded. "They fired missiles at helicopters that tried to cross their airspace. Likewise they used heavy weapons, including anti-tank missiles when the local authorities came to their border in force. There are no armories there—so they had to have gotten outside help."

"That makes sense, and is disturbing," the President said. "If it's Newmerica, that doesn't surprise me. There are other powers out there that might like to take advantage of our civil war—and that worries me deeply."

"Confronting them in an armed fight right now could backfire on us," Trip said. "Right now the majority of Texans don't support secession. Many are sitting back to see how this plays out. If we start creating martyrs out of these folks, it will generate sympathy and patronage to their cause."

"We can't tolerate them leaving America, not now," the President affirmed.

"Agreed sir," Jack said off to Trip's left. "We need some time. We need to find out the lay of the land in terms of who's backing this move. Once we know that, we can set the right response."

"If they are being helped by outside factions, chances are the average person in his little republic doesn't know whose manipulating this conflict. If we discover who is helping them, it might be useful for us to resolve this without further bloodshed," Trip said.

"You're asking for patience," the President said.

He nodded. "I am sir. I'll go there, meet with their leaders—buy us some time. I'll take enough force behind me so that they know we mean business."

"Agreed. By the same token, General, I prefer that we do not treat them with the same respect you would a foreign nation. I don't recognize this Republic of Texas any more than I do Newmerica."

"Understood. Right now, this is contained to a few counties. We don't want it spreading; nor do we want support for the movement to grow. We need data."

"If push comes to shove, will you fight them General Reager?" the President asked.

It was a heavy question to consider, and Trip took a moment to formulate his response. *I am Texan. Firing on my own people—that's something that people would never forgive or forget. Then again, I have been fighting a civil war already—shooting and killing other Americans.* He struggled to balance his response. "I was born a Texan and will die a Texan, sir. I am also an American—born and raised. I didn't ask for this civil war. I don't like having to kill my fellow countrymen. They made the decision to rise up against our nation. I am true to my oath as an officer.

"If these people continue with their illusion of being a separate Republic, I will do what I have to in order to bring them back into the fold. If they choose to fight, then that is their decision. I have a duty I must perform. Otherwise my commitment to the nation and to my own words as an officer mean nothing. I will hate every minute of it. It might mean I can't call Texas home when this is all over … but if I must fight them, I will do what I have to do."

Charlottesville, Virginia

Doctor Victor Morose sat on the back porch of his modest house just outside of Charlottesville, flipping through a book. The porch was a glassed-in affair, obviously heated against the chill of a late January in Virginia. He was an older man, slender, wearing a thick sweater, that, when combined with the bright sun that was showing, gave him enough warmth to be outside.

As David Steele watched him through the scope of his rifle, it appeared that the man didn't have a care in the world. Living in a nice house, the professor of the University of Virginia was a man of means and from what David could tell, a touch of arrogance.

Dr. Morose had been his sister's academic advisor before her brutal murder. Maddie had told their father, Grayson, that he had warned her that people were watching her—that she needed to be more active on campus politically. Maddie had tried to blend in, but it was too little, too late. She had been lured off campus with other conservative students like lambs to the slaughter. Maddie had surprised her assailants, killing some of them before she was murdered and her body dumped into a creek.

The loss of his beloved sister had dominated David Steele's life since then. He, his father, and a family friend, had extracted revenge on the group that had committed the crime—a campus secret society called the *Grays*. David had penetrated their group, then left pipe bombs at their meeting place. They had been killed, all of them, in one fell swoop, consumed in an explosion and fireball that still lit up David's memory in the dark times when he found himself alone. He had killed them all, and the part that bothered him most was that he had enjoyed it. Still, it wasn't enough for him or his father. Maddie demanded more.

David and his father had been conducting surveillance on Dr. Morose for several days. David eyed his prey and considered his actions. *The man had known that Maddie was a target, but had done nothing to protect her. He had warned her, but that was little more than to ease his own conscience. He had to know what the Grays were going to do to her. He deserves what is coming.*

"What's he doing?" his father asked from the front seat of their car.

"Reading," David said, lying flat in the trunk of the car. They had modified the vehicle, allowing him to fold the rear seats flat and lie down concealed in the back. A small hole had been cut in the rear of the vehicle, one that could be covered with a plate when not in use. It looked like a rust spot. It was the perfect camouflage for a mobile sniper.

"Any sign of his wife?"

"None," he said calmly. "He's just sitting there reading." Seeing the man's house reminded him of the home that his family used to have, when his father had been a member of the House of Delegates. When the Fall happened, the family had adopted new identities and been hiding in seclusion ever since. *We had to lose our house, had to give up everything, so that men like this could prosper.*

After the destruction of the Grays, his family had committed themselves to try to fix the problems at the universities which had led to Maddie's murder. His father had pointed out that the problem was with the administration, the professors who fed the students a diet of intellectual hate. Student activist groups fed that hate even more. They had dedicated themselves to resolving the problem. As his father had said, "They are a cancer, and you have to cut out the tumors when you find them."

Dr. Morose was one of those tumors.

"I can take the shot," David said slowly in a low tone.

His father didn't respond for what seemed like a minute. "Dad," he urged. "If he goes inside, we won't have this chance."

David knew his father. He was a lawyer, a man who believed in justice, despite everything that had happened to their country. The fact that he was hesitating wasn't bad; it was good. *We are not cold-blooded killers; we are trying to get justice—real justice.* If his dad had reacted quickly, it would have surprised him more.

"Take the shot," his father said.

David had been hunting several times in his life. His father and grandfather had trained him on how to handle weapons, shoot, and all about gun safety. This was different though. It wasn't a ten-point buck in his sights—it was a human being.

Drawing a long breath, he began to let it out slowly as he aimed. A number of factors came into the shot—the distance, wind, possible deflection from the window panes—all of it was a complex math that came into play. Concentrating more than ever before for a shot, David slowly squeeze the trigger.

The kick was hard against David's shoulder, but not painful. Dr. Morose's head exploded with the retort of the rifle firing. The bullet didn't break the glass of the porch windows, but simply punched a hole in them a millisecond before hitting his target. Crimson gore covered the far windows as the dead man toppled over sideways onto the porch floor, out of sight. The crack of the gun in the trunk of the car was loud; his ears ached from it despite the plugs he had in place.

David put the cover patch in place, obscuring his sniper hole. "Drive," was all he said.

Grayson Steele started the car and began to drive away. *One down, thousands more to go ...*

Nashville, Tennessee

The headquarters for the American National Security Agency was not nearly as impressive as the facilities under the control of the Newmerican government. It was an old bank, one of those that had shuttered its doors during the waves of economic recession following the Fall. Where the old NSA, now part of Newmerica's NSF, employed thousands, this one employed hundreds. They had vast arrays of computers at their disposal, courtesy of the plunder-taxes that the Ruling Council had imposed after they seized power.

Kiff Renner wasn't intimidated by the numbers of those that stood against him. He knew some of those people from his time at the Department of Homeland Security. Most were good cyber-people, but lacked real-world experience. They did things by the book, literally. The mainstay of what they did was to produce hefty manuals on how to protect their nation. Creativity was discouraged in favor of consistency.

You can't fight cybercrimes with a manual. That was something he had tried to convey to the DoD and the DHS for years. They turned a deaf ear to Kiff. He was, after all, a cybercriminal himself, an outsider to Washington DC and the twisted thinking of the deep state. *I had a track record of successes, but it wasn't enough to convince them that my way was right.* Kiff knew he didn't fit in, but he loved his work, especially since the alternative was prison time. Ultimately, it was his being an outsider that nearly cost him his freedom. He didn't like to think back to those days, not long after the Fall. The FedGov had brought their unique combination of fear and hate down on him.

Now he was the Assistant Director of Cybersecurity for America. While the title sounded glorious, he spent little time managing operations, and still spent his days hands-on, waging a form of digital warfare against the Newmericans, Russians, Chinese, North Koreans, Iranians, Saudis, and every other nation that was more than willing to pick at the beleaguered country.

Kiff had been heads down at his desk and didn't hear the footsteps of the man approaching. Looking up, he saw Jack Desmond, arms crossed, a wry grin on his face. "Hello Kiff," he said.

"This can't be good news," Kiff quipped back.

"What makes you say that?"

"Is it good news?"

Jack shook his head. "I like to think of it as a great opportunity for an old friend."

"Every time you say we are friends, bad things happen to me," he reminded Jack.

"I need your, shall I say, unique set of skills," the President's Chief of Staff said. "And this one comes from the top."

"Fire away Jack. God knows I owe you."

Desmond closed the distance between them; then he closed the door to the small office that Kiff called his domain. Jack seemed to survey the trinkets and things that Kiff surrounded himself with, fixating on a bust of Green Lantern—not the newer versions, the old-school Hal Jordan Green Lantern. Kiff embraced his geekdom fully, with batarangs and Captain America's shield on full display. "Have you heard about what is happening in north Texas?"

Kiff shrugged. "I caught bits and pieces. I don't trust what the TRC brands as official content. If the story is true, there's some counties in Texas that are declaring themselves a country."

Jack nodded. "This is one of those rare times where the TRC got it right, though they are making it out to be a bigger thing than it is. They have claimed they are seceding from America. The thing that sticks out is that they seem to have a lot of backing. Military hardware they shouldn't possibly have—supplies. This seems bigger than them having some millionaire backers. The intelligence community suspects they are getting help from our enemies."

"Of course they are," Kiff said. "Why not? We are in the middle of a civil war. If you ever wanted to inflict some pain, now is the time to do it."

"I don't like getting kicked when I'm down," Jack said. "I also don't like the thought of our enemies exploiting this opportunity. It's not a level playing field, and it rubs me wrong."

Fair fights were not something that Kiff was familiar with. As a kid, he had always been a geek. That made him fair game for bullies. His father had preached ignoring the bullies in school … that they would eventually go away. Kiff learned quickly that ignoring them only invited more attacks. After several vicious pummelings, he tried fighting back, but the odds were two to one and these were football players. The lesson was clear. Don't fight on their terms. The Internet was a great source for him to figure out how to pick locks on high school lockers. After school one day, he planted homosexual porn in the lockers of the two football players that had beaten him, followed by an anonymous tip to the principal from a fake email account. The bullies were pulled out of school, accused of being homosexuals—then when they protested— homophobes. He leaked the story to the local press which resulted in school board meetings, news crews in the kids' front yards, the whole shooting match. Both kids were pulled from the school, thus ending the attacks on him. From that point forward in his life, Kiff refused by play by the rules that the bullies set, both in school and in life.

"So you want me to help you level this playing field?"

"The way we see it is simple. If they are getting help from the outside, depending on who that is, it is going to help our case with the public. People who might back such an effort if it is organic, will cringe if the bad guys are involved … and from the look of it, someone has been helping them. I have suspicions that fit the facts, but that isn't enough. I need tangible evidence. The kind of stuff that you are good at getting."

One of the things Kiff liked about Jack was his trademark bluntness and honesty. *I hope he appreciates it back.*

"Alright Jack, I can help you. You need to understand some of the limits I'm facing here."

"Make me wise."

I have to remember that line. Kiff shifted position in his seat, then spoke, "Since the schism between Newmerica and America and that little attack you pulled off to take down the East Coast's Internet, the Big Tech companies have been building what we are calling a blockade around their net. There are holes all over the place, but each day they plug more and more. It makes my job infinitely more complex if you want me to peer into PCs and accounts on the other side."

"For now, just the leaders of this little rebellion in Texas."

"That's easier, but still complicated. If they are getting help, chances are it is pretty sophisticated. It's not going to be a simple wire transfer. They will bounce this all over the globe to try to hide it from us, including on the Newmerica side of the fence. If these guys are smart, most of the stuff may be local on their hard drives—not easy for me to snatch and grab."

"Are you trying to tell me you can't do it Kiff?"

"No. I'm setting your expectations. There may be only so much I can do without having their hardware in-hand."

Jack nodded for a moment, then continued. "For now, do what you can from here. If you need the hardware, there are ways for us to get it in your hands."

"Alright," Kiff said, wondering how Jack could secure their hard drives. A part of him wanted to ask, but a part of him didn't want the answer. "I assume this is high priority."

"*Very* high," Jack returned handing over a folder of information. "This is what we have so far on the leaders of this pain in the ass. Get what you can. Help me build a case."

It's going to be a late night or ten. "I'm handling it personally. I'll do my best."

"Thanks Kiff. I hope that's enough. The fate of Texas may be in your furious little fingers …"

Smyrna, Tennessee

The Tennessee National Guard base in Smyrna, Tennessee was an older facility as far as National Guard bases went. Out in front of it were a tank, an artillery piece, and an attack helicopter on display – the usual lawn décor of a military installation. The majority of the facility had a look of a 1980s college campus; plain brick buildings lacking any distinction. The family housing on the base was older than what had been at Arnold Air Force Base, a bit more beat up, but Caylee couldn't complain. After Raul's kidnapping from the Air Force base, the commanding officer of the Smyrna base beefed up his security to ensure that the same crime would not happen under his watch. *There are times this inter-service rivalry works to our advantage.*

Raul and his sister Maria lived on the top floor of the townhome where Caylee took the small bedroom on the first floor. If someone did try and penetrate the home, it put her in a better position to deal with them. *I don't need much space anyway … I don't own a lot.*

They were still attempting to fall into some sort of routine. Maria didn't want to ever be separated from Raul; she always wanted to sleep in the same room as him. She didn't talk much about her time in the Social Quarantine Camp, but Caylee sensed that it had been a horrible experience. *I don't blame her for not wanting to be far from him … that camp took their mother from her.*

She and Raul worked out daily. He had come out of the Supermax in better physical shape than she had ever seen him. They used the base gym where he insisted that she continue their hand-to-hand combat training while Maria watched. Raul listened well and seemed to thrive on the physical stresses she put him through.

Caylee was concerned about their self-imposed isolation, especially with Maria. *It's not healthy to remain indoors all of the time.* She convinced the young girl to join them when they went running, which seemed to help. Bit by bit, Maria was starting to normalize. Caylee could see it when she finally laughed for the first time.

Tonight would be good for them. The doorbell rang and Caylee pulled her weapon and checked outside through a side window, rather than through the peep hole. Smiling, she called, "All clear," and Raul opened the door.

Standing there in the dark was Travis, Charli, and Andy. Raul let them in, giving them a brotherly hug as each came in with the exception of Andy who held a crock pot. With Andy, they bumped elbows as they came in.

Charli moved to hug Caylee, but they paused half-way, awkwardly looking at each other, and then proceeded. Caylee wasn't a hugging person, but for Charli, she would make an exception. There was a bit of mutual admiration between the two of them. Travis gave her a nod, his arm shifting in the sling that he still wore. He had been shot at the Supermax and was still nursing the wound. Andy shuffled in. "I made chili," he said, putting the crockpot on the counter.

Caylee had invited them all to dinner under the pretense that it would be good for Maria to socialize with others. The other reason was far more private. She liked her small circle of friends. Together, they had done the impossible—break Raul out of the Supermax—the first successful breakout from there. She found herself missing them for the last few weeks after their return to America with Raul. *I used to think I didn't need friends. As it turns out, I was missing this in my life.*

The dinner was fun. Andy was a decent cook; the chili was hot which she liked, and everyone was laughing, joking, and poking fun at each other. Caylee eyed Maria and saw her laughing as well as they relayed the stories of planning Raul's liberation. They retired to the family room space with a few cold beers.

"So Caylee, what is next for you?" Charli asked.

"I'm here for the time being," she said, realizing she didn't know how to answer the question. *What is next for me?* It was a query that was as perplexing to her as it was to Charli. "I assume at some point Mr. Desmond will be offering me an opportunity to test my skills again. In the meantime, I'm here." She glanced over at Raul who gave her a nod.

"What about you Raul?" Andy asked.

"They are doing things in those Social Quarantine Camps differently now. From what Maria has told me and what Charli and Caylee learned, they are more death factories now than reeducation. They were bad before. Now the government is using them to exterminate their enemies. We can't let that continue. We have to save as many of those people as possible."

Travis took a long sip of beer, then spoke up. "Those camps are a real challenge. Most are only lightly defended, but getting the people out and to safety … it's a logistical challenge."

"We have to do it," Maria said, surprising Caylee by joining in. "They killed our mother. They will keep on killing people. It may be hard, but we have to try."

Caylee felt strangely moved by Maria speaking up. She had been so quiet for weeks, and now she was finally emerging from her shell with someone other than her brother. *It's healthy for her to engage like this.* "Travis is right; it's a challenge, but it can be done," she said.

"Every person we get out hurts Newmerica," Raul said. "They will tell their stories, and it will confirm people's fears about those camps. Someone needs to be held accountable for this slaughter."

"That's the trouble," Andy said, seated on the arm of the sofa next to Charli. "You can take down the camps, but the people that gave the orders to kill those people, holding them accountable for their crimes, that's a different challenge. History shows that it is easier to bring the underlings to justice, but the big fish, they tend to get away or cheat justice."

"Why is that?" Raul asked.

Andy leaned back. "History is full of people beating the legal system. Herman Göring committed suicide to avoid the hangman's noose. A number of Nazi war criminals went to South America and died of old age before their identities were found out. Those that are caught, like Eichmann, never admit what they did was wrong. Justice is a pretty elusive thing when it comes to the big war criminals of history."

"That sucks," Raul said.

"It's reality," Charli replied. "It doesn't make it right, but it is how the world works unfortunately."

"The biggest challenge you are going to face is reaction to liberating a camp," Travis said, shifting the topic back to the original. "When you hit Valley Forge, the result was that they reinforced security all up and down the East Coast. Since you can't liberate all of the camps at once, the minute you start in an area, it will force the authorities to beef up security everywhere else. Each subsequent camp you hit is going to be harder. Also, since they are using the camps to kill people, once you start freeing people, they will escalate the killings. Less people alive means less people to testify against them."

Charli nodded as she began to speak. "The good news is that if we do pull something off like this, it will syphon off SE and NSF resources to have to deal with protecting the camps. The more they are sucked into that job, the less the army will have to deal with." *Jack Desmond will appreciate that aspect of all of this ... and we are going to need his support for such a plan.*

"It almost sounds like you're trying to talk me out of this," Raul said.

"*On contraire,*" Caylee said. "We are professionals. It is our job to look at the obstacles and come up with a way to overcome them. You should have sat in during the sessions we had when we planned to spring you from jail."

Raul nodded, clearly thankful she was not dissuading him. Caylee continued. "If you're doing this to save lives, it means we have to stage this on a larger scale. That means greater logistics."

Charli looked at Maria and at Raul. "We shouldn't talk so much shop. You just got free and reunited with your sister Raul. This is a time to kick back, get your bearings again. That time in prison couldn't have been good for you."

Raul crossed his arms as Charlie spoke. "It was rough," he conceded. "At the same time, I hadn't had time to relax except for the time I spent with Caylee after she got me out of Pennsylvania." He cast her a glance, and she offered a thin smile. "Before all of this I was just a kid in the Youth Corps. Now half of the country thinks I'm some escaped domestic terrorist."

"Raul, you know you're not a terrorist," Caylee said.

"I know," he said. "The thing is Caylee, I have been on the run, and the whole world is constantly coming at me. Deja Jordan, she tortured me. They were going to try me and kill me … that was their plan. The made me run; they hunted me down, kidnapped me, beat me." It was clear he was getting emotional, more than usual. Charli reached over and put her hand on his shoulder, but Raul pressed on.

"This cost me my *madre*. She died thinking I was a terrorist." He paused, visibly shaken by his admission.

Caylee opened her mouth to talk, but couldn't form the words. This had been coming for a while, and a part of her was glad that he was letting it out. *He's been hurt … badly.*

Raul drew a long breath, then continued before anyone could speak. "The thing is, I haven't been in control since Valley Forge. They have had me reacting to them. I'm tired of that. Planning to get those people out, to save them before they are killed, that is the first positive thing I've been able to do in a while."

Caylee never felt as proud of her friend as she did in that moment. A rare chill ran up her spine. *He's right. This is something that gives him purpose, and it is something positive. He needs this.* "Alright then," she said, summoning control over her emotions. "Then we plan it—together."

Raul's face lit up. "Really, you'll all help?" his eyes swept the people in the room.

"Of course," Charli said. "I think you more than deserve some payback with the Newmerica government."

"Sounds like fun," Travis Cullen said, finishing his beer.

Even Andy smiled. "We *are* kind of the experts in prison breaks."

Caylee settled back in the chair. A part of her was just as excited as Raul, though she would never show it. *This is going to take time and thought to pull off, but we're just the people to do it.*

CHAPTER 3

*"There are no police—the NSF is a
social support organization."*

Berlin, New Hampshire

The Massachusetts National Guard patrol slowly made its way
down Jericho Road heading south, easing through the town of
Berlin. Su-Hui watched from the roof of the sporting goods store
as the patrol made its way through the city, the turrets of the Bradley
fighting vehicles sweeping each building as if they were afraid of an
ambush.

There had been a few angry arguments and heated debates, led by
Herb Fletcher, to do just that. Herb seemed to thrive on creating strife
for Su-Hui. The idea of ambushing the patrol in the same town they used
as their base of operations was foolhardy, but Herb insisted, loudly, as if
that somehow made him more right. Su-Hui eventually told him to shut
up. *There is a time for debate, and a time for rational thought. Herb
doesn't understand the difference.* One of the members of his cell had
told him not to take it personal. From what he had been told, Herb's wife
had left him before the war. Given his abrasive personality, it was easy
for him to understand his wife's departure. He had gotten himself fired
from his job for being obstinate. "Herb is one of those guys that works
hard to find new ways to screw up his life, then blame everyone else for
it. He has a self-destructive streak. His big mouth is his worst enemy."
It had told him a lot about Herb as a man, but not how to manage him.

Su-Hui had ordered the Sons of Liberty to hunker down and hide
when a patrol came through. Engaging the enemy National Guard would

be fighting on the Guard's terms. Setting off an IED in town would force them to begin a search, one that would put the SOL at risk of being discovered. *To fight this war, we must not wage it the way the enemy wants. They desire a set-piece battle where the odds will be even. I do not want even odds. I want to win.*

Su-Hui watched the patrol snake through the city, and his legs didn't cramp until they were out of sight. The walkie-talkie he carried crackled as the New Hampshire National Guard troops who were charged with protecting Berlin weighed in. "They are on their way Su-Hui," signaled the sergeant who was observing the perimeter. "I think we are safe for now." It was only then that he let himself relax. Working his way down the ladder at the rear of the building, he went inside where the SOL were armed and ready to fight, in case one broke out. "We are clear," Su-Hui told those present.

"Hiding isn't fighting," Herb snarled as the others began to relax. "I came here to fight."

Su-Hui wanted to ignore him, but experience with the man had taught him that he would not let up. "We will fight, when the time is right."

"Where?" another voice, a female named Rachel, asked.

Su-Hui knew that was a decision that had been made by General Griffiths before his departure. "Our target is outside of Boston. It is the National Guard Joint Force Headquarters at Hanscom Air Force Base."

"Boston?" an SOL leader from Ohio spoke up. "That's hours from here."

"Yes, it is," Su-Hui said. "And it is across the border which is protected with checkpoints. Between here and there are thousands of enemy troops just looking for the opportunity to engage us.

"It is a difficult assignment, but one we drew. There are other raids planned with adjoining states by other SOL groups. Hitting the enemy in their home states will scare their leaders. They will fear worse attacks. Taking out the Joint Force Headquarters will cripple them even further."

"How can we do it? We can't use snowmobiles that far," said another SOL member with a distinct Bronx accent.

"General Griffiths presented an approach. We need to go there in vehicles—National Guard trucks. Some will be loaded with explosives; some loaded with us. We will blend in as a convoy returning from

New Hampshire. Once we are in the base, we will park the trucks with explosives and extract the drivers; then get out. The bombs will do the rest of the work."

"I don't know if you've noticed or not," Herb said. "But we don't have any Massachusetts National Guard trucks, let alone enough explosives to do any real damage."

Su-Hui eyed him carefully. *This is not the time and place for a confrontation, in front of the others.* "I am well aware of that. We will need to steal some trucks. As for the explosives, the General has indicated he will provide them. Add in some falsified orders and credentials, and we should be able to drive right across the border and get into the base." The crowd of freedom fighters began to murmur, talking about the plan among themselves. Su-Hui could see that they were generally in approval, which only made Herb Fletcher fume a little more.

"This sounds risky," a deep voice came from a dark-complexioned woman of color, a recent SOL volunteer.

Su-Hui nodded. "It is. Most of us are not strangers to the risks we've faced. We have been hunted by the enemy. They destroyed our base of operations in Lisbon, killing some of our loved ones. This is war, and at any time, something can go wrong and lives can be lost."

Bowing his head slightly, Su-Hui drew a deep breath, then continued. "Risk is something I am familiar with. My family is from Taiwan. We were there when the Chinese attacked. They devoured our military. We counted on help from America, but the Ruling Council refused to send the aid we were promised. Our people fought hard, with spirit, but the numbers were against us.

"In that chaos, I got my family to our boat and sailed off. I had rarely sailed out of sight of the shore, but set out blindly, across the ocean. The enemy jets roared overhead. We found other boats and stayed together. At any moment we could all have been destroyed.

"We were picked up by the Navy. My family struggled in this new nation, Newmerica. A group of Social Enforcers attacked my wife and daughter. We moved away from California and the madness there. I never forgot the America of my youth—the land of the free and the home of the brave. So when the chance came to join the Sons of Liberty, I did … we both did," he cast a glance at his wife Hachi who smiled proudly.

"My entire life for the last few years has been risk upon risk. You are all here for your own reasons. Just getting to New Hampshire was full of risk. Every day and night risk stalks us all. It is easy to give into your fears," Su-Hui said and cast a quick glance at Herb, which only made the portly man blush with anger. "But we do not. So yes, sneaking into Massachusetts is dangerous. It is filled with risk. I, for one, think the risk is worth the reward of further crippling their war on the people of this state. I accept the risk."

The nodding of heads and the smiles of determination washed over Su-Hui as Herb and his tiny cadre of followers fumed and made their way to the rear of the crowd. "You heard the man," Trudy spoke up. This burly lumberjack from Michigan had been Su-Hui's partner. "We need to figure out where we can get our hands on some trucks!"

The District

General Hollings Rinehart was ushered into the Newmerican President Daniel Porter's office by his assistant, a skinny non-binary person with fading orange streaks in their hair. The Vice President saw the military as pompous, and there was little reason to think of Rinehart any differently. While the office was Daniel Porter's, the VP was far more of an authority figure in the room, and she knew it.

Rinehart had come on the recommendation of the Army Chief of Staff, though that meant very little to the assistant as the man came in and was shown a seat. The VP had wanted a person of color or someone that checked off all of the right boxes – to show that the people of Newmerica were properly represented. The Pentagon had insisted on Rinehart, over her protests. They claimed he was the man to get the job done, someone that could fight the civil war swiftly to conclusion and victory. *The Pentagon said that same sort of glowing things about General Donaldson, and he cost us Atlanta and left us with a quagmire in New Hampshire.*

"General," President Porter said as the officer shifted in the seat next to the Vice President. "I appreciate you coming right over."

"No problem Mister President," he said, sweeping back his old-man's blonde hair with his left hand.

"General Donaldson left us with quite a mess up in New Hampshire," Daniel said as the VP watched the reaction on the older General's face.

"Insurgencies are tricky beasts to begin with sir," Rinehart said. "With the winter conditions up there, it is hard to press your enemy into the kind of battle that's easy to win."

"What would you do differently General?" the Vice President asked.

"I don't want to speak ill of the dead, but General Donaldson was a bit too soft on these people. Cutting off electricity in Gorham for a few days was a minor inconvenience at best. Destroying Lisbon was a good start, but it was too small and isolated to serve as a good example.

"What I would do is stop pussyfooting around with the Governor and his people, trying to get them to accept the election results. They need to be imprisoned or dealt with in some other way." There was something in the way that he said the last bit that told her they might be facing a firing squad, which she approved of.

"We need to build off of what was done in Lisbon—on a larger scale. Let them see the downtown of a major city blasted apart if they support these insurgents. We need to put some camps in place, round up people helping the enemy, and intern them for the duration of the conflict. We need to bring in a lot of additional troops as well, surge and surge hard." His voice rattled off the ideas at a consistent and angry pace.

Daniel seemed to soak up the details. "I tend to agree. A number of these terrorists came to New Hampshire from other states. We have SEs in those states. I think we should go after their families if we find them."

"That's a good idea," Rinehart said. "Once they see their loved ones shipped off to Social Quarantine, they might think twice about staying and fighting in New Hampshire."

"What about St. Louis and the offence in Iowa?" the VP asked.

"We learned some good lessons from Atlanta," General Rinehart said. "Sieges are nasty things. We need additional combat forces in the St. Louis autonomous zone. If you can spare some SWAT teams from the NSF, they would be perfect to get in there. St. Louis has small reservoirs but gets most of its drinking water from the Missouri. We will need to reinforce the purification plants, but that puts that city in a better place than Atlanta where they were cut off from fresh water.

"Breaking out, the way that they tried in Atlanta, was a hot mess Mr. President. General Kotter was a fool for trying it, and Donaldson shouldn't have approved it."

"He was worried about the civilians being without food and water," President Porter said.

"The looting and hoarding were the root of that problem," Rinehart said. "We have much more of an NSF presence there to avoid that kind of shit. The food supplies need to be under military control for rationing from the start. Also, we need more troops in the zone before they tighten the noose around the city."

"And what about Iowa?"

Rinehart drew a quick breath sighing it out slowly. "It's a damned good diversion at best. Yes, we needed to secure the Rock Island facility, but this is aimed at keeping our enemies focused elsewhere. Inflicting some pain on Davenport is good; it forces the enemy to respond, but that's about all. Strategically, it doesn't help us much other than siphoning off troops to deal with it."

"We still have Iron Scorpion," the President said.

That ushered in a rare grin from General Rinehart. "I planned Iron Scorpion to be the knockout punch. We are massing National Guard troops in Virginia for the attack. Right now, we have them poised to appear to be a strike into North Carolina. Our drones have seen a buildup in that state in response."

The Vice President grinned. The plan for Operation Iron Scorpion had been proposed by Rinehart, and she loved it. *The enemy thinks they are so safe in Tennessee ... not for long.* The best way to defeat the enemy was to cut off their head, and that was what Iron Scorpion did.

"Will they be able to counter it?"

"It's possible," Rinehart said. "This General Reager of theirs seems to be a sharp cookie. So far he's handled his affairs quite well. Iron Scorpion is the boldest offensive we have planned. If we catch him with his pants down, it has a good chance of succeeding."

She loathed the respect that the General gave to his opponent ... a telltale sign of toxic masculinity as far as she could see. Daniel nodded and she remained quiet. He glanced at her, and she gave him a single nod of approval. Only then did the Newmerican President speak up. "It sounds like we have the right man for the job. You will assume overall command of the Newmerican military forces immediately."

Rinehart flashed another small grin as he rose to his feet. "Thank you sir," he said, saluting. He did a fast about face and walked out of the President's office, leaving her alone with Daniel.

"You are being remarkably quiet Alex," Daniel said.

She stirred slightly in her seat before responding, "I have doubts about the military—I always have. For generations we have spent far too much money on military hardware and gadgets that could have better been spent on social programs."

"Agreed. For now, we need them," the President said. "When this is over, well, we will need them less."

"As for Rinehart … he says all of the right things. Then again, so did Donaldson."

"I've come to the conclusion that the Pentagon sent us Donaldson to get rid of him," Daniel conceded. "He was the one that made sure that no one from the military came to the aid of the Traitor during the Liberation. Having him die the way he did was fairly convenient for them. It removes a key person that might make them look bad if this war ends up in our defeat."

Alex nodded. "I thought the same thing. The problem with the military is that we have control over them, but we don't have eyes and ears in the field. Otherwise, we might have spotted some of the mistakes that Donaldson made and could have corrected them before they ended up being disasters."

"What are you suggesting?"

"I think we need people's officers embedded in the military. People from the SE ranks that are loyal to us, rather than to the Pentagon. We can give them the power to form Tribunals if they see officers not acting in the best interest of the nation. Having our people, *loyal* people, in with the military ensures our desires are fulfilled."

"Commissars?"

"Of course we won't use that name," she said with a cringing expression. "It has too many negative implications. We can call them the People's Wardens, or something like that. It will ensure morale is where it should be and give us more control of the military."

She had been waiting for the right opportunity to spring the idea on Daniel, and Rinehart's appointment had served it up to her perfectly.

The President of the Newmerican states hesitated. "I tend to agree.

At the same time we have had tacit support from the military. While I don't trust them, I think we need to think this through a little bit before doing something that might alienate some of their officers."

She was a little surprised. Daniel had always been decisive, but now that he had the title of President, he was dithering. *Where is the man that brought about the Great Reformation?* Her mind raced with how to convince him. *He needs a story ... something to remind him of who he really is.*

"Daniel, I'm reminded of a story my mother once told me. Have you ever seen a dead squirrel on the road?"

He was puzzled, but paying attention. "Of course."

"Do you know what killed the squirrel?"

"I assume a car tire."

"No. Most people think that though. You're a thoughtful person, so you'll understand. It wasn't the car that killed the squirrel; it was indecision. You've probably seen it dozens of times in your life. A squirrel runs in the road, sees the car, and panics. It starts running one way, hesitates, then turns back the other way, then panics more, and eventually is just gets hit in the road. Why? It froze, so focused on the car, it couldn't make up its mind. Indecision killed the squirrel.

"We are at a crucial point in this conflict. The enemy has had some victories. We need to keep the military in line. Remember, they turned their back on the Traitor President when we came into power. There's always a chance that they will flip back." *There—let him chew on that.*

Porter nodded. "You're right. Thank you for clearing my head on this. I have never fully trusted the military either. They have stayed on the sidelines, giving us bits and pieces of what we need, but refusing to commit to the cause. They are waiting to see who wins rather than jumping in with all of their might. Having our own people, these, let's call them Warden Officers, in with the troops will ensure that the military doesn't turn against us when the chips are down."

There's the Daniel I have come to know! "Rinehart and others will protest," she said.

"Let them. I am the President and have the authority to order this," he said with pride.

She rose slowly. "Then I can go and make preparations?"

"Of course. Thank you Alex. I can always count on you."

Smiling, she walked out of his office. *He was as easy to manipulate as always. Now my people will be in with the military. With the NSF and SEs already in my control, I now will have my grip on the military as well.*

Momma would be so proud of what her little girl has become!

Jackson, Michigan

The Standard Goods warehouse was a dark red brick structure that stood three stories tall. In its prime, it had probably been storage for everything from industrial dies and molds to people's house contents. Its prime was long behind it now. While the building itself was structurally sound, the company that had owned it went out of business years ago. Since then it had been purchased by a holding company. The majority was owned by an off-shore investment firm that was backed by the Chinese government.

As Dr. Liu pulled into the structure's big, ground floor, the metal door closed behind him. Standard Goods had been a staging point for him. Jackson Michigan was situated almost dead center between Chicago and Detroit on I-94. In the days before the Liberation, the Chinese had used the warehouse to smuggle drugs into the United States. Back in those years, it was less about making money than about creating lawlessness and moral decay in America. No one suspected the Chinese being involved heavily in the U.S. drug trade ... he had organized several gangs and other criminal groups to handle his distribution. Flooding drugs into major urban centers increased crimes, put strains on law enforcement, and cost the Americans millions to try to fight the epidemic.

Things were different now. After the Liberation, instability could come from the massive socialist changes that the Ruling Council had inflicted. Liu remembered the days when militia groups had tried to rise up against the gun control laws. ... Arming them had increased bloody and politically embarrassing standoffs. Pitting Americans against each other was even easier with a government in power whose political alignment was so close to his own nations' ideology.

The small group that greeted him were not Chinese nationals, but Americans that had been bought and paid for. In every nation there were people whose allegiance and loyalties could be purchased. It was a simple matter of how much it cost. If anything, under the Newmerican flag, it was easier to find people who were willing to sell out their values. That was what Reparation Points did—it turned neighbor against neighbor for money—rewarding behaviors that the state sanctioned. The taxing of the upper and middle classes made prosperity difficult, and with Social Enforcement in place, anyone trying to get ahead became a target. *These people like to think they have such lofty ideals, but in the end, there are always those that turn traitor if presented the opportunity.*

Some of the men were his own security detail. They came in an SUV. They wore black clothing and made no qualm about showing their firepower openly. They were not locals, not like the others in the warehouse. These were people that he had turned long ago, true loyalists to the Chinese nation. Their presence was less for his security, and more of a show of force.

It was the same back home in China. The Triads, organized crime gangs, not only existed but thrived. Some of the groups were covertly backed by the government, while others were completely rogue. Despite generations of indoctrination, the black market always seemed to prevail. Weber remembered as a youth when the PAP—the People's Armed Police raided a small grocery store in his neighborhood. He remembered the family that ran the business; they seemed like nice people. Little did he know that they were supplementing their income by selling goods provided by one of the Triads.

In the raid the PAP found boxes of black western products. The couple was sent to jail—their business boarded up. It was fitting; they were traitors after all, working against the interests of the people as a whole. A few weeks later, word spread that the Long Zi Group, one of the Triads, had established another front for their smuggled-in goods. It was a lesson Liu took to heart. *The lower people will be the ones to go to jail if we are caught—not the leader.* From that point on, he made sure he was that person.

Liu moved over to the pile of crates, partially covered by a gray tarp. One of the men working for him pulled it back to reveal the metal boxes, marked: Medications—Do Not Expose to Light. Several Canadian maple leaf stickers were slapped on the crates as well indicating custom's approvals.

"The Canadian's did exactly as you said," the tall man said pointing to the crates. "No one in their customs wanted to open them fearing it would ruin the medical supplies."

Having the goods come in through Canada had been easy. With the instability of their southern neighbor, Canada had slid closer to the Chinese government as a reliable trading partner. The 'medical supplies' had simply been looked over.

Liu nodded to the tall man who snapped the latches on the cases. The black plastic interior was sealed, so that even a casual check might look like protection for medication. When he peeled it back, the inside showed the long, dull green tubes, four of them, perfectly packed. Additional metal components, small boxes, and sealed tubes were packed alongside them just in case the Canadians decided to somehow x-ray the contents.

Perfect, just what I need for our friends! The tubes were portable anti-tank missiles, the HJ-12. Liu knew that at some point, the Americans were going to have to force their hand with the rebellious Texas Republic … and when they did, they would get a surprise … an armed response that could destroy their most potent conventional weapon—the Abrams tank.

The shipment represented much more than that. *It is time that the Newmericans feel some of the same pain as their comrades to the south.* "Excellent. Arrange to smuggle four of these crates to our contacts in the Republic of Texas. Take the other four and transport them to our facility in Ishpeming."

The men exchanged glances, unsure why they would be taking the missiles north to Michigan's Upper Peninsula. *They are curious, but cautious.* It was one thing for them to offer their services against the Pretender President and America. It was another if the weapons were being stored for some reason in their own state. Their moment of angst somehow made him feel good … powerful. Liu glanced at his security detail who simply shifted in place, gripping their weapons even tighter. The traitors he was meeting saw the gesture and understood that asking questions was not something that would be wise on their part. "You heard my orders?"

The men nodded. "Good. Make the arrangements to get them to

Texas in the next two weeks. I have transferred the first half of your payment into the off-shore accounts we set up for you. You get the rest when the job is complete. Understood?"

He got more nods in response. The professor moved back to his vehicle where the driver was waiting, and his security detail moved to their SUV behind him. As he pulled away, Weber Liu allowed himself a broad grin. *My nation wins by making sure that this country never unites, that it remains in chaos and divided.*

CHAPTER 4

*"The Great Reformation is only possible by
inconsequential sacrifices on all of our part."*

*Texas Military Department (TMD) HQ,
Camp Mabry, Austin, Texas*

For General Trip Reager, coming back to the headquarters of the Texas National Guard felt odd. After the dissolution of his family and the loss of his business, the National Guard had become his life—his home. Most of what he owned was in a storage unit in College Station, Texas. His simple quarters off-base was modest, deliberately devoid of photographs or anything that might offer a chance of a memory of his past. The rise of Newmerica had stripped him of his former life, one precious piece at a time. Dwelling on it didn't help make the pain any easier. What did help was fighting to put an end to the half-decade nightmare of a progressive American state.

He shook hands with Colonel Lance Meade of the Oklahoma National Guard. The stately black officer had a chiseled expression of grimness about him. Trip had read the dossier on the man and knew he was a tough, hardball officer. After the Fall, they had taken him into custody, shipping him off for three years in Social Quarantine. He had gotten out just before the recent election and had personally led his troops to liberate the camp he had been held in. For Colonel Meade, the civil war was personal and Trip respected that.

Captain Judy Mercury came in and took her seat next to him as they all settled in. Meade's aide, a Second Lieutenant whose name badge read Mathews, gave Judy a nod as they settled in across from each other.

"Thank you for coming Colonel," Trip said.

"Thank you for asking nicely," he said cracking a smile so thin that it was almost invisible.

Trip settled into his seat opposite of Meade. "I'm activating the 45th Infantry Brigade Combat Team and placing you under my command. I've discussed it with General Moorehouse, and he suggested we talk."

"Very well, General," Meade said, his face offering little expression. *This is a man I would not like to play poker with.*

"We need to destabilize the Newmerican forces that have crossed into Iowa. Most of Davenport is under their control. The Iowa troops are dug in on the outskirts of the city, but they are in a defensive posture. The Illinois forces are currently staging for a final push."

"The Thunderbirds will not let you down sir."

Trip was happy to get that kind of response, though he did not doubt he would get it. Bravado and the military were joined at the proverbial hip. "If we want to slug it out with them in Davenport, it's going to get ugly. I wanted to call this meeting to do a little strategic shit-balling and see if we can find a way around this problem rather than sending good men and women into a meat grinder."

Colonel Meade nodded. "I think we all can appreciate that."

"The challenge is that the Illinois troops, along with the NSF and SEs, have a strong natural barrier to defend, the Mississippi," Trip conceded. "I'd love to get in behind them, force them to either withdraw from Davenport, or surround them there and starve them out."

"Chances are they know that," Meade replied. "Unless their CO has a brain full of horseshit, he will have some mobile units behind the river defenses. If we try to force a crossing at a non-bridge location, he will respond and hit us before we can have a strong bridgehead."

"That is what aerial reconnaissance has told us," Trip said. "With St. Louis being an autonomous zone, it limits our crossing points dramatically. I am interested in your insight into this, Colonel," he said as he rolled out a map of Iowa and Illinois showing the best estimates of troop placements on both sides.

Meade leaned over the map and studied it for a long, few, silent minutes. "Assuming they have most of the bridges wired with explosives, we don't have a lot of good options here sir."

Trip had felt the same thing.

He had brought Captain Mercury with him for a reason, but didn't tell her. Trip remembered how she had earned notoriety in Iraq while serving under him. *Judy is the kind of person that doesn't play a traditional game of war. She's aggressive as hell and she thinks creatively, something many career officers lack. I need to take advantage of that kind of thought process.* "Captain, what are your thoughts?" he said turning his head slowly to her.

"Sir?" She had been caught off guard, but not entirely shaken.

"Captain I didn't just bring you in here because you are on my staff. You're here because you have a certain knack for not following the usual military conventions. You pulled it off against the Iraqis; you did an outstanding job at Stone Mountain, and I need a bit of that brilliant thinking you are known for."

Her slightly darker skin went red in the cheeks with his comments. "If I may be so bold sir, I think the key with these people is to fight them where they aren't."

"What do you mean Captain?" Meade asked.

"Sirs," she said, clearly composing her thoughts. "If you move to encircle them, you still have a sizable force of Illinois troops who will get increasingly desperate. As we saw at Stone Mountain, they will try to force their way out of a shitty situation, one we would create for them."

"Go on," Trip urged.

"You need to get them to withdraw, preferably on their own, not dig in," Mercury replied, gathering her composure even more. "I would not try to come in behind them. I would give them something else to think about, something that would force them to get out of Iowa." Her finger hovered over the map for a moment, then stabbed down on a city.

Springfield! Trip couldn't help but smile. *The state capital. That will certainly get their attention.* "That's a long way behind enemy lines," Meade said. "Abrams and Bradleys eat a lot of fuel. The Abrams run on fuel you can't get at the nearest Exxon station. You drive in that far and get into a fight, you're going to be fighting some hellacious logistics."

Meade's point was incredibly valid. It was not strategy and tactics that won battles. It was logistics that often was the true god of war. Judy was undeterred by his comment. "I understand that sir, but there are ways around that."

"How?"

"I haven't come up with that yet?"

"How will you get a raiding force on the other side of the Mississippi?" Trip asked.

This time it was Judy who flashed a bit of a grin. "If we try to fight across, they will blow the bridges and we will lose a lot of people. I suggest we apply a level of, excuse my language, tactical fuckery sir."

"Go on," Meade said, leaning back and eyeing the Captain carefully.

"Both sides use the same gear in this war—same vehicles, tanks, guns, armor, everything. We should take advantage of that. We can disguise ourselves as Illinois National Guard forces. Forge some orders and pray for a little incompetence, and they will let us drive right into Illinois."

"Damned risky," Colonel Meade said, followed by a pause. "I like it. They'd never expect us to strike at their state capital; nor would they expect us to camouflage ourselves like their own troops. It's just crazy enough to work."

Trip smiled. "Our watchword is audacity. For the time being, I'm attaching Captain Mercury to your staff. If anyone can work this out, it's her." He glanced at his subordinate and gave her an assuring nod. Judy's blush only grew.

"Welcome to the Thunderbirds, Captain," Meade said, extending his hand.

Charlottesville, Virginia

David Steele sat in the Runk Dining Room on the University of Virginia Campus, pretending to be looking at his iPad. The dining hall was a low buzz of discussion, occasional laughs, and occasional clatter from the back area of plates and silverware being cleaned. The smells were enticing as well. A part of him wished he had a student ID just to eat some of the food. *Dad said when he went to college that dorm food was horrible—but these kids eat like kings and queens.*

His eyes studied the students while he masked his disdain for them. This was where his sister had gone to school before she had been murdered by her so-called peers. While they all appeared to be nice kids, he knew the truth; many of them were committed fanatics in support of Newmerica. Colleges were less involved with educating than they were with indoctrinating the students. He had sat in on numerous classes and had seen the instructors in action. Any student that questioned the narrative that America was a corrupt rebellious state was quickly scorned, not just by the professor, but by fellow students. He had seen one student driven into humiliating silence in front of his peers by the teacher's mocking. *This is what it must have been like for Maddie. She simply kept her mouth shut, but in the end, even that was not enough.*

David had attended the memorial protest over the murder of Dr. Morose. Some students were impassioned and they were openly weeping, which forced David to suppress a sneer. The leaders of the protest claimed that Morose had been killed by "fanatics who want to take down our country." He didn't see himself that way at all. *They are the fanatics—they riot regularly; they created a culture that allowed innocent kids to be slaughtered.*

When he spoke to his father about it, Grayson Steele had told his son his perception. "They are everything they claim they aren't. They call anyone that doesn't believe the way they do Nazis or racists. In reality, they are the ones that use the same tactics that the Nazis did. They label groups and assign negative traits to them. They support Stormtroopers by allowing Social Enforcers to operate. They are the ones that embrace a form of national socialism. They are everything they claim the other side is." David found himself unable to disagree.

He had come to the dining room, not for a meal, but to conduct surveillance on another professor, one Dr. Carmen Mikolitis. She was the chair of the Political Science Department, the literal heart of student programming. Dr. Mikolitis had an olive complexion with very short black hair that looked at times more like a helmet than a hair style. David's eyes were always drawn to her fingernails, which were long and painted glossy black.

Dr. Mikolitis held court in the Runk Dining Room three days a week during lunch. Students, either adoring her politics or seeking to gain favor, crammed into one of the large booths where she sat, hanging on her every word. She seemed to revel in being the center of attention; he could see it in her deep hazel eyes and the smile she flashed. Students peppered her with questions about the war, about the evils of capitalism, and she fed them lines that sounded like TRC approved sound bites. *They worship her. They see her as an inspiration.* David had no doubt that she was seen as the embodiment of the Newmerica ideals on campus.

Which was why she had to die.

She was only some fifteen feet away, and he could hear her talking, only occasionally casting her a casual glance. Bits of her comments reached him clearly. "Social Quarantine is necessary to protect the elements of our society that don't believe in our values. If we didn't have quarantine, they would be targets for justifiable correction. We have put people in the camps for their own good."

David pushed down his anger at what she said. *That was what they wanted to do with my parents—with us.* Grayson Steele had hidden his family because he knew he was a target. *I saw the footage of the people they got out of Valley Forge. They were being starved to death. She's just pushing the same lies that the government does.*

She pecked lightly at her salad, spending most of the time basking in the glow of the students that sat with her. David tried to push past her arrogance, but couldn't. It was the essence of who Mikolitis was. *Her hate brings her admirers and she loves it. ... You can see it in her face and hear it in the excitement of her voice.*

He knew that killing her would not stop the hate on campus. His father pointed out that after the death of Dr. Morose and the killing of the Grays, the deaths only seemed to galvanize the students more. Part of it was fear. David knew that they were worried about what might happen to one of them.

As she finished her late afternoon meal, Dr. Mikolitis got up and left. A trio of students followed her, as did David, but from at least twenty feet back. She walked to her car, a candy-apple red electric Subaru, thanked her followers, and took off. *She's predictable. She follows a pattern.*

Pulling out his phone, he called his father. "She's on her way home," David said as his father picked up.

"Good. It's the same every day," his father replied. "I'll see you at the apartment."

Today was surveillance only. His father was checking to see where security cameras were and where there were dead spaces. They had done the same with Dr. Morose before killing him. David knew that killing Mikolitis would not bring back Maddie—but it might give the students and faculty a dose of the fear they were serving on a daily basis. They would be forced to look over their shoulders, feel unsafe even in the comfort of their homes. For five years they had beaten, killed, and imprisoned others without the least bit of guilt. Mikolitis's death would rattle them all.

Turning, David walked off campus as a brisk blast of cool late January air hit him. Following his father's advice, he checked all around him, swiveling his head around to make sure he was not being followed. He knew that he was an outsider, pretending to be a student. It was like being a pilot shot down behind enemy lines. Caution was as important as blending in.

Once he got within eyesight of his tiny apartment, he thought again of the sister that had been taken from him. *Maddie ... we will make them pay for what they did to you ... I promise it.*

Nashville, Tennessee

Kiff Renner had three massive monitors dominating his desk, and all three were a montage of open windows, running applications, and other tools of the trade. Occasionally images would pop up of the people he was looking into. Their data would be sifted, sorted, and stored in secured folders.

His office was dark. Kiff had chosen one without an exterior window, not just for security purposes but because he preferred working only in the warm, white glow from the big monitors. Kiff knew he was a bit awkward—'quirky' was the word his mother used once to describe him. Social interactions always felt forced to him; he made himself deal with people one-on-one. In the digital realm, though, he was in his comfort zone. These streams of data and bits of information, ... this was his universe and in this universe, he was a god.

Booker Hickox, a self-proclaimed General of the Free Texas movement, had organized a militia group right after the Fall, the Hickox Rangers. They had engaged with several SE groups in Texas before being declared domestic terrorists. The newly formed NSF had rounded up most of them, though Hickox had evaded capture. As a former Army vet, dishonorably discharged for insubordination right at the time of the

Fall, he had become a bit of a celebrity in Texas for outfoxing the NSF. *People that evade the law, even for the wrong reasons, always seem to gather followers.*

Salem Marshall, on the other hand, the man that claimed to speak for Free Texas as its President, was a highly successful businessman. He ran a massive shipping company, Trans-Tex, that, despite the waves of recession that followed the rise of Newmerica, still eked out a profit and stayed in business. He was a former U.S. Army officer and had hosted several high-priced fundraisers for his cause in recent months. *This guy is the financial backing for this. Holding the purse strings puts him in charge.*

Miley Hines had been a successful country musician until Newmerica had come into being. Her far-right political views had landed her two years of Social Quarantine and had left her career in ruins except in her home state of Texas. She was far from the attractive young woman she used to be at her peak.

How these three had been drawn together was something that Kiff was curious about, but he knew it was inconsequential. *Let the historians ponder that.* He was more interested in their movement and where it was getting its backing. The state-run firewall that Big Tech was erecting around Newmerica was impressive, but it had plenty of holes in it. It helped that he had some friends who worked covertly for Microsoft and other subcontractors who were deliberately leaving open gaps in the defense. People tended to think of hackers as being loners, but Kiff knew differently. There was a comradery among code-slingers that surpassed politics.

A few months earlier, he had saved some of their lives. Jack Desmond had come to him with an idea about bombing the headquarters of tech companies in California. He had been Jack's consultant on the damage it might cause. It was his suggestions that had avoided the targeting of facilities where Kiff had allies. He was rather proud of that … how he had saved some of the good people out there. While he hated the loss of life that had come from the bombings, he knew how corrupt the Big Tech companies had become. *They are nothing more than tools of the Newmerica state. They have been corrupting the truth, hiding reality from the people, for years.* While some innocent people had died, plenty of individuals drenched in guilt had met their end. *Big Tech still hasn't recovered from what Jack and his people did.*

He had learned bits and pieces about the Free Texas state already. He managed to penetrate one of their email accounts—*what a stupid password—FreeTexas!* Most of the messages were to others that supported the effort, all of whose names Kiff flagged and stored for Jack Desmond to use. It was a little disturbing to see that there were so many people throughout the state of Texas that were behind secession.

From an Excel spreadsheet, he found on one email attachment that a lot of money was being was funneled into the Free Texas movement, though the names were replaced with a series of code names. While a lot of its money had clearly come from Salem Marshall, they had gotten huge influxes from several off-shore accounts in the Cayman Islands in recent months. Marshall had made trips there often in the last year, no doubt managing his affairs and shifting the money around.

So where did those funds come from? Who's really behind this? That had been an elusive bit of information. The banks off-shore were notorious for their privacy and security. That didn't mean they were impenetrable, but simply complicated to get into. He had found a half-dozen deposit sources, all of their account information heavily encrypted. The level of encryption had been a flag for Kiff. This wasn't some geek in his parent's basement whipping up code—this was big-time security, ... *the kind of shit you can only get from a state-sponsored cyber group.*

Some of it had the hallmarks of the Russians. In fact, it seemed almost too obvious that it might be Russia behind the money. It made sense. They had long been a primary source of cyberattacks against the United States. After the Fall, their army had stirred an 'uprising' in the Ukraine and the Russians had swept in, seizing the smaller nation whole in a four-month war. Newmerica had issued warnings, implemented ineffective sanctions, stomped its political feet—but the reality was that the Ukraine was solidly in Russian control. Daniel Porter and the Ruling Council were unwilling to go to war over Ukraine any more than they had been with Taiwan. Putin made no qualms about attempting to bring back the old Soviet Union, and Newmerica was a speed bump to him. *If we had responded militarily, they might hesitate. Instead we send them harsh language. You have to feel sorry for the folks in Lithuania and*

Lapvia ... they are next on the chopping block.

For over three hours he studied the encryption, his eidetic memory crunching tiny fragments of code against things he had seen over his career. To a casual analyst, not one of his caliber, it appeared that all of the transactions were Russian in origin. The more he probed and poked, though, the more he started to see that not all of them were the same. Some were deliberately done to mislead prying eyes, to make people think that the Russians were behind the transactions. *Some of these came from somewhere else. Someone is trying to mislead anyone looking into this.*

Kiff's fingers flew over the keyboard, and he swung his mouse like a saber in battle, shifting windows, moving data, organizing the bits and pieces that he was gathering. As much as he wracked his brain, he couldn't easily arrive at who was behind more than half of the money transfers.

Shifting in his Herman Miller Aeron chair, he only paused to pull a red Twizzler out of the pack on the corner of his desk and chew on it furiously as he thought. Twizzlers were his go-to snack when he was hungry. *I need to back away from this, look at it from a different perspective.* He leaned back in the high-tech chair, surveying the windows and the data. His mind pivoted, attempting to find a new angle. He hit his Mandalorian Bobblehead and watched the silvery helmet bob side to side for a moment as his brain thought about his next moves.

Who has the resources to move money in this manner, hide the tracks, and try to level the blame at the Russians? America and Newmerica had more enemies than it seemed at times. Many had reveled in the coup that had taken out the previous American President. In the dark, shadowy corners of the globe, there were plenty of people that loved the fact that America was divided. More importantly, they would love it if the U.S. never reunited. It would be like the fall of the Soviet Union all over again—another superpower toppled from within. Those thoughts bothered him a great deal, giving him even more concentration on the issue at hand.

Who had the means to try to throw off my hunt? The Saudis had a massive cyber unit that might try such a ploy, but there didn't seem to be a motivation for them. The Germans had a crack team, but again, there didn't seem to be a motive for them to try to destabilize America in the middle of a civil war.

The Chinese were easy to contemplate in the role of villain. They had the resources, well over 10,000 state-sponsored hackers. They would benefit greatly from keeping America in turmoil and as far as blaming the Russians, it was not inconceivable for them to do so.

Some of the encrypted transactions he saw definitely had Russian hallmarks. No doubt the Russians were involved with funneling money to the upstart Texans that were trying to form their own country. The other accounts ... they were different. Kiff understood the digital cloak and dagger thing that his opponent was trying to do, laying the blame at the doorstep of Russia. *Maybe someone else would fall for that, but not me.*

As he eyed the open windows, he felt the pains of frustration. He cast his eyes to the clock and noticed that nine hours had passed. He winced. *No wonder I'm hungry. I've done it again, gotten in so deep that time has slipped away.* Running his save instructions, the windows blinked out. When done, he shut down his PC and powered down the terminals. *I need to go home, clear my head. There's only so much I can do from here. Tomorrow I will poke at the overseas traffic hubs, see if I can tell where the transfers moved through.*

One thing was sure, the Free Texas movement was being propped up from the outside by less than honest players.

CHAPTER 5

*"If you distrust the government, you distrust
your neighbors and family as well."*

Lancaster, New Hampshire

Lancaster, New Hampshire was situated where the Connecticut and Israel Rivers converged, right along the Vermont state border. After the successful raids that the Sons of Liberty and the New Hampshire National Guard had mounted, the border had become more of an armed picket line. One of the Newmerican bases of operation was Lancaster, nestled in the Riverside Camping and Resort.

Su-Hui and the small team of National Guardsmen and SOL troops with him surveyed the base, and he found himself cringing. There had been a one day warming of the weather, and the melting of the snow revealed that the Newmerican forces had used the last few weeks to hunker down. Sandbags and barriers prevented anyone from directly approaching their base. Razor wire on new fence poles formed an outer perimeter. When he had last seen the post, it had a single guard tower. Now there were five. Trees had been recently felled leaving clear fields of fire for anyone that might be approaching the base.

"You almost get the impression that they don't want visitors," said Lieutenant Olsen of the National Guard as he lowered his binoculars.

"They are adapting," Su-Hui said as he lowered his own binoculars. "They are afraid." His voice rang with disappointment. He had hoped to launch a raid at Lancaster, one where they could capture the trucks they needed for their strike in Connecticut. Leading an attack on the base now would result in a large battle, one they might not necessarily win. *Even if we did defeat them, chances are we would be destroying most of their motor pool in the process.*

The problem was they needed the trucks. You could paint trucks to make them look like Connecticut National Guard vehicles, but the license plates would be a dead giveaway. The New Hampshire National Guard didn't have the vehicles to spare, not with spring only a month or more away. When the snow melted, they were going to need the transportation as the fighting would turn from being a guerilla effort to more of a straight-up conflict. *We have to find our own transportation for this.*

"This is all bullshit," Herb Fletcher snarled from the back of the small group. Su-Hui had brought him along, hoping that involving him in the operation might take some of the edge off of the man. It didn't. Herb seemed to revel in questioning everything that Su-Hui said or did. *I have no idea where his bitterness comes from; nor do I care.*

He slid down the snow bank to the huddle at the bottom of the hill that had hidden them from view. "We need to get creative on getting transportation."

"If our intent is to hit the Joint Force Headquarters, it is on an Air Force base. It will be heavily defended. We are going to need at least a few companies' worth of force to breach it," Corporal Abernathy spoke up.

Su-Hui could feel the cold from the snow penetrating the seat of his pants as he sat down in the snow bank. "It is possible that we have been looking at this all wrong from the start," Su-Hui said. "If we were to capture a half-dozen trucks in a raid, it might very well tip them off that we needed them for a reason."

"So what are you thinking Mr. Zhou?" Lieutenant Olsen asked, his breath hanging in the air like a small cloud between them.

"Rather than mount a strike to grab a large number of trucks, perhaps we should shift to Humvees. There are more of them in the state, easier to secure."

"We'll need more of them," Trudy added.

"That's true. But most of them we've seen are armed with machine guns or missiles. Their patrols can be taken, and we can capture them a few Humvees at a time," he offered. It wasn't the approach that he had intended, but, if done correctly, it might work.

"You'll need too many of them," Herb said. "You can't hope to drive a convoy that long into an enemy state. The whole idea is stupid."

Su-Hui rose to his feet from the snow and stood in front of Herb. "I am in charge of the Sons of Liberty. I did not ask for it Herb. The others chose me. They did not choose you."

"It was a damned popularity contest," Herb replied as if he were struggling to hold his anger in check.

"I was chosen for a reason, regardless if you agree with it. As such, I speak for the Sons in such matters. If you are uncomfortable with that, you are welcome to depart."

"This whole operation is going to get a lot of people killed. We're still no closer to ending this war."

This time it was Lieutenant Olsen who weighed in with Herb Fletcher. "That's where you're wrong. Guerilla wars are not won in big battles. We are fighting a war against their morale. We are challenging their moral fortitude to continue the fight. We are siphoning troops that might be used elsewhere. This is a long-term campaign. Every time we strike at the states that sent guardsmen and SEs into New Hampshire, we are making them wonder why they are here and worry that their friends and families back home might be the next targets. This is exactly the kind of war we need to fight."

His face filled with unsatisfied rage, Herb scoffed at the small huddle at the far end of the table. *He has no rebuttal, only his hate.* Su-Hui made sure he made eye contact with all of the others in the cluster. "The Lieutenant is right. Randy always told us we were playing the long game. We must honor his memory and those we have lost by finishing what he started. We need to seize enemy Humvees. That is where we need our focus to be for now. When we have enough, we will take the fight to Massachusetts and make them regret they ever came here."

Nods came back from everyone other than Herb and the one, lone person that stood with him. Slowly they began to make their way through the tramped snow to where they had parked their rides. Trudy, his friend and snowmobile driver, moved on one side of Su-Hui, with Corporal Abernathy on the other.

The young Abernathy spoke in a low voice as they trudged one deep step at a time through the snow. "Look Su-Hui, we can't tell you what to do. You folks are militia—irregulars. But I have some advice for you."

"I welcome it."

"This Herb fella," he said, nodding ahead where Herb and his compatriot made their way through the snow. "He's going to be a problem. You're going to have to deal with him. If you don't do it now, you'll have to do it later."

Su-Hui nodded. "There is still a chance that he will come around."

Trudy leaned in. "Give me the word, and I will break his legs," she growled. Su-Hui stopped, and looked at her, hoping that she was joking. It was nearly impossible to tell from the expression on her face though.

The District

The Vice President stood in the empty Tribunal chamber where the trial was going to be held and savored the ambiance of the courtroom. The last time she had been there had been for the Tribunal of Senator Lewis. Now Becky Clarke, the former head of the Truth Reconciliation Committee, would face charges of treason.

The VP's Secret Service detail was outside. They had insisted that they be with her, but she had ordered them outside of the room. It wasn't just her disdain for the people in the Secret Service—she found them overly cautious and smothering. *Glorified cops.* No, she did not want any ears to hear what she had to say. *This is between me and Becky ... one last chance for her redemption.* The fact that she was even calling the meeting demonstrated just how magnanimous she really was.

Becky's guilt had already been determined—the Tribunal was for the people of Newmerica, so that they could see the price that traitors pay. The fact that Becky was actually innocent was a mere technicality to the Vice President. She had directed and overseen the creation of the evidence that framed Lewis, Clarke, and others in the assassination bombing of the Ruling Council. It had been necessary on her part to play her hand on her political foes. *The last thing the country needed was divisiveness in our ranks. This fake-assassination attempt has removed a few minor political speed bumps and ultimately lays the crime at the feet of the American President and his people ... as it should be.*

Becky could still perform a useful purpose for the state. She had tried to convince her once before, but doing it here, in this empty chamber, would drive home on her one-time-rival just how grave things were. *I hope she sees this room and realizes what is about to befall her.*

Two NSF guards brought the shackled prisoner in. Becky looked as if she had lost twenty-five pounds, if not more. Her cheeks were hollow; the skin under her chin seemed to sag slightly as she shuffled in with the leg irons on. Becky's hair was still short, but looked as if it had been trimmed with a weed wacker. Her eyes, however, were as angry and piercing as ever while she locked gazes with the Vice President.

"Leave us," she said. Both guards hesitated for a moment, then left to join her NSF Secret Service detail. Becky took time as they departed to look around the chamber.

"Grand isn't it?" the Vice President asked. "It really comes across well during the broadcasts."

"I would have gone for lighter colors," Becky said turning back to the Vice President. "It creates a bit more of a sense of hope."

The Vice President smiled slightly with those words. "You know, you might just be right. I always thought that your job was hard and thankless, but since I assumed control of the TRC, I've found aspects of it to be fun. Some aspects are like interior decorating. I never realized I had a knack for that."

"I can't tell you how happy I am that you are enjoying yourself," she replied with a sarcastic twist in her voice.

The Vice President tipped her head slightly. "Aw, hurt feelings still, Becky?"

She dipped her head slightly as she responded. "You know I'm innocent Alex. You set me up. You know the truth. I had nothing to do with the assassination attempt."

"The truth is what I say it is. You used to run the TRC—you know that as well as I do."

Becky mumbled something, just under her breath, then spoke up. "What is it you want from me?"

"This Tribunal will be brutal on you Becky, and it doesn't need to be. If you would be willing to confess, claiming that the American President sponsored the assassination attempt, I think I could arrange for a reduced sentence—perhaps just some time in Social Quarantine."

"You want me to lie."

"You did it for a living, running the TRC and all. Aren't you the one that coined the phrase: 'Lies are truths if they are positioned properly?' You above everyone else knows that what people think is the truth is really a matter of what is presented and what their perspective is. You don't want to hang by piano wire like Lewis. The old man voided his bowels on television when he died. You don't want that. You were once on our team, bringing down the conservatives, bringing about the Great Reformation. Wouldn't it be better for you, your family, everyone, if you simply implicated the American President?"

"You want me to take one for the team. Is that it?"

"If that helps you process it, yes."

Becky lowered her head more, almost as if she were looking at her feet. She muttered something, but the Vice President couldn't quite hear. Stepping forward, she still could not make out what Becky was saying. "What was that?"

The murmuring continued; her eyes were averted. The prisoner seemed to slouch, bending her legs slightly as if she didn't have the strength to stand upright. The Vice President took a half step closer and leaned in, trying to make out what Becky was saying.

Becky bent a little more, than sprang at her with handcuffed hands in front!

The Vice President had been lured in close, and Becky had come at her with a rage and fury that she had not expected. Becky collided with her mid-flight, her hands digging into the Vice President's throat. She lost her footing and fell, with Becky landing on top of her. She jabbed her hands at her assailant, but Becky was lightning fast. She drove her handcuffs into her throat, tearing at her skin. For a moment, the Vice President couldn't breathe, and panic took over. Clawing at her attacker, she got Becky to slide to her left on her throat.

"My name is Rebecca!" she snarled, sinking her fingers into the Vice President's cheek. One finger caught her earring, pulling it hard. "No one calls me Becky ... no one! Especially you!" The rage in her eyes was like something out of a horror movie. It was clear that her intent was to kill.

The Vice President tried to cry out, but for a moment couldn't. One of Becky's hands shifted, hitting her in her right eye and pressing hard.

The VP reeled attempting to twist from one side to the other.

Finally she managed a cough; a rapid fear-filled gasp of air managed to get in. What is that emergency code word the Secret Service gave her? In the fury of the assault, she couldn't remember. "Help!" she managed to blurt out weakly.

"You framed me for a crime I didn't commit you bitch!" Becky said. She leaned in, mouth open, and bit her high cheekbone. A ripple of pain shot across the VP's face, and she could see blood in Becky's mouth. She felt one of her hands grab some of her hair and pull. *Oh God ... she's going to kill me!*

Suddenly there was a rush in the air to her left and someone hit Becky, tackling her and pulling her off of the Vice President. She was still struggling to get air as the Secret Service pounced on her attacker. She saw a baton come out and repeatedly strike Becky who managed to land a kick into the knee of one of the Secret Service agents, sending him toppling. The other one tore into her with furious determination, getting her hands cuffed in record time. The two guards moved on Becky, one landing a kick on her for good measure, while the Secret Service agent moved to her. "Stay down ma'am," he urged. "You're bleeding."

The VP coughed again and felt a bit dizzy. As she saw Becky being picked up to her feet, she saw a clump of her own black hair in her attacker's hands. The baton attack had caught Becky's cheek, and it was already fire engine red, turning purple. Despite the tackle and hits, Becky looked at her and grinned. "How's it feel bitch? That fear of death. It's coming for you. You know I had nothing to do with that bombing. For every one of us you frame, you are adding to the number of people that want you dead!" The guards violently pulled her away, leading her out.

"We have an ambulance in route," the Secret Service agent said. "I need you to stay put. None of the wounds look bad, but we need to get you to a hospital. Remain calm ma'am."

Calm? Is he crazy? It had never dawned on her that Becky would attack her. If the Secret Service hadn't come when they did, she would have been killed. "I'm fine," she said numbly, rubbing her neck where the handcuff had dug into her and seeing a little smear of blood in her hand. *She is insane to have done that.*

A few minutes later the EMTs arrived and began checking her. Her hands … no … her entire body was trembling. Her usual calm demeanor was gone. *She almost succeeded in killing me. Another few minutes, and I'd be dead!*

"We need to get you on the gurney ma'am," the EMT said kneeling in front of her and gently touching her sore spots. As she trembled, she felt aches and pains everywhere. Out of the corner of her eye, she saw one of her black pumps nearly ten feet away, a testimony to the struggle she had endured.

"No," the VP stammered. "Get a camera crew down here on the double. Have them film me. I want the world to see what Becky did to me, I want them to see me get on the gurney on my own. I want them to see me as the victim I am … and know that I'm stronger than this."

The Secret Service agent attending her was stunned for a few moments at her request, then began to bark out her orders into her shoulder mike. *The world is going to see me as strong. It's what my mother would want, for me to rise above this,* the VP thought.

As the shaking began to fade, she closed her eyes in deep thought. *You will die slowly for this Becky. No one will blame me for what I do to you after this. I will be the greatest hero of Newmerica once this footing is shown.*

Maysville, Iowa

Captain Judy Mercury stared at the map for the hundredth time, and all it offered her was dismal frustration. She glared at her half-cup of coffee, contemplating a sip, but realizing that it was hours old and far too cold for her. The National Guard had taken over the North Scott Senior High School and was using it as their temporary headquarters. Judy was situated in a history classroom that had been turned into an ad hoc planning room for her attempt to cross the Mississippi. As she glanced up where the flag was usually hung in the room, she saw a blank spot. Iowa had sided with the American President, and had torn down its Newmerica flags. She contemplated the blank spot for a moment to clear her head. *I wonder how many companies are scrambling to make the stars and stripes again?*

Outside the wind whipped a flurry of snow past the window. A storm front had moved in, an Alberta Clipper. It only added to the misery of not being able to come up with an answer to her dilemma. As she rubbed her eyes, she heard the door to the classroom creak open. Turning, she saw a lean, sandy-haired Lieutenant Colonel standing at the door with two cups of coffee. On his flight jumpsuit was the distinctive red and yellow patch of the Thunderbirds, a stylized American Indian bird. On his chest was his pilot's wings. "I wasn't sure how you wanted it, but I figured you might need one."

"And you are?"

"I'm Lieutenant Colonel Mihalek," he said with a grin, walking to her and putting the coffee in front of her. "Colonel Meade thought I might check in with you."

She embraced the warm cup and pulled it across the table to her, savoring the aroma for a moment. *I'll bet it's more along the lines to see if I've made any progress.* "Thanks for this," she said.

"A hell of a challenge, eh?" he said taking a seat across from her.

"I think I solved at least a few of the logistics challenges," she countered.

"How's that?"

"Most of our vehicles run on diesel, which means we can hit local gas stations and fuel up. The tanks are a big challenge because of their unique fuel needs."

"Agreed," he said taking a sip of his coffee at the same time she did. "You don't want to get deep into Illinois and run out of fuel."

"Correct," Judy said, pausing to sip her own coffee. She preferred cream and sugar, but this was not a time to be choosy. "We have a lot of flatbeds though. If we put the vehicles on flatbeds, disguise them as battle damaged Illinois tanks, we can drive them right into Illinois. All we have to do is fuel up the flatbeds—which is a hell of a lot easier than fueling a full attack column. Hell, we could even bring along a tanker truck of fuel for the tanks if we want to."

The Lieutenant Colonel stared at the map, then back at her. "That might just work. You'll need some orders, documents to bluff any checkpoints they have."

"If they give us shit, we have fully armed and crewed vehicles. I mean, who would want to get into a shouting match with a bunch of tanks?" she countered. "But yeah, some fake orders will help. Technically, we can't fight under the enemy colors, so whatever Illinois markings we have need to be temporary, something we can easily remove. If we get caught, I don't want anyone facing war crimes trials."

"The Newmericans don't play by the rules," he said with a grin. "They'll execute you long before a trial."

She chuckled because he was right. Their enemy was ruthless, reckless, and without morals. "From what our intelligence reports, most of their forces are on the state borders and in Davenport. They seem more worried about protecting Chicago than anything else."

Mihalek nodded. "I noticed that too. Chicago has a lot of factories, so they see it as a strategic center."

"This raid isn't about strategic resources. It's about sucking troops away from Davenport so it can be taken back."

"So Springfield then?"

She nodded, sipping the coffee and wincing slightly at the hot bitterness on her tongue. "This is about to get real for a lot of politicians." With those words, she offered the Lieutenant Colonel a smile.

"You won't be able to hold it."

"I don't have to. I just have to make them turn around and come after me."

"You won't be able to get back," he cautioned. "They still hold the bridge crossings and have the bridges wired. You try and force a crossing, they will nail you."

Judy nodded. With her finger, she drew a course across and down the map from Springfield to where she intended the raiders to exit." Mihalek leaned over, squinting slightly as she did so. When she finished, he raised his gaze to her. "Well, they certainly won't see that coming."

"My thoughts exactly."

"So why the struggle?"

"I need a way to get our fake convoy into the enemy lines. Flatbed trucks, even when they are loaded with vehicles, are vulnerable as shit. We can't just drive into Davenport without getting shot up, and one thing I hope to avoid is getting shot up."

The Lieutenant Colonel looked at the map. "One thing I learned over the years is to ask the right questions. So if I understand you correctly, you need to find a way for the Illinois forces to take you into their side of the lines openly, so they want to do it? Is that correct?"

The way he worded the question was interesting to Judy's mind. *I haven't thought about them wanting to take us in?* I've been looking at this as a penetration—our convoy somehow punching through the front. Maybe that's the wrong angle. "That's one way of looking at it I guess."

Mihalek nodded. "The Colonel asked me to check on you, but I think a part of that was to make sure your plans were workable. Hell, I think using trucks is downright brilliant. It's all moot if you can't get them on the other side of the front. You've been looking at this as if the front is static."

"It is right now."

He nodded. "Right now. But the front can move. In fact, we can take efforts to move it, if we so desire."

"So rather than take the trucks through the lines ..."

"You move the front lines instead."

Leaning back, Judy looked at the map, then to the Lieutenant Colonel. "That just might work. We'd have to find the right spot, stage it just right—but it might just work." Her mind danced at the ideas, propelled by black coffee, exhaustion, and a surge of creativity.

"Alright," he said, leaning back. "So how do you think you can do this, and what do you need to pull it off?"

Outside a gust of wind whipped snow against the window so hard that it reminded Judy of sand hitting glass, like in Iraq. *I'll need a place that can hold the trucks and personnel, something out of sight. I'll need to have it look right, so that nothing seems out of place. We'll need the right location on the front, one that won't compromise the forces holding the outskirts of the city.* For the first time in days, Judy Mercury allowed herself to smile.

CHAPTER 6

*"Defending yourself at the expense of
others makes you the aggressor."*

Smyrna, Tennessee

The commander of the National Guard Base in Smyrna, Tennessee took no chances when it came to the safety of the Lopezes. The security presence was visible and formidable. Caylee approved of their presence after Raul's kidnapping at Arnold Air Force base. There would be no fake pizza delivery people showing up now.

Raul and Maria settled in slowly to the new reality of their lives. Both had done numerous interviews for the American free press—talking about the horrible life in the camps, the extermination of humans, forced labor, etc. When pressed for how Raul got out of the Supermax prison, he went with the official line, "With the help of some very good, patriotic friends." It was never enough for the media, who wanted details, but he offered none.

Ted, the former senator that Raul had been imprisoned with, spoke at length about the tortures he had endured and offered little more than Raul did about his rescue, saying that, "A crack team of individuals had gotten both he and Raul out." She shook her head the first time she heard that. *We were never 'crack.' We were determined, organized, and lucky.*

Maria and Raul passed their time working out, three times a day. She showed him moves she had learned over a lifetime in the Army and as a contract employee for the CIA, as well as her time as an operative. Raul took to her training with an almost fanatic zeal. Caylee enjoyed it—the strains, the physical contact, the polishing of her own skills, teaching what she knew was somehow rewarding all on its own.

Raul had his own project, trying to figure out how to liberate the remaining Social Quarantine camps in Newmerica territory. He had a computer map of the United States and, thanks to information that Charli provided him, he had plotted the known camps. Once she walked behind him and saw the sea of red dots on the screen that marked the locations. *I never realized there were so many of them.* As an operative, Caylee had seen more than a handful of them—but from what Raul was assembling, it was a staggering number of camps. *I doubt that anyone, even in the SE or NSF has any idea of the full scope.* Every Governor allowed the SEs to set them up as they saw fit, and Social Quarantine was both useful and profitable for Social Enforcers. It's a criminal operation. *They send people to the camps without trial, confiscate whatever they own, and take it for themselves. The result ... it encourages the SEs to do more of it.* The more she saw, the sicker she felt. *I was part of that machine being an Operative. I arranged for people to be sent to Quarantine. I never appreciated just how big this really was.*

A part of Caylee wanted to help Raul, but she checked herself instead. *This project is his. It's almost like therapy for him, something to occupy his mind. When he needs or wants my help, he'll ask for it.* In the meantime, she let him work on the myriad of problems liberating the camps posed.

Maria was coping with the quasi-freedom differently. She was afraid to be alone. She slept in a separate bed in Raul's room. When Raul and Caylee worked out, she stood at the door and silently watched. At first, Caylee thought it was creepy. She spoke, but it was usually in a low tone, her head bowed down as if she was afraid of Caylee's reaction to her words—regardless of how innocent they were. Bit by bit, she began to understand the younger woman. *Maria has been through a lot. They killed their mother and she was alone in the camp. God only knows what they may have done to her.* When they ate, she took scraps of whatever was on her plate and wrapped them in her napkin, tucking them away. *They starved her, and she is so conditioned to rationing her food, she can't help it.*

Caylee had tried to console her, crack her shell of relative silence. Maria finally would talk to her about mundane things—like what she wanted for dinner.

Caylee made sure that Charli, Andy, and Travis came over for meals and to watch old movies. The stuff coming out of Hollywood since the Fall had been a crap-fest of wokeism. The movies were less about telling good stories, as it was pushing political and social agendas. Filmmakers painted the years leading up to 'The Great Reformation' as oppressive, hate-filled times. They were almost always filmed with filters to make them look dark and dismal. They avoided contemporary movies, favoring classics like Die Hard or Elf, movies that did not make anyone think about politics.

Maria concerned her because no matter how hard Caylee tried to reach her, the young woman seemed to turn her away. It wasn't a chilly relationship, she simply would not open up with Caylee. When Charli came, however, Maria did seem to let her guard down more. Caylee watched Charli's interactions with her, hoping to learn how to duplicate the results, but thus far Charli's magic with Maria had been elusive to her. She never would admit it out loud, but she was jealous that Charli had success with Raul's sister and she did not.

As Caylee turned on the dishwasher one morning, she received a call from Jack Desmond. He told her that Ted was coming to visit with her and Raul that night. When she said that Andy and Charli were already coming, Jack had said, 'Perfect.' It made her instantly suspicious.

She ordered in food from Olive Garden … cooking was never her strong suit. Charli and Andy came early in the evening and everyone, even Maria, was chatting. When the knock came to the door, Caylee checked the security camera feed in the kitchen and let the guest in.

Ted, the former Senator that they had rescued along with Raul from the Supermax entered with a big smile. "Ah, Caylee, my favorite trained killer," he said, opening his arms for a hug.

She hugged him back, if not awkwardly. "Come on in."

Ted looked better than the last time she had seen him in person. He had put on some weight, not a lot, but his cheeks no longer sagged. His ragged beard was now professionally trimmed, and his energy level was high as he went around the room, shaking hands, hugging people— maneuvering like a politician. *It's probably a good thing we don't have a baby for him to kiss. He'd be all over that.*

Dinner was good, with Ted commenting, "I used to hate Olive Garden … after prison, it's a feast!" During the meal, he asked how everyone was doing, what they were spending time on, engaging. Maria was a bit standoffish with him, but even she seemed to smile and get drawn into conversation when he asked her if she was going to be attending school soon.

When they finished, they retired to the small family room area and sat down for more chatting. Caylee knew if Jack Desmond had arranged for Ted to visit them, he had come with a reason. So far, he was keeping that close to his vest. After what seemed like hours, she finally came out and asked him directly, "You must have come here for a reason Ted. What is it?"

He glanced at her and smiled. "I love dealing with someone who is blunt." He then turned to the group. "The President has asked me to look into how we manage the states as we bring back territory into America. Specifically he asked me to look into protecting historical and cultural works and relief of the Social Quarantine camps."

Raul stirred. "I have been looking into the camps, trying to figure out how to liberate them."

Ted nodded. "So I heard. That's one of the reasons I'm here. I could use your help."

"So we are going to get those people out?" Raul asked excitedly.

Ted drew a deep breath before responding. "It's tricky Raul. From what we gathered from your sister and the folks here in this room, some of these camps, if not all of them, are shifting from punishment to slow extermination. There's a real concern that if we start launching raids to liberate the camps, we may save the people there—but the Newmericans may get fearful and escalate their efforts to kill their prisoners."

Caylee heard his words and understood their logic. "He's right," she added, immediately getting Ted's attention. "It will get worse as we start to take territory. They will want to kill all of their prisoners rather than face war crimes. Parading starved survivors into court is something that will make them afraid. They will do away with all potential witnesses."

"That's exactly what they'll do," Maria said coldly, her own experience creeping at the edges of the tone of her voice. "You have to do something."

Ted nodded. "We will. I have suggested that we organize teams to be with the front line troops, people who can advance just ahead of the army and liberate the camps—get them the medical attention they need, arrest the SEs running the place. It's not going to be easy, but we have to save as many of those poor people as we can."

Caylee could see a bit of disappointment in Raul's expression. "I had hoped we could just go and start liberating them."

"There will be some of that Raul," Ted said, "But we need the army's protecting to ensure we can protect these people. That means being on the front lines, ready to get to the camps quickly, before they decide to kill everyone there. We will need medical specialists, the right kinds of foods for people that are starving, and the means of getting these people out of harm's way. I could use your help with this. You have started to compile the camps. You liberated one already. We learned a lot about them after the election when the states that sided with the President shut their camps down, but you are a bit of a resident expert."

They had all seen the footage of the quarantine camps being liberated. In Kentucky, right after the Fall when the Governor released almost 90 percent of the prison inmates. The prisons had been 'repurposed' into Social Quarantine camps where the inmates had suffered under conditions that had not been in place for convicted felons. In Georgia, the camps were open air affairs, leaving many to suffer from sickness or die from exposure. Even in Texas, a state that had resisted Social Enforcement, camps had been established and the inmates forced to do road repair during the steamy hot summer months. Everywhere the camps were liberated, the story was a variation of the same theme—brutality, cruel treatment, near-starvation, and death.

"I—I want to do it, but this is big ... even bigger than what I can do," Raul said.

"You must do it," Maria said in a louder voice than Caylee had heard her use since they had met. "You have to try Raul. You have to help those people. They took our *madre* from us. You have to make sure no one else suffers the way we have." She put her tiny hand in her brother's and squeezed it.

"What will happen to the people that ran these camps?" Raul asked Ted.

"Well, in Georgia, we have arrested the Lieutenant Governor who was in charge of the camps. He's been in custody and we have caught a large number of the Social Enforcers that were running camps. In Kentucky, we've begun to round up the people who were behind their camps, the same with Texas and the other states that fell in with the true President. These people will face trial for their crimes."

Caylee's eyes narrowed with his words. "Some will use the legal system to get off. There are other ways to administer justice."

Ted nodded at her. "You told me your background once we got out of the Supermax. Personally, I'd love to turn loose people with your skills to hunt down these people and handle matters. But we are not the enemy, and those tactics, tribunals in the middle of the night, vigilante justice and killings ... that's not who we are. We are better than that."

"When we play by the rules, sometimes we lose," she countered.

"True enough," Ted conceded. "Some would say our adherence to the rule of law is what cost us. It certainly cost us Washington DC and let the nation slip into a totalitarian regime. Our enemies are not burdened with morals or ethics. But when the fighting is over, and one day it will be, we need to be holding the moral high ground."

Caylee looked at Raul and saw him drink in Ted's polished words. *The man speaks like a politician, but he is right.* "I will help you with this."

Ted beamed a big smile. Andy spoke up, "It's a noble cause Raul. You're doing the right thing."

Ted turned to Andy. "I'm glad to hear you say that Andy," he said. "Because part of this is preserving our historical monuments, architecture, and documents. Jack said you would be the perfect person to head that up in our new organization."

Andy turned beet red. "I ... I ..."

"He'll do it," Charli said for him.

"Hey!" he said, reeling around to give her a mock scornful look.

Charli looked up at him. "You were born for this, Andy. You saved the Constitution, the Declaration of Independence, and the Iwo Jima flag. Besides, you were saying you needed to find something to occupy your time. You need a bigger purpose. This is perfect for you."

Andy stammered for a moment. "I'm not a trained historian," he countered.

Ted shook his head. "I know. Jack filled me in on your background.

I don't need a historian. I need a good soul, someone who respects our history. Jack tells me you are that man."

Andy closed his mouth and nodded. "Alright. If Raul can do this for his mother, I can do this for my father." Andy and Raul looked at each other, and in that moment, Caylee could see they had a new bond that tied them together.

"Is there a name for what you are doing?" Charli asked.

"Jack gave us a code name for this project, Seraphim."

"What is that?" Caylee asked.

It was Raul that responded. "They are celestial angels, of the highest order," he said. "They are guardian angels."

Caylee nodded in response. "For the first time in my life, the government named a team correctly," she said, offering both Raul and Andy an approving nod.

Pampa, Texas

Trip looked up the long, flat, treeless strip of State Highway 70 in Gray County Texas, right up to the barricade that had been thrown over the road, a half-mile out. It was winter. Only late winter wheat remained in the fields, seeming to stretch as far as his eyes could see.

Just two weeks ago, three Texas counties; Wilbarger, Ochiltree, and Dallam, had declared themselves Free Texas—proclaiming themselves as the Republic of Texas—a nation of its own in the heart of America. Word came forty-eight hours ago that Gray County had now thrown in with the rebels. As Trip looked up the long highway stretch with his binoculars, he saw the barricade was two cement mixers parked to block the road. Given the flat terrain, the obstacle could easily be skirted, but he suspected that the Texas rebels had reinforcements nearby, out of sight.

Trip hated being there and facing this. On one level, as a Texan himself, he understood the spirit of independence that the fledgling republic stood for. On another level, he hated it. Having part of Texas break away from America, in the middle of a civil war. It felt horribly wrong and, in some ways, engineered. *Their timing is far too convenient for our enemies. ... Newmerica has to be behind all of this.*

This was a task he had to handle personally. He knew that the leaders of the co-called Texas Republic would only respect a fellow Texan.

While he knew they had to be reasoned with, he also understood that was a daunting if not impossible task. *I don't want to have to use force to pry them out.*

Captain Harnessy, his G2 intelligence officer, stood at his side, looking down the stretch of road. "They have a few Technicals parked behind that barn off to the far right. Our people also spotted an up-armored bulldozer in a ditch up there, out of line of sight. All it would take is a little push, and they would be forced to fall back."

"I'm not here to fight … not yet," Trip replied. "I'm here to try to convince them of the folly of this play of theirs."

"Do you really think you can talk them out of this, General?"

Trip shook his head. "They are committed at this point. I won't be able to get them to back down." He had a cousin, Billy, who lived in Gray County. Trip spoke with him two days before to get the inside story of how the county had joined the Republic of Texas. It had not been a vote, or a decision on the part of the locals. The Republic had simply come in and captured the County Council and the Sheriff. It had been bloodless, fast, and anything other than a mandate of the people. Billy had told him that for the most part, people were keeping to themselves, not sure how any of this was going to play out. Trip's last words to his cousin were simple, "Keep your head down. I'll handle this." It was not just an assurance; it was a commitment.

Trip moved over to the stripped-down Humvee with a white flag that fluttered slightly in the cold breeze blowing across the Texas plains. "Look Captain, this is simple. We are there to warn them, tell them about the blockade; do what we can to keep this from escalating."

Harnessy moved to the driver's seat as Trip took the passenger position. "These good old boys are not exactly playing by the rules sir. What if they decided to take us hostage?"

Trip had considered that, but was trusting that they would not seize an American General, a fellow-Texan. *The odds are in my favor, meaning I am as prepared as I can be.* "If they try something that stupid, command will pass to General Horrocks, and he will be far less open to talks than I am." *That, and we have a sniper team in position out in those fields. They move on us, and they will start dropping.* He slammed the door and nodded down the road. "Let's go slow and easy."

The Humvee made its way down the highway closing on the pair of cement mixers. As they got closer, Trip noticed the machine gun positions from behind the tires of the big vehicles. He also noticed what appeared to be an anti-tank missile launcher. *This is more than some good old boys and girls. They have gotten their hands on firepower—a lot of it.*

Captain Harnessy stopped some twenty yards in front of the vehicles, and a pair of men got out. Trip slowly opened the door of the vehicle and stepped out, Harnessy doing the same. He held his hands up to show that he was unarmed. The two figures that approached them were the leaders that Trip had been briefed about, Booker Hickox and Salem Marshall. Booker wore fatigues visible under his military winter coat, faded, but clearly his. Marshall was dressed more like a businessman, a trench coat covering his portly belly and starched blue shirt. "General Reager I presume," Hickox said, standing in front of Trip.

"Mister Hickox," he replied. "This is Captain Harnessy of my staff."

"*General*," Hickox said. "My rank is General."

"If you say so," Trip said, refusing to commit. "And you must be Salem Marshall."

"*President* Marshall," Hickox said with a hint of bitterness in his voice.

Trip didn't respond verbally, but with a nod in Marshall's direction. "I thought it might be best of us to talk face-to-face," Trip opened. "I doubt that any of us want this matter to get bloody."

"Respect our sovereignty, and there won't be any bloodshed," Hickox.

Marshall was quick to join in. "What the General is saying is that it isn't our intent to engage in violence."

Trip eyed the man carefully, slowly gathering his thoughts. "You mean like taking the Sheriff and County Council prisoners?"

"We are invited into Gray County," Marshall said. "We took them into custody to protect them."

"I've heard that line before. It usually was used by Social Enforcers putting people into Social Quarantine," Trip countered. "Regardless of your alleged justification, you need to know that it needs to stop here."

"Or what?" Hickox asked. "You going to order your troops in to fire on your fellow Texans?"

Trip gave him a small grin, if for no other reason than to throw him off. "We are implementing a blockade of the counties that you claim are part of your little Republic. No one will be allowed in or out of the counties that you are in until this matter can be resolved. If you decided to export your politics to surrounding communities, you will be met with deadly force."

"You want to try to starve us out? Well that won't work," Marshall said.

Trip shook his head. "I don't think you understand Mr. Marshall. This isn't to starve you out, it's to bottle you up."

"You may think you can walk over us," Hickox replied. "But we are a hell of a lot stronger and better armed than you think." He nodded to one of the cement trucks where Trip saw a man armed with an anti-tank missile launcher. He tried not to look too interested in it, but at first glance, it didn't appear to be one from a U.S. stockpile. *They are getting help from the outside.* "Yes, it seems you are fairly well equipped."

"We are not some hayseeds you can bully with tanks," Marshall cautioned. "We have a lot of men and women who feel the same way we do. America is a failed experiment. The rise of Newmerica is proof of that. Being an independent nation is what is best for the people of Texas."

"I'm not here to engage in political ideology," Trip said. "I'm a military man. For me, my life is about loyalty and honor. I find that makes things easier for me when I put my head down on my pillow at night. What you are doing here is waging an insurrection. For now, my orders are to contain it, and I will do just that."

Marshall looked right and left. "What about your loyalty to Texas?"

"I have sworn an oath to the United States."

Marshall was not swayed. "This is a hell of a lot of ground for you to cover. Are you really going to commit the troops to protecting hundreds of miles of our border?"

Trip grinned a little more, then glanced up, squinting for a moment. "You see that Predator drone up there?" nodding skyward at the high white wisps of clouds that obscured the bright blue sky above.

Both men shielded their eyes with their hands on their brow and swept the skies. "I don't see shit," Hickox finally said.

"And yet, it's up there, cameras on us right now. You didn't think that I'd come here without protection did you?" He let his words sink in.

"I might make a suggestion that you think carefully about who and what you are up against. We are the United States of America. If it comes to a shooting match, I will come with what I have access to, and you do not want that to happen.

"You want to call yourself a country, that's fine for right now. You want to cause trouble for America, well, you are going to get a 500-pound explosive rectal exam from a drone. It's really that simple." His words took some of the color out of the face of Marshall, and added hints of crimson to Hickox's leathery skin.

"You will find we have the means to defend ourselves quite well General Reager," he said firmly. "We shot down a police helicopter that crossed our airspace just yesterday. We have the means and the resolve if we are pushed. The Republic's sovereignty is not to be underestimated."

Trip glanced once more at the man with the missile launcher. "So I see. It is clear that you have some help. No doubt there's a few people out there that like to see America with our testicles in a vice. I'm sure they love this war with Newmerica and would love to see a good fight within Texas. Consider this, General Hickox: Just how much support would your people have if they found out where you were getting your help from?"

Those words hit him, confirming for Trip that they were getting aid from the enemies of America. "It won't matter to them where the help comes from. What matters is our independence!" His words were defiant, so much so that Trip smelled their insincerity.

"One thing I have had to learn while commanding troops in the field is when the enemy is bluffing," he countered. "You think on that for a while General. Because once people learn the truth, there's no putting that genie back in the bottle."

The Texas Republic General glared at him through narrowed eyes. "So that's it; you've come to threaten us?"

"I'm not threatening. Think of me for what I am, a fellow Texan who's warning you not to trespass on my property. We've talked; you know where we stand, and I feel I understand who you are now. For the time being, no one needs to get hurt on either side."

"For the time being," Salem Marshall said.

Trip nodded. "Mr. Marshall, think on it this way. I represent a neighbor that respects me, but there's only so much pushing around I'm going to put up with. You have declared yourself a nation, but that was not by the will of the people; it was because some people with guns took things over. The last group that did that, during the Fall, is getting their asses shot up all around the country right now. Do you really think that the President is going to put up with this kind of cowboy bullshit forever?"

Trip turned slowly and walked back to the Humvee. Captain Harnessy got in and started it, turning it around and driving away from the blockade.

"General," Harnessy asked.

"Yes Captain."

"Do you really have a Predator on-station here?"

Trip smiled. "No. But they don't know that. Paranoia is a potent weapon. I don't have the forces to surround their insurrection. So let them worry that I have the Air Force watching them. For the time being, it gives me flexibility elsewhere."

"They might call your bluff."

Trip nodded. "It's possible … but not right away." *I just need some time to resolve matters in Davenport, and repair and refit from Atlanta. Once that is done, this Texas Republic bullshit will get resolved.*

Charlottesville, Virginia

David Steele peered through the small sniper hole in the trunk of the car as his father sat in the front seat. They were a block off of campus, on Chancellor Street, right across from the burned out shell of an old fraternity house. From what David's father had told him, the house had been the home of a business fraternity on the University of Virginia campus before the Fall. During the riots, some students had torched the building, citing the evils of their targeted businesses. David didn't understand their logic. *Even if you assume that big business was bad, those students had nothing to do with it. They were just students.* The lesson was clear. The students didn't care if their rioting and carnage made sense to the rest of the world—they felt justified in everything they did.

That was part of the problem with Newmerica—there was no balance between actions and justification. The Ruling Council had undertaken actions against half of the country with no real reason other than they didn't like how they thought. His family knew others that had been rounded up by Social Enforcers. Sometimes they were beaten; other times they were taken away to Social Quarantine camps. *They never need a reason or excuse for what they do; they are in charge.*

Campuses thrived on a self-perpetuating, vicious circle of hate. Professors indoctrinated students, brainwashing them into loathing every aspect of America. They encouraged them to take part in riots … convinced them that it was the right thing to do. Violence was always justified if it was applied to conservatives or those suspected of not fully supporting Newmerica. Big business, the wealthy, people who worked hard to get ahead. … They were all valid targets.

David saw it for what it was, toxic and deadly. It was the twisted culture on campus that had led the Grays to slaughter innocent students—including his sister. Did they mourn the death of Maddie and the other students they killed? No. They were devastated by the deaths of the Grays, the ones that he and his father had killed. They martyred the killers, not the victims. It was so bizarre and backward that every time he thought about it, the imagery infuriated him. *Who mourns for Maddie? We do. And even that is done in private out of fear they will find us.*

He and his father had taken steps to make it difficult for investigators. They were using a different brand of ammunition for one thing. Second, they used a different rifle; this time it was his father's. That would stymy investigators attempting to connect the murders. *Let them wonder if there are more shooters, if this is a group coming after them, not just my dad and me.*

As he looked through the scope, he saw Dr. Carmen Mikolitis walking slowly with a clutch of students. She was the head of the Political Science Department on campus, one of the lead instigators of the mayhem at UVA. As he watched her, he could see that she was enjoying the small group of students that walked and talked with her. *They are feeding her ego, and she loves it.* He had seen it countless times during his surveillance of her.

That was about to end. His father, Grayson, had said that they needed to change where they struck back, not just to throw off the investigators that would look into the murders, but to make the professors that were responsible for the horrific environment and nervousness wherever they were. "I want them to worry about leaving their houses. I want them afraid to walk the campus," his father had said.

David adjusted the scope slightly, keeping Dr. Mikolitis in his crosshairs. "I have a shot," he said as he lay in the trunk, his legs jutting into the back seat.

His father would be looking around, making sure no one was near the vehicle. They had already made sure that security cameras for the block were taken out. It was often as easy as cutting the wires or spray painting the lenses. Most people were so lazy; they rarely looked and few would want to go out in the winter and fix the problems.

"You are clear," Grayson said in a low tone from the front seat.

David eyed the professor and aimed at her chest. Just as he had done when deer hunting, he drew a long breath and let it out slowly as he gently squeezed the trigger. The gun roared in the trunk of the car, kicking him hard as it sent its full metal jacket projectile into the chest of the Dr. Mikolitis.

A squirt of blood from the hit splattered one of the students in the leg. Dr. Mikolitis dropped, as did the young woman standing behind her, twisting as she fell. David had not intended to hit anyone else, but did not flinch at the realization that he had struck two victims. The small group of students ran from the fallen bodies, fearful that there was an active shooter. Dr. Mikolitis lay on the sidewalk of the campus, her arm flopping as if she were trying to move but couldn't.

His father started the car as David put the patch metal over the sniper hole in the trunk. His ears were still ringing as his father made the turn into an ally that led to Liberation Lane. David crawled into the back seat, leaving the rifle in the trunk. The smell of expended gunpowder came with him as he folded the back seat up and buckled in.

Grayson Steele said nothing from the front seat as they drove away from campus. In the distance the sound of NSF sirens, along with ambulances, seemed to move past them, heading back to the scene of the crime. "We can't just go back to the apartment," Grayson said. "I don't want anyone seeing us to make the connection that we returned right after this went down."

David understood—leave no pattern for authorities to follow. "I'm hungry," he said. "Can we stop somewhere and get something to eat?"

His father nodded, saying nothing about the assassination they had just orchestrated. As they drove, David savored the terror they had caused. *They will finally get a dose of the fear they have been putting out for years. These professors and students that have ruined our lives are now going to feel the same anxieties they have been pushing since the Fall. After this, there will be no denying what is happening ... that they are targets.* It was a strangely satisfying thought, of others having to deal with the same fear he and his family had. While it wouldn't ease the pain he felt over the loss of his sister, it did give him a warm sense of fulfilment.

CHAPTER 7

*"Justice, equality, and equity are all the same
thing ... escape from our racist past."*

Chicago, Illinois

Weber Liu entered the Hyatt on the Loop in the heart of Chicago with a sense of purpose and satisfaction. He checked his phone and the hotel map on his way to the conference lounge on the rooftop. Taking the elevator up, he exited and was greeted by a trio of men in business suits. Instinctively he held his arms out and let them sweep him for bugs and check for weapons. It was a standard precaution given the men and women taking part in the meeting. Once he had been checked, one of the men gestured that it was okay for him to proceed into the large meeting room.

Cocktails were served, and Liu got a slender glass of champagne which was sweet and bubbly. He savored it for a moment before putting it on the bar. This was not the time to get intoxicated, though the Chinese representatives in the room no doubt felt they had a lot to celebrate. The United States was embroiled in a civil war, which meant its gaze would be inward—leaving much of the world open for exploitation. The most potent of the superpowers had hamstrung itself, first with the coup, then with the rise of the former Vice President to resurrect America. For his homeland, the longer the United States was divided, the better. *We can finally exert our strength, and there is no one there to stop us save the Russians, and they have their own interests for the time being.*

Lori Lemon, a popular CNN commentator and professional colleague came over to him. "You are to be commended Dr. Liu," she said. "The

99

Texas Republic … who would have thought that could be brought into being?" She held up her glass, tipping it to him in respect.

He cracked a thin smile. "I did nothing but water the seeds that had already been planted."

"There are many such gardens to be fertilized and allowed to grow," she added, taking a sip of her cocktail. "America has always been so large and intimidating, but it also allowed for a wide range of division. Our homeland would have never allowed such divides to take root and grow. Here, the Ruling Council and the Democrats before them went out of their way to foster more division."

"The strength of this nation, its freedoms, is also its greatest weakness. We would be fools not to exploit it."

"This civil war only highlights their differences." Lori Lemon had been a commentator for three years on CNN, not only touting the TRC's messaging, but making sure the stories that she highlighted were those that would excite or infuriate her loyal followers. Weber admired her as a professional. *As a newsperson, she has done more damage to this nation than most, and with remarkably little effort.*

"Every bullet fired, every mortar shot launched, the so-called United States is hurt. Whatever side wins and leaves us stronger."

She took a sip, but their sponsor cleared his throat; it was a clear signal for them to assemble. The twenty or so guests took their seats around the large table. Liu knew that this was not all of the cell leaders in North America … no one person knew how many Chinese were operating in the region. The faces he saw, for the most part, were familiar—having attended other such summits. There was comfort in being at the large table, a feeling of being instrumental in his nation's cause.

Their sponsor, Aiguo Lung, stood at the far end of the table. "I thank you all for coming. You have all been instrumental in keeping the United States anything but united. Our work, however, is far from complete." There were no comments from the attendees; they all knew their place and the power that Lung wielded. Instead, there were simply nods of acknowledgement.

"We have done well in the last decade to bring a superpower to its knees. With the introduction of a virus barely more potent than the flu, the politicians overreacted and took actions that gutted the heart of capitalism and small businesses. All we had to do was sow the seeds of fear in the media and, as always, the weak-minded did the heavy lifting for us. They imposed mandates and restrictions that not only crippled the world economy leaving China strong, but devastated their supply chain even to this day. We used social media to plant doubt in people's minds to the point where when a vaccine was offered, many refused it. The politicians of both parties never suspected our hands guiding their actions. All of you are to be commended for that.

"America's being toppled in a coup was an unforeseen boon. What replaced it was a nation that was more in line with our own. Thanks to some of our efforts and those of the politicians, they adopted socialism willingly. While they criticized our nation for our prison camps, they set up Social Quarantine facilities everywhere, locking up their own political opposition. As much as I would like for us to take full credit for it, they were more than willing to look the other way as we defamed and smeared the political opposition. They became totalitarian without ever realizing it."

Lung paused, taking a sip from his bottle of water. "The Russians, the Arab states, the Europeans ... we all had a role, some larger than others, in fertilizing the rage that the progressives here felt. We didn't corrupt them—we merely gave them the unseen support they needed. We gave them a nudge ... they did all the rest, just as we knew they would.

"They have defunded the police. They released prisoners in hopes of garnering votes. Their political prosecutors refused to do their jobs, and they implemented bail reform, all under the auspices of fighting racism. Then the same politicians used the lawlessness that followed as the impetus to turn law enforcement into an army of occupation. The NSF is more an implement of state terror than any other police agency in the world. We simply posted memes and spurred one-sided online debates that supported the actions that they put in place. Even in our wildest dreams, we could not have concocted such an elaborate plan." He paused for a few chuckles from around the table, Liu included. He is right. *America is its own worst enemy. It has always been such. The left had been looking for justifications to take harsh actions, and the virus and lawless rioting gave them the excuse they had been looking for.*

"We could have simply shut down our efforts ... they were hardly needed. The Newmericans were splintering and dividing the people of their nation into such small little factions that none of them really had a voice in their own affairs. They were so excited to be labeled some distinct group that it never dawned on them that they were surrendering any hope of true influence on matters. We could have walked away from this; the damage had been done. But we did not. You all continued your hard work for our homeland, and in doing so, you have found new and exciting ways to keep America divided and its people at each other's throats.

"Weber Liu, you are to be commended for your actions with the Republic of Texas," Lung said. Such acknowledgement, by name, was rare and a deep honor. "It is that kind of effort that will keep these two warring nations further divided." Liu bowed his head. "I was merely doing my duty."

"It was innovative, which is what we must become," Lung said. "We are entering unprecedented times. The former United States is at war with itself. We have fostered divisions everywhere, and need to continue to do so. These people cannot even reunite under some false pretense of patriotism because one side has made that word a crime. It is not enough for America or Newmerica to emerge crippled from this civil war; they must be in a position to never again rise as a world power.

"We have already convinced elements of their people to purge their history. They have turned on Washington, Jefferson, Roosevelt, and other historic figures. Thanks to our efforts on social media and in the halls of the Newmerica Congress, we have been able to convince them to do away with their holidays like the Fourth of July. This year, you will all need to push hard for Thanksgiving to be removed as well as Memorial Day. We encouraged them to replace Christmas with Worker's Respect Week, and that proved successful. Those that still practice their Christian holiday are seen as enemies. The people only care that they get the time off of work, not what the holidays are called. As long as Americans get their 'Black Friday,' they won't care that Thanksgiving is changed to Privilege Atonement Day. You will tell your resources that these are tied to Alt-Right Christianity and America's warring past, and as such, is demeaning to people of race. Make these holidays targets, and it will only incite more frustration from America and the churches around the continent. Memorial Day is nothing more than the glorification of United States imperialism. We will tell the masses that putting veterans on pedestals insults the normal working person. We will plant the seeds that the unemployed deserve more reparation points since they don't get the holidays off. The Newmericans will love that concept. Going after these holidays will pit more of these people against each other—which advances our ultimate goal."

Liu understood the thinking. Race had always been a weak spot for the United States. It was easy to convince people that the problems of their life could be traced to their race. It was easier for them to believe than accepting responsibility for their own decisions in life. Where possible, they had recrafted races—Latinos became Latinx, for example. *We are masters of using their own language against them. We create new words, change the definitions of sayings, corrupt their vocabulary ... all with the intent of further dividing them.*

Lung turned to one of the females seated across from Liu. "Kaili Sung, your efforts in penetrating Congress and local governments continues to be impressive," he said as the slender woman dipped her head in reverence. Liu knew she had members of her cells embedded in the staff of many of the Newmerican politicians. They whisper ideas in the ears of their so-called superiors, getting them to take even more radical actions. Some did it in the office; others did so from their beds, snuggled close to the leaders they were sleeping with. Sung was the Queen of Whispers, wielding power on levels that no one suspected. Weber made eye contact with her, and she offered him the thinnest crack of a smile. *She is a comrade, but always a rival.* As with the others at the table, Liu made sure that he never forgot that. *While we are united in our cause, each of us vies for recognition and greater authority.*

Lung surveyed his people slowly as he spoke. "Newmerica is going to push for a Constitutional Convention so that they can throw out the very foundation of laws that made this country. From our people embedded with Congress, we have already seen bits and pieces of this new Constitution. Gone is the bedrock of united states ... state's rights are dominated by Federal law. Their proposed new Bill of Rights alone is over 200 pages long. This convention will further split and partition the people. Some will see it as more free things; others will see it as further trampling on the past of the United States. While the Newmericans seek to tighten their grip, they are simply making the resistance even more determined."

Lung turned slowly from the head of the table, making eye contact with all of them. "On other fronts, we have seen the reports of the Social Quarantine camps being used to exterminate conservatives. This is not a crime—it is an opportunity for all of us. Newmerica is destined to lie and claim these are falsehoods. The Americans will demand justice. We will use our positions to turn these camps into a renewed fear for both sides. The Newmericans will fear that the truth will be laid bare as to what they are doing and will fight hard to cover their activities. They are married to their ideology of extermination, and it is a marriage bond that cannot be allowed to be severed because it is useful to us. The Americans will want vengeance. As such, we want these camps to remain operating as long as possible. We will use our contacts in the media to obscure the truth on both sides. Doubt and denial have long been the tools of the media, and we will continue to use them." Lung's gaze centered on Lori Lemon, who dipped her head in acknowledgement.

Lung continued his summation, "I have word that North Korea will, at our nation's covert insistence, create tension for Newmerica on their West Coast. It is not enough to unite them, but it will give the Newmericans something they must deal with … as will the Americans who will feel obligated to protect their former nation." Weber Liu had his own thoughts about how to create problems for the Newmerican regime, but those could be spoken after the meeting with Lung, in private.

Lung continued. "The people of these two nations have no idea we have been guiding them, and it must remain as such. If they ever develop a common enemy, it might serve to unite them … and we cannot allow such a travesty to occur. Let them wallow in their hate. Encourage them to resort to violence against anyone that does not think the way they do. Nudge them into distrust of each other. If that all fails, weave fear into your messages—fear of what the other side will do, fear over the economy, fear over the Theta variant of COVID. As long as we are whispering in their ears, feeding their egos on social media, and manipulating their media, they will remain divided and weak, which is where they need to remain."

Applause broke out as Lung finished his opening comment. He felt a surge of pride in the actions he had taken. *We fight a war against these people that no one will ever see. We have helped China from the shadows. We are heroes to our nation, though none will ever know of our deeds. ... and all it cost was crippling the most powerful nation on this planet ...*

Dixville Notch, New Hampshire

State Highway 26 slithered along the frozen shoreline of Lake Gloriette in the snow-covered pine forests of northern New Hampshire. At Cold Springs Road, at the far eastern edge of the lake, the logging truck was stopped, turned at a sharp angle with the front end of a Ford Predator seemingly rammed into the cab. Road flares were tossed on the highway, burning hot pink, sending wisps of smoke into the bone chilling air.

On the opposite side of the highway from the lake, a dirt embankment rose upward some ten feet leading into a dense forest of old pines. The snowplows had thrown most of the snow onto the frozen lake surface, but the depth of the snow was such that the embankment itself was a major barrier. Two cars were stopped behind the accident, their driver's out looking at the scene.

Su-Hui surveyed the staged scene as he heard the rumble of the military patrol coming from the east. The fake accident would bottleneck the troops between where he and his people were hidden, above the high embankment and the frozen lake. While he had been told that Lake Gloriette would most likely be able to support a Humvee driving on it, Su-Hui was counting on the fact that the National Guard troops driving them would not like to experiment with the depth of the ice.

It was a good place for an ambush, but this time his resistance group was not going to be destroying the enemy vehicles, but attempting to capture them. As he looked down the highway, he saw the patrol coming. The wind stung at his eyes, and a tear felt brittle on his face as he saw them come into view.

The patrol stopped as they reached Lake Gloriette. Su-Hui had been counting on them getting closer, but the National Guardsmen were clearly cautious. There were contingencies for this, but they weren't behaving as he had hoped they might. *They are learning to be wary of us, especially up this far north, so far from their bases.*

The short column of six Humvees stopped, and only the lead vehicle advanced, slowly, cautiously inching closer. From his concealed position, he could see the men and women get out of the vehicle, weapons at the ready, staring for any sign of IEDs or his people. Behind the convoy, two vehicles pulled up and were stopped as if waiting for them to move on.

Patience was something he had slowly mastered. His wife liked to say that he had been getting more patient since they had arrived in Newmerica—refugees fleeing from Taiwan during the Chinese invasion. Su-Hui knew better. He had masked his impatience in those years, when the Social Enforcers had assaulted his daughter, leaving her an empty husk of the brilliant young woman she used to be. *I faced my inner demons and held them in check ... that is not the same thing as patience.* Patience had come from the missions he had gone on, holding his fire when the urge was there to trigger an explosion or fire a weapon. It was a learned trait, one he honed with experience.

As he watched the lead vehicle creep up on the roadblock, he knew that his people, hidden in the snowbank and behind the logging truck, had their guns at the ready. He held his own AR-15 poised for action as well. Everyone was waiting for his word, and he had enough intelligence to hold the word for his people to move.

Below, the Humvee stopped, and an officer from the Connecticut National Guard got out wearing white and gray winter camouflage. He advanced on the semi truck slowly. The driver, wearing a heavy, dull green winter coat, got out and walked over to him. "Hell of a thing," Valerie Turner of the Sons of Liberty said with a big smile. "Damned brake lines must be frozen."

Her words seemed to make the officer relax, as was intended. He approached her and spoke, but Su-Hui couldn't hear their conversation. Valerie had done her job and done it well; she had lured him over near the cab of the vehicle, oblivious that weapons were trained on him.

For a moment, his body stiffened, just enough for Su-Hui to notice. *He knows now, and is trying to make up his mind. Fight or flight.* Su-Hui raised his own weapon and aimed it at the driver of the Humvee, knowing that the exposed officer was already amply covered.

The officer didn't move for what seemed like a half-minute; then slowly he called out for the other members of his Humvee to join him. *Good, just as we planned.*

As they exited the safety of their up-armored Humvee, they were woefully exposed. He was about to climb down the embankment when suddenly one of the troopers raised his weapon, aiming at the truck. *Shit!*

No order could be given; there wasn't time. The pop-crack of the weapons fire rang out. The lead officer was knocked down by Valerie with a haymaker punch. The other three occupants of the Humvee reeled before they could pull their weapons out. A spray of blood hit the snow covered pavement as they dropped.

"Cover the rear of the convoy," he said into his shoulder microphone. "Intimidate—get them to surrender."

The roar of gunfire from the rear of the column told him that things were already out of hand. One Humvee, at the rear of the line, exploded in a rolling orange and black ball of flame and smoke. The purr of machine gun fire from one vehicle tore at his ears. "Secure this vehicle; move in on the rear of the column," he ordered. A squad of his SOL and National Guard peeled off, running down the highway toward the erupting gunfight.

Su-Hui moved down to the Humvee in front of the logging truck. One of the enemy troopers, sprawled on the snowy pavement, stirred with an agonizing moan. Su-Hui kicked the M4 out of the reach of the man moaning and bleeding at his feet. The trooper rolled over quickly, pulling his SIG Sauer M18 pistol and aiming at Su-Hui standing over him. A pair of cracks of gunfire tore into the soldier's raised gun arm, one hitting him at the base of his throat. His body went limp at Su-Hui's feet. For a moment he wondered if he had been shot, but couldn't feel any sign of it. Looking up he saw Valerie, her weapon still aimed at the man. "You gotta be careful chief," she said with a slight New York tone to her voice. *I was sloppy—he was wearing body armor—I should have assumed he was not incapacitated. Damn it!*

Their conversation was cut off with another explosion down the road. A Humvee tore out and was heading down the highway to their position. Su-Hui didn't hesitate. Lowering to a kneeling pose, he barked out, "Aim for the driver," and opened up with small, controlled bursts.

The bullets thwacked on the armored glass, cracking it slightly. Others joined in, from all over the embankment and the log truck. Several bullets sparked on the long, flat hood of the careening vehicle while most slammed into the glass protecting the driver.

The Humvee, wavered, then turned hard, hitting the snowy embankment he had been hiding on top of, skidding around. Su-Hui tore open the passenger door and jammed his weapon in. The driver held her hands up, shaking, blood trickling from several spots on her face. "Don't shoot—I surrender!" she called. "Out," he ordered, and she exited into the arms of several of his people.

The sounds of gunfire disappeared in the distance. This had been intended as a bloodless effort. Now two Humvees were destroyed—and those were the ones he knew of. As he shot a fiery glance down the road, he saw a line of National Guardsmen being led in his direction, their hands on their helmets in surrender. They were escorted by members of the SOL in their ad hoc camouflage gear.

Su-Hui walked toward them and was greeted by Herb Fletcher. "What happened?" Su-Hui demanded.

"They were making a move against us," Herb snapped. "So we hit them first." There was a bit of pride in his voice.

"We needed those vehicles," he said. "That was our mission. Not destruction. You should have stuck with the plan."

"I made the call, and it was the right one," he said arrogantly. "I came here to kill these Newmerican shit-holes. You should be thanking me for what I did. Besides, this whole plan was a joke to begin with."

Su-Hui was about to respond when Corporal Abernathy spoke up. "What do you want us to do with the survivors sir?"

"Strip them of their gear. We'll take them to General Griffiths for his people to process."

"Fuck that," Herb said. "These are the enemy. I say we shoot them here and be done with it."

"No," Su-Hui replied. "If we start down that path, they will do the same with our prisoners."

"They already are," Herb fired back. "Have you forgotten what they did to our people in Lisbon? I say we shoot them now. It's better than these Newmerican assholes deserve." More than a few of his people nodded in agreement.

"I am in command here Herb; my orders will be followed."

"Or what?" he said, taking a step toward Su-Hui.

"Or I will make you a headless motherfucker," Valerie said from behind him. Su-Hui turned and saw that she had her weapon aimed at Herb's face.

For a moment, no one talked—the tension filled the road and the people standing on it. Valerie shattered the quiet she had kicked off. "Go ahead Herb; say something fucking stupid right now."

Herb glared at her angrily. "Fine," he muttered, holstering his pistol. "You want to follow this Chink, go ahead. He's going to get all of us killed."

Su-Hui walked up to Herb, getting right in his face. They stared for a long second, eyeball to eyeball; then Su-Hui delivered a straight jab into his solar plexus. Herb dropped, gasping for air, sliding across the blood splattered roadway, his face straining as he struggled to get his breath. "I am not a 'Chink,'" Su-Hui said, walking over to him and delivering a strong kick to his ribs. The blow was enough to get Herb's diaphragm to start working again. He moaned, breathing heavily. "I'm more American than you are. You are out of here."

Herb looked up at him. "You can't kick me out. I lead a cell of the Sons. I have every right to be here."

"You can go fight elsewhere," Su-Hui said firmly, contemplating delivering another kick to the man at his feet. "You have no place with my people. I do not care where you go, but you must leave."

Herb struggled to his feet, slipping slightly as he stood. "You'll pay for this," he said angrily. "Before this is over, I'll see you dead."

"You keep swinging your dick around, and you'll be dead right now," Valerie said, her weapon still on him. "You heard the man. You're out of here. We don't need your racist bullshit here. We're fighting for something better."

Herb glared up at her. "You haven't heard the last of me," he said, motioning to his three followers who fell in beside him. They walked back down Highway 26 where the two burning Humvee's billowed smoke in the wind. "You'll pay for this."

Valerie moved in beside him. "Say the word, and I drop him and the others. No one will think less of you for it. Pop, pop, pop … down they drop."

There was assurance in her words. *She is right; it would solve a lot of problems.* Then his mind went to his family—Hachi, Akio, Ya-ting. He wanted Herb dead. His last threat was tangible and filled with hate. The thought of what he would have to tell his wife if he gave that order was too much for him. *He needs to be gone, … but not now, not by my hand.*

"Thank you, Valerie," he said giving her a nod. "We have plenty to do and little time. Men like Herb are not worth the effort or the bullets," he replied.

"You're in charge chief," she said. "But trouble is like a boomerang. You throw it away, and it has a way of coming back at you."

The District

The Vice President adjusted herself on the chair. Behind her, with half-dimmed lights, was the Tribunal room where she had been attacked by Becky Clarke. The hot lights of the camera crew caused the makeup on her face to feel like setting plaster, but she ignored it. This interview that she was giving with *60 Minutes* was important. It was not just about generating sympathy for her, though part of her was counting on that happening. If the interview went well, she would be able to turn the attack against both Becky and the American President.

She wasn't worried too much about the questions—they had been submitted for her approval in advance, and she had only rewritten a few of them. The makeup people had highlighted her bruises and cuts. She was already scheduled for some cosmetic surgery to prevent scars. With the right application of colors and highlights, she looked every bit the victim of a brutal assault.

Becky had surprised her with the viciousness of her attack. Since the beating, the VP had nightmares about Becky on top of her, choking her with her handcuffs, ripping her hair. She had never felt terror on that level before, that her life was truly in danger. *I've always controlled life and death situations.* Strangely, she found herself excited by such nightmare – and not in a bad way. Still, they did conjure darker thoughts. A part of her wondered if that was how her mother and brother felt when

Caylee Leatrom had murdered them. *Did they know they were going to die? Were they afraid like I was?*

The interviewer, Rachel, sat next to her, and she turned slightly. For a normal conversation, it would have been an awkward position, but for a filmed interview, it was something that the VP was used to.

"Tonight I'm with Newmerica's first Vice President. As many of you know, several days ago, she was nearly killed in an attack by the former Director of the TRC, Rebecca Clarke. Despite her previous injuries, she agreed to take part in this interview. Before we begin, madam Vice President, how are you recovering?"

She forced an expression of penance to her face. "Rachel, thank you for asking," she said softly. "The attempt on my life is one that will leave me with scars as long as I live. That is something I have had to come to grips with. I've always known that I was taking risks for our nation. I've never been afraid to stand up for what is right as I'm sure your viewers know. The savagery of this attack is something that I will carry with me forever." She paused for a moment to dab an imaginary tear from the corner of her left eye.

"You were badly beaten—nearly strangled to death by the time your Secret Service agents were able to pull Rebecca Clarke off of you. I read your medical report. You have severe cuts on your throat, damage to your scalp, and as our viewers can see, you have a black eye and cuts on your face. Did you suffer any psychological damage from the attack?"

The Vice President nodded quickly several times. "The trauma of this kind of an attack is more than just physical. What I went through was akin to rape in many respects, or so the experts have told me. I have been working through what my doctors have told me is a form of PTSD … just like what a soldier experiences in battle. I have nightmares about almost every night, waking up in a cold sweat." Some of what she said was true—she did wake up at night in terror. The PTSD was simply added to make her more relatable.

"That sounds horrible."

"We all have our duties," she said, pretending to muster some courage. "I could have just stepped down from my role for a while, but the people of Newmerica need me. I have been blessed with so many get well cards and emails from well-wishers. They have really helped me through this physical and emotional crisis. It is a burden, but it is no more than the burdens that many of our people are enduring."

"I'm sure many of our viewers want to know the answer to the same question. Why were you alone with this terrorist in the first place? She is on trial for being part of the Capitol bombing conspiracy. Why would you want to meet with her here, in this very chamber?"

The Vice President paused for a half-second to make it look as if she were summoning the courage and strength to respond. "Rebecca Clarke ... Becky and I have known each other from the Liberation. I honestly thought that we were friends until this entire assassination plot was uncovered. I thought that if I sat with her, spent some time with her one-on-one, old friend with old friend, she might confide in me and say who was really behind the bombing. Maybe, just maybe, she might tell me why she had gotten sucked into such a scheme to topple our government."

"Did she tell you anything?"

Nodding quickly, the Vice President had been expecting the follow-up question since it was on the list she had tweaked prior to the interview. "She did. She bragged about how the American President, the Pretender, had been behind the plot. He wanted to decapitate our movement by killing the Ruling Council. If it had worked, she would have been the sole survivor and would have reinstated the horrific policies of old. Fortunately they were unskilled in their bomb-making abilities.

"Becky ... my dear friend ... had been offered power by the upstart false President down in Tennessee. She had been corrupted to embrace the old ways, our racist and twisted past." She admired the well-scripted story that she was unleashing.

"That had to be devastating for you to hear."

"It was," she said, locking her eyes on Rachel and not the camera so that it would seem more personal. "I've been through a great deal in the last few months, with the murder of my mother and brother by the upstart President's thugs. Hearing her say that she was so willing to turn on our cause, a cause I thought we both believed in—it was terrible. I thought she was confessing to me, but in reality, she was maneuvering to try and finish what she started and kill me. Before I knew what was happening, she was on top of me. From what my doctors said, I was lucky. She nearly succeeded in murdering me right here—in this room." The last bit was a white lie, one calculated to show her level of sacrifice for Newmerica.

"Your bravery in something that should be an inspiration to everyone," the interviewer stated, putting her hands on the Vice President's in a sign of support.

"Thank you, but this isn't about me. Becky was as loyal as anyone of our people. She got lured into a plot by a Pretender to the Presidency, a man that falsely claims he won the last election. A lot of our people have probably been questioning their marriage to our ideology. I'm sure a few have considered even supporting the Southern President. Some people might find themselves being seduced by the words that white-haired old man says ... it makes them feel, I don't know, nostalgic. Others will end up like Becky; they may think that it is to their individual advantage to support the Liar and Chief.

"I have always believed that we are more than that though. We know that the needs of a lone person are nothing compared to the needs of the whole. We know that a strong central government is the key to maintaining order. I think that Becky can serve as a lesson to everyone. As tempting as it might seem to support this Pretender, in reality, it is a pathway to violence and chaos. I feel sorry for those that waver in their support of our administration—I truly do. After all we have done for them, they still don't really believe in what we have given them."

Rachel almost teared up on cue. "It amazes me, and I'm sure it amazes many of our viewers, that people would bother listening to what the Pretender President says, let alone back a government that would try to murder its opposition in cold blood."

The Vice President bit her lower lip for a moment. "This is a chance for them, an opportunity to think through their choices, and to ask themselves what is the greater good."

"You are a victim," Rachel said. "And as such, a true hero."

"I don't see myself that way," she said cracking a smile as she lied for the camera. "I am just like the millions of people out there. I am working hard, doing what is right, trying to hold together everything that our Great Reformation has brought us."

Rachel turned and offered a few more observations of the Vice

President's performance as she marveled at her own performance. *People will see me as fighting for them. They will feel sorry for me. More importantly, if someone starts talking treason, starts voicing support for the Pretender, they will find themselves turned in.*

I am a true hero to the cause ...

CHAPTER 8

*"Business owners are a low class of
society that are known exploiters."*

Kiff always got fidgety when someone looked over his shoulder at his screen. Space was important to him and his office; with all of its Funko and sci-fi paraphernalia was *his* domain. Having Jack Desmond hovering behind him made him squirm in his chair and drum his fingers nervously on the desk.

He had spent half an hour going over what he had found on the people behind the so-called Texas Republic. His investigation had netted a wealth of information, but he had no way of knowing if any of it was truly useful. That was why Desmond was there, hovering like a hawk stalking a mouse in a field.

Kiff wheeled around in his chair and looked up at the man looming over him with crossed arms and squinted eyes. When Jack spoke, it made him think about what a father might sound like. "Pretend for a minute that I'm not as smart as you Kiff," Jack said, darting his eyes down to him. "Can you dumb it down for me?"

What Jack was asking for was hard. The details of data was how Kiff looked at the world. Things were not simple, as much as he wished they could be. It was difficult for him to summarize things, despite the constant demand for it. He paused for a moment, drawing a lone breath of air, closing his eyes during that time attempting to organize his thinking. "Jack, it's like this. They are being funded heavily from outside sources. That much I can prove. From what I can see, from here, a lot of fingers are pointing to the Russians … almost deliberately."

"So you think that's a red herring? Pun intended."

Kiff cocked his head. "I'm not following."

Jack actually chuckled. "Different generation. I still remember calling the Russians the Reds."

"Oh," was all Kiff could muster. "You do realize I'm going to have to search for that."

"Move on Kiff."

"Alright. The transactions may look like the Russians and North Koreans behind them, but it's almost too much. I mean, wouldn't the Russians go out of their way to conceal that they are meddling here in the United States?"

Jack said nothing in response for what seemed to be an intolerable amount of time. "But this is a hunch, not proof."

"An evaluation based on experience," he countered. *I hate the word hunch.* Reaching out, he took a sip of his Monster Energy® drink.

"Can it be proved? Can you confirm they are getting outside help and prove where it is coming from?"

"Those … are excellent questions," he admitted. "Yes, it can be proved. If I had access to the hard drives of the machines, there are some tools I could run that could help me pin down some of the local encryption. Part of the challenge I have been facing is that they don't leave their machines on the Internet for a hack and run. These guys are smart enough to keep their transaction times on the net short."

"So all you need is the hard drives?"

"And time—but yes."

Jack mused on the idea. "If we take their PCs or pull their hard drives, they are going to know what we are doing."

"That seems logical to me. I mean, if you broke into my house and stole my PC, I'd assume you had access to my data from that point on." Kiff wasn't sure where Jack was going with his thinking, but he found it titillating to contemplate.

"How much time would it take for you to sit down with the PCs and run these tools?"

"Hours, maybe days. It's not quick and easy to break encryption. The stuff I have is from the NSA. If Newmerica is behind this, it will be fast—but my digging shows there are multiple sources feeding these good old boys money."

"Can you copy their hard drives?"

"Yes. Depending on the amount of data, I can mirror a copy fairly quick, even if encrypted. We have a tool kit for doing that. We're talking a half-hour, tops. That would at least give me a copy I can work with. Kind of a suck-and-run thing."

"Does doing that require any sort of special skills?"

"Define special?" *Everything I do is special and unique.*

"Can you train someone to do it?"

Kiff shook his head quickly. "Nope. There are, how do I say it, nuances to what you have to do. Not every PC is the same. They may have some physical security lockouts, local hard drive encryption, any number of measures that I will need to possibly overcome. You have to do this with a tool kit of apps and hardware. If it was one of my staff, I'd say no problem. It's a lot more than what you see in the movies. It's not just putting in a flash drive and watching the countdown."

Jack rubbed his chin in deep thought, saying nothing in response. "You could do it though."

"I'm fairly sure. There's always a chance they have something that might throw me a curve ball, but yeah, I'm more than up to it.

"The question is kind of moot, Jack. From the traces I have run, these guys are in some place called Vernon, Texas. To do it, I would have to be physically there and from what I've seen on the news, that isn't an easy proposition. They have turned that town into a fortress. You'd have to be some sort of ninja to get in there, do the snatch-and-grab on the data, and get out."

Jack stared at him intently, then forced a smile. "Alright then, that's what we'll do."

"You did hear me right? I'm not James Bond material."

"I know people—very good people, who are. We'll get you in, you grab their data, and we'll get you out."

A part of Kiff was nervous and afraid, but it was trumped by the part of him that was excited at the prospect. *This is some serious 007 shit!* "You have access to a ninja that can pull this off?"

Jack's grin broadened. "As a matter of fact, I do."

Maysville, Iowa

"Say that again," Colonel Lance Meade of the 45th IBCT demanded as Captain Judy Mercury's pitch for inserting her team had hit a rough spot. She felt the eyes of the Colonel and of General Moorehouse boring in on her, and it was hard to hide her expression of determination as her face went crimson.

"For this plan to work, I need you to let the enemy take back the area east of the airport, where the warehouses are," she said firmly.

General Moorehouse leaned in. "You do know that we fought like hell to take that area just yesterday."

Judy nodded. "I am aware of that sir. For this plan to work, I need to get a sizable combat force across the Mississippi. What this plan calls for is for us to move into one of the warehouses, put our force on their tractor trailers, and hide them in the rubble. You put up a fight, but concede the ground where we are going to be positioned. They then will 'rescue' us; we drive back across the bridges into their rear area. When we get near the objectives, we deploy off of the trucks and strike."

Colonel Meade shifted on his feet. "How do you know they won't just take you into custody?"

The question was fair. How she answered it was the crux of the plan, and she expected push back. Judy looked about the classroom she had been using along with Lieutenant Colonel Mihalek to plan the operation, and she saw his face. He gave her a smirk and a firm solid nod of support from behind his superiors. "We will convince them they have rescued us."

"How in the hell will you do that?" General Moorehouse demanded.

"Guile."

"Guile?"

"We will be in a warehouse, covered in debris, with vehicles all marked as Illinois National Guard with fake battle damage. We will tell them that we were trapped behind the lines when your forces took that area and that we hid there, waiting for relief. They'll fall for it because the thought that it is anything other than we say it is, will be alien to them."

"General," Mihalek spoke up. "It plays to their egos. Everyone wants to be a hero that rescues fellow soldiers. They'll just get them out of there as quickly as possible, move them out of harm's way. If it is sold to them properly, they'll buy it."

"You'll have to do it so that no one sees us move those flatbeds in," Moorehouse stated.

I've got this. "We will need a heavy smoke barrage. The enemy will assume it is preparations for a counterattack so it won't surprise them," Judy countered. "When the smoke clears, they will simply assume that we called off the attack."

The classroom-turned-planning-room went quiet with Mihalek's endorsement as the two senior officers looked at the map and the logistics that Judy had displayed on her laptop screen. It was tempting for her to speak up, to shatter the silence, but she had learned long ago to let such moments do their job—forcing others to think. "It's a hell of a gamble," Colonel Meade said. "We must ask ourselves: Is this the best way to get a raiding force across the Mississippi and behind enemy lines?"

"We looked at barges to ferry us across, but they are essentially large slow moving targets, and they have pickets looking for such a move on the shore. The Illinois forces hold the bridges and the chance of us getting one intact, even one far from Davenport, is practically nil. And if we did, they would know immediately that we were starting an offensive operation," Judy replied. "If we do it this way, they don't know we are deployed until we decide to let them know, and by then, it's too late."

General Moorehouse planted his fists on his hips, stared at her and squinted. "If this goes south, those are my people that are putting their lives on the line."

"With all due respect sir, my ass is with them." She felt her jaw set forward as she spoke, as if it were a matter of pride.

The older man studied her face. "It cost me good men and women to take that neighborhood," he said. "And you are proposing that we give it back to the enemy, an invading force in this state."

"I am," she said. "Because once we hit them where it hurts, they will be forced to withdraw to home. They most likely pushed into Davenport to maintain the Rock Island Armory and to distract us from other operations. The Iowa Guard has done a good job of containing them, but we need to give them a good reason to pull out of here. I can do that."

"Once you start inflicting some pain, it will be like kicking a bee hive," Colonel Meade said.

"Yes sir, I'm counting on it. We will have plenty of ammo and from what we have seen, they are already spread thin trying to hold the borders. They have damned little in the way of reserves right now. Their interior is an empty paper bag. They'll have to react, and the only reaction that they can have is to fall back out of Davenport to come after us."

General Moorehouse looked at the screen, using his fingers to zoom in on one of the objectives, studying it carefully. "We aren't going to win this war with half-measures. I spoke with General Reager about this, and we both agree that daring and boldness is what is going to win the day. He seems to think you're the right person for the job Captain, and from what I see, I tend to agree."

"So we have the green light sir?" she asked to confirm.

He nodded at her. "You do. Get your task force ready. Coordinate with Colonel Meade on placement of your troops and anything else you might need."

"Thank you sir."

Moorehouse cocked a smirk on his face. "Don't thank me yet Captain. You are going into the heart of enemy territory, alone, unsupported."

"They'll never see us coming," she said proudly.

"You'd better hope that is the case," he said as he turned and left the room. Judy looked down at the material she had assembled for the strike. Colonel Lance walked up to her. "You did good work selling the old man on the plan, Captain," he offered. "Now that you are approved, this operation is going to need a code name."

Judy had been thinking about it. "Grab Ass, sir."

Colonel Meade chuckled. "Grab Ass! Wonderful. It has the virtue of never having been used before." He paused. "Get our teams prepped and ready Captain ... you are going on a raid."

Roanoke Rapids, North Carolina

Trip saw the troop dispositions along I-95, one of the major highways running north and south from Virginia into North Carolina. The day before he had been in Henderson, along I-85 and had seen similar field fortifications. The ground commanders had picked good ground, had cleared fields of fire in the woods, and had put earthwork bunkers with anti-tank missiles poised to destroy anything coming down the highways.

Somehow, it still didn't feel right.

Intelligence indicated that Newmerica was concentrating troops along their southern border with North Carolina. Drone overflights had shown that to be the case, but for General Reager, it wasn't settling well. It was too much out in the open. *The enemy is giving me time to prepare, which is something that an intelligent officer wouldn't do.* "I don't like it Paul," he said looking out over the defensive positions.

Captain Harnessy looked puzzled. "You want to change some of the positions sir?"

Trip shook his head and frowned slightly. "No, these positions are solid. Anyone trying to push through here is going to get their asses chewed up badly. No, none of this feels right."

"Sir?"

"If they are planning to strike into North Carolina, the only viable military target is in Fayettville, where Fort Bragg is. To get there, they had to punch through our defenses here, go through at least one major urban center at Raleigh, then hit Fort Bragg. Their logistics lines are going to be stretched thin."

"Why concentrate along this border?"

"Why indeed," Trip replied, crossing his arms. "You're my G2. You tell me."

"They could be planning a mere incursion into North Carolina, like in Davenport. Something to distract us from something else."

The mention of Davenport struck Trip oddly. *Judy's up there and will hopefully take some pressure off of that situation soon. If anyone can, it's her.* As he thought about Davenport, he seemed to look at it differently. "With Davenport, we have assumed it was to force us to tie down troops or to ensure they held onto the Rock Island Arsenal."

"Yes sir."

"What if that was a distraction?"

"For what?"

You don't send troops into battle for no reason. People die in combat, and the fake President wouldn't be that stupid to waste troops for no purpose. "Show me the enemy troops concentrations." With a few fast jabs of his fingers on his iPad, Captain Harnessy pulled up the latest information.

"They are in Emporia, South Hill, and a contingent in Danville which we presume is a reserve of some sort," the intelligence officer said as he studied the map.

For several minutes, he looked at the map, saying nothing. I'm missing something here. "Give me the rundown of my opponent again?"

Captain Harnessy nodded, taking back the iPad and pulling up the necessary files. "General Hollings Andrew Rinehart graduated West Point, middle of his class. He did two tours in Afghanistan, nothing entirely remarkable. When the Fall happened, he changed his middle name, Lee, to Andrew."

"A virtue signaler of the highest order."

"More than that. He led the diversity efforts in the army after the Ruling Council seized control. As we both know, that was little more than an orchestrated purge of the officer ranks of so-called corrupted soldiers. They claimed they were targeting 'extremists,' but in reality it was anyone that had voiced a conservative outlook."

Trip remembered the diversity and inclusiveness sessions during that period, after the coup. *They forced a lot of good people out of the service. Those they didn't drive out were mercilessly hounded and given the shittiest duties.* Men like Rinehart were a blight to the military, pandering to the politicians, using the armed forces for social experimentation and a source of pork spending projects in their districts. *Worse than that, they weakened the military which invite our enemies into places like Taiwan and the Ukraine. Rinehart and the creeps like him have cost millions of people their lives and livelihoods, slaughtered or enslaved under the auspices of political correctness.* "Tell me something about his combat experience. Anything from a strategic sense that might help me get a handle on what is happening here?"

Harnessy didn't have to refer to notes, a sign that he was more than prepared. "Rinehart likes things big and bold. His maneuvers tend to be sweeping and fast. He likes to go for the jugular, to cripple the enemy's command and control early on, old school shock and awe. At the same time, he seems to have little regard for the lives of civilians that get in his way. In an incident in Shirzay Kalay, he brought down artillery on a position where it was known that there were civilians. His court martial on that fight came out in his favor, but it is an indication that he doesn't care about losses to noncombatants."

Trip drank in the words from his G2 carefully. *He's put those troops there along the border for a reason. Everyone thinks it's a drive south, but Rinehart likes stuff that is bigger and bolder than just crossing into North Carolina. He's a true believer in the Newmerica cause too, and that makes him even more dangerous. But what is his target?*

Ultimately he came to the conclusion that it didn't matter what the objective was. *I don't need to outthink him yet. I just need to have the flexibility to respond to whatever he has planned.* "Good work Paul. I think this son of a bitch is going to do something big based on his past experience and patterns."

"What sir?"

"I don't know yet. I do know we need to have a rapid reaction force prepped and positioned, ready to counter any little tricks this guy tries."

"What do you have in mind?"

"I'm going to have the President activate the Mississippi National Guard's 155th Armored Brigade Combat Team and their supporting troops. We will move them up to someplace along the western border of Virginia west of here."

"I might recommend the Cherokee National Forest. Even in winter it will provide them cover from aerial observation. It is close to I-81 along the western edge of Virginia as well, being positioned to cover Winston-Salem if he tries an end run in that direction." Harnessy pulled up the map on his iPad again and showed the position to Trip.

Good highways in and out—well suited for a counterpunch if this guy moves. "We'll have the Tennessee units assemble another mobile reaction force in Knoxville. That should give us the ability to respond quickly if he tries something to the west. Let's redeploy some of the North Carolina Guard to Rocky Mount as well, just in case he decides to run down the coast."

"I will prepare the orders immediately sir," Harnessy said.

"Good. We need to be prepared. He didn't assemble those troops just for shits and giggles. He's got something in mind." *I'm not sure what it is, but I need to be prepared for the unexpected. I only hope I'm not missing something else, something big.*

Smyrna, Tennessee

Caylee knew he was coming—he had called in advance. While she appreciated Jack Desmond, somehow she had a feeling that his arrival at their home was not something she would enjoy. Desmond was the President's Chief of Staff. He could have asked her to come to Nashville and meet in his office, but he was coming to her. *That means he wants something.*

He knocked at the door and she checked to make sure it was him before opening it. "Please come in," she said courteously. She noticed that his hair was grayer than it had been even a few weeks before. The silver and white strands of hair on his head betrayed the burden of his role. She appreciated that Desmond was not one of those men vain enough to dye his hair. For years he lived undercover, bringing together the cells of the Sons of Liberty. Now that the war had become more open, he was enduring it, but the signs of strain were showing in the deep wrinkles on his brow. "Thank you Caylee."

She ushered him into the family room where Raul and Maria were. Jack shook their hands and greeted them warmly. Caylee offered him coffee which Jack politely declined. After a few moments of formalities, Jack took a seat on the couch.

"I have to ask, Mr. Desmond, what brings you to Smyrna?"

He grinned at her words. "You can call me Jack, Caylee. I've told you that before."

"I suspect you are here for more than a break from the office," she countered. "And if we are going to talk business, I'll stick with Mr. Desmond." Caylee smiled back.

He chuckled. "Guilty as charged. I came here to ask a favor from you." Glancing over at Maria and Raul, he then turned back to her. "If you prefer, we can talk in private."

"These days I prefer no secrets," she said, casting a glance at Raul who gave her a nod. "We are all friends here. Anything you have to say, I'm comfortable with you saying in front of Raul and Maria."

Desmond nodded. "Very well then. I am in need of someone with your unique talents."

"Go on."

"You've heard about the ruckus in Texas with this self-proclaimed

Republic," he stated. Caylee nodded in response as Jack continued. "Our cyber people are fairly sure that the effort is being funded by, shall I say, 'outside interests.' The challenge is in determining who is behind this. From what I have been told, the only way for them to do that is by looking at the data on their hard drives."

"So you want me to steal some PCs."

Jack winced slightly. "I wish it was that simple, Caylee. If we take them, it tips them off. What we need to do is essentially copy what is on the PCs without them knowing."

"Why is that information so useful?" Raul asked. *That's a good question.*

Jack leaned back on the couch slightly. "Right now this little rebellion looks organic. It appears like it is a group of Texans that want independence. That appeals to a lot of people, even outside of Texas. We are in the middle of a war fighting for our freedom, and it makes coming down on this Republic of Texas difficult since they are asking for the same thing.

"If, however, we can prove they are being propped up by some foreign element, or even Newmerica, it sours their story. It will look like this is meddling by some outside elements; it will hamstring their support. We believe that things will collapse from within if the people there find out that this was some plot by our enemies.

"The President would prefer for this to fall apart rather than make us go in there guns a 'blazing. So would I. If we can prove our theory, gather some tangible evidence that this is outside interference, it will go a long way toward ending this crisis and allow us to focus on the real threat, Newmerica."

Raul nodded in response. It made sense to Caylee as well. *This whole thing seemed suspicious from the start. If they wanted independence, why not do it when Newmerica was in power?* "I was hoping to have a little more downtime before jumping back into things," she stated with a frank tone.

"I know. Doing this will save lives if you're successful."

"I have a lot of cyber in my background. I'll need some tools and a little training to do this."

Jack seemed to wince a little bit. "Well, there is a minor complication to that."

"There usually is."

"This isn't something you can just get trained on. To do this, you'll need to take in one of our best hackers to do the nuts and bolts work. Your job is to get him in and out."

Caylee didn't even try to conceal her frown. "Does he have any background in covert ops?"

Jack shook his head. "He got involved in a scrape or two after the Fall, but nothing like what you are hoping for."

"So you want me to play bodyguard and infiltrator for some geek? Is that accurate?"

"I prefer to think of him as an uber-geek, but yes, you've got the right idea."

Sighing, Calyee relaxed in the easy chair where she sat. *At least we're only going into Texas.* "When does this need to happen?"

"Yesterday, if not sooner," Jack quipped.

"You're asking a lot Mr. Desmond," she said.

"The way I see it, you do owe me for a helicopter," he said with a smile. There was a bit of truth in that. When breaking Raul out of the Supermax, their rescue helicopter had been shot down. The fact that Desmond referenced it made it hard for Caylee to not crack a thin smile in response. She glanced over at Raul and Maria for a moment. *My commitment is to protect them. I don't want them exposed because I'm off running some errand for Jack Desmond.*

Raul could read her emotions and nodded. "You need to do this Caylee," he replied. "If it will save lives, you have." Maria joined him with nods of support.

"I want Maria and Raul protected while I'm gone," she said, issuing her sole demand.

Jack understood. "I think I can convince Charli to take a few days to stay here. You aren't going to get better than Secret Service protection."

If it is Charli staying here, he is right. Still, the thought of leaving Raul and Maria tore at her. *I was away when he was kidnapped.* There was more to it than fear of another attempt on Raul. Caylee found the time with the Lopezes relaxing. Downtime was something she had always seemed to be able to avoid in her career. Somehow, the strange little family situation they formed was comforting to Leatrom. It wasn't just healthy for her. Maria was slowly starting to come out of her shell. Going on this mission would separate her from the relaxation their little home provided.

There was one comforting thought in all of this that she appreciated, and that was Charli's involvement. *She's good ... very good.* Charli had prevented a Presidential assassination and handled herself well in the field. *In another life, she would have made a great operative.* "Very well Mr. Desmond, I will need to prepare."

"I will have your partner, Kiff Renner come over. Our intel folks have information on the target people and locations already prepped." Jack rose to his feet and extended his hand. "Thank you Caylee. Kiff is a friend. I wouldn't trust his life with anyone other than you."

She gripped his hand hard and squeezed it as she shook. "I'll do my best." She was careful not to commit to an optimistic outcome. While this mission was only in Texas, she had not seen any of the details. As a covert operative, she knew better than to assume success until a mission was over.

INTERLUDE

"There is nothing that the government cannot fix."

Twenty-two years earlier ...
Huangyan District, Taizhou, Zhejiang, China

Jianyu Liu was manhandled by the People's Armed Police officer and shoved into the room of the bookstore where he worked. The officer was so close that Jianyu could smell what the man ate the day before from his perspiration. The other employees were there as well, all appearing as confused as he was. The armed PAP officers kept their guns on the staff, clearly designed to keep them in line.

Jianyu had seen businesses face a police incursion before, but had never been a part of one. Fear chewed at him, despite the fact that he hadn't done anything wrong. The dour faces on the PAP officers was enough for him to know how serious this was. *What could have happened that led to this?*

"At least one of you knows why we are here," the lead officer stated. It wasn't a question; nor did Jianyu have any idea why a squad of PAP would come to the tiny book shop.

Mr. Hsiung, who ran the shop, was an older man, almost grandfatherly. He bowed his head respectfully to the lead PAP officer. "Respected sir, I have no idea why you are here."

The officer's face revealed no emotions as he paced in front of the employees. "Two days ago we arrested a man. He was in possession of a book, a banned book. Under interrogation, he told us that he bought that book here."

Hsiung's wife, Ju, bowed her head as she spoke. "We do not sell banned material here. We are loyal citizens. My husband is a ward watcher for the party. There must be some mistake."

"The PAP does not make mistakes. We have the book," the officer said flatly. "We have his confession. It is now only a matter of determining who among you has been part of this treasonous activity."

Jianyu felt his face get red with anger and frustration. He had always thought that the Hsiungs were good people. To hear that someone in the store was in possession of illegal material and would be propagating it was offensive and vexing. A part of him wanted to proclaim his innocence, but he knew that speaking to the PAP might be misinterpreted. His father had always told him it was best not to talk to the police unless he was asked.

The officer reached the end of the line of employees, then turned around. "We will tear this place apart to see if there are any other illegal books here. So whichever of you is responsible will be uncovered. It would be best that you confess now. Perhaps you can spare your fellow workers the punishment that is bound to come."

Silence was what the officer got back in response. The officer waited, pacing slightly in place, eyeing them all, demonstrating more patience than Jianyu felt. Finally he spoke up again. "So none of you will talk? Very well, then it is to be considered a conspiracy. You will all suffer the punishment for subversion."

I am to be punished for something I did not do? The outrage made Jianyu shift on his feet as he glared at the other employees. He was not alone; another student employee, Fen, looked from the other end of the line, seeing him. "I had nothing to do with any illicit book," Jianyu said. "Whoever did, you need to confess what you did!" he demanded. None of them responded.

"That is enough," the PAP officer said. "Take them away. A few weeks of isolation will jar their memories. In the meantime, toss this place."

Five Years Earlier ...
Abilene, Texas

"So you're just going to pack up and leave me?" Wanda said as Judy packed her uniforms and gear into the bag sitting on her bedspread. She had been on enough deployments to know that extra underwear, socks, and deodorant were likely necessary. As she moved, the old wooden plank flooring of her house creaked and moaned. It wasn't much, but she almost had it paid off.

"I was called up," she said, glancing at her girlfriend. "I have to go." *You know that ... we've had this discussion before.* "You've seen what is going on everywhere ... the riots, the killings. We have to protect the capital."

"Why you? What if you just don't go?" Wanda demanded.

"You know full well that I'm in the Guard. When they call, I go. That's how it works. We've had this discussion before. The Governor wants us to protect the capital in case ANTIFA or some other group tries to grab it." Judy had been tempted to say, "It will only be for a few days," but she knew not to float that with Wanda. *She'll hold me to it, and I can't promise that.*

"Don't go. Don't get involved with this," Wanda pressed. "They've got that bastard President in custody. Now that he's out of the picture, things will calm down."

Judy checked her facial expression of sadness and paused for a moment, looking at her lover as if to say, "Do you really believe that? Wanda, I have an obligation."

"What about your obligation to me?"

There it is ... the classic Wanda move. It is always about her and her needs. Wanda had dropped that bomb before, when Judy had gone on her last tour of duty overseas. *It's as if she doesn't understand my commitment. Or worse, she doesn't care.*

That was the core of the problem, and Judy knew it. This was an argument that had been a long time coming. Wanda was so far left that she didn't think that the rules applied equally or fairly. She saw the National Guard as a 'side gig' rather than a patriotic obligation. Wanda was in school full time, working on her master's degree in women's studies. To her, college was the real world—where Judy knew the reality of the situation. *She refuses to question her instructors. They have brainwashed her almost completely.* It had gotten worse over the years of their living together, and moments like this only made things bad.

Judy looked at her, stopped packing for a moment, and put her hands on Wanda's shoulders. "You know what I feel about you."

"You aren't showing it."

"It's my duty to protect Texas." They were not just words—it was who Judy was.

"This entire state is fucked," Wanda snapped and Judy pulled her hands back. "A bunch of redneck white trash, wallowing in their privilege. Big oil companies exploiting the workers and polluting the entire planet. The fact that you would want to defend that system and those people makes me sick."

"So you are saying I'm a redneck? That I have white privilege?" It was almost laughable given that Wanda had lighter skin than she did.

Wanda glared at her. "Just because you don't see it in yourself, doesn't mean that it's not there."

Judy drew a long breath to calm herself and to buy a few moments to get her thoughts together. "Look, I get it; you're pissed off that I have to go. That doesn't change anything. I still have to go."

"If you go, I won't be here when you come back," she said like a petulant child throwing a tantrum. "I'll leave you."

And there it was, the words that Judy knew her lover had been waiting to say all along. They hurt, more from the fact that Wanda would act so childish ... that their relationship meant so little. She's stooping to extortion. The wave of sadness that came over Judy was less for herself over the end of their relationship. It was pity for Wanda. *She's too immature for what we have.* "Then you should pack your bags now. I'll have my dad come over and change the locks. He'll be looking over the place while I'm gone"

"You don't think I'll do it. I will," she said with tears streaming down her face.

"I know you will," Judy replied, as a wave of resolution overcame her. "And I am going to have to deal with the emotional fallout from your decision." *I will move on.*

"If you will just stay ..." she pleaded.

"No Wanda," Judy said. "I get it. You are willing to let your hate take priority over what we had together. While you preach tolerance, what it really means to you is that I do what you want. I am a soldier. I have a commitment. It's not just words; it's about who I am. You see my obligation as a job. It's not. It's about honor, pride, and duty." *And you don't have those things in your life. All you have is your anger and hate.* For a moment she wondered if she had said the last line out loud or had only thought it.

"I don't have anywhere to go," Wanda said.

Because you've spent your life burning your bridges ... blaming other people for your bad decisions. She felt a wave of sympathy, but pushed it down. *You need to fix this yourself.* "Go back to your parents in San Antonio," she offered. "You can transfer to a college there if you want. I ... I don't care where you go. You just need to leave here."

"I'll need some time to make arrangements," Wanda sobbed, wiping the tears from her cheeks. "Maybe I can stay here until you get back. We can work this out when you get back." *Another classic Wanda maneuver was unfolding, stalling the inevitable, trying to back pedal. There's a part of her that thinks this can be fixed.*

Not this time.

A growing resolve came over Judy. *I'm not going to let her off the hook this time. It's not good for her, or for me.* In the past she had always folded, always taken back Wanda after one of her explosions. *This isn't a relationship, it's a support group for her. I can't do that again. It's not fair for either of us.* "You can have a few days. All of the utilities and the mortgage are in my name. The furniture is all mine. You need to pack up your stuff and go." As she spoke the words, she realized how little Wanda brought to their relationship besides the feelings they had for each other. *I have been supporting her financially and physically and convincing myself it was love.*

"Why are you being so mean?" Wanda asked.

Judy shook her head. "This isn't about me. Then again, it never is. It's about you and your issues. It's about your beliefs that you try to inflict on others. Until you get on top of your feelings or find someone that thinks the way you do, you won't be happy. You aren't going to find that happiness with me, and I'm not going to be happy staying with you. Go back to your parents, Wanda. Get your life together."

Wanda sulked out of the room weeping, and Judy returned to her packing. Like when she went overseas, there was a feeling that she might not be coming back for a long time.

Five years earlier ...
The District

Kiff's supervisor, Joseph Eckhart, stepped into his tiny office and dominated the doorway. Eckhart was a Director of Domestic Cyber Security with the DHS and had spent most of his civil service career figuring out ways to reorganize the department he was in charge of. Kiff respected him, slightly. The man had a background in technology, but for the most part was a mid-level administrator. His one redeeming quality was that Eckhart knew to hand Kiff an assignment and leave him alone. Kiff tolerated him, but barely. *If he was micromanaging me, it would be hell to be here.*

For Kiff, the months after the Fall had an almost ominous feeling. The Ruling Council, who had no standing under the law, was making changes almost daily. Most of Congress was dead; Kiff had watched the grainy footage of the slaughter the night that the Fall happened. Those members that survived followed the orders of the Ruling Council lock-step, rubber-stamping their directives and mandates. They packed the Supreme Court so that nothing stood in their way of running the country as they saw fit. *It's understandable. Anyone speaking up has a way of simply disappearing.*

Renner had seen the greatest nation on the planet overthrown in a bloody coup, and damned few people seemed willing to resist. The Ruling Council was ordering the rounding up of guns, which was starting to lead to a wave of dangerous standoffs. Counter protests had come in the weeks following the coup, only to result in violence and mass arrests.

A lot of rumors were running around, talk of rounding up conservatives and sending them off to prisons. The press embraced the coup, and was apparently elated about the announcement of some sort of clearing commission, the Truth Reconciliation Committee, that would vet news articles for accuracy. While many saw it is as a necessary and positive step, to Kiff it was government censorship—plain and simple. When the Ruling Council had ordered Fox News off the air, stripping them of their FCC permits, there had actually been people cheering in YouTube videos. *They don't want any dissenting voices out there. Their supporters are too blind to see themselves as the baddies in this drama.*

He had looked up to the military in his youth. After the Fall, he eyed them with suspicion and outright contempt. They had stood down when the White House was burning and Congress was being slaughtered. In doing so, they had sanctioned what had happened the night of the Fall— or the Liberation, as the TRC referred to the event. *It was an insurrection, an armed uprising, but they paint it as something positive.* What was more disturbing was the fact that so many people seemed to embrace the branding rather than be sickened by it.

Kiff had seen the handwriting on the wall. He had taken down his photo of the man they called, 'The Traitor President.' His MAGA bumper sticker that he kept in his office was discarded. This was not a safe time to be a supporter of the man that the revolutionaries had killed.

As he looked up at Eckhart from his pair of large monitors, he saw the consternation on his supervisor's red face. "Kiff, we need to talk," he said in a low tone, entering the office and closing the door.

It sounded serious, and he nodded to Eckhart. "What is it?"

"Kiff, I'm sorry about this," Eckhart said.

Renner was instantly confused. "Sorry about what?"

"They sent out edicts for every agency. We were ordered to identify employees that are conservative or right-leaning."

"Why?"

Eckhart shifted on his feet side-to-side. "I don't know for sure. I spoke with some of my peers, and they have sent over FBI to take them in ... the people on their lists."

FBI? Why would they want to talk to me? A wave of anger rose for the young man, followed by a feeling of betrayal. His face was hot and he rose to his feet, almost face-to-face with his supervisor. "You ratted me out because of how I voted?"

"I didn't have a choice," he said. "Other people in the department know that you supported the President. You didn't exactly hide your affiliation. If I didn't turn you in, and someone told the powers that be, then they would be coming for me too. I didn't have a choice." His voice wavered. It was as if he wanted Kiff to pity his plight, but Kiff had bigger problems of his own.

"So you sold me out to save your own ass," he stated.

"It's not like that."

"It totally is, Joseph," Kiff snapped. "So the FBI is coming for me?"

Eckhart seemed confused by the question, shrugging slightly. "I don't know that for sure. I've heard they are taking some people into custody. I have no way of knowing if they are coming. Maybe nothing will come of this?"

For a few moments, Kiff said nothing. A part of him felt he had nothing to worry about, that he should simply sit down and see what happened. *I haven't done anything wrong.* Then again, neither had half of Congress, and they had been slaughtered. Guilt wasn't the issue. *They don't care that I haven't done anything wrong. This is payback for not thinking the way they do.* His flight response overrode his fight response. "This is my life you asshole! The people running the show now are more than willing to kill people that don't follow them lock-step."

"Now Kiff, don't overreact."

Renner started gathering up his personal items, stuffing them into his backpack. "Overreact? Why would they ask about my political affiliation? They are putting together lists of names of people like me for a reason, you *dick*."

"Where are you going?"

"Why would I tell you?" he said, grabbing a small framed photo of his mother and stuffing it into his backpack. "You've already shown you can't be trusted."

"Kiff—if you take off, they are going to know I told you."

There it was; *Joseph is thinking about himself.* "That's your problem. You've already sold me out."

"I didn't have a choice," he said in a dejected tone.

Slinging the backpack over his shoulder, he shoved his way past Eckhart and started for the hallway. "Consider me on leave," he said, not looking back. He started for the elevators, but paused. That was a potential trap, and his brain registered it as such. *I need out of the building, but nothing obvious.*

Bolting to the left, he started down the stairs. At the first landing, he heard the shuffle of footsteps below. "We have a team in the lobby; we will hold here," a voice said. "Roger that. There are ten targets on the list." The voice seemed to come from a walkie-talkie and echoed upward. *Aw shit! I'm not the only one.*

Kiff looked at the window on the landing and the fire escape just beyond it. As much as he hated heights, the thought of being in the hands of a radicalized FBI was worse. *We're only five stories up—I can do this.* Kiff knew he was no athlete, but he was not entirely out of shape either. The long walks to and from the Metro stop every day helped. With his father long gone, the maintenance of his mother's place where he lived was something that fell to him. While he hated ladders, he hated the thought of what the FBI would do with him even more.

The window resisted opening. He banged on it. Then he heard the voices below. "What was that?" There was commotion below him, the sound of leather shoes hitting the stairs.

Aw fuck!

CHAPTER 9

*"Desiring wealth is a sickness. A rich
society is inherently corrupt."*

Berlin, New Hampshire

Su-Hui stood in what was the motor pool for his resistance group, watching the experienced people work on the Humvees they had captured. It had taken four different raids to capture the number of vehicles he felt necessary for the operation. While he never would admit it to the others beyond his wife Hachi, he felt that things had gone better without the dark presence of Herb Fletcher. The man was always in the back of the room, taking verbal pot shots at each and every decision he made. *I miss having his people here, but not the voice of his dissent.* It had been almost a week since Herb's stormy departure, and with it had come a noticeable increase in morale. *Negative people are like a virus; they infect people indiscriminately.*

The Humvees were not just being checked over for a long road trip, but were being equipped for the operation. Some were being converted into car bombs with explosives and charges being put into them or on them in ways that did not attract attention. The external jerry cans for fuel were packed with explosives on the vehicles that were going to be used to devastate the Joint Force Headquarters. Cartons marked as spare parts or MREs were filled with high explosives. Every nook and cranny on the Humvee that could carry something devastating did so. The four bomb Humvees, dubbed by Trudy as 'The Four Horsemen,' made Su-Hui nervous, so he wanted to watch them be prepared himself. *One of these is probably enough to do the job. Four of them are indeed the apocalypse.*

He wanted to be sure that nothing might accidentally set them off.

The other Humvees that were parked in the old Mountain Tire garage were being equipped for a heavy gunfight. Additional armor plating was being added, and the Humvees were being loaded with heavy ammunition. Two of them were already equipped with Hellfire missile launchers when they had been captured, giving the force even more firepower. The others were being loaded with ammunition. *It isn't enough to get in and destroy the headquarters. We need to be able to get back to New Hampshire.*

Su-Hui was still working on the plan for the operation. He had sent a pair of Valerie's SOL cells to sneak across the border into Massachusetts to do preliminary scouting. The moment the attack began, he knew that the entire state would light up with response. *They will come at us with everything they have.*

Leaning out of the vehicle that was being worked on, he saw Hachi holding a cup for him. "It's soup. You missed lunch," she encouraged.

The warm cup came with a whiff of tomato. He sipped it, found that it was already cool, and drank down the heavy tomato soup. "I worry about you when you miss your meals," she chided him.

"You worry too much my dear," he said taking another deep sip.

"I am in command," he said. "I worry for the others."

"This operation of yours is risky," she said. Hachi always used a small number of words to say a great deal. Having been married to her for decades, he knew how to read them. *She is fearful that something will happen to us, that we may be facing some sort of trap.*

"I am taking every precaution possible," he tried to assure her. "We knew we would be facing risks just coming to this state and joining the fight."

Hachi nodded. "We had to come," she said. "Our homeland had been invaded, and the nation we fled to was not what we had dreamed or envisioned. These people took everything from us, our hopes, our daughter, our financial security. We were made out to be foreign trash. They looked at us as worthless refugees when we risked our lives to get here. These people took the American dream from us simply because of where we came from."

She won't even say 'Newmericans.' She simply calls them 'these people.' Su-Hui rarely saw such a display of emotion from his wife. It was something that he understood all too well. California had been as bad if not worse than what he pictured mainland China to be like. *Now that same tyranny is in our homeland of Taiwan.* It ate at him to think of what social order was being pushed down on the survivors of the Chinese invasion of his former home. At least that came at gunpoint. *The Newmericans struck like cowards and overthrew their government—they killed their leaders. Rather than try to change things, they simply acted like spoiled children and took what they wanted ... what they thought they deserved.* The Chinese were far more up-front and honorable when compared to the people he was fighting against.

A young man came running into the garage from the front of the tire business. "Sir," he called out to Su-Hui. "Something is on the TV right now ... you need to see this."

He took another fast sip of his soup and handed the cup to Hachi. They followed the runner back to the front of the shop where the waiting lounge had a television hanging in one corner. As he entered almost a dozen people were already crammed into the room, watching the screen.

The image was in front of the State Capital in Concord. The front lawn was covered with deep snow. It wasn't the fresh powder, but instead was dirty, smeared with mud and speckled with bits of black. Standing on the lawn was the Governor and Lieutenant Governor along with a number of older men and women. They were not wearing winter coats, despite the cold, but were dressed in suits and professional attire. Wisps of their frosty breath masked the stern resolve and anger on their faces. The Governor had several days of gray beard growth, and his hair was disheveled, catching the light breeze blowing through.

A General stood at a podium. The video banner under him stated that it was General Hollings Rinehart, the man that had taken the place of General Donaldson, who Hachi had shot dead. The man had a grim expression on his face; his thin jowls reminded him of the actor, John Goodman. Unlike the politicians, he wore a military issue olive drab winter coat to protect him from the weather.

"For far too long we have struggled with New Hampshire denying its people their rightful place in the Newmerican government. Rather than simply accept the voice of the people and acknowledge the rightful and lawful election to the Presidency of Daniel Porter, these people have put their own interests above those of the electorate.

"Their so-called 'Defiance' movement has spawned domestic terrorism in the state. Innocent service men and women have died at the hands of the insurgency that these people propagated with their words and actions. They even led to the death of my predecessor, General Donaldson." That mention made Su-Hui glance to his side where Hachi stood, huddled next to him.

"I am a reasonable man and have tried to work with the administration of this state, despite its obvious corruption. These leaders that many of you have looked up to have refused to accept the reality of the circumstances. They have clearly suppressed the votes and rights of the citizens of New Hampshire for some misguided belief that America has a right to exist.

"My predecessor was too lenient with these traitors," he said nodding at the cluster of politicians that stood some seventy-five feet from him. "His kind-heartedness with the people of this state was mistaken for weakness. It encouraged outside agitators to come here and take innocent lives for a cause that is unjust and illegal." He paused for a moment, no doubt to allow the teleprompter that was in the corner of the image on the television screen to catch up with him.

Su-Hui's worst thoughts came to the surface as he stared at the TV. *I know what totalitarians do. We saw it after Taiwan fell.* Many had continued the fight after the military had surrendered. The Chinese were not tolerant of resistance. *His patience is gone ... but he doesn't have to do this to make his point. Please ... don't do it.*

General Rinehart continued. "The bombings, the deaths, and illegal detentions of military personnel must end immediately. While we have tried to work with the current administration, we have found their positions ridiculous and untenable. Worse, by stonewalling, they are encouraging further resistance." His words were firm, solid, and damning.

"This afternoon, both the Governor and Lieutenant Governor were presented reasonable terms and conditions for ending this conflict. They have refused this generous offer." Rinehart paused for a moment, then nodded to someone off-camera.

"Ready," a distant voice barked. "Aim ... fire!" The crack of a number of weapons went off simultaneously. The echo of the blast carried through the television speakers seeming to shake each person in the small room. Both of the civilian leaders dropped backwards in a spray of blood. An audible gasp rose in the tire center waiting room from Su-Hui's people. *He did it. He actually executed them.* His predecessor had killed people as well, but this … *this is murder.*

"Given the state of martial law that already exists in New Hampshire, and under the expressed authority granted me by the rightful President, Daniel Porter, I am naming myself temporary military Governor of this state. As my first action, I hereby ratify New Hampshire's ballots in the Electoral College as being for the Newmerican President. This state is once more, part of the greater United States of Newmerica."

He paused, seeming to glare into the camera. "And to those who follow the banner of terrorism and continue to mount your petty little 'Defiance,' I have this to say. Look at what happened here, this afternoon. This is the full measure of our resolve to keep the country whole. Those that would stand up against us will meet the same fate as the Governor and his subordinate.

"Leave now … while you still can." The image shifted back to a local reporter, the TRC logo emblazoned in the lower right corner. Someone got up and turned the television off.

It was as if the life had been sucked out of the room. Su-Hui knew that he needed to say something to turn this around. He spoke up, louder than he had anticipated, but with a deep resounding voice. "This was an act of desperation. It speaks to the nature of the people that we are fighting against. When they are done slinging words and catch phrases at us, they come with bullets.

"I know some of you are as sickened as I am by this. It angers you. Some might feel fear. We all knew what we were signing up for when we came here. Many of you," he said making quick eye contact with Hachi who gave him a quick nod, "already experienced this kind of desperation when they destroyed Lisbon and tried to kill us all there. We persevered through that, and we will push on through this."

As he paused, one woman spoke up. "They aim to kill us all." There was no fear in her voice; it was a statement of fact for her.

Su-Hui nodded. "That has always been what they wanted, … what they desired. You've seen some of the footage coming out of the Social Quarantine Camps—you've heard the stories of what goes on there. They always intended to wipe us out.

"That leaves us with a choice. You could go home, hide, put this behind you. Deep down you know that sooner or later, they will come for you though. That is who they are. It is their very nature.

"Or you can stay here with us and fight on. I would prefer a single minute of resistance against such men as this over a lifetime of cowering in fear. The nature of tyrants is death and destruction. I lost everything because of this accursed Newmerica. It would have been easy for Hachi and I to stay at home and hope that someone else would fight them. But we came—as did all of you.

"I say we take the fight to them—hard and fast. We show this Rinehart that he is not really in charge, no matter what title he wishes to laud on himself. I say we avenge this war crime, and make it so that they have little choice but to leave here once and for all."

"Hell yeah!" called out one of the New Hampshire National Guardsmen that was in the room. His cry brought verbal responses from all that were present. They howled loud and proud; the roar of their voices was almost deafening.

General Rinehart has overplayed his hand ... and now he will suffer for it.

Jackson, Michigan

Weber Liu studied the inventory list once more, comparing it to the email he had. There was no doubt in his mind; someone was skimming ammunition and explosives from his shipments. He had security people working the Los Angeles ports, ensuring that his containers avoided customs inspection. The truckers on the payroll were from the homeland. They came with impeccable credentials and references.

That left his own people working the warehouse. As he sat in his car outside of the red brick Standard Goods warehouse, he wished that things were different ... that he did not have to take action. It wasn't the amount of what was being taken; it was a small crate every now and then. It was the fact that they dared steal from him. *Lessons are necessary in such instance to ensure that people understand the authority of the state.*

Nodding to his security detail, they opened the door to his car, and he was greeted by the musty aroma of the old facility. As he stood he saw the staff of the facility. They had no idea that he had uncovered the betrayal by one of them. As he walked before them, he surveyed their faces, hoping to see a hint of guilt. None was offered. *Such a shame.*

"Good day," he said in a low tone. "I presume you have delivered the goods as ordered."

A burley man named Dash Murren spoke up. "Just as you requested sir."

"And there were no incidents along the way?"

He looked genuinely confused by the question. Liu did not mistake it for a mark of innocence. Those that broke their faith in the state often concealed their crimes with acting and deception. "No sir. We didn't have any problems at all."

"And your shipment?" he said looking over at his other driver, Mark Durst.

The man shook his head. "No problems at all sir."

"I see," Liu said. "And here, in the warehouse ... any issues with security?"

"No sir," his local man from Jackson said. "The locals know to stay away from this place, as does law enforcement." There was a hint of pride in his tone, which Weber noted.

His security detail slowly shifted to the flanks of the men as he took two steps to his crew. "The problem I have is that two boxes of ammunition are missing, as is one carton of grenades." Liu paused for a moment so that it could sink in with the men. They looked down the row at the others, each seeming to try to spot the guilty person.

Weber Liu drank in the image and it reminded him of his youth, when he was Jianyu Liu back in the homeland. *What follows is necessary for all of them, not just the guilty man.*

"So none of you will talk? Very well, then it is to be considered a conspiracy," Weber Liu said, glaring over the tops of his glasses. No one spoke, but the looks of panic on their faces meant that they understood the plight they faced. Their dismay was to be expected. He had been on the other side once in his life when someone had done something reprehensible, and he and other innocent people had been blamed. Memories of the bookshop where he worked in his youth, and of the lesson he learned there stood out clearly for him. *Fear paralyzes. Fear compels. Fear unites us all.*

"Organizations such as mine demand loyalty. We pay for it … we expect it," Liu said slowly as he paced in front of them. "One of you has betrayed my trust. Given the gravity of the work we do, you will understand that we cannot allow such a transgression to go unpunished. Speak up now; admit what you have done, and you will spare the others what is to come."

There was no response other than an elevation of panic. For a half moment, he said nothing, letting the silence eat at their nerves. "A shame. It is one thing to be a thief. It is another to be a coward. Then you will all pay a price for this." He nodded to his head of security. Two of the guards grabbed the man at the end of the line, Dash Murren. The big man struggled, but the men with rifles jabbed the butt end of their stocks into him hard, one knocking the wind out of Murren. They dragged him forward to one of the crates on the floor of the old warehouse. While one security man held a knife at his throat, the other two put his hand out on top of the crate.

Another security person, the lanky John Quang, slipped on a cheap, clear, plastic poncho, then reached into his kit pack and pulled out a Ryobi battery-powered reciprocating saw. One thing Liu respected the most about John Quang was that he took his work seriously, never once questioning an order regardless if its horrible implications. The florescent green/yellow of the saw made it stand out. The big cutting blade on the end was white, pristine, having never been used. Liu knew they would need a new one, a clean one.

Seeing the saw Murren struggled harder, only landing another blow from the butt of an assault weapon in the square of his lower back making him grunt and moan at the same time. "We will start with each of you, removing a single finger. If the person who stole from us does not confess, we will take another, then another. Once you have lost your fingers, if you haven't bled out yet, we will take your hands—then your arms, then perhaps parts of your body you care more about. If the guilty person has not confessed, well, by then, it will not matter … I will be hiring a new crew." This was not a threat coming from Weber Liu; it was a statement of fact.

Looking at the eyes of the men who worked for him, he saw their stark raving terror. "I didn't do it!" Murren pleaded. His words meant nothing to Liu. It was very possible that Murren was innocent. That was why Liu was starting one finger at a time.

With a nod to the man with the saw, the blade started to purr to life. He lowered it slowly as Murren struggled. There was a loud wail of agony from the big man as blood splattered all over the crate. The guards let him stand, and he clutched his left hand, now missing a pinky finger, blood squirting through his other hand as he tried to stay the bleeding.

The expressions on the others in the row went from terror to outright horror. One looked as if he were going to faint when Murren sobbed and staggered his way back into the line. "As you can see," Liu said. "I am a man of my word. If the guilty person wishes to step forward, he will spare his comrade the pain that Mr. Murren has experienced."

One young man, Benny Orly, shaking with fear, started to cry. "I—I did it. I'm so sorry," he pleaded. The other men that flanked him stepped sideways, away from him. "I didn't think anyone would notice. I didn't mean any harm." Snot ran from his nose as he cried and tried to explain himself.

Benny stood alone; his composure was gone. Liu nodded to his man with the saw. In two brisk strides he was standing in front of Benny. The saw hummed back to life as he drew it across Benny's neck. There was a gurgle as the blood rained down on the security man's poncho; then Benny dropped to the floor hard, making the sound of a bag of potatoes hitting the concrete. His body twitched slightly as the saw stopped running.

"My apologies," Liu said to Murren who was still clutching his hand. "You will be compensated for this unfortunate incident."

Turning back to his black sedan, Liu waited for his security people to open the door for him and he took his seat behind the wheel. *There will be no more thefts. They have all learned a valuable lesson today. Their loyalty will be complete because it is laced with fear ... and fear is what holds the world together.*

CHAPTER 10

"Erasing the past paves the way to a brighter future."

Davenport, Iowa

aptain Judy Mercury heard the nearby rumble of artillery going off, and a thin screen of dust fell from the rafters, covering her helmet and uniform. There were no lights other than what the troops had on them. The trucks had been shut down, lined up in the warehouse bay of the massive old print shop. Bits of debris covered the tarped tractor trailers to make it look as if the nearby explosions had rained down insulation, trusses, and other bits of roof on the semis.

Inside the concealed vehicles were two companies of infantry, well hidden inside vehicles that were made to appear that they had been damaged in battle. Of course it was all a façade, a carefully crafted ruse to mislead anyone that might pull the tarps back and peer underneath. A platoon of M1 Abrams tanks, a handful of Bradley fighting vehicles, an M1126 Stryker, and a pair of LAV-25s were joined with a number of Humvees. All bore the markings of the Illinois National Guard, right down to their license plates. She had even ordered two of the truck windshields shot at and cracked to make it look as if they too had taken some damage. *For this ruse to work, we have to look and act the part.*

More artillery made the building vibrate as it went off. As the last of her people finished making the trucks appear that they had been hidden, she ordered them under the tarps and into their vehicles. Turning, she saw Lieutenant Colonel Mihalek tossing several cider block chunks onto the front fender of the lead truck, to add to the camouflage.

"It looks like you're about ready," he said.

"Ready as we'll ever be."

"I've alerted the Indiana and Kentucky National Guard and given them the appropriate codes. General Reager has assured us they will be ready."

That was comforting to Judy. *If Trip says they'll be ready, then they will be.* Judy had been with him both overseas on deployment and when he had come back to the Texas National Guard full time. *We've spilled blood on a lot of the same ground over the years.* "I think we've got this."

The Lieutenant Colonel checked his watch. "I've got to go. Good luck," he said, giving her a salute. She returned the gesture quickly. "Thank you for all your help sir."

"Don't thank me yet. If this doesn't work, you are going to be in the middle of a tornado of shit pretty damned fast."

"It will work," she assured him. *It has to work.*

He took off out the back door, hunkering down as a nearby mortar round went off, peppering the metallic sides of the structure, punching a dozen holes on top of the hundreds that were already in the building.

As she climbed into the cab next to her driver who was balled up on the floor, she realized just how alone they were. *The friendlies are going to pull back and we will be behind enemy lines.* It was a frightening prospect, despite the fact that it was her idea. Still, General Reager had sent her here to do just this—change the front lines.

Curling up the best she could on the floor of the truck cab, she waited. Her driver, Corporal Ted Spears shattered the silence between explosions outside. "We've got this Captain," he assured her. "And if they decide it's a scam, we will unleash a buttload of fuck'em-up on them." His Midwestern drawl was different than her Texas accent, but it was still present.

He's right about that—they'll regret it. While her raiding party was on trailers and made to look like damaged vehicles, they were fully manned and ready for action. If the Newmericans somehow pierced their disguise, well, they would be sorry. "Just wait and play along," she said as she shifted, trying to find a relaxing position. The banging of distant machine gun fire, in small bursts, came from several directions near their building.

As she lay on the floor of the cab, she remembered when the Governor had called up the National Guard right after the Fall. It had been a time of chaos, with Washington DC taken hostage and several state capitals under siege. She remembered when the Ruling Council had made its presence known and how much that had angered her.

Thinking back to those times, Judy remembered Wanda, and that made her mentally wince. It was an old wound but one that still ached. Looking back now, she saw that Wanda had taken their relationship for granted. Their romance had been one way. Thinking back to the last time she saw her former lover was something Judy tried to suppress but couldn't. The image was branded into her mind, every minute detail. That image made her close her eyes and struggle with the tears that inevitably came. *Goddamn San Antonio!* As much as she tried to emotionally lay the blame with Wanda for what eventually happened, her own responsibility was something she could not escape. It didn't define who she was, but it was a reminder of the price of freedom.

As Judy shifted on the floor of the truck, a cramp in her left hamstring tensed up. She tried to reach back to massage it, but there was very little room for her to maneuver. *Damn Charlie horse!* After a few moments of pain, it passed and she was thankful. The only good thing about that was it made her forget just how cold she was. *I will never come to Iowa in the winter again.*

They had been there for hours as the sounds of the battle seemed to drift further away from the building where her raiding force was hidden. That had been the plan all along; the Iowa and Oklahoma troops were going to fall back and let the Illinois National Guard 'save' them. She listened intently for some sounds, any indication that the enemy was outside, but heard nothing beyond the occasional roar of diesel engines from combat vehicles.

Then it came, a voice barking out orders. It wasn't nearby, but other voices seemed to get closer. They were accompanied by rustling in the large bay, like debris being moved. *It's show time!*

Turning, she raised herself up to peer out the windshield and saw a squad of infantry coming from the far end. She held her hands up so they were visible. "Don't shoot!" she called out just loud enough for them to hear. Flashlight beams hit her making her wince. Slowly, she squirmed to the door and slowly opened it as the troops closed on her.

"Keep your hands where we can see them," ordered the Lieutenant as she climbed out.

"Jesus, she's one of us," a voice said as the flashlights continued to blind her.

"Christ, Captain," the Lieutenant said. "How did you end up here?"

"It's okay," she called out. "These guys are friendlies!" The drivers all began to sit up, and the flashlight beams hit the trucks.

"We were ordered to recover this equipment," she said and gestured with one of her raised hands. "We got overrun. They never came in here. We've been here for three or four days waiting for someone to find us—hopefully someone on our side."

"Holy shit," the Lieutenant said, lowering his flashlight. "They didn't find you?"

She shook her head. "No. I had my people stay put. We could really go for some grub and water," she said. The Illinois National Guard began to pass their canteens and pull out MREs, handing them to her and her drivers. Two men climbed up on her tractor bed, lifting the tarp to check the vehicles. *This is the true test to see if our fake battle damage passes muster.* Her heart pounded in her chest as she took a deep swig of the cold water.

"You saved our asses," she said to the Lieutenant, handing back the canteen.

"The enemy is just two blocks from here in force," he said. "They are holding onto the airport like a tick on a dog's ass."

Judy glanced back at the tractor trailers. "We need to get these things out of here and back to the rear for repair and refit," she said. "The last thing we want is for them to counterattack and capture them."

"Right," the Lieutenant said. "Alright, listen up; we need to clear those doors," he ordered the squad that was with him. "Clear a path for these trucks." The infantry slung their weapons and started work immediately.

"Thank you Lieutenant," she said. "What's your name?"

"Matt Orlowski," he said.

"If we get out of here, I'll let my CO know your name. Hell, you might just get a commendation for this." The line was deliberate on her part; she was playing to his ego.

"Hurry up," he ordered his troops.

"We are overdue," Judy replied. "Any chance you can call ahead and let them know that we are cleared to get back into Illinois?"

"Not a problem Captain," he said. "It's a damned miracle that you were not captured when they took this area. I will let HQ know that you are heading to the rear."

"I appreciate it," she said.

The clearing of the staged debris took fifteen minutes. Her 'rescuers' never bothered to do a detailed check of her cargo; they took her at her word. Finally the doors opened at the far end of the bay, and the snow on the other side cascaded into the room. Judy clamored up the side of the truck, leaning down. "Thanks again Lieutenant Orlowski. We'd have been toast without you."

"Yes sir," he said.

The trucks started up, one after another, belching black diesel fumes into the building. Her driver, Sergeant Hart, said nothing, but could not conceal his smirk as the truck lunged forward and started out. She wanted to chide him for his expression, but she empathized with his feeling. *We fooled them this far. Now all we have to do is get to Illinois. Once there, we can get this party started.*

Nashville, Tennessee

Kiff Renner eyed the muscular female and wondered where Jack Desmond had come up with an MMA fighter on such short notice. There wasn't a hint of fat on her, and the way she moved was almost cat-like, so smooth and sleek. Everything about her screamed control, of her words, her body, and her thoughts. Her short hair wasn't as much styled as it was cut with precision. She stood in his doorway casually leaning on one arm that was in the doorframe, but to Kiff there was nothing relaxed about this person. Just standing there made him feel that his darkened office was somehow smaller.

"Mister Renner?" the female asked.

"Um, yeah."

"Jack Desmond sent me," she said entering, then closing the door.

"I just got the call you were coming," he said, shifting in his chair. "Have a seat," he said gesturing to the chair. The woman sat down, her eyes clearly drinking in every details of his office.

"I'm Caylee Leatrom," she said, leaning back slightly.

That name had meaning. He remembered the data dump a few months ago, all of the nasty secrets of the NSF's operative program. *Shit ... she's that Caylee Leatrom. Jack sent a trained killer here!* "I, uh, have heard of you."

"Good," she said. "That saves me going over my resume'."

"Jack said he was sending me someone that could get me into and out of the Texas Republic. I didn't expect—well—*you*."

"I prefer people to not expect me in my line of work," she said. "During the drive over, Jack gave me the rundown on you. He said you were some sort of super-hacker."

Kiff flinched at the last word. "I hate that word—hacker. It's not really accurate. I'm a cyber security expert. I have a knack for getting around security systems, sifting through the data, breaking encryptions, that kind of thing."

For a moment she looked as if she were almost bored with what he said. "So you're what? A geek?"

I've been called worse. "Yeah, sure. Geek will do."

"So tell me about this data grab." There was no small talk with this person.

"It's two computers. I'm assuming one is a laptop, the other a desktop. The desktop system is at a static address; it always logs on from the same IP. The laptop pings off of several different IP addresses, which is how I know it is mobile." He slid a piece of paper listing physical addresses where the computers were known to be.

"The desktop unit, is it in a home?"

He nodded. "It might be a laptop system, but it doesn't connect to the Internet from any place other than that address."

Caylee studied the paperwork. "Obviously the mobile PC is going to be the trickier of the two to hit," she stated flatly. "How long does it take you to suck off what you need from the hard drives."

"It's not really sucking. It's more like—"

"Mr. Renner," she cut him off. "To me, it doesn't matter what it is called."

"*Kiff,*" he said

She was confused for a moment; then he continued. "You can call me Kiff. The whole Mr. Renner thing is a bit strange."

Caylee gave him a single nod. "Okay, Kiff. How long?"

"Times vary. It depends on the level of hard drive encryption that the systems are running. I have a lot of tools to get in, but it isn't an exact science. A lot of this is more art and instinct."

"The time?" she asked once more, clearly not satisfied with his answer.

"About an hour, maybe two."

"Mr. Desmond said you can't just rip out the hard drives ... that we don't want them to know that we have pulled the data. Is that correct?"

"Yeah," he said. "Pulling the drives would be best, but if we do that, they know we are on to them."

Caylee shifted slightly in her seat, then leaned forward, closer to him, entering his personal space almost deliberately. "Mister—*Kiff*," she corrected herself. "These kind of things can either go smoothly, or with hiccups. My job is to get you in and get you out with the data. Doing so is done with risk. For me to do my job, I need to know a little more about you. Have you ever been in a situation where your life was on the line?"

Kiff paused, thinking carefully back to the months that followed the Fall. He had remained at the Department of Homeland Security, still working hard. The country was changing. The Ruling Council had claimed to be running the country, and the former President had allegedly died of a heart attack while in custody. It was a time of chaos and violent change.

Then one day, they came for him. He hated that memory and what followed, despite the results.

"Yeah," Kiff said looking Caylee in the eyes. "You could say that I have been in a few situations where my life was on the line." Memories of fleeing his job in Washington DC and the confrontation at his mother's house swept over him. It was as if five years had not passed at all, the emotions, the tension, all of it came rushing back at Kiff full-throttle.

Caylee must have seen it in his face because she didn't react for a few seconds. "Good. Then you know the importance of you doing exactly what I say, when I say it. We are going to be entering the world where I work. These Texans are playing a pretty deadly game. They are not going to appreciate anyone poking around in their business."

The full gravity of what he was going to be facing was sinking in fast. "Gotcha," he said. "You say jump, and I jump."

She nodded once. "Have you ever handled a gun? I'm not talking Call of Duty. I mean the real thing."

Again, the memories from his flight into obscurity came back at him. "Yes," he said with a hint of indignation in his voice. "I know how to handle a real gun. I've had to fire one once in my defense too."

"Excellent. That means you have no qualms about shooting at another human being."

"You think it's going to come down to that?"

She had the perfect poker face; it revealed nothing. "I always anticipate the worst. I make plans, and my plans have fallback plans. Something can and will go wrong; it almost always does. While I don't cherish using violence, I recognize the need to do that as part of my job. The fact that you can take care of yourself, even to a minor bit, is helpful. While you rely on me for safety, I have come to appreciate that I may have to rely on you at some point."

Kiff nodded in response. She's a professional. Jack wouldn't have sent anyone who wasn't. His trust in Jack was easy to transfer to her. Caylee looked the part of the tough person. Her chest and shoulder muscles were the product of hours of working out. *If half the stuff I read on the net about her is true, she is one tough hombre.* "When do we start?"

She offered a razor-thin smile to him. "We already have."

Charlottesville, Virginia

The speaker with the megaphone stood in front of the boarded up Rotunda building on campus, and his voice rang out for the gathered crowd. "We are being targeted," he said, allowing the protesters to murmur sounds of agreement. The speaker adjusted his black gaiter mask. Many of the students wore masks as well. Some wore masks because of the Theta strain of COVID, but more recently, students and professors had taken to wearing them to hide their identity. The school newspaper had encouraged it, making it hard for killers to target individuals. The student speaker's voice roared from under the material wrapped around his face.

"Someone is coming for us. Not a warrior, but a coward. This killer is an assassin, no doubt some alt-right refugee from Social Quarantine. They have come to this campus and are killing those that are standing up for what is right.

David Steele was in the crowd and looked around him. Since the death of Dr. Mikolitis, the University of Virginia student body had become nervous, afraid, and paranoid. While the NSF had not publicly linked the deaths of Mikolitis and Morose, some student groups did. Between classes and at night, students moved in small groups rather than walk alone. One fraternity was providing armed escorts, complete with body armor. There was a feeling all around him that they were being stalked, hunted, and executed.

Good.

The crowd was calling for justice, demanding safety for the students, which made him want to smirk. The hypocrisy of it was all around him. *They want to return to their comfort. They want to get back to their lives of tormenting and even killing those that didn't believe what they did. They took Maddie from us. They are nervous because for the first time ever, they are on the other side of the gun sight. No one cried for all of the people that the Grays murdered; there were no protests, no memorials. Now that they are the targets, they are afraid.*

He shuffled slowly through the crowd of angry and frightened students. There were cries for the NSF to provide them with protection. "It's not safe anymore because of these terrorists!" the student with the megaphone cried out. "We need more student safety patrols. We demand protection!" David saw the irony. A significant piece of his life had been spent hiding under assumed names. Steele was just one of the names his family had been forced to adopt. As he looked around, the students gathered in front of the old building. He could tell they were a mix of afraid and angry, finely blended by him and his father. *They are finally getting a taste of what it is like to live in the world they created ... a place of fear ... and they hate it.*

Some speakers called for guns for the students, which made David's urge to chuckle escalate even more. *They all claim that guns are bad, that guns are responsible for killing people. The Ruling Council banned guns, rounded them up. Now, at the first hint of danger, they are willing to toss aside what they believe in for their safety.*

His father had summed it up a few years ago. "The morality of these progressives is not like ours. Theirs is flexible; it's situational; it's subject to change based on their little needs and desires. That is where they are weakest. We have principles that we stand behind. For them, everything is based on what they feel at the moment." At the time he didn't understand what his father was talking about. There, on the UVA campus, it was painfully clear how accurate his dad was.

David eventually reached the edge of the protestors and started to walk off campus. *This will complicate things. They now know that Dad and I are out here. They are taking measures to protect themselves. We have to get more creative.*

As much as he hated the fact that they were aware of what he and his father were doing, a part of him reveled in the fear that the students were finally feeling ... a small dose of what they had inflicted on others for years.

CHAPTER 11

"Standards and rules are important but need to be flexible based on factors we determine as relevant."

The District

The Vice President of Newmerica sat in the gallery as Becky Clarke was led in before the People's Tribunal. The VP had ordered a camera set up to catch her expression as Becky was ushered in. Rehearsals and test screenings of her facial expressions showed that watchers wanted to see her in pain, then rally and stand strong. That was what the Vice President was going to do, give the viewers what they wanted.

Becky had been prepared for the presentation every bit as much as the VP. They had fitted her with a mask that was eerily similar to Hannibal Lector in *Silence of the Lambs*. It was more of a muzzle to prevent her from biting anyone, but the similarities were there and quite deliberate. Her hair had been cut almost erratically to make her appear wilder. With her loss of weight, and the fact she was denied even a sports bra, everything on her face and body seemed to sag. Her hands were double-shackled with the lower cuffs leaving no room for her to attempt to choke anyone. Her fading orange prisoner jumpsuit had a stain above her left breast.

Becky ignored the VP in the audience focusing her attention on the Tribunal members. More than half of them had been changed out after Senator Lewis's tribunal. TRC polls had shown that some of them, including Lewis's Tribunal leader, did not resonate well with watchers. Replacement candidates were brought in and vetted with test audiences.

It was critical to create the illusion that justice was prevailing, and that those delivering the justice were of a fair-minded and diverse community. While conviction was all but guaranteed, the appearance was more important than the substance of the evidence presented.

The new Tribunal leader was an older black actress, one that had been on television for years. Her face was one that was well known and respected. Her talk show and podcast had millions of followers, and her devotion to the Newmerica cause was solid. As Becky was chained to the podium where she would face her charges, she stared intently at the leader.

"Becky Clarke, you stand before this People's Tribunal to determine the full extent of your guilt in plotting and executing an assassination attempt on the Ruling Council and to determine if you are in league with the Pretender President's administration in committing treason. Furthermore, you are charged in a second assassination attempt on the Vice President." The Tribunal leader gave a nod to the gallery where the VP sat, giving her a tiny dip of her head in response.

"Rebecca," Becky said.

"Excuse me?"

"My name is Rebecca. No one calls me Becky," she said in a half-growling tone of voice. Her eyes rolled slowly to the gallery and for the first time, she locked gazes with the Vice President. It amused the VP, how much Becky hated the fact that she used her nickname. When she had tried to kill her, she had cried out, "My name is Rebecca!" while she had clawed at her face. *I'm so glad that I had the script for the Tribunal Leader changed so that it referred to her that way.* Despite the desire to smirk, she kept the dour face of a woman who was facing her attacker … playing up perfectly for the cameras.

"We are a Tribunal of the people," the leader said, her long, white dreadlocks swaying as she cocked her head to the side. "We will refer to you as we see fit."

Becky's face, what could be seen of it from under the mask, went red. "I demand representation."

"You will hold your mouth," another member of the Tribunal said angrily.

"This isn't some court of law where you would get to parade around your privilege, one of the females on the Tribunal responded. "This is where the will of the people is doled out. This is where real justice happens."

Becky shifted on her feet. "This is a puppet court and you all know it."

"Continue to speak up," the leader said slowly, "And I will have no choice but to see you gagged." Her words seemed to suck the air out of the chamber, and Becky went quiet. "Alright then, how do you plead?"

She stiffened, summoning what little pride she had left as she spoke. "I am innocent. These charges and the evidence against me have been manufactured."

The Vice President savored the indignity that Becky was trying to endure. She had once been one of the leaders of the Great Reformation … the recrafting of America into a progressive paradise. Now she stood accused of crimes that the VP knew she had not committed. The only real charge was her second attempt to kill the Vice President. *Oddly enough, it took her being accused of being an assassin to actually become one.*

The presentation of the evidence, the falsified text messages, the footage of the explosion, the fake emails—it all took hours. While some of it was forensic in nature, they had learned from the Lewis Tribunal that when technical information was presented, readers were more likely to change channels. This time around the data was dumbed down to ensure maximum ratings.

For her part, Becky said nothing. Where Lewis had interrupted in a vain attempt to try to clear his name, Becky remained mute. She was angry. That much the Vice President could read in her masked face. There were times when Becky's eyes would dart over to her, clearly signaling her out in the gallery. The VP ignored such momentary stares.

The morning proceedings went on, and at noon the leader of the Tribunal called for a lunch recess. The NSF guards came forward and unhooked Becky from the podium. As they were about to bind her hands in front of her, she appeared to cough, raising her hands to the face of the mask for a moment.

The guards reacted, pulling her arms down, seeming to struggle with her. *What is she doing?* Becky staggered to her left slightly, then dropped down on the cold concrete floor of the Tribunal on her knees. The guards were pulling at her mask, attempting to get it free, but struggling with the clasps on the back of the face restraint.

Becky seemed to go limp, as the people in the room suddenly froze, fixated on her. The Vice President rose from her seat, not sure what her former colleague was doing. One guard finally pulled the mask off and threw it near the elevated bench where the members of the Tribunal were all standing, leaning forward, attempting to see what was transpiring with the accused.

The guards lowered her to the floor, and when the Vice President saw her skin; it was already starting to look pale. *What did she do?* She started to move past people in the gallery, pushing people aside to get closer to Becky. Why aren't they giving her mouth-to-mouth? One guard was on the radio, his voice loud enough for her to hear. He was calling for an ambulance.

She maneuvered over Becky so she could see her eyes, staring skyward, devoid of life. Her mouth seemed almost frothy, like a rabid dog. Under the bubbly froth, it looked as if Becky was actually smiling. *She's dead ... how did it happen?* The Vice President was still unable to process what was unfolding. "What in the hell is going on?"

"Stand back," the NSF officer said, reaching down for a pulse. "It looks like she has taken poison of some sort."

The Vice President stood rigid at those words, taking a half-stride backward. *Poison! How did she get poison? She had to have gotten it from a guard or someone in the prison.* Her mind danced with scenarios. *This is a conspiracy. Someone is cheating me of justice!* Moments of confusion were replaced by rage.

"She had no right to escape justice. None! Goddamn it, I want to know who in the hell gave her poison? I want the name of the traitor, and I want it right now!" Her words fell to gathered people who all seemed to stare at her in silence for a second or so.

She didn't care how she looked to the cameras or to the public. This was an event she had meticulously staged, and now Becky had usurped it by committing suicide. *This is an outrage! People watching want justice and she robbed us of that.* "I want every guard that had contact with her placed in custody—now!" She was barking orders to the very men that would be impacted by what she said.

She robbed me of my moment of victory. She stole from the people. They deserved to see her face her judgment! She had not felt this angry since learning of Caylee Leatrom's murder of her mother and brother. Worse yet, there was no one to take it out on. Becky had left the building.

Carroll, New Hampshire

Su-Hui looked out at the Patio Motor Court and thought for a moment that he had somehow time traveled back to the early 1960s. The part campground, part motel, had some upgrades, but for the most part it was a slice of America that was long gone. *During the summer months, they must do a better business.* This early February, and while there had been a few warmer days, it had not brought the tourists. With the war going on, he was fairly sure that tourism was going to be dead in New Hampshire.

He entered the office, and the stocky man behind the counter got up, coming around to face him. "You're Mr. Zhou, right?" he asked, tucking in the one exposed flap of his blue and black flannel shirt.

"I am," he said as Valerie Watson entered the office, carefully eyeing her surroundings.

"A mutual friend said you were coming. He said you were a 'defiant' person." The hint to the resistance name, Defiance, was not lost on him.

"I am a man of peace who has been forced into conflict," he replied with a smile.

"Aren't we all?" The man gestured to the green, vinyl covered chairs that were in the tiny lobby area. Valerie took a seat, as did Su-Hui. "The name is Tate—Tate Palmer. Can I get you some coffee?" Palmer asked.

"No thank you Mr. Palmer," he replied, feeling the broken strap of the chair under his seat on the left side. I take it our mutual friend told you what we were looking for."

The man nodded, running his hand once through his thick reddish beard in a failed gesture to straighten it. "Our friend said that we were like-minded folk and that you were looking for a place to fall back to."

"Indeed," Su-Hui said. One lesson that had come out of the destruction of the SOL's base in Lisbon was the need to have a second place where they could retreat if necessary. *We will be gone for several days striking into Connecticut. I will not leave our loved ones behind without a plan and place to go.*

"Well, we have twenty-two rooms here, not to mention two campers that can be pushed into use if needed. I've got a bunch of army surplus cots in storage too; we used them when the Boy Scouts used to come up here and camp. We have hot and cold running water. We have basic cable. I used to have HBO, but tourism has been a trickle over the last few years with those damned libtards calling the shots down in DC."

"Discretion will be the key, Mr. Palmer."

"Call me Tate. Everybody does," he said with a smile.

"Alright Tate. We have a lot of vehicles that would be coming in. If the out-of-town visitors were to see them all parked here, it might draw a lot of unwanted attention."

He nodded quickly in response. "We butt up to Mt. Washington. The KOA campground next door went out of business during the first COVID outbreak. We can park some vehicles there, under their shelters. That would keep any aircraft from spotting them. There's two trails I can clear with the tractor up to Mt. Washington. Plenty of places back in the pines to park. Out of sight, out of mind."

Clearly Tate had already put some thought into this, which Su-Hui appreciated. "It may not ever come to pass, but we need to be assured that if our base is hit, our people have a place to go."

"I saw the videos out of Lisbon," Tate said, dipping his head. "I had a cousin that lived there. She never said you folks were in that town; people up here don't stick their noses too much in other people's business. They destroyed her home, her car, both her cats, and she lost her left leg. They said the folks there were 'harboring the enemy,' or some bullshit like that. Tilly wasn't harboring anyone. She just lived there, and they damn near killed her."

We have all lost a great deal in this war. Su-Hui remembered Randy Birdsell who had died in the bombardment. *General Donaldson didn't care who he killed, he just wanted to destroy the town send a message.* "I am sorry for her injuries. Our enemy is a bit ruthless."

"I saw them shoot the Governor too. I didn't vote for him, but he held his ground right up to the end. When he wouldn't play along, they put a bullet in him." It was clear by the slight wavering in Tate's voice that the events upset him deeply.

"We appreciate your offer of shelter. We do not have much in the way of compensation—"

"Aw to hell with that," he said waving his hand as if to brush the words out of the air between them. "I'm not doing this for the money. This is personal. They are stealing our votes and trying to paint you and the other folks as terrorists when you are trying to keep us free. Don't you worry Mr. Zhou, we know who the *real* enemies are. If they come here, they are going to find out just what kind of shot I am with my deer rifle too."

Su-Hui turned to Valerie at his side. "We are going to want to set up some communications with you. If something happens at our current base of operations, we will need a way to let you know that we are on the way."

"Sure—just show me what you want," Tate said.

"We may want to pre-position some food and ammo here too," Valerie added. "It's easier than us trying to haul it with us if we are on the run."

"The rooms are empty, as you can imagine. I will give you keys to numbers 2 and 6. You can put whatever you need there."

Su-Hui rose and extended his hand. "I want to thank you for this. Hopefully, we will never need to come, but it is nice to know that we have a place to go if things get out of hand."

Tate's calloused hand seemed as if it were twice the size of Su-Hui's as he gripped his and shook it back. Tate said, "My youngest, Colin, he was hoping to go to school to learn diesel repairs, but with the travel restrictions because of the Defiance, they aren't allowing him to go. He's a hell of a tracker and hunter. He'd like to come with you, join the fight."

Su-Hui paused for a moment. There had been a steady trickle of recruits since the destruction of Lisbon. The people of the Granite State were angry at the power cut off in Gorham, and they were outright furious at the destruction of Lisbon. *As much as Newmerica thinks they are putting the squeeze on us, they are helping with recruitment.* At the same time, Su-Hui was always wary. *They will try to infiltrate us, identify, and pin us down.* The Chinese had done that right before the invasion of Taiwan, sneaking in agents and police as normal citizens. *I trust Tate. He's been checked out by other locals who know him, so his son is likely safe as well. Others ... well, we have a protocol in place should they show up.* "We would be honored to have him with us," Su-Hui said.

Tate called in his son, a lumbering 6'6" man that looked more like a lumberjack than even Trudy. "Get yer gear boy; they are going to take you with them." A smile washed over the youth as he darted to the back of the office and out the door.

"He won't let you down Mr. Zhou; you can count on that."

"I'm sure he won't." As Tate moved back behind the counter, Su-Hui turned to Valerie. "It's a good place."

"Let's hope we don't have to use it," she said.

"We need to be prepared for every contingency," he replied. "Our enemy has resources we do not. They are showing themselves to be ruthless and brutal."

"They've always been that way," Valerie said, tugging on the zipper of her coat to prepare to go and face the winds of winter. "People are just starting to see them for what they really are. For most people it's going to be a rude awakening. They have leveraged the system, cashed out on reparations and other programs. It was all shits and giggles until the President was sworn in. Now they are seeing Newmerica for what it really is, a totalitarian state."

"Let's hope that's enough to turn the tide of this war."

She cocked her head and smiled. "I love your optimism Su-Hui ... no matter how misplaced it is. A lot of people will turn on them, but more will fight to hold onto the benefits they have gotten out of the system. The only thing that is going to turn them is spilled blood."

He hoped that Valerie was wrong, but a nagging voice in his head told him that she was likely telling the truth.

Ann Arbor, Michigan

Dr. Liu heard the knock on the door of his office at the University of Michigan at exactly 1:00 p.m., as expected. One thing he could count on with Zack Taylor was that the youth knew the value of being prompt. "Enter," he said.

Zack was a student of Asian descent with long, almost ash colored hair, an oblong face, and almost pale skin. His American mother's traits, namely the hair and the skin tone, along with the brilliant pale eyes, were present. Zack wore a crimson 'What-would-Che-Guevara-do? T-shirt.'

The young man had been a student for two years at the U of M, but had been an agent of China since birth. He was a second generation spy. His father had been born in China and had posed as a student, then a businessman at General Motors for decades, constantly feeding the homeland with every little innovation that GM came up with. Zack's mother was oblivious to her son's real purpose in life which was to spy for China. That was something that his father had ensured—a tiny bit of plausible deniability should he ever get caught. Weber Liu used Zack to help him with cyber security for his operations. The young man demonstrated signs of brilliance at times with his digital camouflaging of the money transfers that Liu required. The fact that he had asked for the meeting was rare, and it usually meant something disturbing.

As Zack entered, he quickly bowed his head in respect as Liu gestured to one of the two chairs opposite his desk. Closing the door behind him, Zack plopped down in the seat hard, almost carelessly. "It is good to see you Zack."

"Thank you for agreeing to see me Dr. Liu. Something came up, and I thought that it might be worth a few minutes of your time."

"What is it?"

"I've been monitoring not only our systems, but those of the people you send money to. A few days ago, I detected something that, well, kinda surprised me." That part was no surprise; it had been an order from Liu. It was not enough to make sure his systems were secure; he needed to ensure the people he dealt with were as protected as possible. Of course, he hadn't bothered to tell them of his behind-the-scenes monitoring. *That is the price of doing business with our nation.*

"Go on."

"These TR people you are dealing with," he said, using the slang that was starting to emerge in Newmerica about the Texas Republic. "I got an indication that someone was poking around their systems. Not a full-blown penetration, but more like precise little jabs at the security."

"Were they able to obtain anything incriminating?" Liu asked.

"Nothing that we didn't want them to get," he said. "The bits and pieces they were able to glean were the bait we left out there—that this was pushed by the Russians, North Korea, and even a hacker group in Bulgaria. There was nothing in what they grabbed that didn't point somewhere else."

Studying the face of the young man, he could see his left eyebrow wrinkle upward, a hint of deeper thought. "But you are still concerned?"

"I am," Zack replied. "First, there was a level of sophistication in this hit that had all of the marks of a pro. I'm not talking some college kid looking for something bribable. Whoever this was poked around our off-shore accounts, ran some traces that I still haven't been able to fully crack, and got in and out without leaving a trail that I could follow. More importantly, I found signs that they may have tracked some of the information back to campus. Whoever these guys are, they are good ... state-sponsored good."

That was disturbing to Liu. *Someone is trying to piece together the nuts and bolts of our financial arrangements.* "You are sure they did not get anything that could be of use against us?"

Zack nodded. "For now. I did some digging on my own. These Texas folks have got some data on their systems we didn't put in place, masking some other transactions. That stuff was easier to identify. It had NSA written all over it. From what I could tell, they have been getting some assistance from Newmerica as well."

"So the NSA has information on their systems. Is it possible that Newmerica was behind this probe of our data?"

Sighing deeply, Zack shook his head. "I don't think it was them. If it was, they went about it all wrong. Since they already have a cloaked app on their hard drives, they could have used that as a bridge to get to the data. This came from another source, somewhere else. That points to another player."

For Liu, it made perfect sense for Newmerica to attempt to prop up the Texas Republic. *So who could be trying to learn the depths of the Texan's finances?* The obvious thought was America. After all, it was far more damaging to America than it was to Newmerica to have Texas secede. He had not thought that they possessed the cyber capabilities to perform such a penetration. *Was it the Russians?* No doubt the Kremlin wanted to know everything about what was happening in northern Texas to exploit the opportunity. More disturbing was that it might be some other player, a nation that Liu was not considering.

After a few moments of deep thought, he finally framed the question for Zack. "What can we do about this?"

"There's some defense measures—little micro-apps—I can install on their systems. It will further mask what we've been doing and will give us a better idea of who is poking around on them."

"Then do it."

"There's the rub. I can't do it from here. I need hands-on access to their systems."

Liu considered the issue carefully. The Texans were not likely to simply give him access to their computers. While they had a relationship, the trust was limited. That meant that Zack would need to covertly get access to their hardware. While he was a cyber genius of sorts, he was not a typical field operative. *He will need help.* "You realize what you are asking?"

"I do," the young man said. "There's no other way that I know of. This is a clandestine op, the kind of thing that has to be done without their knowledge."

"I will send someone with you, someone who has skills that are well-suited to this kind of effort." There were several members of his team that might suffice, but the one that came to him first was John Quang, the skinny security person on his detail. Quang had a cold-blooded ruthlessness about him, rarely speaking, always achieving his objectives. "Of course, if you are detected or captured, the Texans cannot know who sent you or what your purpose was." What he was really saying was darker, more sinister. *If you are caught, you need to do whatever it takes to hide who you are, including death, if necessary.*

Zack seemed to understand fully, not immediately responding, but soaking in the words of caution. "I won't fail. I will make you and my father proud."

CHAPTER 12

"Higher education is a right and proof of intellectual freedom."

Charlottesville, Virginia

David Steele watched from a small café halfway up the block as Dwight Clemmons, the Public Safety Director for the University of Virginia, waddled up the street and into the small community market. His father had suggested Clemmons as a target for a number of reasons. He was in charge of the student security on campus when Maddie had gone missing and had been killed. When his father had met with the man, he had blown off her disappearance, making it sound as if Maddie had just sneaked off for some fun.

The casual disregard for his duties ate at David and his father. Students had been lured off campus for years by the Grays and possibly other student groups, only to be killed. Clemmons was a broken cog in the wheels of justice there. This was a man that didn't follow up when students disappeared. *He turned his eye the other way to what was going on, and that makes him just as guilty as the people that pulled the trigger.*

Clemmons was a creature of habit; his father had determined that from his own observations. On Wednesdays and Saturdays, around noon, he went out for a walk to the local market just up the street from where David sat. He would buy two large paper bags of groceries—the era of plastic bags had come and gone with the rise of Newmerica—yet the oceans were still polluted. Clemmons would walk down Freedom Park Avenue. He would stop at the small hobby store for a few minutes of browsing, then continue on to his modest, little apartment some five blocks away.

With the heighted sense of insecurity on campus, their traditional form of assassination was shelved in the case of Clemmons. The local NSF was increasing patrols, looking for anyone that might not fully fit in with the campus community. The police presence created the illusion of security, but David and his father had not given up on their quest for vengeance. *A big part of this is that we don't want them to be safe. We want them to be worried. They have acted with no consequences for far too long. We are those consequences!*

In planning to kill Clemmons, the initial thought was a more personal attack … a stabbing or perhaps a poisoning. The problems were the myriad of security cameras. The days of walking up and stabbing someone were fading away. The key to their success so far was that it was difficult for the NSF to connect their crimes, and they had avoided detection. The NSF had little to work with. Clemmons, however, was very public in his travels. Disabling enough security cameras might, on its own, attract unwanted attention.

David wanted the death of the Public Safety Director to be public. *The students all suspect the crimes are connected; I want them to know it. They need to experience some of the same fears my family has.* His father reluctantly agreed, somewhat to David's surprise. "They took my little girl from me and put this family through a living hell. They need to eat some fear, a big plate heaped of it, choking down every bite!"

The plan had been crafted when David realized they still had some bomb-making materials left over from when they had killed the Grays. The pipe bomb was actually two small pieces of pipe, wired with a crude detonator made from parts purchased from a Home Depot garage door opener they had purchased for cash in Richmond, so that it would be harder to link to them. There was enough difference in the construction of this device from the ones that killed the Grays to make the NSF question a connection, but the Steeles knew that it would escalate the tension with the students.

Planting the explosive in full view of cameras required some careful thought. David's father noticed that there were two garbage containers on the path that Clemmons walked when he went to the market. These were only emptied once a week, on Saturday. They put the bomb in a paper bag and casually discarded it in one of the containers, as if throwing away trash. It was done at the beginning of the week so that by the time the NSF gathered up surveillance camera footage, chances were high that the images had already been overwritten.

His father had dropped off the bomb, wearing a fake beard and some clothing he had picked up at Goodwill so they could be thrown away after the drop took place. David had watched him do it, and there was nothing out of the ordinary in his gestures, nothing that might attract any attention. He had even managed to use a fat man standing in front of the small bakery's trash container, positioning the man between him and the bakery security camera for cover.

The tension, while waiting, was hard for David to mask. As he sipped his coffee, he realized that the caffeine was probably not helping his state of mind. *We get one shot at this.* David had already seen Clemmons enter the market further up the block on the opposite side of the street.

People were walking along the sidewalk, oblivious to the fact that they were walking past a bomb. David knew that innocent people would be injured by this killing. It bothered him a little, but not as much as it should have—which was worse. He was not looking for a body count, but early on they realized innocent people were going to be hurt as well. *How innocent are they? They live in this community; they thrive here because of the university—a place that condoned the murder of my sister. None of them was raising a finger against the almost weekly protests. They weren't even shocked that Maddie and the others disappeared, or that they had been found dead. None of them said that what the students were doing was wrong. As long as they have jobs and a sense of security, they don't care what happens to other people … just as long as it doesn't happen to them.* Despite that, he and his father had chosen a Wednesday for the attack to minimize damage to others.

When Clemmons finally came out, his arms weighed down with the paper bags of groceries, David felt himself tense up. Under the napkin on the small café table, he held the garage door opener with his thumb poised over the button that would set off the bomb.

Clemmons looked happy, his chubby face showing a broad smile. He had no idea what was coming. As David watched, his eyes went to a family that was walking up the block, toward his bomb and the target. It was a couple and their little girl. She was small, probably only four, and clung to her father's hand as they walked.

His mind tried to calculate if they would pass the bomb before Clemmons did. Seeing the little girl reminded him of Maddie, and for the first time during one of these covert missions, David Steele hesitated. Clemmons has to die, but the thought of killing the little girl ... that was different. Grimly, a realization hit him. *I can't kill a little girl.*

Just before they reached the bakery where the bomb was placed, the family turned and went into the bike shop next door. David let out a ragged sigh of relief. His moral dilemma resolved itself. The only other people walking on the sidewalk were two college girls, sporting their campus colors of blue and orange, at least three stores down.

Clemmons strode to the bakery and stopped, turning to look inside the window—his back to the garbage container with the explosive. *Now!* David pressed the button on the ad hoc detonator.

Nothing happened.

A moment of terror hit him as Clemmons turned to continue on. David jammed the button again, and instantly there was a loud whoomp followed by a jarring boom as the bomb went off. Glass shattered from the shops all along Freedom Park Avenue. The café waitress only a few yards away dropped her tray, sending scalding hot coffee on a couple who were thrown on the ground. The window in front of David cracked from top to bottom from the concussion of the explosion up the block. Several car alarms went off, screeching down the street. People ran in every direction, away from the epicenter of the explosion. A vehicle swerved in the street, colliding with a van, the crunch of metal adding to the cacophony of chaos.

Smoke rolled from the bakery, ugly blackish gray smoke. There was no sign of Dwight Clemmons—the blast had devoured the man instantly. People ran out of businesses all over to see what had transpired, and a flicker of flames rose from the front of the bakery.

David got up and slid the garage door opener into his pocket. He saw the family rush out of the bike shop, shaken and afraid, but very much alive—which made him feel good momentarily. Clemmons was dead. It might be a while before he could be identified too. Once he was identified, given his position at the university, they would realize that these incidents were not isolated. That didn't concern David; many students already felt that way. *Perhaps now they will realize what they have been doing is wrong. Consequences have a way of blowing up in your face.*

Davenport, Iowa

Judy Mercury's covert caravan had been queued up on the entrance ramp to the I-74 bridge over the Mississippi for half an hour or more. Traffic was congested and the rumble of distant artillery only seemed to make matters tenser for her and her driver, Sergeant Hart. Off to her right, she could see the Rock Island Arsenal on an island in the river. As darkness was setting in, she could see the fires from artillery hits on the facility burning in the distance.

It had been a slow slog to get to the checkpoint. The Illinois National Guard, along with units of militia from a half-dozen other states, were still viciously clinging onto Davenport. Trying to pry them off of the west bank of the river was going to be a costly affair. She felt she could make that easier once they got into Illinois—but it was all moot if they didn't get across the river. *Once we start stirring up trouble, they will have to send troops after us.*

As the vehicle ahead of them started across, her own driver lurched the truck slowly to the security detail. "Orders?" the corporal asked as the window came down, bleeding out every bit of the warmth in the cab.

Judy handed him not only the forged orders, crumpled, folded, and a bit damp for effect—as well as a note she had obtained from Lieutenant Orlowski, who had been leading the unit that had 'rescued' them. The corporal clung to the papers tightly as a gust of wind whipped at them. Using a flashlight, he seemed to scrutinize every word. She could see his lips move ever-so-slightly as he read.

Checking his clipboard, he handed the orders back. "You're not on my list."

Fear knotted in her stomach. She knew that this was a critical moment. On the bridge ramp, if it came down to a fight, it was going to get messy, and it would be ugly fast. There was no room to maneuver, and there were both sides of the bridge. Even if they did deploy, getting across the bridge could be iffy at best. *This whole operation could be FUBAR if this moron doesn't buy our story.* Leaning toward the driver,

Judy summoned her guile and called out in her best command tone. "You should have a message from Lieutenant Orlowski; he was going to call ahead. We're the ones that were trapped behind enemy lines."

The young man seemed to stare back at her blankly, then checked his clipboard once more. "You're just not on my list Captain."

No shit, Sherlock. "I don't give a damn about your list, Corporal. Take a look at what we are hauling. I've got a bunch of damaged tanks and vehicles back there on the flatbeds behind me. We are on our way to the repair depot in Princeton." Judy used her best crisp command tone of voice.

"I understand Captain; it's just that I'm not supposed to let anyone across who isn't on the list."

Judy drew a long, deep gulp of air which gave her some time to gather her thoughts. "I appreciate that. Now appreciate where I'm coming from. My people have been living in our truck cabs for days, most of that behind the enemy lines. None of us have not had food, showers, or a decent shit for days out of fear of getting our asses captured. I'm tired, hungry, and starting to get a little pissed off."

Her words were starting to rattle the younger man; she could see it in his face. "I understand sir, but I have orders to not clear traffic that isn't on the list."

She unbuckled her seatbelt and stepped outside, storming around the front of the vehicle. "Call your superior over—now," she said, getting in his face.

Fumbling for the shoulder mic, he requested some Lieutenant whose name she couldn't hear. It took two minutes for the Lieutenant to show up. It was hard to tell if it was a man or woman, but Judy really didn't care. Her feigned anger was full-on. "Is there a problem here?" the Lieutenant asked. Her sewn name badge read *Hobbs*. From his deep voice, he could tell he was dealing with a male, if not in spirit, in body.

"You could say that, Lieutenant," she said, emphasizing his rank. "I'm Captain Mercury with the 404th," she said turning so that he could see her fake unit insignia on her shoulder. "My people have been trapped for days behind enemy lines. Lieutenant Orlowski saved our collective asses and sent word ahead that we were coming. I've got a damned convoy loaded for repair, and your 'bridge attendant' says we can't go across." Out of the corner of her eye she saw Sergeant Hart shift enough to expose his sidearm. *Don't pull that weapon ... not yet.*

The Lieutenant bit their lower lip slightly. "They are not on the list?" he asked the corporal, who shook his head in response. "No sir."

"I'm sure you heard of us," Judy pressed. "If you don't believe me, radio Orlowski—he will verify our story."

Lieutenant Hobbs looked at her, then leaned out to look down the long line of queued up vehicles. "These are all with you, sir?"

"Yes. I just want to get back on the road and finish my mission. We've been holed up in a warehouse hiding from the enemy for days. Chances are that's why we aren't on your current list. If you feel the need, go dig up the paperwork from three days ago. You'll see we were cleared then. Frankly, I think it's a waste of time." She prided herself on planting seeds that this might all be a misunderstanding. Further, she knew that the last thing anyone wanted to do was jam up traffic on a bridge, during a battle, looking for paperwork. *Sometimes administrative bullshit works to your advantage.*

"You understand that we have to be careful, don't you Captain?"

Judy gave him a nod. "Honestly, do you think the enemy would be coming through the middle of our occupation zone hauling damaged vehicles?" Saying it out loud helped her keep from laughing.

Lieutenant Hobbs walked back to her flatbed and pulled one of the bungies off. Peeling it back, it exposed a Humvee, painted in Illinois National Guard colors, its paint job charred black all along the driver's side, courtesy of some blow torches to simulate the damage. The crew that had doctored the vehicles had used the torches to cut the armor, marring it to make it look as if it were hit with a glancing explosion. Even with gusts of wind, she was sure that he could detect the smells. *Is he going to check all of the trucks?* Inside each vehicle was a crew, laying low. *If he opens a door, this goes south fast.* Instinct wanted her hand on her sidearm, but Judy knew not to take any action that might spoil her ruse.

Hobbs stopped though, reconnecting the bungie cord for the tarp, then turned to her. "I apologize for the inconvenience Captain." Turning to the corporal, she said, "You did the right thing Corporal. Log them as overdue, grab their plate data, and get them over the bridge."

Judy nodded to Lieutenant Hobbs. "Thank you Lieutenant." She rounded the front of the truck and climbed back in. Sergeant Hart leaned out toward the Corporal. "Sorry for that. We've been looking up the ass of a dead dog with fleas for days now. We're all a bit crusty around the edges."

"No problem, Sergeant," he said. "Proceed."

Hart rolled up the window and Judy's lead truck started across the bridge over the Mississippi as the others followed behind her. Glancing at her driver, she asked, "Looking up the ass of a dead dog with fleas? Where did that come from?"

The older Sergeant cracked a smile. "My grandfather used to say it. I wanted that Corporal to think we were strung out. Dropping a one-liner made sense."

"Good call," she said. "If the military doesn't work out for you, you can always take up improv."

As she saw the Illinois side of the great river looming in the distance, she curbed any sense of relief that was wanting to creep out. *We have a long way to go. The worst thing I can do is allow myself to relax. Letting my guard down will get us killed.* As she saw a dusting of snow blow past the windshield, she remembered a line from a poem. "… and miles to go before I sleep."

Nashville, Tennessee

Caylee found Kiff's office intriguing if not cluttered. The nerdy trinkets that he had, right down to the Lego Star Wars fighter on his credenza might fool some people into thinking that he was childish. Her experience was that such people were not immature; they were creative. She saw the small statue of a gnome wearing a Captain America uniform and touched it gently as Kiff's fingers sped across his keyboard with a speed that she knew she could never equal.

"You like him?" Kiff asked, never slowing at all as he typed.

"Who is he?"

"Captain Gnomerica … get it?"

"No," she replied flatly.

His hand shifted to his mouse, and he began clicking on a number of icons on the screen. "Alright, Wilbarger County has all of their stuff online, a pay and play access. I used a bogus credit card and downloaded the blueprints from the planning office for the Trans-Tex offices." On his screen the floor plans flickered up in multiple windows.

She had asked Kiff to see if it was possible to get the plans, and he had delivered. Trans-Tex's offices, owned by Salem Marshall, had been turned into the seat of government for the self-proclaimed Texas Republic. One of the computers they needed to access was there. The other was a laptop in possession of Booker Hickox.

She leaned in and pointed to one floor, and without a word, Kiff enlarged the image for her. In the semi-darkness of his office, she leaned in and looked at the floor plans. This is not a secured building; at least it wasn't at the time it was built. Chances were fairly good that they had upgraded their security since their declaration of independence from America. Those kinds of changes were not likely to be on the original blueprints. *We will have to do some surveillance. By now that facility could be an armed camp.*

"What about the surrounding area?" she asked.

It took five clicks for him to pull up an aerial photograph of the building. "This was harder to get. The NSA controls most of the satellite coverage, and the NSF controls the NSA. I still have a few sneaky little passages into their systems. As it turns out, they have the facility under their cameras. So, I boosted some of their satellite images."

Caylee studied the photograph. The parking lot had been turned into something resembling an armed camp. Trucks, tents, sandbagged emplacements. It was no surprise to her; it simply meant that things were more complicated. Surrounding the building were several strange objects spaced at the perimeter. "What are those?"

"I asked myself the same question," he said, zooming in on one of them. "A quick perusal of the CIA's systems paints those babies as Pantsir missile systems. Usually they are truck mounted; that's what made things a little complicated in the identification. They have two of them deployed there."

"Greyhounds," she said coolly.

"What was that?"

"The Pantsir's NATO designation is the Greyhound SA-22," she said. "I've never seen ground mounted ones before." *Someone has been shopping for some fairly heavy military gear.*

Kiff turned his head slowly to face her. "How do you know that?"

Caylee gave a small shrug. "Let's just say that I spent some time working for the agency and leave it at that."

Kiff smiled, crookedly, but a smile all the same. "Cool. Jack didn't give me your entire resume."

"I doubt that Mr. Desmond has my full resume. These guys are some serious backing to afford that kind of hardware. Those are Russian systems."

"I don't think it's the Russies," he said, pronouncing it as if it were the word, 'pussies.' "Too obvious. There's too many people that still hate the Russians. Whoever has armed them is giving us bread crumbs aimed to mislead us."

"You can't prove that though," she cautioned, standing up straight and putting her hands on her hips.

"Not yet," Kiff admitted, spinning his chair to see her better. "Once I get a copy of their systems, I will though." She admired his confidence and hoped that it was merited. "All of this," she said pointing to the satellite image, "means that getting in and out is going to be tricky."

"I assumed as much," Kiff said.

Good. He knows what he is signing up for. "What do you have on the laptop?"

"I had to get into Verizon's system to pin down the physical location of the IPs where that is showing up. One a business, owned by a leader of this little rebellion—Booker Hickox. It is used during the daytime hours out of his office in Vernon. Trans-Tex uses some software to make pinning down the IP hard, but I'm fairly certain it is being used there. The other location is a Budget Inn in Vernon. That pattern shows mostly on weekends, starting on Friday nights. Hickox is fairly consistent as to when and where he is logging on.

The motel—he has to have a reason for going there. "Has he got someone on the side he's sleeping with?"

"I had the same thought. I haven't found the person yet, but from what I pulled up on the Budget Inn, it's a shithole. There have been two murders there in the last five years not to mention an abnormal number of drug arrests, so it's not exactly the Ritz. I doubt he's going there to get the free Showtime."

Caylee's mind processed what she was hearing and seeing, attempting to sort through the data and organize her thinking. For her, it was like filling out an outline. Two targets, two ops, one a hardened target, one with a vulnerability, and a soft target. For several long minutes she said nothing, simply stared at the screens and organized her thoughts. Kiff finally shattered the silence. "You're not brain-locked are you?"

"What?"

"Brain-locked. I get it sometimes too. You get so deep in thought that you kinda tune out everything around you."

"Perhaps," she conceded. "I was trying to do an assessment of what we have to do when you've told me how much time you may need with the systems."

"This isn't going to be easy, is it?"

She turned from looking at the monitor to him. "Parts of it are bound to be easier than others. From what Mr. Desmond has provided me, these Texans right now are fairly tense. They expect the Army to come at them and are gearing up to inflict as much damage as possible if and when that happens. We need to be discreet about how to get into this so-called Republic. That's the first step—our penetration. Then we need to go for the hardest target first, the Trans-Tex PC. After that we will need to craft a visit with Mr. Hickox for his laptop, preferably at the Budget Inn."

"Trans-Tex has been converted to a military base," Kiff said, pointing at the satellite image. "They probably aren't going to like us sniffing around."

That is an understatement. "I will grant you it is difficult. Mr. Desmond wouldn't have asked for my involvement if it was easy. I will get you in so that you can work your techno-magic. The key is for you to do what you are told."

"Got that from our previous talk," Kiff said. "So what is next?"

"We'll need some gear prepared and pre-positioned. I have a friend that can help with that. Next, we need to practice with our Texas accents. Then, we need to go shopping."

"Shopping?"

Caylee grinned. "Clothing—boots—we need to look the part." *Even*

if we do look like the locals, this is going to take more than subterfuge;
it is going to take some good character acting on the fly.

Cherokee National Forest, Tennessee

General Reager looked over the mobile response force that he had ordered positioned and was generally pleased. On its own, the rolling Southern Appalachian Mountains, covered with dense growths of trees, provided ample cover from aerial observation. The ground forces had taken other precautions, using felled trees and even sod to erect partial covers for the vehicles, helping mask their heat signatures from probing drones or aircraft. The heavy shelters they had put up and camouflaged would look like small mounds of forest from the air—some even had planted small pines on top to further add to the illusion that there was nothing underneath.

Colonel Dan "The Dancer" Ricketts in command of the rapid reaction force that was hidden there, stood at his right. Captain Paul Harnessy stood at his left. "Colonel, you've done a damned fine job of digging in here," he said.

"Thank you General. We are ready for action whenever those people make their move. Any indications as to when that might be?" The older Colonel hiked up his camouflaged pants.

Trip appreciated the question. "We think it is soon." He turned to his G2 officer, Harnessy. "Paul, show him what our drones picked up."

Harnessy pulled his iPad out and displayed the photos that they had gotten the day before. "These are images of Highway 58 that runs east and west in Virginia along the North Carolina border," the Captain said, angling the iPad for better viewing by the two officers. "As you can see, they have put out a lot of construction barrels along that road—over eighty miles worth, all poised to move. In Volney and Independence, Virginia, they have cut off the highway altogether."

Ricketts's face wrinkled, and the ends of his white mustache rose, as he squinted at the image. "Captain, I've driven a lot of highways over the years. I have to tell you, I've seen a lot of construction barrels along the roadway. My sister lives in Michigan, and half of that state has cones and barrels in place year long."

Trip weighed in. "I felt that same way at first Colonel. But there's nothing on the books about roadwork planned for that road—and usually a big project like this would have had public hearing, planning sessions, maps—but Virginia has nothing on record about planned work there."

"Also sir," Harnessy weighed in. "If they were planning for major construction, they would have staged some actual construction equipment somewhere along the route. There is none that we've been able to find."

"Let me see the highway on the map," Colonel Ricketts asked. When Harnessy pulled it up, Ricketts stared at it intently, taking hold of the iPad himself and zooming in. "No wonder you positioned us here."

Trip was pleased to see that the Colonel grasped the risk. "They are staged as if they are going to drive south, into North Carolina. They may very well be planning that. But with this highway prepared, they could easily swing west, right into Tennessee." The Newmerica General Rinehart was given to big sweeping maneuvers—always driving for the knockout blow. Trip understood that thinking all too well and was preparing for it. That didn't guarantee success. *They hit us hard enough and fast enough, and they might get through at Knoxville and head right for Nashville. We are going to have to hold them off, enough for our own counterattack.*

"We aren't enough to hold off everything he has," Ricketts said.

"I know. We have forces poised in Knoxville as well, and you'll be coordinating defense with them until help can arrive. As of this afternoon, we've Captain Paredes's air support force deployed west of Knoxville for tactical air cover. We've also shifted some of our air assets to Nashville and have deployed some air defense batteries around that city and Knoxville."

"I heard all about him from Stone Mountain," Ricketts said. "I appreciate that kind of support."

It had taken a lot to replace the helicopters and crews lost in the fighting in Georgia, but "Lariat" Paredes was ready.

"Knoxville is the key," Trip said. "Of course that comes with a lot of ifs. *If* they drive west, *if* we can hold them there long enough, *if* we can redeploy what we have in North Carolina fast enough."

"We'll do our best sir," Ricketts said. "Just give us the go signal and we will be on the move."

"I can't ask for much more than that," Trip said. *Hopefully your best will be enough, if it comes down to it. If not, our temporary capital will be overrun, and the enemy will generate momentum for their cause ... something we cannot afford to let happen.*

CHAPTER 13

"We will take care of your retirement years
... put your trust in the FedGov."

The District

The cardboard box was larger and heavier than the Vice President would have expected. It dominated her pristine desk, looking remarkably plain and nondescript. This was a package that she had been expecting with a suppressed bit of glee. When her assistant, Trey, had carefully placed it on her desk, she did so as if it were somehow tainted. *No doubt she went and washed her hands afterwards.*

Using her letter opener, the VP cut the top off carefully. Inside was a thick, clear plastic bag, roughly the size of two bags of flour. It was tied off at the top with three big twistees, one dangling a label. Holding the tag in her hand, she saw the words, "Human Remains." With a heavy heft, she pulled the bag from the box, setting it down in front of her.

The ashes were gray, almost tan in color—far finer than she expected. Staring at the contents as she lowered herself to her seat, she could see bits and pieces of what she presumed were bone fragments in the mix. Having never seen cremated remains, she did not know what to expect when they had arrived. *So this is all that is left after they burn you.*

The Vice President was glad that she had not done that with her mother or brother. This seemed so impersonal, so dull. For Becky, it had been a fitting way of disposing of her body. Someone had almost released her remains to her parents, but the VP had stopped that. Becky's parents became indignant, issuing demands for their daughter's body, but she had used the vagueness of 'national security' to essentially tell them to fuck off. *They don't need her to mourn. Besides, I have a place for her.*

The VP didn't want Becky's body buried like her own mother and brother. Becky still had a lot of supporters in the TRC, though few dared admit it openly. A body, with a tombstone, would be a draw for her allies, a place for them to go. *There will be no shrine for her; no place where she will be remembered.* Reducing Becky to ashes and keeping them prevented that. It was also a way for Becky to remain part of what was unfolding. *From your new home on my bookshelf, you can watch me take Newmerica into the future.*

Staring intently at the plastic bag, she remembered Becky's public suicide. Thanks to the time delay during the incident, only a little bit of her death made it on the air, too much for her tastes. The TRC had put up a 'Technical Difficulties' screen right after she dropped. The editing crew had been so caught off guard by the death that they had allowed some of the footage out before cutting it off. The Vice President made sure that the editors were fired and would be denied their unemployment benefits. *Maybe next time they will pay more attention, if they ever land a job again.*

Their debacle had let the world see Becky drop, which meant a cover story for what happened had to be crafted and done quickly. The official story was that Becky had suffered a seizure, was taken to the hospital, and died shortly thereafter. There were rumors out there, some dead-on accurate about Becky's suicide. None of that mattered; the official story was out there and, thanks to some crafty editing of the footage, it seemed that was what had occurred. *Creating doubt in the minds of the masses is far more useful than the lie itself. It means we don't have to refute the rumors; we just make people question them on their own.*

Becky had been one of the founders of Newmerica. That was reality, and even the Vice President accepted it. While the public knew the persona that she had put forth, that could be changed. That was the true power of the Truth Reconciliation Committee. ... It set and controlled the narrative, and the Vice President now controlled the TRC.

I will see her slowly removed from mentions about what we have accomplished. Our official history of the new nation will give her scant credit. Mostly, I can hang on her what happened to Congress the night of the Liberation. Over time, the story we will tell about Becky is a minor role, with all of our misdeeds laid at her feet. If there is ever a time when the people want a villain in what we have done, we will provide them one in the form of Becky.

From behind her desk she pulled out the bright blue urn with a seal bearing an up-thrust fist ringed with stars, one of the first flags that Newmerica had flown and one that Becky had designed herself. The Vice President had toyed with simply purchasing an inexpensive urn off of Amazon to hold her former colleague, but there was no one to enjoy such a final dig. This one had been expensive, custom designed by her for her old comrade. She set the urn next to the bag and looked at both of them, wondering if all of the ashes would fit inside. No matter, if it didn't, the rest could be flushed down the toilet or thrown out with the trash.

Pressing the button on the small control pad of her desk summoned her assistant a few seconds later. "Yes, Madam Vice President?"

"Please put these remains in the urn. When you are done, I want it over there, on the top shelf." She gestured to the place she had cleared off for the urn.

Her assistant looked flummoxed at the order. "They are just ashes Trey," she said in an almost offhanded tone. "Just pour them in."

Trey's complexion went slightly pale, but she knew not to ignore a direct order. "Of course ma'am," she said, grasping the top of the thick plastic bag with one hand and the urn with her other hand. "If you don't mind, I will do this in the restroom."

"Of course, whatever it takes," she said as Trey left the room, and the automatic door system closed behind her. The VP set the empty box next to her mahogany banded, reddish waste basket, and then looked carefully at her desk to make sure that no particles of Becky had somehow been left behind.

Leaning back in her chair, she looked at the empty space where the urn would go. *We will have plenty of time together old friend. You will see everything you dreamed of come to fruition, but you'll never get to enjoy it. You may have cheated me of your execution, but you are mine now—forever.*

Berlin, New Hampshire

Su-Hui looked out with a bit of pride at the eleven Humvees they had captured over the last few weeks. They filled the old service garage to capacity. While they all had New York or Massachusetts markings, they were fully outfitted for the mission at hand. More than half bore marks from battle, bullet, and blast scars. The severely damaged ones were patched up enough to get them on the road. The ones filled with explosives looked as if they were filled with standard issue ammunition crates to hide their deadly surprise. The others were loaded down with fuel cans, munitions, grenades, etc.

A small number of civilian vehicles were also prepared, many with steel plates added to the interiors for armored protection. They were designed to be scouts, looking for checkpoints, running ahead of the small task force to make sure that there were no surprises. It was a precaution he had added to the operations at the insistence of the New Hampshire National Guardsmen. A prudent thought. *No one would think that a couple of people driving a simple civilian vehicle are part of a larger military operation.* It was one of the big advantages that the Sons of Liberty had—they could easily blend in when they had to.

He had gathered the personnel that would be going on the mission with the vehicles and the support and family members. *They all need to know what we are doing and the risks involved.*

"If I may have your attention," he said as he stood on a footstool. Given his short height, it only seemed to elevate him slightly. "I want to say a few words before we depart.

"We are going south, through an occupied state. It is our intent to disguise ourselves as our enemy, but at any juncture, this can go wrong. For those of us going, it is critical that you follow orders. Anyone panicking and opening fire too soon can turn a tense situation into a full-fledged battle." Su-Hui paused to make sure that his words were landing on the people in the raiding party. The nodding of heads told him his message was being heard.

"The enemy will not make this easy. There will be checkpoints, road blocks, places where they will question who we are and where we are going. We have given them a great deal to be frightened about. They will not make this easy on us.

"Once we get across the border, we will proceed to the Joint Task Force headquarters. We will place our explosives, park our car bombs, and depart. If we do this right, our bombs will devastate them. More importantly, it will send a message to the people of Massachusetts— 'Stop sending your soldiers to kill people in New Hampshire.'" Those words brought even more nods of agreement.

"Getting back will be difficult. They will try to box us in. Make no mistake, there will be shooting. Our goal, however, is not to get engaged in a fight on their terms. We will split up once we are back in New Hampshire and make our way back here."

He swept the crowd for a moment until he made eye contact with his beloved Hachi. "The last time we went across the border, they came for us." Memories of the bombardment and devastation of Lisbon surged to the forefront of his mind for a moment. Seeing his wife's face and the firm smile she offered him gave him purpose; it gave him the confidence he needed. "We have people that will scout to make sure that no one makes a move on our people. If they attempt to do so, we have a fallback position we will use. We are leaving very little to chance this time." *We learned our lesson the hard way, with blood and death.*

Drawing a long breath of the diesel fumed air, he continued. "This will not be easy, but it is strategic. It is aimed at splintering the support that Newmerica has. Our efforts in Vermont have drawn many of their troops out of this state. We hope that the same will happen with Massachusetts. Even if it doesn't, it will make people there afraid of what we might do … what we can do.

"They will learn that our Defiance is not just a slogan—it is who we are!" His last words brought about cheers, hoots, and applause.

Slowly Su-Hui lowered himself. Hachi came up beside him through the crowd. Leaning in, she kissed him on the cheek. "You have become quite the leader."

Someone patted him on the back as they passed, but it did not shake his focus on her. "I am nothing without you."

Her eyes almost seemed to glow with his words. "You must take care of yourself, my love," she said in a low tone so that only he could hear it over the din of voices and movement around him.

"I always do."

"I am serious," she said scornfully. "Your children and I rely on you. You are our strength. If not for you, we would be living under communist Chinese rule back home. You got us out and saved us."

The mention of his children hit him hard. Ya-ting, once so bright and vibrant, had been taken from them. Not physically, but mentally and emotionally; it was as if she were a blank slate. It was a crime that the government had ignored her rape and beating. Only a vigilante police officer had sought to set matters right. It had been a lesson for him. When you see a wrong, you take action, no matter how violent, to correct it. "I understand. By the same token, you know that I have to do this."

"I do. I only fear this is not as easy as you described it."

He conceded her comment with a single nod. "You may be right. Our enemy has become much more ruthless in the last few weeks." Memories of the Governor being murdered were still etched in his mind. "If you suspect that you are at risk, you know where the fallback site is. Don't hesitate to go there."

"I will," she assured him. "Just make sure you get back."

Su-Hui hugged her tight. It was easier than making a commitment that he wasn't sure he could keep.

Sedan, New Mexico

Since the election, the fate of New Mexico was one of those that hung in the balance. As Dr. Liu looked at the village of Sedan, he understood why no one was fighting there at the moment. The area was long, wafting dead fields of grass, a dull brown in color. The only things that broke up the flat monotony of the landscape was the occasional barbed wire fence or a distant windmill … not a sleek modern one, but an old 1930s one that had somehow defied decay and still stood.

New Mexico had voted for the Newmerican President but had won by the narrowest of margins. When an audit and recount was called for, a large number of mail in ballots had proven to come from non-existent voters—enough to bring the vote back to the American President in Tennessee. While their Electoral College votes went to the American President, the Newmericans claimed that New Mexico's votes had been suppressed and that the state had been stolen. The progressive Governor refused to acknowledge the American President, so the state was left in a quagmire as to where it fell, with both sides claiming it as their own.

Liu had come here with his delivery team because Sedan was just over the border from Dallam County of the new Republic of Texas. They had flown their cargo into Santa Fe, had rented the big white panel truck, and had driven to the border of the fledgling nation. Booker Hickox was there, with his own Trans-Tex truck, and a half-dozen men with weapons waiting at the border. The two vehicles were poised on the border, some twenty yards apart, as if there were some invisible barrier between them.

They look like they strolled out of central casting. The men wore jeans, not designer jeans but actual working pants. Their shirts were covered with a fine dust, kicked up over the New Mexico plains. Cowboy hats and boots were worn, not as Liu usually saw them, as fashion statements—but rather as work attire. They all stood out in contrast to his men who wore black slacks, starched white shirts, and black blazers. The only commonality between the two groups was their firearms which were openly displayed.

Liu walk out on the deserted road, and Hickox moved out to meet him. "You folks are prompt, I'll give you that," he said with a deep Texas drawl.

"We take care of our friends," Liu responded. He nodded back to his men, who opened the back of the truck and began to unload the boxes. "As we agreed, munitions and missiles. We have also made a rather generous donation to your cause."

"So I've been told," Hickox replied. He waved to his men who moved out and began to pick up the boxes and take them to his vehicle.

"My backers have been most curious; what are your plans?"

Hickox looked at him, narrowing his eyes. "Expand of course. We have four counties right now. We've got folks poking around in other counties, stirring up interest."

"Don't you worry that the American army will simply move in and squash your little uprising?"

"It ain't an uprising," Hickox retorted. "Texan independence is a patriotic act. It is native to our people. We are just doing something that has long been overdue. We should have split off right after the damned Fall."

Clearly Liu's words tugged at Hickox's sense of patriotism. "I meant no offense. But even with the arms we have provided you, the Americans present a threat—as do the Newmericans for that matter."

"Don't you worry about the Newmericans," he said, grinning just a bit. *We have them in our pocket, and they don't even know it.* "They think our efforts are helping them. I don't trust those commie bastards as far as I could throw them. They probably think we're a bunch of rednecks that they can manipulate. Well, their money is just as useful as anyone else's and we don't dance to their tune.

"As for the American army, well I hope they come at us. Anyone they kill will be a martyr to the cause. It will look like the big bully on the block beating up on the little kid—and that will fire up a lot of people to side with us. One thing the last five years has taught us is that a lot of fine folks in Texas hate big government. They get pissed off when the government starts telling them what to do and when to do it. It started with that COVID vaccine shit and went downhill from there." Hickox paused for a moment, reeling in his emotions.

"Besides, their top General is Trip Reager, a good old Texas boy if there ever was one. We had a little pow-wow with him. He knows that if he comes in guns a 'blazin', he will never be able to set foot in Texas again. We think the world of the man right now, but if he starts killing us, well, folks are going to remember that."

"I find it hard to believe that the Americans are going to simply sit back and let you peel away counties from Texas, Mr. Hickox," he said as the men behind him continued with the transfer of weapons and ammunition.

"You're right about that. Sooner or later, they'll come," he conceded, tipping his black Stetson back slightly. "When they do, we'll be ready for them. We don't have to beat them, just give them a bloody nose and a kick to the ball-sack … just enough for people in the state to see them as the oppressor and us as the victims. The one thing that Newmerica has given us is the sense that all victims are somehow heroes. People have had that drilled into their heads. So if they see any military come at us, they will feel sympathy for us and our cause. When they do come, they will be generating more support for us than you can imagine."

There was a simple logic to what Hickox was saying, thinking that showed him to be more intriguing than Liu had first expected. *This is not an impulse on their part. The people that are behind this Republic of Texas have weighed their options carefully.* "Eventually, they will be forced to respond to you."

Hickox nodded. "Eventually. While they have parked troops along our border, there are plenty of gaps, as you can see." He gestured to the wide plains that surrounded them. "Besides, they have plenty to keep them busy. That autonomous zone in St. Louis, the invasion in Iowa … for the time being they have bigger fish to fry than us."

That was true. The American Army was being stretched thin. He had received word from his operatives in Virginia about a large buildup of Newmerican force there. The Civil War was pushing both sides to their limits, especially with the Pentagon and the regular army standing down for the most part. "Your assessment seems valid."

"Damned right it is," he said with a hint of pride. "People are underestimating Salem and me. We caught a spy from Newmerica snooping around. Let's just say he won't be doing that ever again."

Getting Zack Taylor to give access to their computers was going to be riskier than he had anticipated. He would have to get word to John Quang and Taylor to warn them before they made their penetration attempt. "It goes without saying, that if anyone were to find out that my people were backing you, it would hurt both of our causes."

Hickox nodded in response. "I understand that. Nothing would piss off Texans more than to find out that China was backing our independence movement. All I can say is don't you worry about that. We have some top notch security in place. Your transactions are routed, rerouted, and rerouted again. Between what you do before we get your money and what we do after, there's no way that anyone could figure out your government was backing us."

There is always a way. We were able to penetrate what security you have in place and have seen the gaps in your digital barriers. Liu was tempted to offer him technical support rather than sneak in Zack Taylor to do the work covertly. His instincts told him that the Texans would refuse such help. *They are proud, perhaps too much so. The last thing I want to do is make them feel we don't trust them or their capabilities.* "As long as that information never reaches the public, we shall continue our arrangements," he said calmly.

"We appreciate your support," Hickox said, offering his calloused hand.

Weber Liu took it, his own hand dwarfed in the Texan's, and gave him a firm shake. *We do not care if Texas becomes its own nation or not. All that really matters is the further division of these people, and for now, our support serves that purpose. If our support is ever made public, it would be a disaster for both nations.*

CHAPTER 14

"Ask not what your country can do for you;
ask what you can do for your country."

Wilbarger County, Texas

Kiff sat in their faded blue Dodge truck, struggling with his mix of nerves and excitement. Caylee had told him they could sneak into Texas from Oklahoma with few problems—the Red River level was low at this time of the year. But the ground was flat. There was scrub brush but few trees, and without a vehicle, sneaking across would take longer and be more difficult. It was not snowing there, but the wind was penetrating with a sting of winter. Kiff was not the kind of person to like the outdoors that much anyway, so driving across had some appeal.

There had been a highway patrol checkpoint on the Oklahoma side of the river. They had issued a lot of warnings about the Republic of Texas, that there was a threat of military action, that it was not formally recognized, etc. They had searched the truck to make sure they were not smuggling anything into the Republic in the way of weapons, somehow managing to not find any of the weapons that Caylee had stored. She had told them that they accepted the risks of going south into the breakaway republic. Of course Kiff knew if that didn't work, a quick call to the Southern White House would have quickly resolved any impasse.

Caylee had drilled him on his cover story, despite him proving he had memorized all of the details. That was how Caylee was, thorough. He tried to fake a southern drawl, but no matter how good he thought he sounded, she said it was an epic failure. "Just talk; respond with the answers I prepared for you. I'll handle the rest," she assured him. It was odd, but he believed she would do just that—handle it. A part of Caylee inspired confidence, especially when she was plying her craft.

Their truck was a beater, fenders dented in from years of farm abuse. He swore one dent on the tailgate was a hoof-print. It had been faded dull in the hot Texas sun for years. Mud was caked near the rust holes on the driver's side fender. It had a smell inside that was a mix of hay, manure, and other people's sweat. In the back was a jumble of things that Caylee had put there, a tool kit with a hidden pouch for her special tools, a small tank of gas that was marked oxygen, and a few other camouflaged items.

Caylee was wearing an old, thick, padded, dull gray winter vest over her flannel shirt and thermal top, courtesy of the Salvation Army Resale shop she had taken Kiff to. *We needed worn clothing. Showing up in brand new stuff would have made us stand out.* Kiff had suggested cowboy hats, but she had opted to ponytail her hair and string it out the back of a beat up, frayed and dirty ball cap with the Ranger's logo. As they approached the checkpoint on the Red River Bridge, Kiff saw that the Texas Republic was taking securing seriously. Two trucks were mounted with machine guns on the back. A dozen or so people were armed with rifles and pistols, and one person had what appeared to be a hand-held missile launcher flung over his back. As they got close, the weapons tracked them meticulously, clearly preparing for a fight.

"Remember what I told you and whatever you do, don't overreact," she said in low tone as she brought the Dodge to a stop some ten yards from the road block.

They slowly enveloped the truck. Three went to the bed of the truck while two stood by the doors on either side. The others were standing, weapons at the ready, aiming at the vehicle. One man had two German Shepards on short leashes, no doubt to take down anyone stupid enough to run. In a weird way, the dogs were more intimidating than the men with guns. It wasn't that Kiff hated dogs; it just seemed that most dogs hated him. The canines only added to the air of inevitability if things went south. *Even if we wanted to shoot our way out of this, we'd be doomed.*

She lowered her dirty side window, and a man with a big thick beard leaned in, almost in her face. "So, where are ya'll headin'?"

Caylee smiled, broader than he had ever witnessed. "We've got some friends in Dallam who called us and invited us to come. One of them has a PC that died, and my boyfriend here is a bit of a computer geek."

Kiff grinned slightly, as they had rehearsed. The burly man asked for their driver's licenses, which both dug out. They were fake, but had been provided courtesy of the State of Texas and a phone call to Jack Desmond. They took them back to one of their vehicles and pulled out a handheld police scanner, usually issued to law enforcement. *These guys are more sophisticated than they appear.*

It seemed to take forever and he was getting more nervous with each passing moment. Caylee slowly turned to him and locked gazes with him. It was as if he could read her mind. *Relax ... this is part of the game.*

The man came back without their IDs. "Who were you going to see?"

Caylee rattled off the three names quickly. He asked for their phone number. "I have it on my phone," she said, pulling it out and scrolling. "I haven't memorized a phone number in years." When they had rehearsed, she had said she used lines like that because it was something everyone could identify with. Now he was seeing her technique in action.

The names she had given belonged to some Texas loyalists that Jack had provided. If called, they would vouch for their story. Caylee seemed very relaxed given the firepower that could be dropped on them in a moment's notice. She had stashed a number of firearms in the truck, cutting out pieces of metal to conceal them. The nasty one, a sawed off shotgun, was behind a false door panel right next to her. Kiff was fairly positive that she had at least one gun on her body as well, if not more.

The man speaking to her jotted down the number. "Wait here." He went off while the other slowly circled the truck. It seemed like it took forever, and for the first time since they had arrived, Kiff felt hot. A nervous sweat broke out and he wet his lips slightly while the man seemed to be making phone calls. A glance over to Caylee returned a smile, but at the same time he noticed her hand drifting down to the door panel. *Please just be instinct. Please just be instinct.*

After several long minutes, the man ambled back. "I called yer friends. They supported yer story." He handed back their driver's licenses and Kiff stuffed his into his wallet.

Caylee's grin broadened. "So we can go on?"

He shook his head. "No offense ma'am, but we need to search your vehicle and pat you down."

"Is that really necessary?" she asked innocently. "I mean we are already running later than we'd planned because one of us," she said and shot Kiff a fast glance, "couldn't get his ass out of bed on time."

"'Fraid so," he said opening the driver's door for her. She nodded at Kiff, and he opened his door and stepped out. A gust of cold wind hit him, and he made sure his hands were up.

A female, at least he thought she was, turned him around to face the truck. "Hands on the cab," she said, patting him down. She squeezed him hard with each pat, leaving little to chance. She pulled him to one side and grabbed his backpack out of the rear of the cab. She took everything out, checking it over. She turned on his PC and his personal encryption software demanded an ID and password. For five minutes, she went over everything in his backpack, pulling out cables, portable hard drives, flash drives, everything. He wasn't worried; there was nothing suspicious in his bags.

She moved to their luggage, taking it to the back of the truck and lowering the dented tailgate. Pawing through everything Caylee had; the only thing she found was a can marked 'Mace' that Caylee had packed. The female held it up for the others to see. *That won't unload on us over mace ... will they.* Kiff's eyes were locked on the men.

The man patting down Caylee pulled a knife from a sheath on her pant leg. He held it up for her to see. She seemed to get a little defiant. "I'm not going across your Republic without some protection."

An instant later, a man searching the truck pulled out her 1911 that had been hidden in the air vent of the truck. "Gun here boss," he called. In a heartbeat, the Texan's hands dropped to their weapons, and the cold air blowing across the Red River suddenly seemed to get a bit warmer. *Oh shit ...*

Roanoke Rapids, North Carolina

The rumbles of artillery going off a mile away shook Trip Reager's chest. The plumes of smoke snaked into the cold air, and the roaring-hiss of outgoing rocket fire, hitting the advancing Newmerican forces was a sound he desperately wished he didn't have to hear. It was far too familiar, stirring up memories of places like Stone Mountain and the Middle East. Every explosion tugged at those memories and the knowledge that now he was fighting other Americans. *The sooner this is over the better.*

He stood under a copse of pine trees, next to his command Humvee as an explosion went off some 150 yards away. Bits of dirt and fragments of a blasted tree rained down all around the infantry position it was intended for. Dead pine needles rained down from the shaking trees. The troops there huddled deep in their foxholes. The prepared positions were good, reinforced with felled trees and a lot of dirt, but nothing would protect them from a direct hit.

The bombardment had begun an hour ago, right at 0700 hours. It was enough to keep his troops pinned down for the time being. No one wanted to risk exposing themselves as potential targets for the enemy artillery. Based on their misses, they didn't have local observers attempting to adjust the shots. The damage that his force had taken appeared to be more random hits than directed shots. *If I'm right, they are just trying to hold our attention here.* There was an equal chance though that his instincts were wrong—that this was really the prelude to the main thrust into North Carolina.

Major Thorpe moved beside him as Trip lowered his binoculars. "Evacuation of the remaining civilians is as complete as we can get it, sir."

There were always holdouts, people that refused to evacuate regardless of the threat. "Very well Major," he replied, turning slowly to him. "How bad is the damage in the town?"

"Fires are out of control," Thorpe replied. "The Walmart is a total loss—direct hit with their first volley. They are tearing apart the downtown area."

Of course they are; they want to make sure that we think this is the preliminary move to them coming right at us. He was still counting on the deception to be part of the charade. "Captain Harnessy, we seeing any movement?"

"They have advanced out of Emporia, but are moving slow—south by southeast. They are maintaining strong air cover over Virginia right now, limiting aerial reconnaissance. They did bomb our forward positions, but so far are keeping their air support tight over their troops."

"It's almost as if they don't want us knowing what is going on in Virginia," he said with a hint of sarcasm.

"We have some civilian observers, loyalists. They say that for right now, it looks like a gradual advance south."

Which would mean I'm wrong. Trip had no issues accepting his mistakes. It didn't bother him one way or another. His father had always told him what separated good men from bad was that the bad ones refused to accept responsibility when they made mistakes. *If they do thrust south, I need to be prepared to shift our troops from Tennessee.* While it was tempting to give that order right now, patience was still needed. *Timing with an operation like this is everything.*

"What's the status on our air support?"

His Air Force liaison, Captain Hill, stepped forward and cleared her throat. "Sir, per our rules of engagement, we are currently staying on our side of the border. They are poking at us, but so far not a full-on air incursion. We are keeping them back from close ground support missions."

What if their ruse is to make me think that a push into Tennessee is the real diversion? Doubt always was there, but kept in check with Trip. It had to be. Once doubt got ahold of you, it would never let go. *I could go on forever questioning my instincts on this, and in the end I'd be right here, at the same place, staring at the same problems.* "What about along the Tennessee border?"

"Nothing … yet," Captain Harnessy replied. "I've ordered a few Rangers to get close to the main roads heading that way. I have a team in Dansville, which they will have to use on a lateral change of direction. We're using CB radios and codes rather than our milspec comms gear since both sides are using the same hardware. So far, they are at the front door banging on it hard." As if to emphasize his point, another artillery blast went off around 100 yards downrange, shaking them all.

The problems that a push into Tennessee would cause were daunting. If they moved fast enough and overwhelmed the defenders, they could drive on to Nashville. That would be a political disaster, to lose the Southern White House and the seat of the American government. While it was just a city, in recent months, it had become a symbol. *The blow to our morale would be hard to mitigate.* The loss of Nashville would have immeasurable political implications. He wasn't worried about losing his job as the commanding General. Focusing on career advancement wasn't part of his motivational makeup. *I never asked for the jobs I've been given. I am here to serve, period.*

A strategy for dealing with the Virginia military threat had weighed heavy on Trip. The most traditional approach was to swing his own forces to the left, moving to block and engage them if they went into Tennessee. It was simple and eloquent, but it was also costly in terms of manpower and equipment. ... He had seen that at the Battle of Stone Mountain.

A more risky but potentially effective strategy was to swing north and west from their positions along the North Carolina border into Virginia, coming in behind the enemy offensive and cutting off their logistics. It could force the enemy to turn back and attempt to drive them out before they ran out of fuel or vital supplies. There was also a chance that it might make them more aggressive and thrust deeper into Tennessee, grabbing what they needed to operate from the local population. Fuel and food could be taken from the civilians, but not military ammunition. Short term, the Newmericans could wreck a lot of havoc. Long term, they would be an army cut off from vital supplies. *Hard to kill as a cockroach and easy to deal with as a cornered rat ... that's how Dad put it.*

Trip liked the second option best, but had plans in place for both. It gave him a little comfort, having two contingency plans staged and ready. He also had plans for redeploying the forces already in Tennessee if indeed the enemy was intent on plowing through North Carolina. As he watched another explosion far off in the distance, he wondered how long the wait would be. *Are they heading right at us? Or are they on the move in some other way ... something I hadn't seen?*

"Sir," Harnessay said after several minutes of contemplation. "We are getting reports that the enemy has crossed the border just west of here, coming out of their staging grounds in South Hill. Our defensive force is being engaged three miles on our side of the border along I-85. They report fast moving vehicles—no tanks."

Trip kept his reaction in check as his brain processed the data. *If this is a diversion, it's a convincing one.* "Alright then. For now, this is the main show. We fight them here and we fight them hard. Hold them in check for now along the border. But the moment I hear they are on the move, we switch to our contingencies."

"Sir," Major Thorpe spoke up as another rumble of explosions went off on their far right, destroying a clump of trees instantly in a fireball and blast. "What about the forces we have in Knoxville? If this is the main thrust, we are going to need them. Shouldn't we have them moving this way?"

Trip's jaw set forward as he heard the thunk of outgoing mortar fire. Far off, somewhere in the low clouds, he heard the roar of jet engines. He'd had Harnessy put together the profile of his opponent, General Rinehart. All indications were that Rinehart liked bold, sweeping offensive operations. He used deceit to throw off his enemies. *It's his nature. .... It's who he is. I'm not fighting the Newmerican army as much as I am fighting him.* His gut told him that this attack south was bait, designed to make him dig in and hold ground while Rinehart swung around him and headed west into Tennessee. "No, not yet," he said firmly. "This is the opening play. We still have a big game ahead of us."

Wilbarger County, Texas

Caylee saw the bit of accusatorial facial expression in the man who held the 1911 handgun they had found. She presumed they would find a weapon or two in their search, if they conducted one. *Go ahead, have your moment.*

She had been prepared for such an event, firing off a witty excuse rather than attempting to deny the obvious. "Well, duh," she said with an almost perfect southern drawl. "You think I'm traveling without being armed? You want to see my concealed carry permit?"

The man who had found her switchblade on her shin held it in front of her as he took possession of the 1911. "It seems like you are a lady that likes dangerous things."

You have no idea. Spotting the man with the shoulder-launched missile, she noted that a fresh coat of spray paint barely covered the white stenciled instructions on the side. *Someone wanted to make sure we didn't know where that came from.* She mentally noted it, turning her real focus on the discovery of her gun.

"You ain't confiscating my gun," she said in a flat tone. "Or my knife." Nodding off in Kiff's general direction, she went on. "He's a computer geek, not much help if shit goes down. We're coming in to help out some friends. I'll be *damned* if I am going to travel across your little country without the means to protect myself. I'm pretty fucking sure if I was your sister or daughter, you'd expect the same." There was a method in what she said. Caylee knew that if she presented this as a guns-rights issue, or if they thought about a family member, they might be more prone to look the other way.

For a few moments, the bearded man in front of her said nothing, simply looked into her eyes. In her mind she was mentally keeping track of everyone, their potential fields of fire, and the limitations of being on a bridge. *This isn't an ideal location if shit starts to go down.* For a moment, she remembered crossing the Ohio River with Raul, taking out most of an SE team, racing into Kentucky under a hail of bullets. *What is it with me and bridges?*

Kiff shifted in place, as if the tension in the air was stirring him to some sort of action. She gave him a glance that said, "No!" but it was too late. The female next to him saw him shift his stance and drew her weapon. "Hold it right there fella. Don't you be doing something that is going to make me go out and dig a grave for you in this cold."

"I just ... I don't see the problem," Kiff said. "She needs a gun for protection ... that's all." It wasn't a great recovery on the part of Kiff in terms of diffusing the situation, but it was a good start. *Just ratchet this down a notch or two Kiff.* ... "I've got this."

She was less worried about her odds than those of Kiff. She had worked with him, the basics of throwing punches, some firearms training, and teaching him how to protect himself and deflect blows if attacked. Against a drawn pistol, well, his odds were shit. He was smart and a quick learner, but that could all go to hell if shooting started. *If Kiff was killed, the mission was a bust.*

Caylee was in her persona though. Backing down now might raise more raised eyebrows at their story. *I have to push on given the odds. Let's hope that Kiff keeps his mouth shut.*

"Well?" she demanded, shattering the silence.

"You need to understand somethin' little lady," the bearded man said. "Tensions between our folk, Texas, and the American government are pretty high right now. You just passed a state police checkpoint in Oklahoma to get on this bridge. I'm fairly sure they told you that things are big uppity right now. While your story sounds good, none of us know you from Adam."

"Do I seriously look like a threat?" she asked, holding her hands out to her sides and spinning at the hips slightly. "I'm just one woman. What kind of trouble do you think I can cause?" It was a loaded question, and even she admitted silently that she wanted to smirk right after saying it out loud.

The man didn't seem moved by her words. For a long time, he just glared at her, as if daring her to take action. Caylee respected what he was doing. Nervous people hate silence. They sometimes speak up to shatter it. She had used the technique dozens of times in the past and was no stranger to it. *I refuse to play along. If you expect me to be the one to blurt something out, you've got the wrong person in your sights.*

He spoke first, as she knew he would eventually. "You realize that if you come in and something starts, we cannot promise you that you can get back."

"I'm Texan, born and bred," she said embracing her fake identity to its fullest. "If I am in Texas, I'm always home—be it the state or your little republic."

The man looked over at an older gentleman in their small clutch of border patrol. The old man gave him a single nod in response. The bearded man stepped over and handed Caylee her 1911 and her switchblade. "Thank you," she said, bending down and putting the blade back into the sheath on her lower leg.

"We will give you a visa," he said. "It allows you to be here no more than five days. If you don't leave by then, we send folks after you and escort you out."

This is new. ... Our intel said nothing about visas. "Shouldn't be a problem," Caylee replied. "We hope to fix our friend's PC in a day or two."

She moved next to the driver's side door as the older man went to one of the trucks and came back with small, folded, blue cardstock visas. He asked for their driver's licenses again and painstakingly filled out each one with a pen. When done, he returned their IDs and the visas. "Don't lose these," he said cautiously. "You need to present them anytime you're asked to do so."

She gave him a single nod. "That'll work," she said, sliding into the vehicle as Kiff did the same on the passenger side. The bearded man motioned back, and the machine gun armed Technicals backed up, opening the road for their passing. The Dodge started, kicking up a dark cloud of diesel smoke as it rumbled to life again. Driving slowly, she passed the vehicles. For at least a mile, neither she nor Kiff spoke. Finally, the younger man let out a long sigh of relief. "Wow, that was tense."

"Getting in is easy," she said. "Getting out might not be. At least for the time being, we have valid IDs."

"You were so calm back there," Kiff said with an astonished tone to his voice. "Sorry I lost my cool."

"Kid, you never really had any cool to lose."

"I'm not a kid," he said. "I just look like one."

"Point taken. Going forward you have to remember that people read your body language more than anything coming out of your mouth. When you shifted back there, they interpreted that as panic or aggression. If you had pushed it, the whole situation could have gotten messy."

"How do you do it? I mean, all of this. You were so calm—you didn't waver or hesitate. How do you pull it off?"

"Training, experience. If I wanted a confrontation, we would have had one and fast. I didn't—not this time anyway. What was important was that we got across. You did pretty well yourself."

"I was scared shitless," he admitted. "But it wasn't all bad."

"Why is that?"

"It's been a while since a girl felt me up like that," he said referring to his pat down.

Caylee smiled, if only for a moment. "You sure that was a girl?"

Kiff shrugged and grinned. "You have to take your victories where you find them."

CHAPTER 15

"Thanks to your government, you are never truly alone."

Tilton, New Hampshire

Su-Hui's band of raiders had stopped in Tilton, New Hampshire, hiding themselves behind an abandoned Kohl's that had closed years earlier. The National Guard had been using the abandoned store as a small base and with some relatively easy modifications to the rear loading docks, the Humvees of the raiders were squeezed in and under cover.

Their journey had been slow and methodical, just as Su-Hui had planned. Outwardly, the raiders looked like a large enemy patrol. One roadblock had questioned them to the point of recording their license plates, but allowed them to pass. They had stayed off of the main roads as much as possible, using bases of other Sons of Liberty cells or the National Guard for protection. While they were only a few hours from the border with Massachusetts, the Newmerican strongholds of Concord and Manchester were in the way and had to be carefully skirted.

Their hosts prepared venison steaks which were a bit gamy for his taste, but were filling. The locals brought in fruits and vegetables to make the steaks seem more like a feast than a hastily grilled meal for his people. As they settled in and started cutting the last bits of his steak, Su-Hui was approached by a Lieutenant and Corporal Abernathy who escorted him.

"You are the SOL commander?" the Lieutenant asked.

"Su-Hui Zhou," he said as he started to stand. The Lieutenant met him halfway and sat down, so Su-Hui did the same.

"I'm Lieutenant Duwe," he said, pronouncing it as *Do-wee*" though Su-Hui picked up his name from the tag sown on the front of his fatigues "I am the G2 for this area of operations," he said, keeping his voice low so that it didn't travel. Abernathy sat down next to him. "I was telling the Corporal here that we picked up some chatter recently about you."

"Chatter?"

"Comms traffic," he said coolly. "At first we didn't know what they were referring to. Their code name for your force is Dragonrider. We have some loyalists in the Newmerica force that I discreetly reached out to asking for clarification. As it turns out, you folks are Dragonrider. We believe their code name for you personally is Longwang."

Su-Hui happened to like the sound of that. It was the name of a fearsome Chinese deity, the king of the dragons. What he didn't like was the fact that the enemy knew about them and him by name. "So they are tracking us?"

Grimness fell over the Lieutenant's face. His piercing gray eyes narrowed, and his mouth opened for a moment, but he said nothing. *He's disturbed by something ... something bad.* "It's a little more than that. We got indications that they are aware of your operation and your target. They are staging a pretty big ambush at the border. More importantly, they have the names of most of your team."

How could it have happened? Surveillance would not have picked our names. This is the product of treason! His own face tightened. *If they know about us, then our support and families are at risk as well.* His body seemed to tense up at that thought. "We've been through their checkpoints. ... Why would they have done that if they knew where we are going?"

Lieutenant Duwe ran his hand through his short, black hair. "As near as we can determine, they are tracking your movements with the checkpoints. The Newmerican forces are strongest in the southern part of the state. They want to get you deep into territory that they have full control over before springing their trap. After Berlin, they don't want a chance of you getting away, so the ambush they are planning is overwhelming." Duwe's word resonated with him deeply. *This is not about stopping us from doing the raid; it is about crushing and killing us.* The thought that they were being led into a trap chewed on the fringe of his thinking for a few long, silent moments.

He tried to unravel how this could have come to pass. *To have our names, the person would have had to be with us. To know our mission; they would have had to be there.* Su-Hui wondered if one of their team had somehow leaked the information, or if a local who had been giving them supplies had found out about it. *That is highly doubtful. Our people have been told not to talk, that spoken words are daggers that can stab them in the back. Then how did the Newmericans learn about us and where we are going?*

The reality hit him hard. *A traitor! That is the only way! Someone deliberately has set us up.* "We have been betrayed," he said in a low tone of voice.

Lieutenant Duwe nodded. "I don't have all of the details, but our informants say that the enemy apparently captured a group of SOL fighters a few days ago. They got information from them. Since then, they have been shifting more forces south to deal with you at the Massachusetts border."

Herb ... it had to be Herb. Herb Fletcher knew about the operation when he had stormed off. For all of his bluster and aggressiveness, it was somehow easy for Su-Hui to picture him turning on his comrades. *Such men lack the fortitude to do the right thing when pressed.* "This is bad news indeed," he replied. "It was Herb Fletcher and his people—it had to be. No one else knew enough to cause us this kind of hurt."

"I can have my sources check, if you want," the Lieutenant offered.

Su-Hui shook his head. He knew the truth already in his heart. Confirming it would not solve the problem at hand. "If they got it from someone they captured, it was most likely Herb Fletcher. His name needed to be circulated to other SOL groups as a potential risk. If they flipped him, they may try and use him against other cells."

"Good call."

"Our families and support people need to be relocated immediately." Herb had left before they had scouted the fallback position in Dixville Notch. In that moment, he could not help but think of his wife, Hachi. *I won't let her be in danger like when we were in Berlin.*

"We can get that message to them," the Lieutenant assured him.

"We'll deliver it in person, just in case they are monitoring your communications."

The betrayal hurt him deeply. It was mixed with a bit of guilt. *If I had not driven Herb away, none of this might be happening.* Herb likely resisted a little during his interrogations, enough to create the façade of being loyal to the cause, but Su-Hui did not doubt that he had enjoyed ratting them out. *Every war in history has its traitors who seek to turn things to their own advantage.* No doubt Herb Fletcher was one of those men. "Is there any way we can still fulfill our mission?" he asked.

Lieutenant Duwe shook his head. "They have pulled a lot of their forces southward, stripping most of their patrols and borders to the east and west. Every road or trail that leads into Massachusetts is covered from what we have been able to learn. After your raids in Vermont, they are covering the woods, logging trails, hunting paths, any place you might be able to use to go south. Like I said, they are prepared for you heading to Boston."

Su-Hui said nothing for a few moments to gather his thoughts. *Going south isn't an option now. The wise move is to fall back to Dixville Notch and regroup with the rest of his people.* All of his planning and preparations were going to be shelved because he had been outfoxed by the enemy. That made Su-Hui angry, and in that anger, he found the will to concentrate his attention on the details. His mind focused on what Duwe had said. *They are pulling their forces from the eastern and western borders of New Hampshire to block us going south. That leaves them weak in those areas.* "So you are saying that the border to Vermont, for example, is only lightly defended?"

Duwe nodded. "That I can confirm."

"I need a map," he said. Duwe got up for a moment, walked over to another guardsman, and came back with an old printed road atlas that was already opened to the state of New Hampshire. He handed it to Su-Hui who began to study it.

"What are you thinking?" the Lieutenant asked as his concentration fixated on the map.

"From what you have told me, going south will lead to death or capture. If we fall back, they will know that somehow we figured out what they were planning. That will put your spies in their ranks at risk.

The enemy will know they have been compromised. Retreat could cause them to escalate their search for moles.

"They believe they are working with good intelligence information from a traitor. What if that information is *mostly* correct? What if we attack a different target entirely?"

Duwe leaned back and crossed his arms in thought. "Tell me, Mr. Zhou," he said slowly. "What are you thinking?" Even Corporal Abernathy had to lean in to hear what he was saying.

Su-Hui looked around and lowered his voice more. "Where is the New York National Guard headquartered?"

"Outside of Albany, Latham, New York," he said pointing at the map.

"And they have sent most of their forces to the south, to snare us?"

A crack of a grin appeared on the Lieutenant's face. "You're thinking of heading west, not south."

Su-Hui traced his fingers along a string of curving backroads to Vermont. "We cross into Vermont. They aren't expecting us there. We punch across Vermont and into New York. We attack headquarters there. It is the same basic concept, but a different target." The more he spoke, the more he liked the idea.

"Once you start shooting and word gets out, they will scramble to get to you," Duwe cautioned.

Corporal Abernathy stabbed his long finger at the map. "Yes sir, but there are not a lot of big roads running east and west in that part of the state. It will take them time to mount up, and if they do come, it is likely to be a hell of a traffic jam when they do get moving."

Duwe nodded. "We may be able to help with that jam. Some felled trees in the right spots can cork the bottle fairly easily." He paused, then looked Su-Hui right in the eyes, locking gazes. "Shit, it might just work."

"We will need plans for their base, and quickly."

"We may have something to help you. We did a lot of joint exercises before the Fall. Some of my people may have been on the bases. I can send them along as guides."

"Excellent."

"There is a downside," Duwe cautioned. "The folks that told them we were heading into Massachusetts are going to get the shit beat out of them. It will look like they deliberately mislead the army to the south. You may be sentencing those men to their death."

Su-Hui crossed his own arms, mirroring the Lieutenant. "They were willing to send us to our deaths in a trap. Treason comes with an invoice that is always due." If it was indeed Herb who had betrayed them, Su-Hui was more than willing to lay that bill at the traitor's feet.

Princeton, Illinois

The confusion at the gate of the repair and refit yard in Princeton was minor at best. Yes, the Illinois National Guard had no record that Captain Mercury was coming with a small convoy of vehicles for repair. Judy won over the guard with a mix of bravado and bluff that she was getting used to and starting to enjoy. "Do we look like the enemy? Would I have driven here all night long if I didn't have orders to come here?" The private who was a sentry at the gate seemed more than convinced and waved her little raiding party in.

Their journey to Princeton had been without any real incident. There were remarkably few checkpoints and with the two that she passed, she had them confirm her passage with the bridge she had come across, essentially getting two of the enemies to assist her. Understanding the military all too well, she savored the situation using her previous bluffs to confirm her latest ones. *What was that old saying? "The definition of Army is a perpetual bureaucracy with occasional moments of firepower."*

The depot was a series of commandeered warehouses and a sprawling field of tents. There were a number of tanks, armored fighting vehicles, and a sea of Humvees. Some were so badly damaged it was clear they were keeping them around for parts. Others showed makeshift repairs while the majority were just battered and blasted hulks. The snow had been lighter in Princeton; there were only a few inches on the ground, and its covering of some of the damaged vehicles spoke as to how long they had been sitting there. The sheer number of vehicles told her a story all on their own. *Intelligence was right. This is their central repair facility.*

She got down and squeezed her shoulder mic, "Comms check," she whispered, then pulled the top of her coat tighter against the cold Illinois winter air.

"Acknowledged, Grab Ass Actual," came the voice of Lieutenant

Short, commander of one of the Abrams tanks. Judy held her grin at hearing the code name of the operation applied to her comms tag.

"On my order, you will all begin debarkation," she whispered as she rounded the front of the truck cab.

A Second Lieutenant headed over toward her. "Captain, what is all of this?" He gestured to her caravan.

"We're here to drop off," she said calmly. "Fresh out of Davenport."

A number of enlisted personnel began to come out of the nearby tents and approach the trucks. These are repair personnel, trained army mechanics. *If they start poking around, they are going to notice pretty quick that our battle damage is just cosmetic.* Squeezing the *speak* button on her shoulder, she whispered: "All troops, stand by for debarking."

The Lieutenant got close to her. "I wasn't expecting any of this sir," he told Judy coolly.

"What can I say? We were trapped behind the lines for a few days." Out of the corner of her eye, Judy saw some of the depot personnel starting to unhitch the tarps that covered her ruse. "This is Grab Ass Actual, deploy," she said in a firm tone. Her words drew a fast puzzled expression on the Lieutenant who cocked his head to the side.

A rumble of vehicles suddenly started up. The depot teams backed off, startled by the sudden throb of diesel and turbine engines coming to life. The tarps flew back as her command began to uncover them. The Lieutenant, still somewhat dazed, turned in disbelief. "You brought your own crews? What in the Sam-Hell is going on?"

The ramps on two of the flatbeds dropped with a metallic bang as the first Humvees backed off, their gunners mounting the machine guns and clearing the weapons for action. Almost immediately, one of the Abrams tanks rumbled off of a flatbed with its turret turning.

Panic came to the Lieutenant that had come out to meet her. It was understandable to her; chaos had come to roost on his little corner of the civil war. As a Bradley came down, he reeled on her. "What is the meaning of this?"

Judy drew her sidearm with a swift move and aimed it at him in a perfect stance. "You are our prisoners. Order your personnel to stand down and no one will get hurt."

His eyes fixated on the gun more than her words. His mouth hung open, unable to form cohesive words. "I—I … " was all he could manage to stammer.

A shot rang out, a single crack of gunfire from one of the warehouses, and a metallic ping of a ricochet off of armor. *Shit!* She ducked down slightly, as did the Lieutenant. Her people had rules of engagement. If they were fired on, they did not have to wait for her command to return fire. The long period of time cramped in the vehicles had been like coiling a tight spring with her people. Now that spring released its energy. Two of the Humvees opened up with their machine guns, blasting the door of the warehouse where the shot had come from. The short, controlled bursts ripped the thin door apart, and flickers of ricocheted shots danced inside. Another one of her team's Bradleys rolled off a truck, turning its turret on the warehouse.

More gunfire came, this time from a tent. One shot hit the cab next to her as she crouched, making the battle suddenly very personal.

"Form a perimeter," she barked into her mic as the Lieutenant started to reach down for his sidearm. She still held the pistol on him with one free hand, but he was hoping to take advantage of her giving orders and the chaos of an erupting gunfight to get the drop on her. *Damn!* She squeezed the trigger slowly and the gun bucked in her hand. A spray of crimson from the left knee of her target dropped him quickly. Thoughts of grabbing his pistol evaporated as he wailed in agony, both hands attempting to stem the bleeding from what was left of his knee.

A Bradley fired its 25 mm M242 Bushmaster chain gun, a burst of three rapid bangs, tearing into the tents where the shots came from. The high explosive rounds devoured the olive green tents in balls of orange and red flames. The snow on them went flying in every direction. More machine guns tore into the warehouses as the Humvees began to roar away, moving to encircle the facility.

Judy moved up to the fallen Lieutenant. "Order you men to surrender," she snarled at him, reaching down and taking control of his pistol.

He hissed at her, not out of anger but out of agony. His eyes were wide, and his face was now a bright crimson. Both his wound and breath created small puffs of moist heat in the cold air. Gritting his teeth, he seemed to slowly gain control of his pain. "Fine!" he said, exhaling hard. "Hold your fire Goddamn it! Cease fire! Stand down! … That's a fucking order!" His voice was just loud enough to carry over the shots.

Judy's own people were on the move, surrounding the structures, training their weapons and preparing to eliminate any resistance. She was not there to rack up a body count; she was there to sow chaos in Illinois, to draw the enemy out of Iowa. Kneeling next to the man she had shot, she hit her mic again. "Hold your fire," she said as one machine gun sent another spray of bullets into the warehouse, stitching a line of holes horizontally on the metallic siding, easily punching in. It stopped and for a strange moment, there were no shots. Only the rumble of the vehicles deploying.

"Order them out here, hands in the air," she demanded.

"Come out," he called, his voice wavering just a bit as blood oozed between his fingers. "Hands up. That's an order."

Through the blasted warehouse door, a lone private emerged, wearing coveralls caked in oil and grease stains. He came out with a look of fear on his face, followed by another figure—this one a black female. From the tents a line of Illinois troops came out, some fifty in all. Her personnel moved over and began to assemble them in front of the warehouse, patting them down for weapons.

"I need a medic at my position," she said into her mic. Her tiny task force had brought two medics with them, one of whom sprinted over to her to help the wounded Lieutenant. She stood and felt her body tense as she looked out at the surrendering enemy. "Get inside, cut off their communications," she ordered Sergeant Hart who had moved up alongside her. "I want these buildings checked for anyone hiding." Hart immediately ordered a squad into each of the structures as a few more enemy emerged, hands in the hair. Every face she saw was angry, confused or red from embarrassment or shame. That was something she understood. *If the roles were different, I'd be pissed off or humiliated too.*

Smoke rolled from the tents as small fires broke out where the Bradley had blasted. She saw one of the Abrams race behind the warehouses, keeping its turret tight on the structures themselves. In that moment, she let out a long sigh of relief.

Two hours later ...

As the convoy started to pull out, explosions from the fires her raiders had set in the structure threw bits of the blasted warehouses in every direction. The small munitions dump went up next with a chest-thumping explosion. Smoke, sick, gray and twisting, rose in the still winter air. No doubt it would be seen for miles, which was fine by her. *I hope the locals show up. I hope they realize that they are no longer safe.*

The prisoners had been loaded into two trucks taken from the depot. She had considered turning them loose, but these were the enemies—despite the fact that they wore the same uniform she did. *This will get the attention of the National Guard. They will realize that we are in their rear area causing trouble, taking prisoners, destroying their ability to keep fighting. They will have to come for us.*

She had ordered the vehicles stripped of their Illinois National Guard markings. The symbol of the Oklahoma National Guard replaced it. The troops morale seemed to shoot up with that one gesture.

As Judy looked down the road, the convoy turned on a two-lane road heading south. *They will start looking for us, sending out their police. That would be laughable ... police against tanks.* Smiling, she knew the next targets were going to be far more complicated. As Sergeant Hart drove on, she leaned against the passenger door and allowed herself a few much needed hours of sleep.

Roanoke Rapids, North Carolina

The artillery bursts were slow, almost methodical from what Trip Reager could see. He had pulled back his forces to their second line of defense along the North Carolina, Virginia border. The trenches and field fortifications were good, and he made sure that the advancing enemy troops were under a rain of artillery and mortar fire. The ground was churned up, pock-marked with craters. The air stung from expended ammunition and diesel and gas exhaust fumes. There was a hint of pine in the air, not from an air freshener, but from blasted trees whose smoking remains left entrails of white twisting in the air. Voices calling out from their positions were muffled, drowned out by the occasional explosion.

They had one more line of defense if they needed it, on the southern bank of Rapid Roanoke Lake and the Roanoke River, which ran mostly west to east. It would mean yielding the town, but the river and lake were formidable against armored vehicles. It had worked well at Stone

Mountain, and there was no reason for him not to use them for defense on this side of the front.

If this is a diversion, it's a damned convincing one. For a full day and a half, the Newmerican forces were wading into his defensive positions. Both sides unleashed limited air strikes, which added a new tempo to the music of the battle—deep bass explosions that shook pine needles off of trees for miles and devoured armored vehicles, leaving only flames and ugly black mushroom clouds to mark their graves.

Trip Reager's mind went to other fronts where operations were underway. Captain Mercury's raid had started—he had gotten word that she was at least behind the enemy lines thanks to a tactical withdrawal. That didn't mean she wasn't a POW already. *If she manages to not get caught, she'll raise hell in Illinois, that's for sure.* St. Louis was still a sore spot, a Newmerican autonomous zone. Trip knew the enemy was relatively contained in the city, much like Kansas City—but they still represented objectives he had to take.

The Defiance in New Hampshire was doing a great job of tying down a lot of New England troops hunting for the resistance fighters. Every day there were little attacks on the enemy, a casualty here and there. From what he was gathering from his intelligence people, the attacks were more than frustrating for the enemy. There was a risk of overplaying their hand, but the strong-willed people of New Hampshire and their Sons of Liberty allies was doing a great job of infuriating and embarrassing the enemy. *Sooner or later the enemy is going to realize that fighting there is a lost cause.*

Texas was a stalemate … for now. Trip had forces along the Republic's southern border, strong checkpoints. So far the rebellious Texans were staying on their side of the line. It was just a matter of time before someone made a mistake or caused an incident. That was something he wanted to avoid at all costs … these were Texans after all, his kin. *I hope Jack Desmond's people can work their magic soon. The last thing I need right now is a new front in this war.* With that thought, he turned his mind back to the rumble of artillery in the distance.

So far, he had been making the Newmericans pay for every bit of ground that they had taken. Their infantry had been bold in their initial assault, assuming that the artillery had suppressed his forces. They learned that artillery alone does not win battles. Machine guns and well-placed mortar rounds turned an assault into a bloody smear on the brown and dull green winter grasses of North Carolina. To their credit, the enemy rallied and pushed again in another sector. They were gaining yards of ground, but at the cost of soldier's lives. He watched from a position behind a thin line of short pines which masked the command Bradley fighting vehicle at his side.

Trip knew he was taking a risk. He had forces poised to respond to assist him, as well as divert to Knoxville if the enemy was heading west into Tennessee. The longer he waited to deploy those forces, the less likely they would be in position in time. It was like a mathematical computation program that was constantly running in his mind. Every passing minute, he calculated the risks of the Newmericans throwing everything right at him. If he made the wrong decision, if he sent his forces to the wrong front at the wrong time, everything would be ruined, and the chance for victory would diminish.

He had learned in Iraq, Afghanistan, and more recently in Georgia, that patience was a key component of any military operation. Inexperienced officers leapt too soon. He had been in their shoes before and had made the same mistakes. In his youth his father had always told him to, "Stop, pause, think things over before you do something stupid." At the time he had written off those words of advice as simply foolhardy. Being in battles on the other side of the world had taught him how smart his father had been. Unfortunately, by the time he had learned that lesson, and had come home, his father had died. *Well Dad, I'm listening to you right now, whether you know it or not.*

He pulled the customized side hatch on the Bradley open, ducked down and entered, closing it tight behind him. The warmth hit his face first, like a welcome kiss. He unzipped his heavy winter coat and moved over near his intelligence officer. It was tempting to ask, "Have you heard anything?" but he knew Paul Harnessy too well to nag him. *If he knows something, I would already know it.*

"They are gaining ground to our east," his tactical officer, Lieutenant Phipps, said from her workstation. "The enemy has taken Como and is on the outskirts of Murfreesboro right now. Major Platt is holding the city, but is being pressed hard."

Trip digested the information and took a glance at the map to confirm his thinking. "Send two of our reserve armored platoons over to Murfreesboro under Platt's command." *They are certainly pressing us hard if this is a diversion.* Doubt crept into his thinking, but Trip managed to keep it at bay. "Send in some ground air support as well; see if the Air Force can convince them to slow their advance." Phipps acknowledged the orders and began to divert resources.

Trip felt his jaw lock and tense as he looked around the tight confines of his mobile headquarters. Long minutes went by as the rumble of the artillery exchange continued not far from where they were hidden.

Slowly, deliberately, Captain Harnessy turned to him. "General. I just got a message in from our Rangers in Danville."

"Go on."

"A large convoy, at least three brigades in strength, heading west. It sounds like it's the bulk of their armored force."

Bingo! "Captain Phipps, belay that order. Tell Major Platt he needs to hold his ground, and we will be providing relief to him soon." She immediately began to countermand her previous orders without question.

"You were right sir," Harnessy said.

"*We* were right," he corrected. "Get word to Colonel Ricketts, and let him know exactly where the enemy is and that they are coming his way. Tell him to haul ass and get our mobile response units to Knoxville. Tell him … he paused and thought of one of his favorite films, *The Fellowship of the Ring*: 'None shall pass.'" Just saying it made him crack a smile, one that his intelligence officer flashed back in the form of a full-on grin.

Harnessy relayed the orders to the communications officer as Trip settled in a small seat along the armored hull of the Bradley. *So General Rinehart, you're making a run for Nashville as I anticipated. That gateway isn't going to be a cake walk for you. And now that I know what we are facing is just a diversion, you're going to get a little surprise of your own.*

CHAPTER 16

*"We never lower the bar. We adjust the
minimums to elevate everyone."*

Vernon, The Republic of Texas

Vernon was not a large town, but it was the heart of Wilbarger County, now part of the self-proclaimed Republic of Texas. The breeze was chilly, but dry, the kind that stung at his nostrils. Kiff thought there was a quaintness about the town. It had a small-town vibe, though on the outskirts there were a number of newer buildings and shopping centers. When they drove through the heart of the town, with Caylee at the wheel, he found himself looking at the locals. To Kiff, it felt as if nothing had really changed other than the flag in front of the courthouse. Gone was the red, white and blue with the big white star, the state flag. It had been replaced by a blue flag with a white star and Texas was spelled out between each point of the star. Seeing it was a less-than-subtle reminder that they were in a foreign country.

Caylee was quiet as they drove through town, but Kiff saw that she was looking everywhere, soaking in every detail. She was not much of a conversationalist. God knows he had tried. At times she seemed cold and distant, but to him that seemed almost a façade. Kiff understood far too well. In IT he knew a lot his best people were socially distant because they were so intensely focused on the tasks at hand. He wasn't that way; he burned off his intensity with idle chatter, but he understood that kind of commitment to duty. *She's a professional, an expert in her field. I need to let her do her job so that I can do mine.*

They drove by the Trans-Tex headquarters, and he was impressed with the show of force the fledgling Republic had mustered. Sandbags marked anti-aircraft missile launchers at the perimeter. Olive drab tents and white RVs filled the parking lot. A lot of people were wearing fatigues, a hodge-podge of patterns. *It's like someone raided the discount bin at the Army Surplus store.* Everyone carried guns. Technicals, trucks armed with machine guns, were visible. Some had tubes that looked ominously like missile launchers to Kiff. *They are prepared for war.*

As they drove around the perimeter, Kiff made some mental notes of his own. The Trans-Tex building was where his target computer was likely to be. He had studied the layout of the structure, but seeing it in real life was something else. From what he could see as they drove by, it had limited points of access. The employee parking lot had been taken over, and it appeared that temporary parking had been set up in a nearby field. The big truck bays looming over the massive warehouse had potential for access, but he also saw patrols of armed personnel near them.

Caylee said nothing as they drove by, cruising slowly on the roadway that snaked along the northern side of the building. The southern side was a long, clear, sloping grassland lining the banks of a wide creek. Her eyes were narrowed, and he could see that she was noting things he was overlooking. Eventually she made her way to the Hampton Inn on the other side of Vernon. There she checked them in and the two of them unpacked their gear from the truck.

Once the door closed, Caylee sat on the bed, then looked at him. "What did you see?"

"An army base," he said. "Lots of gear they shouldn't have been able to purchase … expensive stuff."

"What about the building?"

He paused momentarily, realizing that she was testing his observation skills. "The south is more open, near the truck bays, but there's no cover. We're toast if we come in from that direction and someone there has night vision gear. If they thought anyone was going to be sneaking in, they'd expect it there."

"Go on."

Am I getting this right? "Going in the front door means walking through that armed camp. No sane person would try that, so maybe that's the way to go." Kiff paused, waiting for a response.

For a full minute, Caylee said nothing; then she spoke. "You're not far off. These good old boys are clearly expecting something. They are probably afraid of a Special Forces raid. Chances are, at night, those Technicals are patrolling with night vision gear, which makes a covert approach more difficult."

"So how do we get in?"

"What would be the last thing they would expect?"

"Us walking right in?" he finally asked.

"Pretty much. The key to an op like this is to be casual and not draw a lot of attention to yourself. If you look like you are trying to break in and you get caught, you are toast. The key is that we need to get in because we belong there."

"So what do you propose?"

"They have to have a security system," she said, leaning slightly forward on the edge of the bed as she spoke, talking more to herself than to Kiff for a moment. "We need a reason to be there. We need authorization from someone in the building so that we walk right in the front door and are shown our way inside. Once we are inside, we can scout out everything we need to, then come back and do the penetration. Their security is all focused outward right now, looking for external threats. If we can get inside, chances are pretty good we can do what we need to, and walk right out the front doors."

Kiff nodded because it made sense and it seemed far less risky. "Let me guess; you need me to sneak into their security system to get us permission."

She raised her eyes back to him and nodded. "Yes. We'll need an excuse to be there, something that won't attract a lot of attention."

"It should be doable. I need your help though. Building and internal security software is usually on a local net, something that I need access to but something that is also not Internet accessible. That building has a lot of structural steel. If their IT guys are worth their salt, they have trimmed the range of the Wi-Fi signals so they probably just transmit a dozen or so yards into the parking area, at best. I need to get access to their Wi-Fi, find their security system, and give us the right credentials."

"So how do we do that?" Caylee asked.

Kiff began to rummage in his bag, pulling out a small, white oval device with two, tiny, thick antennae sticking out the back. "I brought this in my bag of fun. It's a battery-operated signal booster—hard core shit. If we can get this in range of the Wi-Fi signal, it will boost it up to a mile range—more than enough for me to do my penetration. The last time I sneaked inside their system through the net, I left a few little doors open for future visits, more than enough for me to find their security system."

Caylee took the device from him. "It's small, and you need it close to the building."

"The closer the better."

"Okay," she said calmly. "But before we do that, we need to hit that Whataburger® down the street."

Her words surprised him. It wasn't that he wasn't hungry himself; he was; but it just didn't seem like a priority, and from the little he knew Caylee, he didn't want to raise his hunger with her. *I'll eat when she eats. The last thing I want is for her to think I'm a wimp.* "Really, I'm surprised."

"I'm starved," she admitted. "Besides, the bags will be helpful."

"I don't get it," he confessed.

Caylee smiled and to him that grin seemed to say, "You have to trust me."

Two hours later ...

From their parked truck, just outside of the security perimeter, Kiff watched Caylee carrying six bags stuffed with hamburgers and fries over to the soldiers in the parking lot. She had purchased them after they had eaten, catching Kiff off guard. "We're going to feed them?" he had asked.

"You need me in close. This gets me in close," she had replied.

Sure enough, he watched from the passenger seat of the truck and just hoisting the bags was like having some sort of pass. Troops fell in around her as she handed out burgers and milled around the green-clad forces. Even from this distance, Caylee looked as if she was having fun, laughing with the men there who devoured what she had carried in.

After nearly a half an hour of being there, he saw her gather up the bags and refuse, and walk them up to a trash container right outside the main door, stuffing them deep down. Suddenly, he was able to pick up the signal of Trans-Tex's Wi-Fi . *Holy shitballs! She did it!*

He tuned out Caylee entirely; now things were in his world. His fingers flew across the laptop keyboard as he started his search for the security system. In the background he loaded up a penetration routine, something to bypass their security.

She joined him about two hours later, having loitered with the security detail in the parking lot. As she entered the truck, he held his hand up—a gesture for her to remain quiet. He intently glared at the screen, spinning the trackball he brought with the moves of an artisan crafting a vase or bowl on a potter's wheel. It took another thirty minutes, but he finally finished, powering down.

"You got in, I take it?" Caylee asked.

He nodded rapidly. "We are set up as contractors. There's a manager that's on leave, so I put us in retroactively; said that he asked us to come in and work on a database they have. He's out for another two weeks, so we should be able to walk right in."

"Excellent work," she said. "You lived up to your reputation. Mr. Desmond was right about your skill set."

"You too," he said. "I never would have thought about hiding the booster in one of the bags and putting it in the trash. How do you do something like that? I mean at any point they could have caught you and if they did, well, you know," he dragged his finger across his throat.

She didn't blush; then again, he didn't think she would. Instead Caylee smiled. "It is all about believing in yourself. If you believe in yourself, believe you are the person you are pretending to be, then it works. In my field of work, self-doubt and hesitation can get you killed faster than a bad decision."

"Well for the next few days, we have permission to be in the headquarters. We need to find our target PC, and I will need some alone time with it."

"We'll make it happen," she said calmly. "There's bound to be a wrinkle or two, but we can pull this off if we trust in ourselves."

"And each other," he added.

Caylee gave him a single nod. "That goes without saying."

Charlottesville, Virginia

It had taken a little work for David Steele to get the name of one of the student leaders, Bailey Treater. She always wore a large, black mask that obscured most of her facial features. She was an exchange student from South Korea, was short, but had a piercing voice when she had a megaphone in her hand.

David's reason for targeting her was simple. After the bombing on one of Charlottesville's busy streets, Bailey had led the protest rally. She had said that the campus community was being targeted by Nazis, dangerous domestic terrorists. With full passion in her voice, she called for students to turn each other in if they suspected one of them had involvement with the attacks. Bailey had become the voice of student anger and fear.

David and his father had talked after they had listened to the fiery oration on campus that she had led. His father had summed it up succinctly. "It's funny that the people that support the totalitarian regime are the ones calling us 'Nazis.'" David was used to it. The last five years of his life had been about bombastic speeches and violent protests. It had reached the point with him that the words they spoke no longer mattered. All they had was loudness and hate.

As he walked some forty yards behind her on campus, he knew she would be a difficult target. She lived in a dorm, and with the fears spiking at UVA, more cameras were being installed everywhere. From what he had seen of her, she was always in public, always with several other people. While he had few qualms about killing her friends, it simply made it more difficult to get near her to do the job.

His trailing her had shown only a few places where she might be caught alone. One was when she jogged on campus. While there were other students nearby, a shot from his mobile sniper's nest in the trunk of the car might be able to take her down. The problem was she was literally a running target. There was a chance, given ranges and her speed, that he might miss. With security increased, taking a second shot might be risky.

The other opportunity he had spotted with her was that she went alone to the library to study. Bailey apparently liked dark little private nooks in the library. He was contemplating shooting her with a handgun there, up close and personal, but the library posed its own set of challenges.

Cameras captured who went in and left, which meant using a disguise to either enter, leave, or both. Then there was the gunshot itself. A lifetime of television and video games had led him to believe that silencers could muffle a gunshot indoors to nothing more than a *puff!* sound. His father had purchased a suppressor, and they had tried it and at best, the suppressor cut the sound down, but it was still loud, too loud. David knew that the moment he pulled the trigger, others in the building were bound to hear.

His father had suggested poison and was working on a way to get it and deliver it that would be less explosive than gunfire in a campus building. In the meantime, he followed her closely, hoping that some other opportunity might present itself.

As the sky began to unleash a light, misting rain, David decided to break off his pursuit. He was tired ... the nights of no sleep tore at him. He hadn't slept an entire night in weeks. In the middle of the night, he would jerk himself awake, usually in a hot sweat. There were nightmares about his sister, or the bomb going off ... a cavalcade of mental carnage that tore into his attempts at slumber.

His father showed the fatigue as well, but never talked about it. Dark bags of skin hung under his dad's eyes and he seemed to be losing weight. Grayson Steele never wavered though, never complained, and David took that as an example. Neither spoke about their nightmares; they simply remained focused on the job at hand.

He walked back to the small apartment they had rented off campus. He unlocked the door and entered, closing it behind him. His father sat at the tiny table, with several bottles arrayed in an arc before him. *It looks like he's doing some sort of chemistry experiment.*

"How are you?" his father asked, looking up from the small bowl that he was hovering over with an eyedropper.

"Fine," David said. For a moment, he paused. *Am I fine?*

"What about your little friend?"

"Bailey isn't giving me much to work with," he replied, setting down his backpack. "I think the library is going to be our best chance."

"And a risky one at that," his father added. "The good news is that I think I have been able to mix up a fast-acting toxin."

David walked over and looked at the liquid his father had in the small bowl. "How did you do that?"

"We live in a world filled with irony, David. The TRC is big into blocking every bit of conservative content, but when it comes to lethal stuff, there are YouTube videos out there and full recipes for this kind of stuff." He paused and stood up, stretching slightly ... an indication of how long he had been sitting there.

"Will it work?"

His father nodded in response. "We'll need to buy a rat and test it, but it should work. The trick is in the dosage. You have to inject it and from what I have been able to piece together, you need a full syringe of this stuff to do the job."

"Bailey's not likely to simply sit there and let me shoot her up," David said.

"You said she always has a big bottle of water she brings with her. When she goes to the bathroom, you drop a few of these in," he said picking up a paper plate with a handful of pills.

"What is it?"

"Animal tranquilizers ... courtesy of Tractor Supply. If these will put a horse to sleep, it will work on her too. When she dozes off, you inject her, change your appearance, and leave."

David was impressed. There were still a multitude of risks in play. Someone might see him; she might realize she is tired and try to leave on her own, and then there were the cameras.

Suddenly, there was a knock at the door.

Both of the Steele men looked at each other. Grayson took a towel and draped it over his work on the table. David moved over to the closet and closed it so that their weapons would not be seen. Slowly, Grayson walked up to the door and cracked it open.

"Mr. Steele. I'm sure you remember me," a deep voice said from the other side. His father opened the door and standing there, in a long, blue trench coat, was a man with salt-and-pepper hair and a square jaw. David knew instantly it was a policeman, even before his eyes saw the 'NSF,' logo and motto stitched on the breast of the raincoat, "Tutor of Licentia."

His heart began to run like a race car motor inside of his chest. "Detective Schrank," his father said, opening the door wider. "To what do I owe this visit?"

The man was the same height as his father, but he looked bigger in his uniform trench coat. His face was stern and rigid. "We need to talk …" he said, stepping into the apartment.

David felt his face get red. *Shit! They found out what we've been doing!*

Vernon, The Republic of Texas

Kiff and Caylee had walked into the lobby of the Trans-Tex building, shown their fake IDs, and had been given building passes by the security team—proof that his penetration of their security system had worked. They were told where to go and simply found two empty cubicles and set up. While Kiff worked on his laptop, she logged in with the account information he had given her and began to check for information about Salem Marshall's office security.

Usually she had little use for cyber experts other than as subject matter experts. She had some basic hacking skill of her own. As an operative, she carried flash drives that could help here with local system penetration. There was always a little distrust when it came to computer specialists. They possessed knowledge that she didn't have, and there were times when her life depended on it. Most of the time, it was her life that was on the line in the field during an op, while the experts sat in their cubicles far from the action, safe and sound. With no real skin in the game, they risked nothing if things went wrong

Kiff, however, was here, with her, in the field. *If he drops the ball, we are both toast.* There was something oddly pleasing about that. It also increased her appreciation of Jack Desmond, that he would pick people good enough to buffalo their way into a rebel state the way that Kiff did. Kiff wanted to learn too; he listened and did what he was told. Most geeks she had worked with had a rebellious streak when it came to simply following orders. *He's clearly been through some shit in his life to get him to this stage.*

A few Trans-Tex workers came by, introduced themselves, and asked what they were working on. Caylee wove a story about them doing an audit. "I wish I could tell you more than that, but you know how these things are." They seemed friendly enough and smart enough not to press further.

In her mind she had already calculated an emergency egress from where they sat, in case their true intentions were discovered. She knew the fire stairs were the best option if they got caught. She had brought a handgun in pieces in case they did a check of her briefcase on the way in. Assembling it in her lap took only a few minutes, nothing that would look conspicuous to anyone walking by. The two magazines she smuggled in would limit how much shooting she did, so whatever she aimed at had to be dropped, and fast.

In the cubicle next to her, Kiff was deep in concentration. Out of his backpack, he pulled a red Twizzler and chewed on the end of it while he worked. He was typing fast and furious, using a trackball to scroll and click. She saw his eyes darting quickly, reading and processing things he saw on his screen. She admired his skill set and found herself feeling a bit jealous. *I have relied on people like him on ops. I could be a lot more effective if I had those skills too.*

Hours went by, and she pulled out an energy bar which would substitute for lunch. Kiff seemed immune to the passage of time. The only pausing he did was to pull another Twizzler out of his bag. It was around 3:00 p.m. when he finally paused, stretched in his chair, and looked up at her.

"I found the target," he said in a low voice. "Corner office, southwest side."

Caylee moved to his cubicle and leaned in. "What kind of security does he have?"

"It looks like our target isn't in today, which will help. His office has a mag-bolt door lock," Kiff said just above a whisper. "I've got that overridden—all we have to do is enter the code 666 on the keypad. I've written a routine that will put the security cameras in a loop showing the same image of an empty office once I pull the trigger on them. I've got the same thing running for everything on this floor, so to anyone looking down on us, it will look like we are sitting in Cubeville working on our laptops … exactly what they would expect to see. That's the good news. The bad news, … he's got a laser floor grid system in place. Just opening the door will trigger it."

"I take it you can't disable it?"

Kiff shook his head. "They're good. It's a standalone system. If I cut the power, it has a battery backup. While it's tied to a security alarm, I'm not able to use that link to get in and shut the system off. I found the install plans on the security department's server. It's on the floor only."

Caylee said nothing for a second. She had come up against similar systems in the past and beaten them. "Get me the make and model," she said coolly. "I have some techniques we might be able to leverage from the NSF. Also, get me the building specs for the walls of Mr. Marshall's office. I need to know if I can get access from the adjoining space."

Kiff nodded. "It will take a few."

"We have time," she said as she returned to her cubicle.

Charlottesville, Virginia

As Detective Schrank stepped into their apartment, David immediately wanted a weapon. It was one of their worst fears, the NSF showing up. He eyed the closet where their guns were and realized that it was a good three or four steps to get there. If he bolted for it, the detective would be able to easily draw and shoot him.

He glanced at his father who held his hands out flat and low, a signal to remain calm. "Detective Schrank," was all that Grayson said as the door closed behind the detective. *He's brave; that's for sure ... coming in with both of us here.*

"Gentlemen, please relax," Schrank said. "If I was coming here to arrest you, I would have come with a SWAT team."

"Then why are you here?" David's father asked.

Schrank unbuttoned his coat and took it off, folding it over his left arm. He walked over to the small dining table, pulled out a chair, and sat down just inches from the poison his father had been mixing. David's heart still raced with fear as beads of sweat formed on his forehead. "You both have been causing quite a stir. I thought this might be a good time for me to come and offer some friendly advice."

"I don't know what you are talking about," Grayson said, sounding somewhat less than convincing.

Schrank tipped his head slightly to the left, as if to say, "You're kidding, right? It didn't take much for me to piece it together really. You had a grudge against the Grays, and they die in a mysterious fire and explosion. It took some work finding the bomb fragments in the rubble and one of the melted jerry cans used to douse the outside of the building—but we found them."

The detective leaned back in his seat slightly, completely relaxed. "I figured you had gotten your revenge. It was better justice than the system would ever provide you. Then came the other killings and the bombing. If the students could piece it together, how long do you think it would take us to do the same?"

He paused for a moment, then continued. "Rhetorical question: I got myself put in charge of the task force looking into the killings. I had my suspicions that you might be involved—more gut instinct than anything else. I learned you had this apartment. I followed David for a few days … I saw him stalking someone."

"So you're here to try to get us to turn ourselves in?" David asked, a hint of rage in his voice. "Because that's not going to happen."

Schrank turned to him and shook his head. "I wouldn't put myself at risk like that, David. I came here to talk, nothing more, nothing less."

"I'm confused," his father said. "If you think we had something to do with all of this, why not arrest us?"

"Do you remember what I told you the day you found all of those bodies Mr. Steele?" the detective asked. "I told you I had a little girl of my own."

David's mind danced from one possibility to another. *Is he toying with us? Is he helping us? Why just show up this way? Is this some sort of trick to get us to confess?* His distrust of the NSF ran deep, and with good reason. They were the legal strong arm of the Newmerican government. His eyes shot over to his father who seemed to relax slightly at Schrank's words. "So you're here to—" Grayson said slowly.

"Offer you some advice," the detective replied. "Father to father. Parent to child."

"Go on."

"You've attracted more attention than you realize. Word of your actions has made its way into the media. We've had some copycat activity in other states. We are being pressured to bring someone, anyone, in and charge them with these crimes. I have been able to keep the two of you off the other agent's radar until now, but it is a matter of time before someone pieces it together. When that happens you two will be arrested, paraded out for a very public and humiliating trial—probably one of those damned tribunals—then executed for your crimes."

There was an ominous tone to what the detective said. David's tension level didn't drop. He and his father had discussed many times what would happen if they were caught, and now he was getting it confirmed. At the same time, he was pleased that others were out there doing the same thing he and his father were. *Finally, people are pushing back against what is going on in these colleges!* "So what do you expect us to do?"

"Simply put, move on."

David's father stepped forward. "You want us to stop?"

"I didn't say that. If you remain here, others in the NSF will narrow its focus and find you. It's just a matter of time. You need to get out of town, out of my jurisdiction. If you move on to another jurisdiction to continue your little crusade, it will take months for the NSF to piece together that they might be connected. There's a lot of bureaucracy in play, rivalry between jurisdictions. All of that plays into your favor. Bottom line—the time has come for you to leave this school."

He's not telling us to stop. He's warning us. "I don't understand," David said. "Why are you helping us?"

Schrank looked at him and in the man's chiseled face, he saw the look of a father responding to his own child. "Not everyone in the NSF is there because they drank the Newmerican Kool-Aid. A lot of us remained because we were cops, and we wanted to keep our families fed. I come from a long line of law enforcement. One thing I learned from my own father was that justice comes in a lot of forms. While what you are doing is wrong, what they did was far worse, and the system was never going to arrest the Grays or hold them to account—I know, I was on the inside of that investigation.

"There's more than a few of us in the ranks of the NSF. We do what's necessary to ensure that justice is done—that the scales are balanced. That's why you are getting this heads up David. This is your chance to pack up, take your little show somewhere else. You may get caught somewhere else, or you may get away with it … I can't say. I do know that if you stay here, you are going to eventually get discovered and arrested.

"And ... " he said taking a moment for a dramatic pause, "... like I said, I have a little girl of my own."

Vernon, The Republic of Texas
Four hours later ...

Security swung by every two hours, almost like clockwork. They didn't seem to pay much attention to her or Kiff. Caylee knew the glances from them all too well. "If these contractors want to work late, let them." As soon as they passed out of sight at the 7 p.m. hour, she and Kiff went to work.

Caylee opened the office next to Salem's and removed the ceiling tiles to get access to his office. She carefully pulled the tiles to access his office. The laser grid was a great security system, but its surrounding defenses made it something that could be overcome.

She used the ceiling support girder to pull herself up and slid slowly into the space above Salem's desk. As she slowly lowered herself to the desktop, some dust from the ceiling tiles drifted down, illuminating the grid on the floor in one area. Moving almost cat-like, she leaned over the side of the desk near the back, where his credenza rested. *Small moves are safe moves.* She opened the door and found the system inside, its green LED display indicating it was active.

From what she knew, shutting the system down manually required a key or a three-digit code—neither of which they had. It was tempting to try to rifle through Salem's desk for it, but that would take time they didn't have. From her belt, she pulled out a lock pick set and leaned down from the desktop to work on it.

It was a tubular cam lock, a circular one much like a cable-lock for a laptop. While they looked sophisticated, it only took her three minutes of working it in order to get it where she could turn it. The green LED went to yellow—indicating the system was disarmed.

Caylee returned the lock pick and carefully lowered her feet to the floor. In the back of her mind, she wondered if there was another alarm system in place or something that Kiff may have overlooked. Once she was confident they had not been detected, she made her way to the door and rapped on it with her knuckles. The lock purred as he entered his bypass code and slid into the office.

"Awesome," Kiff said in a low tone, moving past her to the PC on his desk. He began to plug in a cable and connect with his own laptop as if she weren't even there.

"How long do you need?"

"One hour—maybe two," he said.

"I'm going outside, just in case the guards decide to come back."

"Thanks," he said as the screen illuminated his face. "I've got this."

I hope you do ...

An hour-and-a-half later ...

Kiff emerged from the office with his backpack and a wry grin on his face. Caylee moved past him to the office and relocked the door. "I forgot it. My bad."

"Don't worry," she said, double-checking the door. "Did you get what you needed?"

"Yup. One down, one to go," he replied. "I gotta say, that was awesome!"

Caylee smiled in response, gathering up her own briefcase. "Relax Kiff. We are still in enemy territory. Just follow along with my lead. We're leaving late, so the front desk security will ask a question or two. Let's not celebrate until we are clear of this place."

"Gotcha," he said. "Can we go and get a burger? I'm famished."

Caylee nodded as they started down the hallway. Kiff was certainly one of the most unique partners she'd ever had.

CHAPTER 17

"You have a right to seek your own reparations
from businesses that have profited from your
oppression. Remember, material goods cannot
equate to the suffering you have endured."

The District

The Vice President sat down across from President Porter and put on her best friendly face. It seemed with each passing week, and the losses they had suffered, that Porter was not proving himself to be a wartime leader. The Defiance that was raging in New Hampshire was proving elusive to pin down and crush; the loss of Atlanta had been a blow. The brightest spot had been the siege of Davenport, Iowa, and even that seemed to be a seesaw battle in her eyes.

The military offensive for Nashville was starting, apparently catching the enemy unaware. Daniel assured her and his cabinet the day before that it was a knockout blow. "We'll be in Nashville in two days, three tops. We will arrest the Pretender and put an end to this uprising once and for all." It had been optimistic and somewhat exciting, but experience had taught her not to count on it too heavily. *The military seems to struggle when achieving victories, despite our input and involvement.*

If the drive on Nashville failed, she wondered how long the people would continue to support Porter. He had been visionary in organizing the liberation of nation, uniting the various ANTIFA, BLM, and student groups in a single cause, to take down the corrupt government. Organizing and leading, as it turned out, were two different things. *The time will come when the people will need to make a choice as to who should lead if and when he falters.* She was confident that she was the best candidate.

"The war is in flux," he confided in her, letting his breath out in a long-winded sigh.

"It shouldn't be. General Rinehart is putting the pressure on in New Hampshire. I was in the briefing where he said he had gotten intel of a raid in the Boston area. He's got an ambush planned, and once he springs that trap, he'll take the wind out of the damned SOL and this whole Defiance bullshit, once and for all. Granted, Davenport is a hot mess; the attack into Tennessee was going to commence soon. If all goes as planned, the Southern White House will be destroyed. Taking the American capital will bleed dry what morale they have."

"Our forces crossed the border an hour ago," President Porter said. "They are meeting stiff resistance."

"We expected them to fight. Hell, we expected them to die," she said.

Daniel squirmed in his seat, as if he were uncomfortable in it. "There's these NSF reports of resistance popping up all over the place. We've got some sort of murder spree in Virginia, going after SEs; there's been two bombings of SE centers in Michigan and Ohio—an assassination attempt on the Governor of Maryland. ... A lot of people are taking advantage of our military situation."

She ran the NSF and had the report prepared for him. "Daniel, we've known each other from the start of this. You had to expect that there would be a few malcontents out there still. You can't purge racism and hate in just five years."

He nodded, rubbing his chin in thought. She could see the red in his eyes, a hint that he either wasn't getting sleep or was drinking, or both. "I know. We've discussed it a dozen times. I just didn't expect everything to happen all at once. The world fell apart when that Pretender turned out to be alive and took the oath of office. People started to remember what America was like before we fixed all of its problems. They were nostalgic for the past. We underestimated how far some of them would go to get back to that time."

"This whole rebellion has cost me personally too," she said. "You'll remember that one of my own operatives murdered my mother and brother. Not to mention several attempts on my life."

Daniel shook his head again. "I still don't understand it. Rebecca was one of us, a hardliner. She was the person that came up with the branding for the Great Reformation. She created the TRC. I just can't figure out what turned her against everything we fought for."

He has doubts ... and they need to be squashed. "She was seduced with the power you and I have. You thought you knew Becky. She seemed innocent and harmless, but behind closed doors she could be vicious. Everything changed with her after the Pretender took the oath of office on national TV. I'm still not convinced she didn't have a part in that—I mean they cut in on a TRC broadcast. Regardless, I think that this alleged President and his people convinced her they were going to win back the nation, and she knew she would be standing trial if that happened. When people are afraid, they do irrational things ... like turning on their friends."

Her words seemed to hit Daniel's concerns, at least enough for him to lean back in his chair. "If they do win, we will face more than trials. This program we've started, eliminating our enemies, ... they will label it a war crime." His voice dropped an octave as he spoke about the activities in the Social Quarantine camps.

"We have no choice," she replied. "You know that's true. We have tried rehabilitating these people, getting them to see the errors of their ways. It comes back at us. We always made sure the camps were tough living ... they always had a high mortality rate. The new program is nothing more than accelerating a process that was already in place."

"Some of these camps are starting to turn into murder factories Alex," he replied. "You showed me the figures. Some people are starting to question what is really going on in them thanks to these raids that freed those prisoners. If the truth ever got out, we might be seen by some as mass murderers."

"We have worked with our Big Tech partners to keep those kinds of accusations to a minimum, thanks to their prudent censorship," she countered. "Yes, there are rumors about the quarantine camps being a bit more than just isolation of discontents, but we are treating them seriously. We are looking to alter the reparation points so that people will be rewarded if they turn in someone spreading such salacious rumors ... a lot of points. That will get the people working for us to identify and target the people that are potentially disloyal."

Daniel nodded with her words. "Good, I'm glad to hear that. I just worry that if we escalate the, shall I say, *removal* of dissidents in the camps now, it could paint us in a bad light. Neither of us wants that."

As he spoke she could almost smell the fear coming from him. *Before he became President, he had been so swift and decisive. It's as if there is something about his job that devours your spine. If I am ever in that seat, I swear on my mother's grave that I won't hesitate to do what is right.*

She nodded, painting a face of mock horror. "I wish it hadn't come to this. We both know that for Newmerica to reach its full potential, there were going to be sacrifices. So far, we have been the ones making those. As long as people are out there who want to turn the clock back and return to the old corrupt nation, we are going to have strife. They have started a civil war Daniel! These are not people; they are radical conservatives, enemies of the state. You know what they are capable of. I don't like it any more than you do, but the only real solution is to remove them permanently from our society. It's the only real path forward."

The words came from her mouth, but she didn't believe them all. *I do like this plan. It is something we started the night of the Liberation when we killed the opposing members of Congress. It's been a long time coming, but these sick and twisted people need to die. It's the only way we will ever have prosperity. Having dissenting voices confuses the weak-minded. It is best that they just do what we tell them to. When we are done, no one will care how we got the job completed; they will only enjoy the rewards of our great society. Truth be told, we should have started this a long time ago.*

"On top of all of this," he said, his voice returning to a more normal, conversational tone, "we have the SOL stepping up activities across the map. The Ohio Patriotic Front attacked a Cleveland City Council meeting, killing three. In Oregon, one of their cells, 'The Cowboys,' attacked a NSF station, killing six and seizing their weapons and gear. Not to mention the Order of the Bell and the Concord Minutemen's activities. The Sons of Liberty were supposed to be dead and buried, but now they are back. Worse yet, they are showing people that they can resist. We can't have that. It will only lead to more trouble."

On this point the Vice President agreed. *We have spent years showing that resistance was futile, and now it is being undone by these terror attacks.* "Daniel, I have assembled a large task force to deal with the SOL. We have NSF operatives that we are going to slide into their ranks. We will get their names, their plans, then take them down once and for all."

"When, Alex? Six months ago they were nonexistent. Now cells are popping up everywhere."

"It's happening right now," she said with a confident, assuring tone. "One by one we will identify their members and supporters; then we will show them what *true* justice is." *We'll save a few for some show trials, but we will show the dead bodies to the media as a sign of what happens to those that break faith with us.*

Daniel seemed satisfied with her words, at least for the time being. "You've always been a rock Alex. The fact that they keep trying to kill you means you are the true voice of the Reformation. We will stay the course, and hope that the military can deliver. ... They have to. We can't afford to keep losing to these people."

She nodded. "Daniel, if you think it will help, I can go down there— meet with General Rinehart ... give him a little focus." She was looking forward to such a chance. Controlling the media and the national police force made her unstoppable. Daniel, by law, controlled the military, but one thing she had learned was that the law was flexible and permeable. *If I can establish myself as a strong liaison with the military, I will have almost complete control of the government.*

"That's not a bad idea," he said. "Why don't you head down to Virginia and see if you can impress on him the full weight of what this fight means."

"I'd be honored," she said. *My mother would be so proud of me ...*

Springfield, Illinois

Captain Judy Mercury looked out from the Humvee she rode in to the Illinois National Guard Headquarters. Situated in an old suburb of Springfield, it was a number of two story brick buildings, surrounded by a tall, black, steel bar fence. The surrounding neighborhood had ranch style houses built in the 1960s or '70s. Along the fence on the other side were several gray buses and a handful of Humvees. *Most of their vehicles are across the state in Davenport.*

The journey to Springfield had only one incident worth noting. Being on the lookout for them, an NSF patrol pulled them over. Judy didn't wait for them to call for backup. As they angled off of the road, she ordered one of the Bradleys to open fire from its trailer. The police cruiser exploded in the night, lighting up the cold roadway with a rising plume of smoke and crimson flames. She felt bad, launching a surprise attack against a clearly defenseless enemy, but it had to be done. *We are at war, and war means that people have to die.*

They debarked outside of Springfield, sending the flatbeds off to their rendezvous point. Her raiding force drove down the streets of the capital city of Illinois with the public seemingly dismayed. No doubt they had seen military convoys in the last few weeks, but this was different. This was tanks and armored vehicles on the streets, driving through intersections with open disregard for the lights or the law.

She knew that most National Guard headquarters were administrative facilities with arsenals and fuel. Destroying it would not change the war much, but it would get the attention of the units in Iowa. They would realize that their supply lines were suddenly in jeopardy. Moreover, they would know that their enemy had somehow gotten to their state capital. *They are federalized by the Newmericans, but the guardsmen have families and friends here. They will be compelled to come back and try to hit us.*

Her forces were arrayed on two of the streets that surrounded the facility. Their presence did not seem to cause much of a stir, and she had no intention of sitting there to give them time to react. *It is time we light this up.*

"This is Grab Ass Actual to the rest of you grab asses," she said with a smirk that she barely kept to herself. I want every building targeted with HE. Hit the vehicles that they have in the motor pool area as well. Spread your fire out; the goal here is to do damage, not level the place. If we start taking fire, get on the move, swing to the west, and hit the flank from Great Liberation Street," she said. The road on her maps had been called Lincoln at one time, but the wave of reforms from the Fedgov had all but erased the former president.

Judy paused for a long moment to give her people time to aim and load. She steeled herself from the open back of the Humvee, a biting cold wind hitting her face. Looking out, she saw several infantry on the other side of the fence, pausing, pointing at her attack force.

"Fire at will," she barked over her shoulder mic. "Say again, fire at will."

The line of vehicles seemed to bark and blast in unison with a roar that made her ears ring. Machine guns from the Humvees riddled the gray buses parked along the fence with so many bursts that in a matter of seconds, one of the vehicles had a bite taken out of it.

Explosions from the headquarters complex rattled her vehicle and made her chest throb. Her own Humvee's machine gun unleashed a series of bursts, the tracers stabbing into the explosions and smoke. One blast rained bits of red brick onto the hood of her vehicle, evidence as to how close they were.

The big cannons of the Abrams tanks came with two deep thudding booms—one from the firing of the shell; the other, a moment later. Both of the exploding rounds threw dust and debris into the air. Judy adjusted her earplugs, but knew it would be to little avail. Shells hit the parked vehicles of the motor pools, leaving each one a fiery gravesite marking where a vehicle once stood. One went up with a blast of its own, sending a burning tire rolling into the steel fence, hard enough to dent the metal from the impact.

A secondary explosion from one side of the complex added a massive rolling orange and yellow ball of flames that seemed to turn over and over in the air as it rose, then opened up as nothing more than a black ball of smoke.

Judy's eyes went to where she had seen the guardsmen pointing at them, but couldn't see any sign of them. If they were smart and lucky, they were lying flat and not drawing any unwanted attention. The parking lot for the guardsmen was filled with their private vehicles which drew machine guns and the ire of a Bradley's M242 Bushmaster chain gun. The cars and trucks went up in their own balls of fire and carnage, bits of them raining down all over the burning complex.

For three minutes, Judy let her people cut loose on the enemy headquarters facility. Checking her watch, she rose again. "This is Grab Ass Actual, cease fire. Hold your fire." The Oklahoma troops followed their orders well. Only one machine gun fired another few short bursts before stopping.

She struggled to hear the cackle and snapping of the flames that marked where the buildings had been, her ears still ringing from the cavalcade of death that her people had unleashed. The stink of the fire, a mix of burning wood, plastic, rubber and other aromas, stung her eyes and seared her nostrils for a moment. Judy coughed, regretting not wearing her protective eye gear. Even from where she stood in the Humvee, she could feel the temperature change. The chill of the winter breeze was gone, eaten by the many fires burning in the distance.

Her eyes watered as she looked at the destruction. There was an odd sense of satisfaction and accomplishment in what they had done, despite what had to be devastating losses to the enemy. *I have to be careful that I don't start enjoying this too much.* Clearing her throat, she activated her shoulder mic again. "Good work everyone. Move out to our primary target. If the NSF tries to engage with us, destroy them."

This will get their attention. ... What we do next will force a reaction.

Ann Arbor, Michigan

The call came in on one of Dr. Liu's five burner phones in his desk. Each used a Chinese state-proved app that encrypted their communications. There was always a lag between individuals talking as the app ran, but it was effective, thus far, against the probing ears of the NSF. The phone made a buzzing sound, like a trapped and angry wasp. Pulling open his desk drawer, he saw the number and knew that it was Zack Taylor. As he hit the answer button, he moved to his university office door and closed it, locking it as he connected.

"Is now a good time, sir?" Zack asked.

"Yes," he said, settling into his leather padded chair.

"We have arrived at the designated town. We made our penetration last night."

Liu said nothing for a moment, wondering what was going to follow. Taylor had gone with John Quang to the Republic of Texas to plant some security apps on the leaders of the Republic's computers ... hopefully without their knowledge. Evidence had been raised indicating that unwanted eyes had been probing into his transactions with the Republic. *If word of that ever got out, it would be damaging to our efforts.* "Proceed," he said, hoping it was good news.

"Salem Marshall's machine has our hidden app installed," he said. "Mr. Quang was able to get me the access I needed."

"That is good news," he replied.

"There is something else sir, something that you should know," Zack said after a two-second pause.

"Go on."

Another pause was followed with his voice. "I found evidence on the hard drive that someone recently mirrored the data."

"In English please," he said. *The problem with technology people is they have their own language and presume we all speak it.*

"Two days ago someone made a copy of the data on their hard drive. Whoever did it overcame their security software and the system in the office and got a complete copy of the hard drive. I found a hidden temp file that they had failed to delete. While I don't know how they overcame the encryption software, the fact that they overcame it points to someone with an above-average degree of sophistication."

That was disturbing. "Does anything you found point to the perpetrators?"

"I tapped their internal security network. A pair of contract employees were in the building that day, and they stayed late to work. The camera footage never shows them going near Marshall's office, but they could have somehow put the system into a loop to avoid showing what they were up to."

"So you know what they look like?"

Another pause, then he spoke with a crackle on the connection. "I will send you the pictures."

Dr. Liu said nothing but nursed his thoughts carefully. *They may be onto what we are doing and are gathering evidence. It could be the Russians, Newmerica, or even the Americans. It is possible if they got ahold of that hard drive, they may possess incriminating evidence against us.* Fear crept into his thoughts. It wasn't a fear of being exposed; that was something he had prepared for a while ago. No, this fear was the repercussions of being caught. He did not worry about the Americans or Newmericans; he worried more about what his own people would do. Memories of his childhood came back in an instant, and he found himself biting his lower lip.

"Put on Mr. Quang please," he said as he rallied his thinking against this new threat.

"Yes sir," Quang's voice said a few moments later.

"John, I need to amend your instructions for this mission."

"Yes sir."

"The people that Zack identified and has pictures of ... they pose a threat to our operation. If you see them, I want you to capture them, and if that is not possible, kill them."

The pause as the voice encryption software ran was anticipated, but seemed longer to Liu than normal. "I will make that happen," Quang replied.

"Excellent. Then I leave you to your work." He hung up and waited until the images that Zack sent came to the phone. They were not incredibly clear, but good enough to see faces. *I need to send these on to the homeland for analysis. Whoever these two are, they have made themselves enemies of the People's Republic, ... and that is something they will come to fear in the days to come.*

Latham, New York

This was not the plan Su-Hui had conceived, not by a long shot. When they discovered that Newmericans lay in wait for him in Connecticut, he had swung west to attack New York. Getting to Albany, however, meant driving through Vermont. At Brattleboro, Vermont, there had been an NSF checkpoint at the border, complete with six cruisers and a dozen or so police officers. It was tempting to order his force to open up with their machine guns and small arms, but that might give the police time to call for reinforcement and issue a warning.

Instead he sent two squads in, crossing the icy Connecticut River under the bridge, using stealth to attack and overtake the police. Under the cover of darkness, the hearty New Hampshire men and women used planks on the bridge abutments to cross, climbing up the bank and swarming the NSF officers before they could even fire a shot. Their bodies were taken out to the bridge and tossed unceremoniously into the waters, opening the doorway to cross Vermont.

No alarm was given. No pursuit by the NSF. New York was part of Newmerica just like Vermont, and there was no security on that border. He used back roads and lonely stretches of country highways to reach their objective. *We have been lucky so far ... but that can change in an instant.*

Now he faced the New York National Guard Headquarters. The screen of trees that surrounded the base were devoid of their leaves, and ice clung to their limbs, sometimes creaking and cracking in the frigid wind. A few older homes dotted the long stretch of road leading in. At the base entrance was a helicopter on display; its fading, olive drab paint was covered with ice, and the rotors had snow and ice on them as well.

The one part of the plan he salvaged was getting into the base. Rather than shoot their way in, he sat in the lead vehicle, wearing his captured Connecticut National Guard uniform, as they pulled up. A convoy of Humvees arriving at a base was not a cause for concern; in fact, the guards were probably used to it.

They pulled to the checkpoint, and the guard leaned in close to the driver, most likely to shield his face from the cold wind. "Good day. What can I do for you?" He was a young man, probably only in his twenties. *This is not your lucky day to be on guard duty ...*

"We have orders to come here for a meeting," Su-Hui said.

The young man checked his iPad; his hand was pink from the cold. In the darkness of the early morning hours, the pad cast a dull, white glow on the young man's face. "I don't see you on the list."

Su-Hui opened his uniform coat. "Come over to my side of the vehicle Private. I'll show you my orders." He reached inside his coat and wrapped his hand around his Sig Sauer M18 and thumbed the manual safety.

The private came around the Humvee and leaned in just as he pulled the gun and aimed it at his face. "Undo your belt and lower your weapon to the ground." His driver pulled his weapon and was prepared to fire at the other guard on duty.

"What ... what is this?" the Private stammered as he began to comply.

"This is war," Su-Hui said. The other sentry moved casually to the driver, as if he wanted to help, only to be greeted with a weapon aimed at his face. "We will pick you up on the way out and take you back as prisoners." Those words only brought angry and frustrated expressions from them.

Su-Hui opened the door of the Humvee and got out, tossing the belt and holstered weapon onto the floor of the driver's side. Pulling out a zip tie, he nodded at the young private who numbly extended his hands.

Su-Hui bound his hands tight and led him to the guard shack where both men were shoved down on the floor, their ankles bound as well. His driver hit the button to open the security fence to allow them to enter.

Su-Hui got back in his Humvee, and a few minutes later, the harassers swarmed into the compound. They wheeled in front of a newer building, the largest on the campus. It was a three-story, white structure, modern looking … far nicer than the New Hampshire National Guard facilities he had seen or attacked. As he got out, the Humvees fanned out in the parking lot. Su-Hi looked around at the various buildings that made up the headquarters, trying to determine the best place to inflict damage.

"Alright," he said as his personnel gathered around him. "We don't have much time. Park one of our surprises right up against the center of his building. Take one over to their motor pool—that is bound to cause commotion. Take our other one over to those structures, and position it between both of them. Park the other vehicles up good and tight to the buildings to maximize effect. Set your charges, load up in the other vehicles. We'll meet over there," he said pointing to a cleared but mostly empty parking lot.

A New York Guard officer came out of the large, white building just as his people were beginning to disperse. "What is going on here?" he asked. Su-Hui saw his rank, a major. *We cannot afford for him to raise an alarm.*

"Just a drill sir," he said, using the Humvee for cover as his hand pulled out his sidearm.

"A drill? Who authorized this? You can't just drive all over the base like this," he said angrily. As he spoke, one of the Humvees loaded with explosives drove through the plowed snow embankment and parked up next to the white building.

We don't have time for this. Su-Hui drew his weapon and aimed it squarely at the major. "This is my authorization," he said through gritted teeth.

The major's face went red with anger, leaving not a trace of fear. "What in the name of hell do you think you're doing?"

"Be quiet! Get on your knees," Su-Hui ordered.

"Like hell I will."

He squeezed the trigger. The shot rang out, muffled slightly by the snow. The major twisted, the shot hitting in his upper left chest, turning his body in place; then he dropped. "Fuck me!" he called out in agony.

Su-Hui moved around the Humvee to get a better angle on him, but his driver beat him to the major. He moved over the prone, groaning man and fired another round into the officer's head. The anguished moaning stopped, and the only sound that Su-Hui heard for a few moments was the beating of his heart in his ears.

He had killed people before in this conflict—set off explosives, fired a gun, but he was rarely this close. Usually the people he killed were distant—they were figures, not people to him. As he saw the red gore slowly oozing onto the pavement near the body, it mixed with a bit of white snow and seemed even brighter. This time it had been close and personal, and that stuck in his mind. The image was seared into his memory.

"You okay?" his driver asked, suddenly shaking him back to reality.

He nodded and started back to the driver's side of the vehicle. "Let's roll."

Fifteen-minutes later ...

The last crew to plant their explosives sprinted across the parking lot to where the harasser force had assembled. The gun shots had brought out a few personnel who were looking around. Two gathered near the fallen major, some one hundred yards from where Su-Hui and his people were parked. His friend, Corporal Abernathy, his bushy blonde hair blowing in the breeze, led the last team in. "We are all set," he reported, then climbed in the back of Su-Hui's Humvee.

Pulling out the remote detonator, Su-Hui drew a long breath. He turned on the remote control unit, made from some airplane or car remote control and saw the green power light. Without a moment of hesitation, he jabbed the small joystick up to the detonate position.

The bombs went off in two waves—just a millisecond or two apart. The one in front of the white structure was the most visible. The shock waves shook the small trees of their ice and snow all around the parking area and the front of the structure buckled back for a moment, then fell forward into a ball of rising scarlet and amber flames that came from the crater. He heard a crunching sound as a piece of the blasted Humvee slammed into one of his raiders, enough for him to turn and see the smoking twisted piece of metal had dented the side armor. Small bits of debris started to rain down on the roof of his own vehicle, enough for him to glance up momentarily.

The searing white ball of fire rose for a few seconds. It showed the devastation inflicted on the white structure. The building was ablaze, but it looked as if someone had taken a big bite out of it. The ripples from the heat of the flames near the base distorted the damage even more from where he was parked.

A car alarm began to try to pierce the cacophony of explosions … only to suddenly drop off, then stop. No doubt the vehicle was destroyed in the blasts, but managed to survive long enough to bark out its alarm one last time.

The other blasts roared in the distance, their deep booms making his body throb. Turning in his seat, he could see fires raging in the distance. Near the motor pool three other explosions followed a few moments later. The pre-dawn sky over Latham, New York looked as if an early sunrise had come. The lights in the parking lot flickered several times, then went off—no doubt a power line somewhere had been severed.

Su-Hui wanted to savor it for a moment longer. Good men had died to make this attack happen, and somehow drinking in the visual images of the destruction seemed the best way to honor them. He knew they could not stay though; the authorities would be onto them soon. Putting down the detonator, he stood in the open doorway on the floorboard so that the other drivers and teams could see him, illuminated by the flames across the parking lot.

"Alright, everyone form up on me," he called out. "We are heading home."

They drove out of the complex which lit up the pre-dawn skies behind him. A sudden memory hit Su-Hui. "The sentries! We forgot to bring them along with us!"

His drive chuckled. "You're right," he said, snickering for a moment. "Imagine the story they will have to tell their superiors."

"You're assuming their superiors survived," Su-Hui replied.

"Touché sir, touché."

CHAPTER 18

"Mandates are for the greater good. Mandates protect all."

Kodak, Tennessee

Trip looked out the ring-mounted periscope that he had had installed on his command vehicle. The Newmerican Apache AH-64s came down I-40 in a tight formation, spraying anything that moved with Hydra 70 rockets and spitting 30mm death and carnage as they roared in. One chopper was followed by a bright light, a ground fired Stinger It snaked through the air, hitting it from behind and sent the chopper slamming into a nearby office building with an explosion all on its own.

A pair of rockets from the remaining choppers landed some forty feet from General Reager's custom modified command Bradley armored fighting vehicle, pinging the armor with bits of blasted soil and sizzling fragments of deadly shrapnel. As he lowered himself into the rear compartment, he noted that the young officers inside, the ones that lacked a lot of combat experience, winced and ducked, as if it might somehow protect them. Trip remembered being that way himself, but it seemed as if it were a lifetime ago. Instead, he remained calm, not reacting to the explosions outside. If the situation was less serious, he might have allowed himself a grin.

"Where in the hell is our air support?" Lieutenant Phipps asked angrily. Up above them, the turret of the Bradley banged off three rounds in rapid succession, making communicating in the rear of the vehicle a bit of a challenge.

"I've got inbound aircraft from Arnold AFB," Captain Hall, his Air Force liaison said, shooting an icy glance at Phipps. "ETA, two minutes."

"We're not the only show in town," Trip replied in his best calming voice. "Colonel Ricketts has our choppers providing his force protection for the time being. There was a metallic dinging sound of a round glancing off of the Bradley near the driver's compartment. "Captain Hall, have them tear the shit out of those helicopters, if you don't mind."

"Yes sir," she replied, pausing to wipe the sweat from her brow as she began to relay orders to the incoming fighter aircraft.

Colonel Ricketts had dug in tight in Morristown, Tennessee, just a few miles up the road, to slow down the advancing Newmerican force. The American combat commanders knew that speed was important to the enemy's advance. The two companies that had been sent in to stall the assault in Morristown had clung on for nearly two hours before they had lost all communications with them. Trip cringed at the thought of them being wiped out, but knew their sacrifice was necessary. It had given him time to start shifting his troops from North Carolina to join up with Rickett's force.

"Where's the head of their column?" Trip asked Lieutenant Phipps as she stared at her armored laptop display.

"About five miles out and closing," Phipps said tensely.

"Call in artillery support for the coordinates for the overpass; target Charlie the minute that the enemy reaches that position. We need to slow them down, so let them deal with some rubble. Then have them fire at the rest of their column. Nothing sustained, just shake them up and hold their advance. If nothing else, it will force them to disperse."

Phipps repeated his orders and then began to relay the information to their artillery support. The big truck mounted M142 High Mobility Artillery Rocket System (HIMARS) that were poised west of Knoxville were easily in range. His forces had pre-targeted several locations on I-40, the main highway from Virginia into Tennessee in preparation for fending off the Newmerican assault.

Several minutes passed. The rockets came in sounding like jets, and going much faster. Trip returned to his viewing portal as they completed their flight. The explosions were massive, making the ground and the Bradley vibrate. While he couldn't see the targeted intersection that the forward observers had designated *Charlie*, the billowing smoke clouds from the impacts told him that they were hitting their targets. If all went as planned, the Winfiled-Dunn Parkway overpass over I-40 would be destroyed, blocking the highway underneath at least for the time being.

Another roar came overhead, this one slightly deeper than the rocket fire. *Fighter jets!* He popped the periscope hatch and stuck out his head, craning his neck to get a glimpse of them. A pair of F-22 Raptors banked in the distance, unleashing their AIM-9 Sidewinder missiles, and then banking away. At first he couldn't see the targets, but a flash of explosion off to his left marked a place in the sky where an enemy Apache helicopter spun wildly down, exploding on impact with the Walmart parking lot; at least he assumed that was where it fell.

Off to General Reager's right, there was another explosion, this one from incoming fire. A friendly Bradley exploded, forcing Trip to flinch slightly. Melted splatter of white-hot metal rained down on the ground, sizzling where it hit. The vehicle erupted in fire, and he saw at least one crewman climb out, his legs on fire, dropping and rolling as several infantry moved in to help extinguish the man.

That was close, ... maybe too close. Memories of when his own Bradley had been knocked over during the fighting in Georgia came to mind. Trip wasn't afraid at all. He believed you had to lead from the front, but he also knew that the Americans needed him alive and able to command.

Dropping back inside, he called up to the driver. "Watney, we need to redeploy to Phase Line Rubicon," he barked loud enough for the Bradley driver to hear.

"Yes sir," he said, and the Bradley roared to life, lurching hard enough to almost throw Trip off balance before he could get to his seat. His ass grabbed hard when he did hit, thankful that he didn't fall down entirely.

Throwing bodies at the Newmericans was not the answer to his problem. Modern armies relied on solid lines of supply. From what his G2 had determined, the forces that had come out of Virginia were from several states, Virginia, Maryland, Delaware, and the District. They relied on I-81, which became I-40, for their fuel, ammunition, and food. Sever that route and the offensive would feel the effects in a matter of a few days. Their choice would be to push on and pray that a victory would require Trip's force to surrender, or to fall back and try to reestablish their supply route.

To that end, he had ordered Major Platt to launch a counterattack on the diversionary force in front of him. If he was successful, it would swing in a long arc north and west aimed at Abingdon, Virginia. His orders were to secure I-81 there, seize or destroy as much of the enemy supplies as possible, and prevent them from sending more to the force that Trip was facing. It was the same sweeping end-run that the enemy General Rinehart was executing, but would work against his foe … or so he hoped.

As the Bradley redeployed to the next line of defenses to the rear, Trip could feel the weight of time working for and against him, swaying back and forth. They will spot our stab at their rear with their air support first. *Rinehart is no fool. He'll recognize the threat and be forced to pull some of his troops off of this assault to deal with that. In the meantime, we will keep him pressed here.*

As another roar of jets raced overhead and the distant throbbing rumble of artillery continued, he hoped he had enough force to do the job. *If I don't, I have to inform the White House they have to evacuate Nashville.* Trip knew that it would cost him his job, to lose the southern capital of the United States. That didn't bother him as much as the thought of losing itself. *We have been lucky so far, and the victories we've won have given people hope in the cause. If we lose a major battle like this now, it will suck the air right out of the movement. It will give people a reason to pause, reconsider Newmerica, worry that they might find themselves shipped off to Social Quarantine camps. Worse they may start to question their backing the American President. We will lose battles down the road; that is destined to happen. But for now, losing a big one is something I simply cannot allow.*

Summersville, West Virginia

After their meeting with Detective Schrank they quickly packed up their flat to head home. His father had used bleach to wash down most of the surfaces while David wiped their fingerprints off any suspect surfaces such as door knobs. If the NSF wanted their DNA, they were determined not to make it easy.

They drove to Summersville, West Virginia, where his mother had recently gotten a job in the court clerk's office. There had been a roadblock on the border of the two states. The NSF had reviewed their identities and grilled his father about what business they had on the other side of the border. The Virginia border officers warned them that if they went, they might not be allowed to return—a clear threat. His father had been far calmer and fast thinking than David had been. He assured the officers that they had family there and were moving there permanently. The officers logged their names and scanned their IDs on their iPads, then let them cross.

The West Virginia State Troopers that manned their own roadblock one hundred yards down the road were far more welcoming. They too logged their names, but didn't ask a lot of questions. David commented on that out loud, "You guys are more hospitable than your counterparts." "Yeah," the stocky female trooper replied. "More folks are coming from Virginia to our state rather than going the other direction." With that, they were on their way.

Gone was the fake surname of Steele, as his father explained. They were the Adair family from this point forward. At a rest area, he threw away both his and David's old fake IDs and handed his son his new ones. IDs were hard to come by, especially the new Federal IDs which were used for almost everything, including vaccine tracking, but their family friend Frank Campbell was a man of many talents and even more connections. This was his third identity change since the Fall, and each time he shed a name, he felt like he was losing a part of himself. *How long are we going to have to continue to hide who we really are? At what point can we get our old lives back?* While he mentally asked the questions, a part of him was afraid to get a response—so he kept them to himself.

Summersville had a dusting of snow on the ground, just enough to lightly cover the hearty grasses that were a dark green. The buildings were old, fieldstone and brick structures, sturdy, standing in defiance of the times they were forced to endure. The American flags on the government buildings were a strange sight for David. For the last five years, it was considered a banned symbol. Here, in West Virginia, they sided with the American President in Nashville. *I'm in a foreign country. No ... that's wrong. This is what America used to be like.*

They parked in front of the courthouse, and a few minutes later his mother came out. They got out of the car and she hugged them, tears forming in her eyes. She got in the passenger seat and David got in the back, moving some of their clothing from the apartment to the side so there was room.

His mother gave them directions to the apartment, and each of them loaded up an armful of their personal items from the car. Inside, the apartment was sparse, but far nicer than the small flat where David and his father had been living. It smelled clean, no doubt aided by the plug-in air freshener he spied in the kitchen.

After his mother made dinner and they ate, his father had explained the visit by Detective Schrank. His mother absorbed the information with few questions. From what David could see, she was unfazed by the information. It made him proud. She was made of tougher stuff than his father and him put together.

The aroma of spaghetti and garlic bread hung in the air, reminding David of better times, fading memories. "So what is next?" his mother finally said, taking a seat on the sofa so that she could face the two of them.

"We can't continue at UVA," his father said. "That much is clear."

"Do you feel like you're done? That you've gotten enough vengeance for what they did to Maddie?" she pressed.

There was a moment of long silence, and David was the one what shattered it. "No."

His parents both looked at him as he continued a moment later. "This was never just about Maddie. Yes, she's the start, but a lot of bodies were found where she was. If they were doing this at UVA, chances are pretty good they have been doing this everywhere. This doesn't feel over to me, not until they stop this everywhere."

"That's a big job son," his father replied.

"I know," he conceded. "We scared the hell out of those progressive shitbags at UVA. They will be talking about this for years, wallowing in their victimhood. We should move on, go to another school, maybe more. We should target the instigators there the same way that they target conservatives. We need to create the same amount of fear that we did at UVA. We need to make them all afraid, all of them looking over *their* shoulders for a change."

"We can't do this alone," Grayson said. "We were lucky to have to have gotten away with what we did for as long as we did. The campuses react; they put up cameras; they organize student patrols; the NSF steps up. For this to work, we need to be hitting a number of campuses, each with different tactics, things that make it hard for the NSF to connect them. Even then, they have a lot of technology working for them."

"We can get others involved," David suggested. "We can't be the only family that has gone through this."

"It will be hard to locate friendly people who are willing to commit murder," his father said.

"Your friend, Frank, he can help," David countered quickly. "This is more than just UVA—this is everywhere."

His mother spoke, surprising both of them for an instant. "David is right," she said firmly. "There are other mothers and fathers out there that have felt the same pain we have. We need to find them. They don't have to kill; they just have to be willing to help. They will too. I am sure there are hundreds of families out there that have suffered the way we do … the way I do. We have to do this. It's beyond Maddie now; it's for all of them, the forgotten ones." A tear ran down her right cheek and fell off into her lap as she spoke.

She's made of tougher stuff than us. I always thought Maddie got her strength from Dad, but I was wrong. It is Mom that is the heart of this family. "We'll need to organize," his father said. "We need to do our digging … make sure we are connecting to the right people."

"We can do it," David assured him, reaching over and squeezing his mother's hand. "We'll do it for Maddie and all of the others that have been sacrificed."

Springfield, Illinois

Judy watched as her vehicles deployed around the state capitol of Illinois. The stately building with its tall, distinct dome, loomed over her as her Humvee swung around, aiming its weapons outward, away from the capitol itself. She knew that the biggest threat would be coming from elsewhere, especially after their attack a few miles away just a few minutes earlier. Even now, the sounds of sirens from fire and rescue vehicles echoed down the stoic structures of South 2nd Street as they rushed out of the city toward the billowing black smoke in the distance that marked the grave site of the National Guard headquarters.

Judy got out, her torso muscles straining slightly under the weight of her plate carrier with blast plates. *I'm probably starting to get too old for this.* She watched as one of the Abrams tanks under her command smashed through the security barrier intended to keep cars away from the capitol, churning up the snow and sod underneath as it backed into position. Down the block she saw an M1126 Stryker under her command tear through the security chains and posts, heading right up the stairs, crunching and grinding concrete as its engine roared.

The wind was biting through her coat, but that was nothing compared to the cold she had endured in Davenport, waiting for the enemy to 'rescue' her unit. Her stomach ached, mostly from the cold MRE she had called breakfast. Only a heavy dose of hot sauce had made the meal palatable.

NSF officers assigned to the capitol emerged, wearing full tactical gear. Her team dropped for firing stances, weapons raised, but he ordered them, "Hold your fire!" They did and after the NSF team hesitated, they came forward toward her. Judy saw them and lowered her hand to her sidearm, blading her body to them as they approached. While they were wearing body armor and carrying automatic rifles, none seemed shocked or concerned by her appearance. One man, a Captain named Landin, walked right over to her. "Thank God you're here."

She had to fight to keep from smiling. *He thinks we are here to defend the capitol!* "No problem. I'm in command here, Captain Mercury," she said, raising her hand from her sidearm to shake his hand.

"I'm Brice Landin, NSF. We were worried when we saw the news that someone had attacked the National Guard HQ. I wish someone had told us you were coming." As he spoke, a squad of her infantry, Oklahoma men and women, moved past the NSF team and into the building itself.

"Well, as you can imagine, this is a pretty fluid situation," she said. "We came to secure this building," she said, not entirely lying. "Can you take me to the Governor? I need to speak with him."

"Absolutely," Captain Landin said. "We'll take you up right now."

She turned to another squad. "Sergeant O'Quinn, you and your troops are with me," she ordered. The beefy sergeant nodded and ordered his squad to follow him. He cast her a cockeyed expression; his right eyebrow raised as if he couldn't believe it either. Judy shrugged for a moment, and entered the old building.

They moved briskly down the terrazzo floors to a bank of elevators with big brass doors. Half of her squad with the sergeant rode with her and the NSF officers up. The rest of the squad following in a separate elevator a few moments later. "How bad was the HQ hit?" Landin asked as the big doors closed.

"Pretty bad," she said. "We were lucky to get out of there."

"Where did they come from?" the other NSF officer asked.

"That's hard to say," she said. The sergeant next to her dipped his head and covered his mouth with a fake cough to avoid chuckling at the discussion. She nudged him with her hip. "No one seems to know how they got here or what their objective is. That's why I need to talk to the Governor."

The doors opened, and Captain Landin stepped out, "Down this corridor, then left," he said, walking briskly. The second elevator opened with the rest of Sergeant O'Quinn's squad, and they formed up behind her as they walked. "I'm glad you showed up. Ever since the news broadcast about the attack, he's been pissing himself. Knowing you are here will calm him down."

I doubt that ... Judy followed him as they marched through the building, finally stopping at a massive, dark wooden door. The gold lettering, painted on years ago, simply said, 'Office of the Governor.' Landin opened the door for her and her team and followed her in.

In the outer office were three clerks, who, when they saw the men, gestured to the inner office. Landin rapped on the door, then opened it for Judy and she and the rest of the group filtered in. Sergeant O'Quinn discreetly tapped his troops, one by one, pointing for them to spread out, subtly surrounding the pair of NSF troopers. "Governor, this is Captain Mercury of the National Guard. Her force is the one that we saw deploying around the Capitol."

The man was old. Bits of gray hear showed at the roots, proof that he died his black hair to maintain its color. He wore a gray suit with a blue tie that was loosened around the collar of his white dress shirt. The Governor's face was long; his cheeks were shallow; and his skin was dark as if he had gotten a lot of sun in his youth. "Thank God you are here!" he proclaimed. Another person in the office was the Lieutenant Governor. She was an older woman of color with an angry expression barely held in check on her face. The Lieutenant Governor stood next to the Governor, her arms crossed in defiance and a furious look in her eyes.

"We need to get you out of here sir," Judy said.

"Why?" he said, his eyes widening slightly with her words. "Are they headed this way?"

"We just need to get you and your Lieutenant Governor away from here," she said.

Captain Landin spoke up, looking over at one of the infantry squad around him. "Hey, you're out of Oklahoma?"

He must have seen our unit patch. "That's right," she said.

"You're not our national guard?" the Governor asked.

"No we are not," Judy replied.

"I don't understand," the older man said. "Oklahoma is siding with the Americans, isn't it?"

"Yes it is," Judy said, reaching down and pulling her sidearm. She gave a single nod to Sergeant O'Quinn, and he raised his rifle on the NSF officers. Almost in unison, the rest of the squad went to 'weapons ready,' their guns aimed at everyone in the room.

"What is the meaning of this?" the Governor demanded, rising to his feet in indignation.

The NSF officers seemed to understand far more than the politicians. They lowered their weapons, and in a matter of moments were disarmed by the infantry in the office. Anger mixed with embarrassment washed over their faces, especially the puffy cheeks of Captain Landin. For a moment, she thought he might bolt and try to fight it out, but his rage and humiliation was held in check by four gun barrels aimed at him. Satisfied the NSF officers no longer posed a threat, she turned her focus back on the Governor.

While Sergeant O'Quinn had his forces zip tie the ankles and hands of the NSF officers, Judy moved around the big desk where the two political officials were, keeping her pistol drawn. "Who in the hell do you think you are, barging in here?" the Governor snarled.

"I am Captain Judy Mercury of the American Army," she said with a hint of pride. "And you two are my prisoners of war."

The Lieutenant Governor took a slow step toward Judy, uncrossing her arms and her trembling hands. She was defiant and outraged, Judy could see it in her eyes. "We are noncombatants," she grumbled. "You have no legal authority to come in here and take us prisoners."

"I have every right," she snapped back, pulling her sidearm up for them to see but keeping her finger clear of the trigger. "My authority is right here. You refused to acknowledge the rightful President; you authorized your troops to cross into Iowa, invading a neighboring state."

"Those troops were federalized," the Governor said. "They are not under my command."

"A technicality," she said flatly. "In the meantime you did not protest their use. I was in Chicago during the election," she added. "They weren't federalized when you sent them against us then. Your people tried to kill me and my comrades under *your* orders."

"I will not be talked to by someone like you, not under duress," the Governor said, rising to his feet. A pair of guns tracked his every move, and as he rose, his eyes snapped over to them.

"Watch your words carefully sir," she said. "I am under little compulsion to bring you with us alive."

The older man's jaw set and for a second, he said nothing but stared at her. "You'll pay for what you've done here," he grimaced. "Mark my words. You'll pay."

Judy had heard those words before, long ago, back in Texas. For a fleeting moment, she remembered going with then-Major Reager to San Antonio … and the night that changed her life …

Four years earlier …
San Antonio, Texas

Judy was appalled at what she saw happening in San Antonio. She loved that city and what was happening was an affront to her on many levels. Her battalion had been deployed to San Antonio to protect the Alamo from a mob hell-bent on destroying it. The night had morphed in a matter of minutes from an angry protest to a raging gun battle.

To people outside of Texas, the Alamo was a tourist site. They knew it because of John Wayne's movie and were always surprised that it was in the heart of the city. To them it was important, but no more so than Gettysburg or any other American historical site. To most Texans, however, it was sacred ground. It embodied that fierce independent streak they had. It was the soul of Texas spirit. The thought that someone would want to destroy it was personal for every man and woman in her platoon. The rioters were not just attacking a building; they were attacking Texas, and that kind of affront was met with a viciousness that was hard to describe.

As the air rumbled with the sound of distant explosions, she saw an orange glow blocks away, lighting up the sky. She hoped and prayed that it wasn't the Alamo, but a part of her felt that the building was safe. Major Reager was there. She had served with him in the Middle East and knew him to be a fast thinking officer. *If anyone can protect the Alamo, it's him.*

She deployed her platoon at the edge of Travis Park where they had been assigned. The one-block square park offered some soft cover, but little in the way of defense. Her people tipped over some concrete benches, kneeling behind them for protection. This was her part of the line and her mission, as the major had explained; it was simple—"Don't let these people through."

She could smell something burning and assumed the source was the glow in the distance. The noise of the riots, mixed with bursts of gunfire, echoed into the park ... an eerie forewarning of what was going to come. "We are deployed Lieutenant," Sergeant Lafever said, crouching low next to her. "Any word from the Alamo?"

"None yet," she said, staring across the park. In the distance people began to pour out from adjoining streets. They carried banners and brandished weapons and Molotov cocktails, chanting "Tear it down!" over and over. More filtered into the park until there were hundreds.

This shit is about to get real. "Riot rounds until I say otherwise," she said. Rubber bullets would hurt like hell, but generally were not lethal. Her National Guardsmen had them, but she knew that the rioters wouldn't be as gentle. If they opened fire, her people were going to become casualties, and quick.

As the crowd grew in size, it surged across the park, crossing the middle ground where the Confederate memorial statue had been taken down. The surge stopped, and she saw them deploying a phalanx of homemade shields to protect their front ranks. *They're organized and equipped. I'll give that much to them.*

Bottles filled with frozen water flew from their second row ranks, arcing high in the air and slamming into her lines. They were just like thrown bricks. Most didn't hit any of her platoon, but she didn't like being under assault. *We're not just going to sit here and let them chuck shit at us.* "Riot rounds and tear gas," she called out, reiterating that they were not to use live ammunition. "Force them back. Fire at will." Reaching down, she pulled out her gas mask and put it on.

The crack-pops of her platoon opened up on the rioters. She raised her own M4 and took aim at one of the shield holders. She didn't aim for the shield; she estimated that was a waste of time. Instead, she aimed at the woman's exposed knees. She fired two rounds and the rioter reeled, dropping her shield.

Tear gas rounds arched high into the air, landing in the middle of the crowd as Judy took aim and fired into the now exposed second rank of the line. Other rioters with shields dropped. She saw one clear plastic shield shatter under the bullets. Some rioters bent down and picked up the dropped shields, but the surge across Travis Park stalled, if only for a few moments.

The tear gas created an eerie almost glowing fog, illuminated by the lights in the park and the lights the rioters carried. Someone picked up one of the smoking rounds and tried to hurl it back, but it landed just in front of their own lines.

The use of tear gas only seemed to escalate matters. The air lit up with Molotov cocktails, four of them, arching into the air from the rear ranks of the encroaching rioters. One fell short, in front of her, shattering and turning a piece of sidewalk into an instant inferno. Another landed at the far end of her platoon's firing line, and she heard a scream as two members of her platoon were set ablaze. They rolled, but the flames kept lapping at them. Finally, with the help of others, the fires were put out.

She focused on her own shooting for a moment, gritting her teeth in anger. Shots rang out from the rioters, one ricocheting off to her left. Judy ducked down. She held up her M4 and switched to full auto, spraying a ten-foot section of the rioters as she ducked behind a hedge and a tiny curve, using it for cover.

Incoming bullets sparked off of concrete and behind them. Her mind went back to the Middle East. She had nearly been killed in a firefight there, and now this was happening, right here, in Texas.

"Sir, we need to go to live ammunition," Sergeant Lafever said, lying flat and firing his own rounds across the park while she reloaded.

"I'm not authorized to do that," she said as a bullet hit her chest. Judy was tossed back and to the side as she landed on her back. It felt hot and searing, where the bullet had collided with her tactical vest. Sergeant Lafever leaned over her as she struggled for a moment to get air.

"Did it go through?" she coughed, finally getting a gasp of air. The gas mask didn't help matters, but she knew enough not to pull it off.

He pulled back her vest slightly and flashed a light for a moment. "Breastplate caught it sir," he said, trying to suppress the pain of the hit.

"Alright then," she managed with a strained voice. Judy sat up, shouldered her weapon, and fired three short bursts at the crowd. Her chest ached with every breath, to the point where she wondered if the Sergeant had been wrong, but she pushed such thinking away. *If it had gone through, I'd be bleeding out by now. It still hurts like hell.*

"I'm hit!" rang out a voice of one of her people farther down the line to the right. "Dam! Me too," came a voice from Corporal Cherie Hebert. We are far too exposed here. "Move those park benches together; form a wall. We'll consolidate there."

Sergeant Lafever barked out orders and the troops, crouching low, pulled the benches over and formed them into a small semicircle with the arc facing the enemy. The rioters seemed to sense that the National Guard's position was collapsing and started to take slow, methodical steps closer as the gunfire intensified. The wounded were dragged into the small position.

"We are fucked here," a private said, fear ringing in his voice.

"Knock that shit off Riggins!" Lafever snapped.

Judy popped up and fired as bullets hit the concrete in front of her, kicking up dust and fragments that glanced off of her gas mask. *They will overrun us soon.* She eyed the live ammunition magazines on her vest. *It will be slaughter if we go to hot ammo.* Despite that thought, she found herself strangely compelled to grab one and put it in … but she somehow managed to keep that urge in check.

A voice crackled in her helmet speaker. "This is Major Reager," he said smoothly. "The use of live ammunition is authorized. I say again, all units, all commands; you are authorized to use deadly force."

One of her personnel off to the left reeled back, his head exploding in a spray of gore as he toppled over backward. *Shit!* Another trooper wailed, "God damn it! They got me!" Another let out a cry that was so high pitched that it sounded like it came from a child.

"Live ammo!" she called out, pulling her rubber bullets and a fresh magazine of real bullets. Rising just over the edge of the bench, she fired four rounds in rapid succession at the advancing line. Three of her targets dropped quickly; their Plexiglas shields were worthless against full metal jacketed rounds. The other individual that she hit reeled, but stayed upright. *He's got body armor.* As she dropped back down behind the barrier, bullets slammed into the concrete.

The members of her platoon popped up and shot as well. Another private, Tommy Dickson, dropped as a bullet hit him in the helmet. He was alive; it was a glancing hit; but he was down for a few moments.

As she rose again, she saw that the protesters were rushing forward in a full sprint. "Light them up!" she yelled, her voice muffled by the gas mask. Switching back to full auto, she aimed low, going for the lower torsos and legs, raking a good fifteen feet of advancing protesters. Many dropped, skidding on the winter grass of Travis Park, limp and unmoving. The rest of her people did the same. Short but deadly bursts of full automatic devoured the advancing protesters.

The rioters fired back too, but their shots were wild and unpredictable. Suddenly they realized that their ranks were being hit; they fell back in the darkness and the waning white tear gas fog. Another Molotov cocktail arced in the air and landed behind her position, missing by a few feet. The shattering of the bottle and roar of the flames illuminated them and Judy could feel the heat spike. She raised up again and firing another short burst at the retreating protesters, emptied her magazine and forced her back down to reload.

"How are we doing?" she asked Sergeant Lafever. Turning to him she saw that his gas mask faceplate was shattered, and his cheek had a long horizontal cut. *Shit, he was hit in the face!*

Lafever was a seasoned vet though. He tore the mask off and leaned toward the burning gasoline, then look down. "We have six down, maybe seven," he said with ragged breath. "They bum rush us again, and we are going to have some real issues." As if to accentuate his point, another pair of bullets slapped into the overturned concrete bench right where he stood, spitting up bits of the bench with each hit.

Judy yanked off her mask and reached up to hit her shoulder mic. "This is Lieutenant Mercury, I am hold up in Travis Park. Need reinforcements," she said. *Come on Trip ... I need you to come through.*

A voice eventually came back, "Help is on the way."

The dead and injured littered the ground between the two forces. Easily half were alive, moaning and trying to move, but few had any luck. The tear gas was dissipating, giving her a much better view of the enemy disposition. She could see that the protesters were falling back, starting to move around their flanks. "Suppression fire," she called. "Keep those flanks clear ... the cavalry is on its way!" she yelled out to her people.

Three hours later ...

Judy felt almost numb walking through the field hospital that had been hastily set up in Travis Park, the site of her battle hours earlier. Help had come just in time to break up the next assault by the protesters. Now she was walking through the rows of people laid out on the grass, trying to find all of her people. The injured protesters were mixed in with the wounded National Guard, which seemed odd given that one side had been trying to kill the other only a few hours earlier. *Getting shot takes a lot out of your ideals that drive your violence, I guess.*

As she started down one row, she spied a face she had not expected. Wanda lay on a green Army blanket, her arm bandaged and her face smeared with black soot. Judy paused over her former lover, surprised to the point that her mouth hung open. There were no words she could say at first. *I never thought she would be here.* The realization that she might have been the person that had injured her former lover hit her hard, but Judy refused to show it.

Wanda saw her and her eyes narrowed. "I should have known you'd be here," she said in a low tone.

"Are you okay?" Judy asked.

"Got shot in the arm by one of your Nazis," she said. "Maybe by you … I don't know. It hurt like hell until they gave me a painkiller."

"The hospitals are overloaded," Judy said. "They'll get you out of here as soon as possible."

"You killed a lot of innocent people tonight," Wanda snarled. "Must make you feel real good."

"I didn't kill innocents," Judy snapped back. "*They* opened fire on *us* first. My people are dead and wounded too. This was a fight you brought on."

"Sure, sure, that's your story. You should stick to that. A bunch of armed rednecks protecting a stupid old building. … I bet you are *real* proud of yourself."

What happened to her? What happened to the woman that I once loved? How did she become so angry and bitter? "Look," Judy said, "Yes, we protected the Alamo. It is a part of our heritage for fuck's sake. The Alamo defines us as Texans. I'm sorry you got shot doing something stupid. That was your choice, not mine."

Wanda's face was filled with rage as she glared up at her. "You'll pay for what you've done here."

Springfield, Illinois

Judy heard the words echo through her memories. She looked at the indignant Governor and smiled. "Maybe I will, but not today," she said. Turning to her squad, she ordered them to tie the hands of the Governor and Lieutenant Governor. Her new prisoners were furious and outraged, but she didn't care. This had been the plan all along. *If this doesn't get the attention of the National Guard to fall back into Illinois, nothing will. It will also let the people here know that they are not safe, that we can bring the war to them.*

"You'll never get back to Iowa, or Oklahoma for that matter," the Governor said as they were led out into the hall. "We already have Guard forces heading for the city. We still control the bridges over the Mississippi. You're trapped."

Clearly you have not looked at a map recently. As they waited for the elevator, Judy looked at him squarely, eye-to-eye. "Two things. First, if they start shooting at us, they might very well hit you. Second, what makes you think I'm going out the way I came in?"

The look of shock and bewilderment on the Governor's face made it all worthwhile.

CHAPTER 19

"We are always on the lookout for the next offense to protest and set right."

Hoosick, New York

Su-Hui and his raiding party barely noticed the sunrise in front of them; the dull, thick, gray clouds blocked any warmth or light that the sun might offer. A few stray beams managed to make their way through the clouds, columns of lights in the sky, only to slowly close off hopes of clear weather a few moments later. Their attack a few hours earlier had gone off without a major hitch. Their attack had caught the New York authorities completely off guard. The only real hiccup had been that they had gone down the wrong road in the pre-dawn hours and had almost gotten lost for several minutes before turning around and backtracking to get on the right road.

As they approached Hoosick, New York on NY-7—it was little more than a two-lane road—he saw the crimson of brake lights and flashing blue lights ahead, flickering off of pine trees and houses. *Damnation!* It was either an accident or a roadblock, neither one being what he wanted to deal with. "Sir … " his driver said, not sure if Su-Hui saw it. "I see it." As they came up and crossed the overpass that rose over the railroad tracks, he saw what lay ahead.

The NSF had thrown up a roadblock. It was unmistakable. Four of their cruisers were lined perpendicular to the road, two of them pinching the roadway to a single lane. Holding his binoculars, he zoomed in on the troopers. They had their rifles out, body armor on, and there were two vehicles ahead of them—some 200 yards down the road. "Slow us to a stop," Su-Hui said, lowering the binoculars.

Hoosick was never a big, booming urban center; if anything it was a smattering of a few old homes and a handful of businesses along the roadway. The roadblock was probably the most exciting thing to happen to the town in weeks, if not longer. Su-Hui saw the vehicles, and he knew in a matter of moments that some officer would spot them. Looking at the roadblock, he saw that while they held the road, it was possible to go around their barricade on either side, driving along the shallow embankment. He quickly formulated a plan.

Grabbing his walkie-talkie, he turned it on. "Here's what we are going to do. We are going to punch it up and drive around this roadblock on both sides. They will open fire as we approach. Gunners, mount up and disable their vehicles and kill them if you have to. We do this fast enough, and they will not be able to signal for reinforcements. Understood?"

A chorus of yeses came back. "Alright then, let's do this ..." He nodded to his driver, and the Humvee's big engine roared to life as the vehicle lurched forward quickly. Su-Hui put his legs out in front of him, bracing his body for what was to come.

As they roared down NY-7, he saw the dark figures suddenly snap to life and dart behind the cruisers. The two vehicles that were stopped in the middle of the road at the roadblock were simply stranded observers of the battle that was to come. He didn't hear the bangs of their weapons fire, but a bullet slapped into the armored windshield hard, causing him to wince and jerk to the side. Another thunk followed, a hit to the front of the Humvee.

Behind him came a gust of cold air as the gunner went topside and cleared his weapon. Then came the purr of the machine gun—first his, then the others. Sparks from missed shots hitting the pavement were few but visible as they got closer. The windows on one cruiser disappeared in a shower of shattered glass, and bullet holes stitched the vehicles. His driver made a slow arc to the right, to drive around the roadblock as Su-Hui heard the roar of other machine guns open up.

He admired the NSF for a second. The troopers were outgunned, but held their ground as their cruisers were turned into Swiss cheese. Su-Hui realized that there was no other location to set up the roadblock. As his own Humvee raced around the roadblock, he craned his neck in time to see two of the officers fly back, riddled with bullets.

The Humvee skidded for a moment, and he clutched the front dash bar as the driver turned to get back on the highway. Three more bullets hit the armored side of the vehicle with thwacking sounds that he prayed did not penetrate. Another cruiser made a puff sound and was on fire, its gas tank ruptured. He saw two NSF survivors attempting to dive for cover behind the vehicles they had stopped at the roadblock. Another cruiser started to move rapidly down the other embankment; its tires squealed on the highway, but it was out of his line of sight. All of the NSF vehicles were shot up badly, their tires deflated, holes riddling their engine and driver compartments.

His gunner didn't relent, despite their passing, swinging around and continuing to fire long bursts into the vehicles. The lights from the tracers seemed to connect the two vehicles as they passed. When they reached the road, his driver didn't slow down but kept the speed up high. Su-Hui craned his neck around to see the other Humvees, but couldn't. As his vehicle swerved, he saw two Humvees and the rising grayish-white smoke rolling out of the carnage they had just inflicted. Drawing a ragged breath, he pulled up the walkie-talkie. "Status," he barked as the gunner finally lowered himself back inside and closed the top hatch, cutting off the ice cold air.

"We've got two wounded," came one voice.

"Superficial shit here," another SOL voice came back.

"One of them T-boned us with their fucking car. My passenger side rear wheel is fucked up," came Trudy's voice, sounding both angry and frustrated.

"Can you make it another few miles?" he asked.

"Yeah, I guess I can."

"We're only two miles from the Vermont border. "We'll turn off on the bypass and go around Bennington. We will pull over there and transfer your people into our vehicles," he said.

Looking down momentarily, he saw his fingers trembling in their gloves, a hint of the adrenaline rush wearing off. *This isn't what I saw myself doing at this age. I was happy back home in Taiwan, before Newmerica abandoned us and let the Chinese take us. I was supposed to be climbing the corporate ladder, getting promoted, starting to enjoy the good life.*

He let his breath out slowly trying to relax, putting his hands down under his butt to rewarm them. *Because of this damned government, I had to flee my home in shame. We had to live where they told us; we had to be treated as second-class citizens—'Boat people!' I had to endure what they allowed to happen to Ya-Ting. They made me who I am.*

"We sure fucked up that roadblock," his driver said with a grin.

"We killed people who were doing their job," Su-Hui replied.

"They're the bad guys," the gunner added from the back seat.

"Not all of them," Su-Hui said with a strange calm in his voice. "Not everyone that wears a badge is against us. Some are doing it for what they believe in; some are doing it because it's their job and puts food on their plates; others are just trapped in their system and have no way out."

As they reached the Vermont border a few moments later, he pulled his hands up and took off a glove. Reaching inside of his uniform coat and through his shirt and thermal underwear, he found the necklace. Three spent brass cartridges—given to him by Angel Frisosky, the only NSF agent that understood. She had given them these after she killed the men that had raped his daughter, leaving her an empty shell of the bright, young girl that she had once been.

As he looked out the windshield of the Humvee, he saw where a bullet had chipped a bit of the armored glass. A little flurry of snow started for a few moments, then seemed to pass. Su-Hui's fingers, still a bit cold, touched his chest and clung to the cartridges hanging around his neck for a moment. They centered him, gave him calm; they reminded him of why he was there. *Officer Frisosky taught me an important lesson; you have to make your own justice in this nation. I have to remember, there is still good out there in Newmerica ... there are good people even in the NSF. We need to find them and unite them with the rest of us.* While he was not a religious man, he found himself hoping that none of the people they shot had suffered.

Abingdon, Virginia

The Vice President's motorcade pulled off to the side of the highway for a few yards, then slowed to a stop. A long line of cars, trucks, and military vehicles were heading southwest on I-81, and the one thing her Secret Service driver wanted to avoid was being trapped in the traffic jam, or so he told her. She let out a sigh of frustration and mentally held her voice in check, reminding herself that they were assigned to protect her. *They are doing this for my own good.*

The military thrust into Tennessee was going well; they were in Knoxville at the last report. She was coming to prod on General Rinehart. *The military needs a kick in the ass every so often, if only to remind them who they report to.* Also, this was a great photo op for her, lending her insights and advice to the troops near the front. She had brought along a black SUV filled with a camera and sound crew and a handful of personally selected reporters who were guaranteed to position her story properly in their media outlets. *I want the world to see that I am more than just a Vice President ... I am a force that is leading our nation to greatness.*

The problem was they couldn't get to the front. For the last thirty minutes, the line of vehicles had only moved a quarter of a mile. For her, it was beyond frustrating, but there was little that she could do. Glancing out the window, she noticed that there was no traffic heading north across the median from where she was. *That's odd. It's probably an accident or some military foul-up. One of the things I intend to do is reshape the military when this little civil war is over. This kind of shit won't happen when I'm in charge.*

As she sat impatiently in the SUV, she could see some commotion up ahead, over a mile in the distance. It looked as if cars were suddenly wheeling about—some using the lanes that had seemed blocked heading north. Then came a billowing ball of black smoke that rolled in the air. *Is that some sort of accident? Maybe a car fire. Great ... we will be stuck here even longer.*

Some of the cars that were turning around were speeding by, driving far in excess of the speed limit. It struck her as odd, enough to lean forward to communicate with her security detail in the front seats. "What is going on up there?"

"We are trying to pin that down Madame Vice President," her new Secret Service detail leader said. After Becky had attacked her, she had fired her former detail. She hated when they called her 'Madame' and planned to explain to them why she thought it was a demeaning word to describe her. For now, her people were on the radio, signaling ahead to the advance vehicle. She caught only bits and pieces of the messaging, but she heard something in what they said ... panic. *This is more than just a traffic accident ...*

A civilian Jeep raced past her on the median, heading in the opposite direction. It was followed by a military truck, churning up the sod as it raced by. Suddenly, her driver sharply wheeled her SUV around as her advance vehicle roared past them. She was tossed hard to the side and for a moment, had a bit of vertigo as she tried to process what was unfolding. "What in the fuck is going on?" she asked angrily.

"Sorry ma'am," the driver said, racing up onto the northbound lanes and merging with the vehicles—not a steady torrent—heading away from Abington and back into the heart of Virginia. "There's trouble up ahead. We need to get you out of this area, *now*."

She winced, putting down the bit of nausea that came with her momentary disorientation in the back of the vehicle. A hot flash hit her, and she ignored it once her stomach settled. "Trouble? What is happening back there?" she demanded as the vehicle accelerated.

"The Americans," her detail leader called back from the passenger seat. "An attack force just hit Abington. They are cutting off the highway heading south. If we had been further up, we would have been in the middle of a firefight."

The Americans ... that's impossible. General Rinehart was in Knoxville, further south in Tennessee. "Are you sure?"

"Positive," the agent replied. "We were lucky to get out of there."

It made no sense to her, why the Americans would attack there. *Unless they were trying to intercept and kill me!* "They must have known that I was traveling that way. This was an attempt to capture or kill me," she said.

"Unknown ma'am," her detail leader said. "From the bits and pieces we got, they seemed to be targeting a military convoy and taking control of the highway."

She heard their words but was convinced that her Agent in Charge was wrong. *The war is in the south with Rinehart. They had to be looking for me. It's the only thing that make sense.* A ripple of fear washed over her. *If they got their hands on me alive, I can't imagine what they would do.* Images of torture, degrading her, or assaulting her, all rushed to the forefront of her thinking. *Without me, Newmerica would fall apart. Daniel isn't strong enough to lead alone ... as it is, he is filled with hesitation. My nation needs me ... now, more than ever.* There was no doubt in her mind that the enemy felt the same about her level of importance to the Newmerican cause.

"Get me back to the District," she ordered as she pulled her phone out to call the President. *When I'm done with him, I will need to assemble some members of the press. They need to know what is happening ... what the enemy is doing.*

Mt. Vernon, Illinois

One thing Captain Judy Mercury noted about southern Illinois was that it was flat. Trees occasionally broke up the landscape, but for the most part, it was nothing but wide open terrain. It was somewhat warmer than Davenport had been with the only snow being the remnants of previous storms, dirty piles in parking lots.

The journey south had been part of the plan all along. Heading back to Iowa would have forced her into a confrontation with the Illinois National Guard, and the numbers might very well be on their side. Instead they headed south. *If we're lucky, we will get into Paducah in two hours.* When she had proposed the plan, she felt it was more important to get to friendly territory than to try to get back to Iowa specifically. The gloomy dark gray, almost purple, clouds blotted out the setting sun, making everything seem blander, more ominous.

There was another benefit to heading south. St. Louis had been declared a Newmerica autonomous zone. If she was spotted in the southern part of the state, it might make the defenders in St. Louis fear that they were next on her target list. *A little fear can go a long way.* She had learned that years ago while on active duty. *Let them wonder for a day or so if we are going to hit them. Sooner or later we're bound to.*

Paducah was on the Kentucky border, on that state's side of the Ohio River. While the bridges along the Mississippi had been wired with explosives to prevent a counterattack from crossing into Illinois, her intelligence report said there were no such indications about the Ohio River crossings. *All we have to do is signal them with the code phrase that we are coming across, and deal with any roadblocks they may have there*. While on paper it sounded easy, Judy knew it was likely not going to be a simple stroll across the bridge, but so far she was optimistic.

For the time being, they were stopped along IL-37, having just rendezvoused with the flatbed trucks that she had sent ahead of the attack force. Fuel was broken out at the exit where they had linked up, and vehicles were topped off. Fueling the big Abrams tanks took a small team, but they were refueled quickly.

The two primary hostages, the Illinois Governor and Lieutenant Governor, were transferred to another Humvee other than hers. The Governor had been sullen and quietly bitter during the trip. The Lieutenant Governor, on the other hand, had been mouthy—telling her what laws they were breaking, demanding that they be released, warning her about reprisals, … it was never ending. At one point Judy turned on her two captives and told the Lieutenant Governor to, "shut up or I will duct tape your mouth shut. Understood?" The woman must have because after that she kept her legal commentary about their plight to herself.

The trip to the outskirts of Mt. Vernon had been mostly uneventful. There were plenty of stares from passing motorists, stunned to see tanks and other armored fighting vehicles on the road. She had listened to local news stations on the AM frequencies who were reporting of an 'incident' at the State Capitol and a 'terrorist assault' on the National Guard Headquarters. The state commandant of the NSF held a short, press briefing to say that, "Matters are fluid in this ongoing investigation. National Guard troops are being withdrawn, pulled back into the state to protect the legislators and citizens of Springfield," and "We ask patience from our citizens as we conduct our investigation." From what Judy could hear, they were still stunned and confused by her attacks and kidnappings. While that was good news, the better news was that the National Guard was on its way back from Iowa. While the action was intended to quell the fears of the citizens, to Judy it was the sign of something else … victory.

As they finished refueling and giving the crews a chance to stretch and eat, she looked south. *We will need to skirt Mt. Vernon. Sticking to the backroads has worked for us so far, but by now every NSF officer is going to be on the lookout for us.* As she climbed back into the lead Humvee, she waved her hand for the others to fall into a column behind them. The roar of the powerful engines, especially the turbines of the hulking Abrams tanks, made her vehicle seem to throb.

They started down the highway, veering onto a dirt road heading west, E. Webb Road. The potholes jostled the Humvee around side-to-side as they took off down the road. A few minutes later they came alongside I-57. While the two roads ran parallel, they were separated by a thick growth of brush, obscuring their passage. They connected with another road, eventually taking an underpass beneath the highway.

Judy craned her head along the passenger side window as they did. Cars roared overhead, and she watched them carefully. Using the back roads, they had been fortunate that no one had come along and seen them.

As they continued and the last of her vehicles roared under the highway, she opened the door, letting the heat out and a blast of cold air rushing in. Then she saw it—an NSF police cruiser. It slowed on the overpass, coming to a stop. *Shit! We must have kicked up enough dust to get their attention.*

She leaned back in and closed the door as her mind processed it. *There's a chance they didn't see us at all, but maybe some farmer on the back roads tipped them off—or they just stumbled on us.* As much as she wanted to be optimistic, she knew that she couldn't afford to, not with the lives of those in her command at stake. Sunset was coming in a matter of minutes, which would both help hide them but also conceal any threats.

It had been her plan all along to stick to the back roads, hopefully avoid detection until it was too late. Now things were different. There was a chance that the NSF had spotted them, and it wouldn't take much to know that they were heading south. Judy steadied her nerves as her eyes narrowed in thought. *Damn it!*

She activated her mic and broadcast to the column. "Alright Grab Asses," she said firmly. "We may have been seen by the NSF back at the overpass. I had hoped we would be careful and keep off their radar. We can't risk capture or a prolonged engagement here in Illinois.

"So the plan is changing. We're hopping onto the highway, and we are going to haul ass to Paducah. No more of this backroads shit; we are going to move and move full speed, keeping in formation. The time has come for us to go to safe ground."

CHAPTER 20

*"Violence against an opposing, corruptive
viewpoint is an appropriate response."*

Knoxville, Tennessee

G eneral Reager heard another pair of rattling explosions nearby. Windows all around him shattered from the concussion of the explosions. The tinkling of broken glass from the buildings around him was a stark reminder of the dangers of fighting in an urban environment. He lowered himself back into his command Bradley's rear compartment. "We've got some forces up on Western Ave," he said to Captain Hill, his Air Force liaison. We need to make them unalive."

"Yes sir," she said, feeding the orders to the air support above.

Trip rose up the hatch to the periscope to make sure they were dealt with. Less than a minute later there was a long series of rumbles, almost like thunder, from the highway that ran over the street where he was parked. He knew that sound all too well, Spectre gunship support—an AC-130H equipped with two 20 mm M61 Vulcan cannons, and a L60 Bofors 40 mm cannon, and a 105 mm cannon, high above and raining down a stream of death and destruction. Several holes appeared in the highway as shells burst through, spraying dust and debris onto the streets and buildings below.

Any abandoned cars or attacking vehicles would be devoured in such a barrage, and he knew that was happening from the secondary explosions echoing amid the incoming fire. Up above there were explosions in the steady rumble; no doubt the vehicles had been spotted a few minutes earlier. A tire, blown off a Humvee flew off and bounced right in front of his Bradley, bounding off into the side of a building and crunching into the door with a loud bang-thud.

The man-made thunder of the gunship stopped as suddenly as it had started. "All targets eliminated sir. The gunship is low on ordinance and heading back to Arnold," Captain Hill said from her seat. Trip leaned over and told her, "Nice work, Captain," then returned to his perch.

He had not wanted to fight in Knoxville. While it was true that urban warfare favored the defenders, he also knew it would tear apart a lot of buildings and put thousands of civilians at risk. Trip had ordered the civilians to evacuate, but there had not been a lot of time, and the roads had gotten clogged heading to the west and south of the city.

The Newmerican forces had been relentless; he had to concede that much to his opponent, General Rinehart. The Americans had been forced back out of Kodak, and had held for two hours at Midway before withdrawing to Knoxville. Now it had become a prolonged slugfest for the city. They had fought throughout the night, especially in the northern parts of the city, struggling to contain the Newmericans and keep them bottled up. His own Bradley had nearly been captured at one point, but the gunnery crew had destroyed a gray and black enemy Bradley at nearly point blank range, giving his driver, Terry, time to redeploy. As he had looked out into the night through the dawn, the skies of Knoxville were aglow, orange from the fires that were raging unchecked on the battle lines and occasionally lit up by stray tracer rounds steaking skyward. It would have been beautiful if it weren't so deadly.

The struggle for control of Knoxville had raged into a full day. Rinehart's forces were paying a high price for the ground they had taken, and Trip understood why. His force in North Carolina had beaten back the diversionary that had pinned them in place, racing in a long arc to Abington, Virginia. They had caught the Newmericans by surprise, seizing their I-81 supply pipeline, effectively cutting off Rinehart's attack troops in Tennessee. Now his enemy had a choice—push forward and hope to reach Nashville before his supplies ran out, or fall back into Virginia. Rinehart was opting for the former option; that much was clear.

Trip came down. "Show me where they are at," he said to his intelligence officer, Captain Harnessy. To his credit, the Captain already had a display of the city on one wall.

"We are holding them here," he said, pointing at the map. "They have stalled roughly in a line along I-275, which is essentially our front. "We are pushing them south, and they are giving ground.

To the south of the city was the Tennessee River, a perfect natural barrier. Squeezing them to the south would bottle them up against the river and force them to go either east or west. *So how do I take advantage of that?*

Trip looked at the map, his years of training and experience noting every detail, drinking in every corridor. *I'd like to get them in some open ground, a place where we can tear into them. Fighting building by building is hurting us and them. I want them more in the open ... like we did at Stone Mountain.*

Then his gaze spotted a splash of green in the heart of the city, just a few blocks from where he was. The World's Fair Park. "What about this park?" he said, pointing at it.

"It's not big sir, seven blocks or so long, three-to-four blocks wide. There are office buildings throughout, but it does have some flat, open areas."

Trip stared at the park and the disposition of his own forces. "We could fall back, have Colonel Ricketts pull his force back, past the Convention Center. Let them think they are forcing us back; draw them into the park. Rinehart won't be able to resist." He spoke in a low tone, half to himself, half to Harnessy. "If we can get them into the park, we can poise our heavy armor on the fringes. They would be exposed. Bring in some ground support from above—and this offense could be halted."

Harnessy slowly turned to him from the digital display. "Sir, we could do that. But if we don't stop them, they will be able to slide past us on Cumberland and slip along the south out of the city. We don't have any reserves in that area. If they get through, we won't be able to stop them."

Trip's mind was a military calculator, silently evaluating the risks versus the reward; the loss of life versus the possible gains. His defenders had been slugging it out for going on two days with the Newmericans— it was time to bring it to an end. In deep thought, he rubbed the stubble of beard growth on his chin.

"Rinehart has got to be feeling the pinch of no fresh supplies by now.

He can't even get his wounded back to Virginia as long as Major Platt sits on his supply line in Abington. If we give him what he wants to see, us in retreat, he won't be able to resist." He said this with his eyes fixed on the map. Trip's decision was made.

"Put me through to General Ricketts," he said, leaning over to the small communications station in the Bradley's rear. The communications officer nodded to him, and Trip pulled the headset on and put the microphone up to his face. "Dan, this is Reager. How are you holding up?"

"Overworked and underpaid, General," he said, the rapid banging of a Bradley's M242 thumping off near where Ricketts was poised. "We are making them pay for every building they take."

"I have an idea, a redeployment," Trip said. "And I need you to pull it off."

"Go on," he said. Another three rapid booms in his headset told Trip how close Ricketts was to the front line.

"I think it's time we serve these invaders a bit of southern hospitality … "

Vernon, The Republic of Texas

Caylee looked around the dark room they had rented at the Budget Inn and didn't flinch nearly as much as Kiff did. It was a dingy room, with thick blackout curtains that held onto every smell that had ever passed through the room. The bedspreads of the two twin beds were designed to be a colorful pattern and while they looked clean, she was thankful that they didn't have a black light with her. The coffee machine was old school, bolted to the desktop where it sat.

Kiff brought in his gear and winced. "What a dump."

"I've stayed in worse," she replied. *When we are through this, I should tell you about my time in Kyiv.*

"You would think that this Hickox-guy would pick a better place to crash than this," he said putting his backpack and suitcase on the far bed.

"My experience has been that people stay at places like this so they are not seen," she said. "I'm willing to bet he doesn't want anyone to know what he's doing here."

"So what is the plan?" Kiff said, avoiding sitting on the bedspread and moving to the lone chair at the desk along the wall.

Caylee moved over to her bed and sat down. "Assuming you need the same amount of time as the job we did at Trans-Tex, we will need to get into the room and make sure that our target remains asleep. Reaching over to a tool bag she had brought in, she pulled out a small black pouch and showed him several syringes.

"If you poke him with a needle, he'll wake up," Kiff said.

"I've used this stuff before. He won't remember a thing. He might start to wake up, but this is pretty fast acting, especially in the dosage that I use. If he has company, I brought enough to dose two."

"So you're just going to break in, drug him, and I mirror his drive—is that it?"

"Pretty much," Caylee said flatly.

"When do we go?"

"It's dark now. We wait. Most people sleep their soundest in the early morning hours, when they are in deep REM sleep. He's in a room three doors down. I saw him enter before we checked in; that was why I picked this room—its proximity to his. These hotel locks are really old, fairly simple to overcome. I'll go in first, slow and silent, shoot him up, and then you come in and do what you have to."

"You make it all sound so easy," Kiff said.

"It's not," she admitted. "A dozen things can go wrong. If he's not asleep or a light sleeper, he might make a move against us. We're in Texas, so I will assume he's armed, especially since he calls himself a General. We know nothing about his guest. Maybe she is awake for some early morning sex. Someone might see us breaking in and call the authorities. There's a lot of places where this can fall apart."

"You aren't exactly pumping me full of confidence," Kiff said glumly.

She tilted her head forward slightly as she eyed him. "You wanted to know, and I've told you. We will go in prepared." She had been teaching him the basics of holding a pistol and some defensive moves. Kiff was stiff, but he was an eager learner, which helped. *Hopefully he won't have to do anything but his techno-stuff.*

She rose from the bed and shut off the light, plunging the room into darkness. Kiff spoke up quickly. "What's with the dark?"

"I need to look out the window, and if I open those drapes now, with the light on, someone might see us. Besides, I want my eyes to adjust to the darkness." With those words, she moved to where the curtains came together and parted them open less than an inch so that she could glance out. The night was dark; the parking lot had about a dozen vehicles in it. Sadly, their beat-up pickup looked like one of the nicer ones, aside from Hickox's big, dark blue Suburban. "We've got a few hours, so you might want to relax."

"Relax?" Kiff said with a chuckle. "We are technically in a foreign country in the middle of America, planning on breaking into the room of the General in charge of this fiasco, to steal data off of his computer in the middle of the night. I don't think sleep is going to be high on my list until we are out of this place."

"Point taken," she said, turning to the window and allowing herself to smile, if only for a moment.

Knoxville, Tennessee

It was nearly midnight by the time Colonel Ricketts' battered and exhausted troops fell back across the World's Fair Park, linking up with a number of stragglers that Trip's HQ had managed to assemble. Often times breaking off an engagement with an enemy in battle was more costly than waging an offense, and that was certainly true in the case of Reager's tactical redeployment. Many of the armored vehicles showed signs of damage. The infantry was exhausted. Trip could see it in their eyes as he helped Ricketts deploy his forces.

Ricketts was an older officer who was fighting the years, gravity, and the enemy. His face was smeared with black soot; his white mustache was wet as he breathed heavily; the cold night air made thin wisps of frosty breath in the air between them. "They held up on the other side of the convention center," he said. "They probably think we are in it and using it to stage attacks from." As if to make his point, several loud high explosive blasts tore into the back side of the large center. Windows shattered across the face of the structure as the Newmerican artillery blasted the building. The ground reverberated with each explosion under Trip's boots.

"You have your positions set, Colonel?" he asked,

"Yes sir," he said. "We are treating this side of the park along 11th as our line. I have snipers in the parking garage, along with some air defense on the roof and missile launchers. We have coverage of the park from ground level with our armor." Another pair of artillery blasts destroyed the upper floors of the convention center and flames burst forth along the roof, lighting up the park with flickers of orange shadows.

Out of the corner of his eye, he spotted the Sunsphere, the large obelisk tower that rose some seventy-five feet in the air. Topping it was a golden orb of reflective plates, looking more like a Christmas decoration than a representation of the sun. It had been put up during the 1982 World's Fair and had been an icon of Knoxville ever since. Now though, several of the golden reflective plates were gone, dislodged at some point by the vibrations of the battle closing in on it and the park it overlooked. It was a silent observer of what was about to happen.

"Here they come!" rang out of voice from the rear of Trip's command Bradley nearby.

Rifle fire began to fill the darkness of the park. Tracers lit up light spider webs, crisscrossing the flat, open fairgrounds. The cracking and popping of gunfire from the enemy was met with return fire, machine guns purring out short deadly bursts. Smoke rolled out in front of the advancing troops as they tried to grope for cover in the open field of fire and death.

Several rounds ricocheted off of the building where Ricketts and Trip stood, forcing both to move flush to a wall to avoid getting hit by stray fire. "You go to the south, and make sure they don't try and skirt us along the river. You're the end of the line Colonel. If you lose ground, they are going to slide in behind us and drive right on to Nashville. You can't give up; it's that simple. Understood?" Trip asked. Ricketts nodded and gave him a grim but determined, "Yes sir!" as he darted down the street to use an ally for cover, one hand holding his helmet in place as he ran. The rumble of approaching armored vehicles could be heard off to the east, rounding the burning convention center.

Trip darted to his Bradley and got in as the small arms fire intensified over the park. He closed the door behind him as several bullets thunked into Bradley's front armor. The 25mm chain gun banged out three rounds in succession; their explosions were lost in the cacophony of the battle that was unfolding.

"Terry," trip called to the driver over the roar of the cannon above him. "Drift us back; get us out of their direct line of fire for now."

The Bradley's engine roared, and the vehicle reversed, almost toppling Trip, who managed to catch his grip on a hand guide to stay upright. Machine guns nearby purred, sending a wall of deadly jacketed bullets downrange. As he pulled himself into his periscope turrets, he saw an enemy Bradley start to race across the fairgrounds. A Hellfire missile, likely fired from the parking garage, slammed into its softer armored topside, punching inward. The Newmerican Bradley erupted in a blast of crimson and orange fire that blew open every orifice and hatch on the vehicle. A sickening sound of grinding metal could be heard as the vehicle died, its flames adding to the light show filling the night skies.

Artillery rumbled to his rear as the enemy attempted to lay down a barrage where they thought Trip's forces might be. They were off, but it was just a matter of time before they isolated his strong points.

We have to hold here ... we don't have a choice.

Vernon, The Republic of Texas

Kiff stood at the doorway to their room while Caylee moved cat-like on the balcony that connected the entire second story of rooms at the Budget Inn. He watched as she lowered herself to a squatting position and began to work on the lock. His own eyes drifted down to the parking lot, which was dark, cold and quiet. Somewhere in the distance, he heard a car horn blare, probably the only excitement in a city as small as Vernon at midnight. From what little he had seen, the local citizens kept to themselves.

While at dinner earlier, he heard people talking about, "... them Republic folks ..." and from the sound of it, most of the locals had been taken by surprise when the Republic seized the county governments and declared them a new nation. Years of living in Newmerica had tempered most of the people he overheard. There seemed to be a wait-and-see approach to what had transpired weeks earlier. To Kiff, it was encouraging. It meant that there wasn't some great groundswell in support of the Republic of Texas that had seized power.

Kiff carried a pistol, a Kimber 1911. Caylee had insisted on it. She had taught him how to hold it; how to shoot; he still wasn't doing that up to her expectations. He had fired a gun before, but it had been a long time ago, soon after the Fall. He joked with her about it, "If you're relying on my shooting to save us, we're both doomed."

Caylee was undeterred. "You never know how an op will go." She had even given Kiff instructions on how to leave the Republic of Texas, should she be unable to join him.

Kiff thought, *It must be odd in her line of work, always having to prepare for the worst case scenario.* Despite all of her prowess and skills, there was a part of him that felt sad for her. *The life that she's living sure as hell isn't an easy one.*

Caylee nudged and poked at the lock with her picking tools, always pausing and checking her surroundings. There was a level of cold calculation in the way she moved and talked that Kiff liked. It wasn't just that he had the skills; she had an air of self-confidence that he respected and admired.

With a smooth twist, the door handle spun, and she slowly cracked it open. Rising, she tucked away her lock picks and slid into the room. Kiff followed, tip-toeing as he walked. He knew it was stupid that he was wearing sneakers, but it was almost instinctual. When he got to the door, he slowly opened it enough for him and his backpack to enter.

Caylee was already standing over the two figures in the bed. One was Booker Hickox, and the other was a female he decided from the flop of red hair poking out from under the covers. Caylee dealt with Hickox first, no doubt because he would pose the biggest threat. She gently pressed the needle into his neck, injecting the syringe. For a moment, he jerked, and it looked, in the dim light of the half-cracked curtains, that his eyes opened. Hickox's body went rigid. Then, a second later, he went limp. His eyes glassed over as he drifted off.

Caylee repeated the process with the redhead, pulling the covers back enough to expose her wrist and injecting there. She made a light yelping sound, then snored. Caylee said nothing as she moved to the window and drew the curtains shut, then moved to lock the door. Only then did she click on the small desk light. "Alright Mr. Renner, you're up."

He opened his laptop and while it booted up, he rifled around for Hickox's. It was in a briefcase, which made him grin. *Hello 1970s! Who carries a briefcase these days?* He wired the two computers together and started up Hickox's.

Hickox had good security on the system, an encryption program that demanded a PIN. He simply plugged in one of his flash drives and saw a tiny light flicker to life as it began to bombard the Texan's hard drive with possible PINs. It took five minutes, but Hickox's PC finally finished its startup, flashing the Windows logo on the screen.

Once he got past the initial security barrier, he found other safeguards on the system that prevented him from mirroring the drive. Those required other tools, and some on-the-fly modifications to the software that he loaded up to penetrate the security. Kiff's entire focus was on the hardware; his finger and mouse moved furiously as he pressed on to connect the PCs digitally. It took another seventeen minutes, but he finally managed to start the mirroring process.

"We good?" Caylee asked from her position next to Hickox.

"I think so," Kiff replied, double-checking the screens.

Suddenly, there was a crack-bang at the door, loud enough to make his ears ache. The door swung wide open and a figure entered, emerging through a haze of smoke from whatever had been used to blow the lock. Kiff saw the weapon in his hand, a pistol with a long barrel—no, a suppressor. It swung at him first as he sat at the desk; then it darted to Caylee, who was half-way through drawing her own pistol.

"Hold it right there!" the voice commanded as the man entered the room. Another figure followed him through the door.

Kiff looked over at Caylee who seemed to hold her hands up slightly to make sure she did not look like a threat. He thought about his own pistol, in his pants pocket—probably the worst possible place for him to have it at that moment. He mirrored her actions, but a feeling of doom came over him. *We've been busted!*

Knoxville, Tennessee

The dull flat green Newmerican Abrams tank thundered fast across the World's Fair Park, sparks of gunfire glancing off of its thick armored hide as it moved. Trip's eyes widened as he could see it heading right for the parking garage off to his left. The big cannon barked, sending a shell into the middle of the structure. The explosion rained down bits of concrete and brick on the command Bradley as the tank turned to the south, its turret still tracking the parking structure.

Trip Reager flinched at the sight. In the last war, he had always been in one of those tanks on the offense. Being on the receiving end of a charge by an Abrams was a mix of awe-inspiring and terrifying. *God damn it; that is magnificent!* He held his fears in check though; he had to. This wasn't their first attempt to shatter his lines, but it was a dangerous one. A pair of enemy Bradley's followed the Abrams by a few yards, their guns firing rounds into the parking structure, no doubt to keep his troops pinned so they couldn't fire their Javelin missiles again. The last such attack lay burning in the middle of the park near the overpass at Clinch Avenue where they had been blasted apart. Five burning hulks roared, their flames lighting up the area, blackening the overpass above.

"Alright Lariat," he said into his shoulder mic as he looked out the periscope portal. "Pave the road with these bastards."

"Yes sir," came the voice of Captain Lariat Paredes, the whoomping of his Apache's rotors distinct in the headset that Trip wore. His platoon of helicopters came in low and fast a few moments later, running north to south over the park. The pair of Black Hawk® helicopters concentrated their machine gun fire on the turret and thin top of the Bradleys, just enough to get their attention for the moment. Paredes's Apache unleashed a pair of Hellfire missiles at the top and rear of the enemy Abrams tanks.

The explosions rocked the fast moving armored vehicle as it skidded into the side of the lower level of the parking garage. The sound of grinding metal and concrete was sickening. Smoke rolled out of the engine compartment of the Abrams, making it hard for Trip to get a view of how bad the damage really was. *Even if the tank loses its engine, that cannon can tear us up.*

He had held back the helicopters for this kind of push by the enemy and was glad that he did. The Bradley's, suddenly feeling incredibly vulnerable, banked hard at around forty mph, trying to turn for the overpass that marked the flaming graves of the last assault. One collided with the burning vehicle, grinding metal hard with the impact. Realizing their attackers were from above, they must have thought that the overpass was somehow going to be safe for them.

Captain Paredes sensed it too. He fired another Hellfire at the Abrams, then at the lead Bradley. The hit on the Abrams threw hot, glowing, yellow, molten metal spraying into the park—which was followed by a massive explosion from within as the tank and her crew died. Bits of armor and tank parts flew into the damaged parking garage and out onto the World's Fair Park.

The lead Bradley was hit in the rear compartment and was immediately gutted with brilliant yellow and orange flames. The driver of the second Bradley was following so closely that when the lead vehicle was hit, it collided with the flaming vehicle, hitting it hard. The collision, the sound of metal on metal, made Trip wince for a moment.

As the enemy driver backed up, bits of the first vehicle, still on fire, clung to the front of the still operational Bradley. The diver must have panicked for a moment, that or they had suffered damage. After backing up a few yards from its dead counterpart, it seemed to sit there, stationary.

The survivors in the parking garage fired one of their Javelin missiles at the Bradley, hitting the side of the armored vehicle. The back hatch flew open and infantry jumped out, some on fire themselves, all rolling to put out the flames or trying to dive for any cover in the wide open park. Machine guns suddenly came to life, shredding the emerging infantry, dropping a handful of them right in front of the burning tank.

The helicopters banked around, and a missile snaked up from the far side of the park, hitting one of the Black Hawks, lighting up the sky. The helicopter began a death spiral downward to the south of the park, some of its infantry occupants jumping out before it crashed into Second Creek, which snaked down from the park to the Tennessee River. Trip hoped that they were still alive, but he wasn't holding out hope.

The remaining helicopters clearly found targets on the other side of the World's Fair Park. Their missiles stabbed down, and the tracers from their machine guns looked like yellow lightning bolts slashing at the targets. After another pass, Trip heard Captain Paredes's voice in his headset. "We just toasted two more tanks. Their access to the park around the convention center is bottled up with them sir," he said.

"Anything else coming up?" he asked.

"Negative. It looks like they were planning another push, ... Now they are as plugged up as my pop-pop's toilet the morning after burrito night," he said with his best southern drawl. "They are plugged up on those side streets. I can make another pass and really plug them up if I take out the rear of their columns."

"Do it," Trip said firmly. A choice loomed before him. *If Rinehart has half a brain, he might very well decide to fall back, realizing that a charge is already doomed.* It was tempting to let him retreat all of the way back to Virginia. His defenders were exhausted already. Pushing his men might mean a reversal if the Newmericans felt trapped. *Cornered rats are nasty things to deal with.*

While it was tempting, Trip smelled the blood of his enemy and wanted to go in for the kill. *If we don't take out this army here and now, I might very well be facing them somewhere else. I have a chance for a knockout blow right now. Letting it pass means fighting these people another day.*

Drawing a deep breath, he turned to his communications officer with a new set of orders already fermenting in the back of his mind.

CHAPTER 21

"Despotism is always a matter of perspective."

Massac Forest Nature Preserve, Illinois

Judy's convoy of Task Force Grab Ass roared down I-24 to the Paducah Bridge and the safety of Kentucky. The highway was a wide open stretch in the pre-dawn darkness, with only a few cars and trucks—most of which were surprised to see tanks and armored vehicles thundering down the highway. Their sound and size was enough to make even the biggest semitruck driver wince and give them room.

The highway cut through the Massac natural preserve, a dense forest. It was set back nearly 500 feet on either side of the four lanes of roadway, barely visible in the darkness. The woods made her nervous though she was unsure why.

They had spotted an occasional NSF police car, all parked with their lights on, no doubt monitoring their rush south. She doubted that the Illinois National Guard would be able to catch up with them at this point given that they had started their fallback from Davenport around the time her task force left Springfield. That didn't mean they were safe. *I won't feel that way until we are in Kentucky.*

The Kentucky side of the river had been told that Judy was coming—it had been part of the plan all along. She didn't have the means to let them know that it was her force, not an Illinois force, which was coming into their state—they were simply told to be prepared to receive friendlies in armored vehicles. *Hopefully they got the message. ... I'd hate to have to shoot my way into safety.*

As they got closer to the state line on the Ohio River, she saw the flicker of crimson and azure lights ahead. A long line of police vehicles was arrayed across the highway, right at the edge of the river. The big steel arched bridge beyond them was illuminated from their red tail lights. Headlights stabbed out at her Humvee.

"Grab Asses, slow up," Judy ordered as her own driver decelerated. She used binoculars to look ahead. The road lights leading to the bridge illuminated the outlines of at least a dozen police cruisers and a number of armored vehicles that the NSF used for riot and SWAT situations. No doubt snipers were hidden along the flanks in the forest, waiting to pick them out as they approached.

The worst thing we could do is get bogged down in a battle on this side of the bridge. The NSF's Bearcat, Gurkha, and Typhoon armored cars were arrayed in front of her. While they were imposing, they were not a match for her own vehicles. She went over the options—including sweeping to the flanks, or engaging at distances that the NSF couldn't reach. The sudden chop of a helicopter rotor overhead told her they had air support coming in as well.

The time for subtlety is over. Reaching up to her shoulder, she toggled her mic open. "This is Actual. Alright, here's the game plan. I want the Abrams at the front of the column. We go in, two-by-two. We are not waiting for them to fire; engage at extreme range. Use AP on the armored vehicles; target them first. We drive at around thirty miles per hour, straight at them. Hit that line of vehicles and drive right over them if you have to; plow the path for the rest of us. I want the Bradleys to open fire on the flank vehicles—HE ... light 'em up. We are not going to give them the fight they want; our goal is to get over the bridge. If something is in your way, destroy it ... plain and simple. I want the rear of the column to use their machine guns on that chopper. Everyone got that?"

A chorus of tense, "Yes sirs," came back.

Judy adjusted herself in her seat, pulling her sidearm. "Alright—let's roll!"

Knoxville, Tennessee

The American counterattack across the blasted and battered World's Fair Park was swift and savage. The burning convention center still had plenty of enemy machine gun nests which rained down a torrent of fire the moment the vehicles of Trip Reager's command began to roll. They fired bullets, and Trip's force unleashed high explosives, gutting entire parts of the convention center with more flames and raining glass down on everyone in the process. It came down like dangerous shards of ice, clinking and shattering further as the ragged force rushed across. The tinkling only added to the deafening roar of the guns on both sides.

There were plenty of dead and wounded in the park, along with over a dozen blown up or burning vehicles. The drivers would do their best not to roll over the injured in the park, but there were no guarantees. Trip knew that, and while he knew he would be labeled something horrible by the TRC for his orders, he stuck to them. *War is death and destruction. If you come to play, you have to know the risks of the game.*

His own Bradley joined the lunge across the park. Its 25mm boomed—spitting out short bursts of three rounds across the park, tearing into the side streets on the opposite side of the park. Burning vehicles there, taken out by the attack helicopters, marked where the Newmericans had been gathering for their next assault. Now they were forced to the role of defenders as Trip's forces unleashed a storm of fire into their ranks.

A Javelin missile twisted and snaked out of the carnage on the enemy's line, slamming into one of the assaulting Bradleys, engulfing it in flames and sending its turret blasting up and off to the side of the gutted vehicle.

Trip watched the tracer fire that filled the park as the rush of armored vehicles reached the far end. Another savage explosion hit the convention center near where the raging fire was roaring still—throwing bits of flaming debris down on a passing American Abrams tank. The big turret swung onto one of the side streets and fired at almost point blank range at the source of the TOW missile. Trip couldn't see the target vehicle, but the brilliant red and yellow fireball marked its death.

As his driver, Terry, made a slow turn with the Bradley, Trip caught himself being drawn into the details of the fighting rather than the larger picture. It was natural, and something that he had to resist. He moved to the communications station. *I'm not running this firefight. I'm running the entire battle.* "Send to Colonel Ricketts that we are across the park and heading east." The roar of multiple explosions outside didn't rattle Trip.

He was hoping and praying that Colonel Ricketts was making his drive from the north into that flank of the Newmericans. Coordinating the attack was always tricky, but so far Ricketts had proven himself to be made of stern stuff. Another explosion rocked the Bradley hard, side-to-side, enough to cause him to lose his footing for a second. He banged his helmet on the side of the fighting vehicle's interior before catching a hand rail for support. Up above, the turret once more spat out a trio of shots as it finished the slow arc of a turn.

Machine gun fire tinged and banged against the Bradley for a moment, and it stopped as quickly as it had started. "We have inbound enemy aircraft—three minutes out," called Captain Hill from her workstation a few feet away.

Trip had expected some sort of response, and now it was coming. The problem was his own CAP was thin. "Comms—send to all commands, incoming aircraft. Get into point blank range with the enemy."

"Yes sir," the communications officer replied. Captain Hill's head turned slowly toward him with an astonished look on her narrow face.

"Nighttime bombing in a city is hard to begin with," Trip assured her. "It's even harder when we are on top of the enemy." It wasn't an assurance of safety, but it was a way to mitigate the sudden incoming surge of air cover.

He shifted to the viewing periscope and could see they were now almost all of the way across the park. Flames seemed to be everywhere as a big part of the burning convention center collapsed inward on itself, throwing sparks skyward into the haze that hung over Knoxville from the battle below. In the distance he could hear the roar of jets overhead, seeming to get closer.

"Advance," he called to Terry. "Get us in tight and snug to the bad guys!"

Brattleboro, Vermont

Su-Hui climbed up the railroad embankment, the snow almost crackling under him as he lay flat to get a good view of the bridges over the Connecticut River. While both were arched bridges and next to each other, one was new, covered in a dull coat of light green paint. The older bridge had simple orange cones blocking it off. From what he could see, the old bridge was no longer open to traffic, but was more of a pedestrian crossing. On the other side of the bridge was New Hampshire and hopefully a bit of freedom.

His harasser force had pulled off of the road at sunrise, taking a trail to the railroad embankment where they had huddled in alongside the tracks. With the sun up, they were painfully visible. *We need to get back to safety and soon.*

When they had come into New York from Vermont, they had crossed at another bridge, a mile and a half south, near the heart of the town. Experience told him not to go in and out on the same roads. He squinted down at the NSF checkpoint on the bridge and saw a pair of cruisers set up. No cars were coming in from New Hampshire; that traffic had ground to a halt with the Newmerican invasion and the imposing of martial law. The police barricade and officers were focused on New Hampshire, not on a threat hitting them from their side of the bridge. One thing was sure. New York had not communicated with Vermont about the attack on their National Guard headquarters. ... Otherwise there would be more than two parked cars to block the bridge. He had been listening on the radio, and while there were reports of an 'incident' at the headquarters, the news media was not saying much more than that. *It means that they either are unsure if it was an attack, or are deliberately withholding that information.*

"What do you think?" Valerie Watson asked as she looked down on the scene.

"One bridge is guarded; the other isn't," he said. "Either way, they have only two cars there."

"We could bum rush them, cross over on the old bridge," she offered.

Su-Hui looked it over. "We don't know how much weight that old bridge will hold. They closed it for a reason. Our best chance is to take the bridge that we know is sound."

"Do you just want to drive over them?" she offered. "Because we can totally do that." There was a hint in Valerie's voice that she wanted to do just that. He understood as the mental picture of the crushed vehicles was oddly pleasing. What steadied him, however, was logic.

Su-Hui surveyed the officers seated in their vehicles; no doubt they were keeping their motors running to fight off the cold. "We want them silenced quickly," he said. "I don't want them radioing the Newmericans that we are coming across here." If they warned the enemy they were coming, they might be able to box them in. The Humvees were good in cross country, and while some of Vermont's snow had melted, a lot was still there. Just blazing off cross country could get them trapped just as quickly as staying on the roads if they weren't careful.

"They are in their cars, so if we open fire, the first thing they are going to do is get low and start calling for backup. I know. I was a cop," she assured him.

"So we have to take them out quickly," he said. "Cripple their ability to broadcast or kill the occupants before they can get a warning off," he said, contemplating his options. The positioning of the cars and the curve of the road limited the ability for someone to sneak up on the cars as they had done crossing into Vermont. With the sun already up, he felt dangerously exposed.

"You have an idea I take it?"

"It won't be quiet, but it will take care of the problem," he said. "We will need to act quickly though."

Vernon, The Republic of Texas

Caylee eyed the man holding a gun on her with a look of icy controlled surprise. She had been caught off guard but wanted to make it look to the newcomers as if she were more frightened than she was. *He has a gun aimed at me; I need to appear as least threatening as possible.* She raised her hands slightly as he moved into the room, followed by a compatriot who was nervously waving his gun in Kiff's direction. "Whoa, whoa," she said almost casually. "There must be some kind of mistake." Holding her hands up, she had put them right where she wanted them, giving her several options for action.

She judged the man holding the gun on her to be the biggest threat. She could tell by the way he was holding his gun. His sidekick was holding the gun as if he were a kid playing cops and robbers. That man had his trigger finger on the guard, rather than just below the rail of the gun, the mark of an amateur. She had grilled Kiff about that, to the point where she taped his finger at one point on the rail to drive the point home. The man holding the gun on her had his hands out in front of him, his left hand wrapped around the front, holding it like a vice in his hands, raised to eye level and aimed at her.

"Drop your weapons!" he barked; she picked up on his slight Asian accent. Both of them were dressed in casual attire; neither wore body armor, and both appeared to be of Asian heritage. He was not wearing military gear, so she assumed he was not some security detail from the Republic of Texas. *I need to keep this situation from getting out of control.*

Surrender was an option, but one she quickly purged. If she gave them up, they would lose the data that Kiff had gathered ... and she was sure they would be dead before she could reverse the situation. *We have to resolve this now!*

Slowly, methodically, she reached down to the pistol at her side. She had three weapons, a small knife in the belt on her back, contoured to her body, her pistol she was reaching for, and one on her shin. "I'm going to take my gun out of the holster," she said slowly.

"Slowly!" he said nervously, shaking his gun once in her direction.

Kiff was on his feet, facing her assailant's counterpart. For a fleeting moment, they made eye contact. She wanted to say, "Remain calm," to him, but had to let her eyes do the talking for the time being. Like her, he raised his arms, using the chair as a barrier between the two of them.

She continued to methodically reach for her weapon as her assailant closed the distance a half step between them. With two fingers, so that he would not mistake her grabbing for the pistol, she gripped the handle and tugged it free from the holster in one smooth jerk.

"On the bed," he ordered.

She bent slightly and put the gun on Booker Hickox's drugged out body. With all of the commotion in the room, neither of the two in the bed had stirred at all. If it weren't for the gun aimed at her, she might have chuckled.

The man facing her was the oldest of the two. He cautiously moved around the foot of the bed and beside her; then bending slightly, he reached out with his left hand to grab her gun and tossed it to the far corner of the bed. "Who are you? What are you doing here?"

"We don't want any trouble," Caylee said. There was truth in that;

she would prefer there was no trouble, but now that it had come, she was mentally prepared to deal with it. "We are just here doing a little work."

Her words seemed to fall on deaf ears. "Close the door," he said off to his side, never breaking gaze with her. His ally moved back to the door whose knob was now hanging by a few shattered bits of wood and metal. He closed the door. It had been opened with a breaching charge—an explosive charge for blowing doors. That told her she was dealing with a professional beyond the way he held himself, his wide footing, and his holding the gun up to aim squarely at her chest.

"Who sent you?" he demanded in a low, almost growling tone.

"Let's just say we are not allies of the Republic. Who sent you?" Caylee asked.

"I will ask the questions here!" he said angrily. "Who are you working for?"

"Tell him," Kiff said, with a nod. For just a moment, her assailant's attention shifted to Kiff who had been quiet up until that moment. She watched his eyes as they dashed to his left.

Three options came to her—her knife was not a good throwing knife; it was a curved combat knife with a relatively small blade, a Karambit. Besides, it was sheathed in the square of her back.

That left the two guns. One was on the bed, closer to her foe than she was; the other in her leg holster. Both presented challenges she did not like. At the same time, she couldn't pass up the distraction that Kiff had given her.

She dropped straight down, her hand wrapping around the Sig Sauer in the leg holster. For a moment, things were a blur, her lowering. Her opponent, realizing she was ducking down, turned his eyes back to her. He had to drop his aim and was doing so, eating away at what few tiny moments Kiff had given her. She raised her gun as he lowered his. There was a bang, and another … hers being second. Something hit her, a bullet, hard, between her breasts. Caylee flew back into the nightstand, the impact sending the lamp falling and crashing down next to her. It was hard to breathe, but she didn't panic; instead she adjusted her aim and fired again.

For a moment, her vision tunneled as the gun went off. Another pair of shots rang out, making her ears throb. *No, not like this, not now!*

The Paducah Bridge, Illinois

The charge of the Grab Asses opened with the Abrams tanks unleashing their deadly 120mm cannons as they raced at the front of the columns. The boom and flash from the big guns lit up the darkness. One Typhoon armored vehicle seemed to disappear as the armor piercing its shell and hit it head on, going through the engine and then the rear compartment. To Judy, it was as if it folded in on itself, tossing the vehicle back nearly a dozen feet. The burning hulk rolled down the embankment, she presumed into the river.

The second tank's shot hit a Bearcat armored car broadside, going in one side and out the other, hitting another police cruiser that was parked behind it. The Bearcat miraculously did not explode, but the police cruiser flipped up in the air, riding a ball of bright red and orange flames.

Gun fire from automatic weapons, small arms, and machine guns flashed all along the police line that had already been breached. Bullets raced out at the tanks of the vehicles huddled in behind them as they roared toward the bridge. Someone in the NSF force thought it was brilliant to fire teargas, and the fog from the noxious substance formed a misty barrier that the bullets and tracers stabbed through.

The Abram's big .50 caliber machine guns responded, as did the main armament. More explosions flashed from the barrels, then almost immediately were downrange. The bright explosions lit up the tear gas cloud, like lightning bursts in a thunderstorm. The deep banging fire of the huge machine guns stitched a line of tracers all along the line of police cars. For a moment parts of the NSF line stopped firing altogether; no doubt the troopers were dead or falling back for better cover.

Judy's force roared down I-24 when a searchlight plastered them from above. Automatic weapons fire sprayed the convoy. One of her flatbed trucks burst into flames, the driver's compartment roaring like a bonfire as it lurched off the road and rolled over. *Damn it!*

She grabbed for her shoulder mic. "I want fire on that chopper, and I want it now!"

Machine guns from the Humvees purred behind her. The searchlight went off, no doubt hit in the initial shots. Craning around to the side of the Humvee that she was in, she saw sparks of shots hitting the chopper; then she heard a sickening sound, metal twisting against metal, and the helicopter began a deadly arc down, crashing into the northbound lanes of the highway not far from where her flatbed truck had crashed.

She wanted to detach someone to go back to the truck, but she knew deep down that might put them and the rest of her force at risk. The urge to not leave men behind, even dead men, ate at her, but she steadied her resolve. *I'm responsible for everyone ... and there's nothing we can do for them.* Bullets thwacked into her own armored windshield, leaving a few more cracks. Her Humvee began to make a strange rattling noise from under the hood, and her heart sank. "What is that?" she asked her driver.

"Don't know," he said. "It's still running. We can do a tune-up in Kentucky," he said nervously.

She appreciated his humor. Machine gun fire flashed from the forest on both sides of the highway; bullets slammed into the convoy. Her own rear gunner dropped down, his right hand missing and squirting blood. He didn't cry out in pain, but tried to stop the bleeding. "Tourniquet!" she called to the rear passengers who scrambled to stem the crimson spray. An explosion off to her right marked the end of the black NSF Gurkha armored car, ... it's parts raining down on two other police vehicles, an axle with tire impaling the hood of one vehicle, the tire ablaze like some strange torch.

Her own Bradleys behind her in line opened up on the source of the tracers with their 25mm cannons, chewing up trees and silencing the guns on both sides as they roared into the tear gas cloud. More shots popped and peppered the side of her own vehicle with one leaving a smoking hole near the rear.

She remembered the sting of tear gas from the riots and basic training. Her eyes instantly stung, and she struggled to breathe as she pulled out her mask and put it on. Snot oozed into the mask, and she could barely focus for a moment.

The tank in front of her lurched as it drove into the police line that was parallel to the river. A heartbeat later, her own Humvee followed, turning sharply as it rose over the police cruiser that the Abrams had crushed almost flat. They dropped hard on the concrete of the bridge, but refused to slow and raced down under the arches of the bridge toward Kentucky.

Pulling her mask off, she strained to look out the back of the Humvee to see how many of her task force made it across. "This is Actual," she said as they reached the halfway point on the bridge. "Are we all here?"

Knoxville, Tennessee

As the sunrise slowly crept over the smoldering heart of Knoxville, General Reager watched as another group of prisoners were led out of the carnage and into a holding area before being sent into captivity. The sunlight of the brisk morning hit the remains of the Sunsphere over the World's Fair Park. The once proud icon of the city still stood, though half of its brass-coppery colored panels were shattered. Through the haze of the fires from the convention center, he could make out where an errant high explosive round had destroyed some of the supports halfway up. The great sphere hung at a slight angle, pointing east ... *pointing to victory.*

Colonel Ricketts walked over to him as Trip stood next to his war weary Bradley. Ricketts looked exhausted; his shirt was soaked with sweat and soot. The smudges of black on his face made the wrinkles on his red skin even more pronounced. "About two companies of them are heading back on I-40. They got out before we could trap them."

"Order in air support to strike at them," Trip said.

"Yes sir, I already did," he said with a smile. "Don't worry; most of them are not going to make it."

"Once we pick up the pieces here, we need to pursue them into Virginia. I want to link up with our people in Abington." *If Virginia wants to play war, it is going to cost them some of their territory.*

The last hour of the fighting had not been as savage as he had anticipated. Once the Newmericans realized that most of them were cut off, they surrendered. It was a trickle at first, then more. At one point, some troops fired on their own people who were trying to surrender, mowing down a half dozen of them before they were taken out by his own American forces. *I wonder if that was an order, or if someone was just a diehard supporter that refused to see their people surrender? I doubt we will ever know for sure.*

"Our counterattack threw them off. They were getting ready for a hell of a big push. We caught them all bottled up. They had the firepower, but no way to deploy it by the time we were on top of them," Ricketts said.

"We were lucky," Trip added wearily.

"I'll take luck any time I can get it."

"Anyone find General Rinehart in all of this?" Trip asked as he heard the first sounds of fire sirens wailing in the distance. It was too late to save the convention center or many of the surrounding structures, but the battle had consumed over half of the city. The sirens demonstrated that things might return to some sort of normal, and he took it as a positive sign. The smell of burnt rubber and melted plastic stung at his nostrils as he continued to survey the devastation.

"I talked to one of their Lieutenants," Ricketts replied. "No one has heard from him since our counterattack hit them. The rumor is that he caught MH-6 and hightailed it out of here heading back to old Virginny, but we have no confirmation of that."

"How soon can you set off for Abington?" Trip asked.

"Give me six hours," Ricketts said. "My people are about to drop as it is."

"Give them ten," Trip said; then get on the road.

Ricketts nodded and said, "Yes sir," in response. He then reached into his filthy field coat. "By any chance, are you a drinking man, General?"

The questions seemed to come from nowhere. Trip nodded. "I drink from time to time, yes. Why?"

Ricketts pulled out a dull steel flask. "I'm a bourbon man. My son got me a bottle of Pappy Van Winkle Special Reserve—good stuff and expensive as hell. For years I have been saving it, carrying a flask with me when on assignments—waiting for the right opportunity to finally try it. I'd be honored, General, if you would join me."

Trip had received medals before for his service. He had been promoted many times, and each one of those moments filled him with pride. Yet this moment, there, in the ruins of the World's Fair Park, he suddenly felt the most honored. Nodding to Ricketts, he took the flask and sipped it. The bourbon *was* good; it was smooth, living up to its reputation. Handing it back to Ricketts, his junior officer accepted and took a long sip himself, savoring it.

"Damn that's good," he said as he finally swallowed it.

"It was … General," Trip said.

"Sir?" the older man was caught off guard.

"I'm giving you a field promotion to Brigadier General," he said. "You did a hell of a job Dan," Trip said, extending his hand.

Ricketts shook his hand firmly; then performed a pristine salute. "Thank you sir."

"No Dan, thank you. We've got a long way to go with this war. Go tend to your troops and then get up to Abington."

As Ricketts left, Trip Reager felt the warmth in his chest from the bourbon as he turned once more to survey the city. *We saved Nashville, but the cost to Knoxville was heavy. I doubt the enemy is ready to toss in the towel just yet. Let's hope we don't have to blow up more cities to convince them of the error of their ways.*

CHAPTER 22

"Renaming something is the same as fixing something."

Vernon, The Republic of Texas

Kiff always thought of himself as a thinker, but now he was going to have to be a man of action. He had told Caylee to tell them who they were working for, blurting the words out in a quasi-panic. The young man holding the gun on *him* looked over at her while the man holding a gun on *her* seemed to start to turn and glance at Kiff.

Then all hell broke loose!

The first shot left him completely deaf, finishing the work of the breaching charge on the door. Kiff jammed his hand down on his holstered weapon, sweeping back his hoodie at the same time. As he began to draw, Caylee dropped low, no doubt to get her gun. The man in front of her fired, and he saw Caylee fly back into the nightstand, the lamp crashing down on the ugly green carpeting of the Budget Inn room.

Kiff wanted to cry out, but his body went to muscle memory as he drew his own Kimber 1911. The young man who was supposed to cover him was now fully distracted as Kiff brought his hands together, gripping the weapon tightly and raising it to eye level with the young man in his sights.

Kiff's mind was afire. Caylee was down, maybe dead, and he had no desire to be captive to whoever these guys were. He squeezed the trigger slowly, and the Kimber bucked in his hands. For a millisecond, he remembered his home in Virginia ... and thought back to a day he would never forget.

Five Years Earlier ...
Fairfax, Virginia

Kiff had run away from his office like he had never run before. He had no idea that men were pursuing him; it didn't matter. His manager, Joseph Eckhart, the Director of Cyber Security at the Department of Homeland Security, had sold him out. Kiff had bailed out of the office down a fire escape, and when he landed, he heard a commotion behind him. He never looked back to see if it was the FBI or simply some concerned citizen. ... He just ran.

It usually was a seven-or eight-minute walk to the metro station; he cleared it in two, though by the time he got there, he was winded and wet with sweat. It was only then that he dared turn around, only to see nothing. Fumbling, he pulled out his metro pass card, went through the turn style, then down to the platform.

A plan, ... I need a plan. Kiff lived with his mother in Fairfax. He would go home, pack up, take his car, and get away. They would be coming for him; he was sure of it. It wasn't that he had done something wrong; he was a target because he was a conservative, and the Ruling Council, or so they called themselves, apparently was apprehending anyone that might not support them. *It's Goddamn 1984! They are arresting people not for what they've done, but for what they might do. For what party they support.*

He rushed home, and his mother was surprised to see him so early. He told her there was a problem at work, and he had to leave for a few days. He didn't bother to fold his clothing; instead he stuffed it in a suitcase. He snagged two of his favorite laptops and assorted cables as well, stuffing his backpack to the brink. Under his collector's edition Dark Knight statue, he kept a stash of cash—the amount was $2,000—for emergencies or to take with him to Comic-Con for shopping.

Opening the top drawer of his dresser, he saw his grandfather's gun. When he was young, his father had taken him shooting several times. After his death, Kiff kept the weapon partly because the memories of his dad were linked to the weapon; partly because he needed a gun with the spike in crime. Almost unconsciously he took the gun and stuffed it into the top pouch of his backpack, along with two magazines. One was already in the gun ... just as his father had left it. "An empty gun is just a hunk of metal. If you are going to have one, keep it ready to use."

His mother was concerned, and he did what he could to reassure her with promises to call and told her that he would be back soon. He got into his older Toyota Camry and was about to start it when there was a rap on the passenger window. Looking up, he saw a man there, and one on the driver's side.

"Kiffin?" one asked, his voice muffled through the glass. "We're friends of Jack Desmond."

Jack? Jack was more than a co-worker; he was a true friend. He lowered the driver's side window and looked at the man there. He was older, probably the same age as his mother. Clearly this was not an FBI or DHS agent. To Kiff, the man looked more like a teacher or a librarian. "My name is Arthur Forrest, and this is David Check. Jack said he knew you were in danger. We sent folks to your office, but the FBI beat us there."

Kiff was at a loss for words, but Arthur continued. "They'll track your car. Come with us. We will make sure you get out of here okay."

Kiff trusted Jack Desmond, but he had heard that Jack was dead, or at least missing. During the fall of the White House, Jack had been stationed there. *If anyone could have gotten out of there, it would have been Jack.* Instantly he felt some relief and was thankful Desmond had survived. "Alright," he said, opening the door. Then as he rose, he looked at Arthur. "Jack's really alive?"

The man smiled, putting his hand on Kiff's shoulder. "I've never met him, but yes, he is. He's something of a coordinator for us. We help get people like you off the radar of these damned dictators."

David grabbed his suitcase, and Kiff took his knapsack. They left his driveway and went across the street to a blue Dodge. David put the suitcase in the trunk while Arthur turned to him. "We need to get you out of here. We have some safe houses in West Virginia and Tennessee."

Kiff opened the rear driver's side door and swung his backpack off of his shoulder when a voice hit them. "Hold it right there, Kiffin Renner. Agent Meuter, DHS. You need to come with me." He turned and saw the man standing some thirty feet away, weapon drawn, and aimed at him.

The older men raised their hands slightly and turned to face the threat. Kiff looked down and saw that the zipper was only half closed on the pouch of his backpack. In clear view was the handle of his father's pistol. His eyes darted to the gun, the door between them, and the man with a pistol aimed at him. *I could make a move for it—he would never know I have a gun in there.*

Agent Meuter took several calculated steps toward them, keeping his weapon trained on Kiff. "Alright, all three of you, keep your hands up and come around to the side of the car. You," he waved the gun at Kiff, "Close that door and turn around, hands on the roof."

Kiff was facing the car already, with Hampton Check at the passenger door. From his angle, he could see that the older man had a pistol in a holster hidden under his sweater. His eyes slowly went up from the weapon to Check's face. The older black man cracked a thin smile, then winked at him, slowly, deliberately.

Everything became a blur around Kiff. Check went for his gun, drawing it smoothly and sidestepping slightly. Agent Meuter, seeing his sudden movement, sidestepped toward the front of the Dodge while Arthur bent his knees, as if to duck.

The bangs of gunshot filled the air so rapidly that it was impossible for him to sort out who fired first and at whom. Hampton Check was hit; he spun and fell next to the sidewalk near the car. Kiff was holding his gun and aiming it at Agent Meuter.

The DHS agent sidestepped again, this time sweeping the gun on Kiff who held his own weapon in front of him. His father would have chided him for the sloppy grip he had, but it was in his hands, trembling. As he looked down the sights, he saw the Agent had a small spot of blood on his left bicep, apparently a light wound from Check's gun.

"Drop the weapon!" Meuter commanded. Check moaned, and Meuter swung the gun in his direction.

Kiff held his gun, the gun trembling from a mix of his fear and excitement. His finger was on the trigger. He knew he should pull it, that at this range, he was probably going to hit the man. Hesitation wrapped him in its icy blanket, and it was as if his muscles would not follow his own orders. It seemed that for long minutes he and the agent were squared off against each other, though he knew it was really a matter of seconds.

Shoot him! He wanted to, but somehow couldn't. At the same time, he couldn't simply lower the gun. Every muscle on his body was locked up.

Another bang went off from the far side of the car. *Check!* The DHS agent flew back, and a spray of blood squirted skyward from the base of his neck where he had been hit. His gun fired at the moment of impact, and Check dropped.

Kiff simply stood there with Arthur Forrest as the DHS agent's legs trembled, twitching, and the pool of blood began to form around him. He had never seen a dead man before, and had certainly never seen a murder. For a moment, he was paralyzed.

"Damn it!" Arthur said. He turned and saw Kiff with the gun still aimed at the space where the agent had been.

"I couldn't do it ..." Kiff said in a low whisper.

Arthur reached up slowly, wrapping his hand around the weapon, and lowered Kiff's arms. "Son, we need to get out of here ..." he said. Kiff numbly nodded as Arthur moved around the vehicle to check on Hampton. The memory of Arthur Forrest shaking his head sadly over Hampton Check came with an overburden of guilt for Kiff. *I caused that. ... This is my fault.*

Everything else from the rest of that journey was a jumble of images in his mind. Kiff didn't remember putting the pistol back in the backpack, nor what happened as they left his neighborhood. All that he could remember was that when he needed to fire his weapon, he couldn't.

Vernon, The Republic of Texas

The flood of memories of the day of his escape came like a tidal wave. Kiff had always felt shame for not firing, that his inaction had cost Hampton Check his life somehow. That hesitation haunted him. It came back at odd moments in his life, or in his nightmares.

Not this time ...

His right hand crossed his body and jabbed down to the weapon. They interlocked and he brought the gun up, aiming it right at the young man in front of him. It was so fast, so smooth, that he was amazed. His finger slid to the trigger and he squeezed.

The weapon kicked hard in his hands, his wrists throbbed from the recoil, but the shot hit somewhere on the right side of the younger man, sending him twisting hard in place then falling. A spray of blood hit the walls and ceiling as his target dropped.

Everything was muffled from the gunfire indoors. The man that had just shot Caylee, suddenly realized that Kiff was armed. The man swung toward him attempting to sidestep, but coming down awkwardly on the arm of his accomplice. There was a flash from his gun as Kiff turned his aim on the immediate threat and squeezed again. The bang was distorted by his popped ears, but Kiff saw the man's right arm jerk back as he also fired a shot while attempting to regain his footing.

Kiff fired again as the man moved, this time missing and hitting the front window of the room. The curtains tugged, and the glass shattered.

The man was in pain from the hit. Kiff could see that. Then he saw a blur rise from the floor, springing like a cobra.

Caylee!

The tunneling of her vision stopped as she gasped air into her panicked lungs. There was no time to look on the floor for her gun; she simply would have to disarm her attacker the old fashioned way. Pushing off, her ribs ached from the impact on the plates of her plate carrier. She lunged at the man who was now starting to turn his aim toward Kiff. She reached out and grabbed the gun extended in front of him. With a tight jerk, she pointed the gun up to the ceiling, and it barked in their hands.

Then, with a deliberate downward thrust, she drove the gun downward; the backstrap of the weapon dug deep into the soft skin between her attacker's thumb and forefinger. Pain in that spot was enough to make the heartiest fighter unable to hold the weapon. He had no control of the pistol as his fingers went off the trigger, and she jerked the gun free from his grip, stepped back, and gripped it for herself.

Her chest heaved another deep breath of air in as the man looked at her, then at Kiff for a moment; both had their weapons on him. He held his hands in the air and squatted low, a good defensive stance, someone trained in the martial arts. "You have no idea who you are fucking with!" he said, glaring at her. Even with her ears ringing, his words seemed crisp and clear.

Caylee eyed him carefully, drinking in every detail. *He's right about that.* She then dropped her aim and fired, hitting him in his ankle joint right below the shin. He fell forward, his hands reaching down for where she had fired. It wasn't a lethal blow, but it would dramatically negate him putting up any more resistance. He grabbed at the bedspread on the way down, exposing Booker Hickox and his partner who, in their drugged state, had not even stirred during the chaotic battle in their room.

"You're right, I don't know who I'm fucking with," she said, still fighting the ripples of pain that emanated from where the bullet had hit her blast plate. "But I will take pieces off of you one at a time until you tell me." What she got back was an agonized moan as the blood began to seep into the dull green carpet.

She turned to Kiff who was still holding his weapon in front of him. "Holster that," she said. "Change of plans. Grab his PC and bring it with us. Even in this dump, this much gunfire is going to draw a lot of unwanted attention."

The younger man lay on the floor face down and began to moan. Caylee didn't hesitate for a moment. She aimed at his head and fired. His head jerked slightly back on the impact and exploded in a splash of crimson that sprayed the walls just a few feet from Kiff.

Kiff nodded nervously, his hands trembling as he holstered his weapon. "So much for the security deposit on this room," he muttered; then he turned to the PCs and started gathering the weapons. He stuffed them into his backpack as she checked her injured enemy for more weapons, tossing a throwing knife she found onto the bed. Looking over at her, he gave a nod to her chest. "You going to be okay?"

Nodding quickly, she pulled out two zip ties. "It hurts like hell, but if it had gone through, I'd be dead by now."

She quickly zip-tied their would-be assailant's hands and raised him up into a chair. Her attacker's angle was so broken that his foot was turned hard to the left, far past where a human ankle could turn. *He may lose that foot before this is over.* He groaned in agony, and she cut part of the bedspread off and made it an ad hoc gag. "Understand this," she whispered in his ear as she tied it tight. "You so much as break wind at the wrong moment, and you will be dead."

The operation had not gone as planned at all. Rather than a covert data heist, it had been turned into a vicious gun battle. *The bottom line is we got the data; hell we got the entire PC.* A part of her was curious as to how the scene would look when police arrived. Signs of a gun battle, blood everywhere, a dead body, and two naked people in the bed who will rightfully claim they slept through the entire thing. *This will confuse investigators for days trying to piece it together, if ever.*

Kiff turned to her and saw the naked body of Booker Hickox and the 'woman' he was with, at first giving them a strange glance. "They slept through the entire thing."

"I gave them enough sedative that we could have done surgery on them, and they wouldn't have awakened," she replied, pulling out her iPhone and snapping a picture of Booker and his bed mate.

The wig the female had worn was slightly askew, and he could see that it wasn't a woman, not entirely. Kiff winced at the sight. "Aw geez," she heard him say as the ringing still dominated her ears.

Looking over at the bed, she saw Hickox with the transvestite. Caylee shrugged. "To each his own," she said, gathering up all of the weapons in the room as well as policing their spent brass. *There's no point in leaving any more evidence than we already have.*

"Yeah," Kiff said, "But *eww*. And you took a picture of it!"

"I assure you, that photo is one that will not play well with many Texans," she said with a brief smirk. Caylee wanted to massage her aching chest, but there wasn't time. "Help me with Mr. Limpalong here," she said. "We need to be far from here when the police show up."

Brattleboro, Vermont

Alongside of Su-Hui, two of his fighters had joined him, looking down over the railroad bed to where the police cars were, some 125 feet away. Both brought their M320 grenade launchers, loaded with 40mm grenades. Su-Hui looked at the two men, and was surprised that one of them was Tate Palmer, who had been recruited just a few weeks earlier. While he was younger than Su-Hui, he was massive in stature, and his uniform coat buttons were straining under his bulk.

"Do you have any experience with that?" he asked, nodding at the stubby black launcher.

"Yes sir," Tate replied with pride. "I've fired it a lot with practice rounds. I can shoot it up the ass of a running rooster at one hundred yards."

Su-Hui wanted to chuckle at the comment, but could not. "I do not need destroyed roosters. I *do* need those police cars destroyed before they can get a message out."

The pair leaned up over the railroad embankment and looked at their targets. "They're close," the other man said, a veteran who had joined the ranks of the SOL. "We should be able to direct fire right into them." Tate Palmer nodded in agreement.

"I don't care how many shots it takes, but I want them destroyed," he said firmly. "After that get to your vehicles, and we will go back into New Hampshire."

The men nodded, and both slid a 40mm round into the gun chambers and set their iron sights for the range. They crawled up on the embankment with Su-Hui off to their side to watch. "Say when." Tate said, aiming down the sights.

"Now."

Both weapons made a deep thunking noise as they fired their rounds almost in perfect unison. One hit the driver's side window of the car, shattering it. The other round slapped into the mud and snow right under the driver's side door, angled slightly under the vehicle. The explosions came immediately, both devouring the cars and their occupants. The one shot that went slightly under the car ,lifted that side some two feet into the air before dropping it. Flames gutted the compartment of the other vehicle.

The men reloaded and fired again. The passenger door of the vehicle that was tossed in the air flew open and an occupant seemed to be trying to crawl out, though it was hard for Su-Hui to see in the smoke and debris. The second round of explosions was equally savage—one threw the contents of the interior of the vehicle straight up, through the metal roof, raiding bits of a burning police car everywhere in the dirt-covered snow. The other vehicle once more rose up on the driver's side, then continued its arc over, coming down on the officer on the passenger side who seemed to be trying to get away. The car crunched down, and its gas tank simply burst into a blazing funeral pyre. The crackle of the fire was mixed with a rushing sound as the gasoline from the one fire sent black smoke twisting over the debris.

"That will do," Su-Hui said. "Let's get across the bridge and back home."

CHAPTER 23

"Hurt feelings are the same as physical abuse."

The District

The Newmerican Vice President sat behind her pristine desk as the interviewer began. The face that she offered the camera was one of grim resolve, well-rehearsed for the occasion. "This is a remarkable story Vice President. For our viewers, you were going to Tennessee?"

"Yes," she said, placing her hands on the desktop. "I was going to see General Rinehart to consult with him, lend him my perspective of the strategy. I thought my insights would be invaluable to him. Sadly, I was unable to reach him in time to avert the events that transpired." She liked that line the best; it made it sound like she could have reversed the defeat in Tennessee.

"Then what happened?"

"A force of enemy vehicles and infantry hit us in Abington, Virginia. They were shooting and blowing up anything that moved. Once we ... no *I* came under fire, I thought it best to have my driver get us out of there."

"So you came under direct fire from the enemy?"

"Oh yes," she said, shaking her head as if to try to remove the false memory. "Sniper fire hit my vehicle. Thank goodness it was armor-plated, or I wouldn't be here today."

"Incredible," the reporter said, shifting in her seat. "It sounds like you barely got out of there with your life."

"Sadly, that's true. I only wish I could have helped some of the

306

soldiers that were there. This was a cowardly attack by the enemy, striking at the rear of the enemy lines. It's a violation of the rules of warfare!"

The next question she knew all too well, since she had prepared it. "Let me ask you this. Do you think they were targeting you Madam Vice President?"

She knew the truth; she had never come under fire. But the truth needed help; it needed adjusting to fit the narrative. "I hate to think that, but it couldn't have been a coincidence that they hit Abington at exactly the same time I was passing through there. I mean … do the math. What are the odds of that being just a coincidence? We have already seen that this Pretender that calls himself 'President' in Nashville has sent assassins after me before. I have little problem doubting that he would do it again." She believed that it was important for people to see her as a target. One thing that the old Ruling Council had done brilliantly was to make victims seen as heroes. That was what she was doing, crafting herself, once more, as the victim … a hero of the cause, willing to lay down her life for the Newmerican dream. *People love a good tale of victimization. Whether it is true or not means so little to them.*

"You are incredibly brave," the reporter said with complete sincerity. The colleges were properly telling budding journalists for years that their role was to promote a progressive agenda, that anything that hurt conservatives was positive. For the last half decade, the reporter had been coming up the ranks in a media machine that was in support of the administration. The press was free as long as it said the right things and promoted the right causes. *Of course she thinks I'm brave. There is no other alternative for her. To say anything else would be the death blow to her career.*

"I don't think of myself that way," she said, lying perfectly for the lens of the cameras. "I am just like everyone else. I know our cause is just. We are close to obtaining true equity. With the exception of our enemies, we have purged ourselves of our past. Brave? No. I'm dedicated to fighting for our people though."

The reporter thanked her; then the lights went off and the camera shut down. "That was perfect," the reporter said. "Unless there's something you want to change."

"No," she said. "I will review it before it goes on the air though, just to make sure."

It took them five minutes to pack up and leave her office. Tess closed the doors to leave her alone to contemplate the recent events. *Daniel thought that Rinehart was the man that would lead us to victory. All he led us to was a body count. Now there's this shit up in New York. The Goddamn SOL destroyed a National Guard Headquarters. The fucking military thought they were going for Boston, but they walked right into New York State and killed almost eighty people and left a supposedly safe base in burning shambles.*

News from Illinois was sketchy. What was known was that the state's leadership had been kidnapped. *They lost their hold on Davenport, which is something that we need to find a way to twist into a positive. How in the hell did the enemy get a force into Illinois to begin with?*

General Rinehart would have to shoulder the blame on both accounts. Tess knew that Daniel would never accept responsibility for what had happened. Now southern Virginia was under enemy occupation. *Rinehart needs to lose his job or his life for this blunder.* She firmly believed that if he was killed, it would send a clear message to future generals. Don't fail.

We've lost ground, but so far we are still in this fight. We can't lose. Rinehart's Operation Iron Scorpion was a bust for us. We lost ground in Virginia.

Despite that, we are destined to be victorious. Even if they take back all of the territory, it will be impossible for them to undo our accomplishments. Newmerica is entrenched in the hearts and minds of its people, and that is something they can't take from them.

Nashville, Tennessee

Kiff was exhausted, both physically and mentally. They had gotten away from the Republic of Texas, though crossing the border had been harsh. Driving through an armed checkpoint with a gagged and wounded prisoner didn't seem to be a viable option. Instead the three of them waded across the Red River into Oklahoma. The water had been frigid … it had taken a day before his legs felt warm again. Their captive made progress slow as well. *I'm sure soaking that injured ankle wound in the dirty water of the river isn't going to help the healing process.*

They had caught a flight back to Nashville, and from the moment he landed, Kiff had been working on the data he had gotten. In the semi-darkness of his office, he ran countless programs to shatter the encryption of the emails and to run traces on where the data had traveled. At one point, a member of his team had entered and suggested he get a shower. He did it, all the while mentally going over everything he had to do.

Jack Desmond had been by twice, both times suggesting that Kiff get some sleep. He did take short naps in his office, especially when he knew a certain routine was going to take a long time. They weren't the kind of sleep his body craved, but that didn't stop him. *After all that I've been through, I need to see this thing to the end.*

As he returned to his office, he took a moment to lean back in his seat and rub his eyes while several of his programs ran on both the mirror drive, and on Booker Hickox's laptop. The growth of stubble on his face was annoying, but he moved past it. *Who knows. I might look good with a beard.*

There had been no news about Booker Hickox being found in a hotel room with a person identifying as a woman, blood everywhere, and a dead body. Caylee pointed out that those kinds of stories were often swept neatly under the rug rather than exposed. This was not something that was going to stay a secret forever … *how could it? How would he even begin to explain all of that?* Kiffen had allowed himself to chuckle over that thought for some time.

A part of Kiff Renner felt oddly calm as he sat there. It was as if a weight had been lifted off of him. At first, he thought it was the exhaustion that tore at him. Despite the Monster energy drinks, he felt like he was in a haze. He knew it wasn't the exhaustion. The memories of the death of Hampton Check had been tucked away in a dark corner of his mind. His escape from Washington DC and Virginia were memories he didn't want to visit. The Sons of Liberty, the original ones, had saved him, and others too. Hampton Check gave his life for his freedom, all because he had hesitated.

That shame felt lifted somehow. When it mattered, when Caylee was threatened, he had not hesitated. The squeezing of that trigger had changed Kiff; he knew it deep down inside. The guilt that he had felt nagging in the back of his mind was forever gone. Redemption filled the emotional gap that he didn't even know he had.

The application he was running chirped ... a sign that it had finished its work. *Let's see what we can see.* Using every bit of his skills, he began to unravel the finances of the Republic of Texas.

Carroll, New Hampshire

Su-Hui's small caravan of Humvees slowly rolled into the Patio Motor Court, belching black clouds of exhaust as it screeched to a halt. It was just before sunset and as he climbed out, he looked west and saw the brilliant pink clouds streaked with dark blue. There was a measure of beauty to America that he never failed to absorb, one that most Americans took for granted. As he stood looking out at it, he allowed himself to relax for the first time in days.

The radio news he had been listening to was finally starting to admit that an attack had taken place at the New York National Guard Headquarters. He had gotten used to the Truth Reconciliation Committee's spin on events. His harasser force had been called, "A group of right wing extremists, and domestic terrorists." Their attack had been labeled 'cowardly' and 'unwarranted.' *They couldn't hide what we did, so they fell on the old trope of calling us war criminals.*

The Governor of New York was demanding justice, offering a million-dollar reward for their capture. At the same time, he was recalling most of his National Guard out of New Hampshire to protect the borders in his own state. *Apparently our showing up just outside the capital of New York was enough to scare him.* Su-Hui didn't care about the name calling or the posturing. What mattered is that the Newmerican forces in New Hampshire were going to be reduced as a result of their raid.

He saw Hatchi as she rushed out from one of the rooms and hugged him. "I'm so glad to see you," she said right before they kissed. She looked him over as she did since he had been wounded, to make sure he was all in one piece. "You have caused quite a stir. I thought you were going to Connecticut."

"A change of plans," he conceded. "They were waiting in ambush for us there."

"No matter," Hachi said. "You are back now. We are preparing a meal for you all. You must be famished."

Su-Hui nodded, unable to find words to put into a coherent sentence. Hachi seemed to understand. "Go get cleaned up. You smell horrible. Put those clothes in the wash bag, not on the floor."

The leader of the SOL Defiance in New Hampshire nodded obediently. On the field of battle, he was in command. At home, his wife was clearly in charge. As other family members came out and hugged their loved ones, he spread the word to get the Humvees behind the motel where they would not be seen.

They had a group dinner in one of the Patio Court meeting rooms. He devoured the wild turkey that had been part of the meal. Someone had broken out bottles of whiskey and passed them around. The television was on but almost muted. People were laughing, smiling, telling the others about their exploits in the raid. He spied Colin Palmer talking to his father, Tate, about blowing up the police cruisers; his wild hand gestures were easy to interpret from across the room.

"Su-Hui," called out Trudy who was near the television. "You're going to want to see this."

The image said that it was live from the front of the State House in Concord. The bright red banner said, "Traitors to be executed."

As he stared at the images, he saw Herb Fletcher and two of his cronies, hands bound, lined up on the exterior of the wall. A General of the Newmerican force was reading something, but by the time the volume was turned up, he had finished.

Seeing Herb there, he could make out the bruises on his face. *They tortured him. You can see where they have covered up some of his cuts with makeup, but you can still see the swelling. I suspected he was the one that told them where we were going to attack.*

A firing squad moved out in front of them and performed their duties with deadly precision. Blood splattered the exterior wall of the State House as the men fell backward. For a moment, Sui-Hui stared at the image, unsure what he was supposed to feel. While Herb had been an irritant, he was also a member of the Sons of Liberty. It was clear he tried to resist. *Was he a traitor, and if so, to whom? Himself?*

Turning slowly he saw that the entire room was silent; everyone was looking at the same image he had seen. The joy and mirth were sucked out of the room, leaving a vacuum of shame and sadness.

Reaching over, Su-Hui shut the television off. Turning to his people, he felt every eye focus on him. It was staggering, but he rose to his full height and looked at them. "We will mourn for those lost. Our cause was their cause, even if they didn't agree with how we're prosecuting this war. They were killed like lambs led to slaughter. They had no justice, merely vengeance.

"This war is far from over," he said taking a long breath to gather his thoughts. "We have earned our right to celebrate. We achieved a great victory. We have taken this war to our enemies' homeland. What we did will save lives here.

"But as we all saw, we have also lost people." He paused, remembering the bitterness when he had expelled Herb from their group. *He did not deserve respect in life, but his death must be honored.* "To those lost, let us bow our heads in a moment of silence to honor them." For Su-Hui, it was one of the longest minutes of his life. He wanted to think about the future, when New Hampshire and all of America might be free—but instead his mind went to his family. *We must all come through this ... the sooner, the better.*

Nashville, Tennessee

It had taken three days for Judy Mercury to start to feel normal again. They had made it across the Ohio River into Kentucky, but the entire operation had come at a cost. Four dead, another six wounded. It made her morose every time she thought about them. Each time Judy found herself momentarily questioning her decisions, wondering if she should have done something different. A part of her wanted to bring the dead back somehow, by at least learning something.

Each time such thoughts came to her, she ended up back in the same place. She wouldn't have done anything differently. This is war, and in war, soldiers die. It was a mathematical reality. For millennia commanders had been trying to fudge the math, to fight war with no losses, but it was a fantasy.

Her prisoners, the Governor and the Lieutenant Governor had been angry, bitter, and in the case of the Lieutenant Governor, filthy. She had shit herself when the bullets started flying on the run toward the river and had to be hosed off when they finally got to safety. They had been formally placed under arrest, complaining every moment of the reading of their rights as they were transferred to civilian authorities. When the Governor demanded to know the charges, they were flatly told, "Treason and Sedition." Hearing those two words seemed to take the wind out of his lungs, and both of them went quiet after that.

After showering and getting a fresh uniform, she enjoyed a meal with her Grab Asses. They were joking, horsing around, enjoying themselves as only warriors can. She offered a toast to them from the beer that the Kentucky National Guard had provided. "Twenty years from now, when you are telling your grandkids about this, they are bound to ask, 'What's a grab ass?' And you will be able to look them in the eye and tell them that it was the best, most cunning, most daring group of men and women you ever had the honor to serve!"

She had been ordered down to Nashville to make a full report and sat in the military command center that had at one time been the AT&T building downtown. Colonel Lance Meade entered the room and she rose and went to full attention. "At ease Captain," he said, taking a seat. She sat at the corner of the conference room table so they were next to each other, just not facing.

"That was one hell of ride you took," the Colonel said, not bothering to hide his grin of satisfaction. "Those traitors in Newmerica are still trying to figure out what happened to them."

"It had the virtue of never having been tried in decades," she said.

"It worked, and that's what matters. Once you hit Springfield, they had to fall back—and did. It cost them a lot of their force, breaking off like that. Davenport is back in our hands. Once we launch our own offensive, there isn't much south of Chicago that can stop us. Between that fight in Chicago, during the election and this incursion of theirs, the Illinois National Guard is beat up—and you took out their HQ, so rebuilding is going to be even more difficult. Damn fine job!"

She felt her face redden with the compliment. "Thank you sir. I had good men and women under me."

"I'm sure the media is going to want to eat up a lot of your time. I just wanted to congratulate you in private. And I wanted to give you this," he said holding out a patch. It was a red triangle set on one narrow point with a yellow bird rising upward in the middle of it … the unit insignia of the troops she had led, the 45th Infantry Brigade Combat Team, The Thunderbirds. She took it in her hands and clutched it tight for a moment.

"Our Governor has signed an executive order stating you are an honorary citizen of our fine state. General Moorehouse has officially put your name in our unit, assuming you are not attached elsewhere. You will always have a home in Oklahoma."

Home ... just the mention of it struck her for a second. Since the Fall, the military had been her home. She was a Texan, born and raised, and that was where her heart belonged, but it was a wonderful gesture on the part of the 45th and the Governor. "Thank you sir," she managed as she regained her composure. "When this is all over, I think I'll spend some time there. Right now I live wherever my gear is stowed. It's good to know I have options."

"We would be better people having you as our neighbor," he said. Of all of the decorations and promotions she had ever received, this simple gesture meant the most to Judy.

EPILOGUE

"People individually can be ignorant and foolish, but the government is always smart and insightful."

Caylee stood with Jack Desmond as Kiff went over the information that he recovered. His presentation was good, though at times far too detailed for her taste. Jack stood stoically, his arms crossed, soaking it all in.

She had been working, but was back at home with Raul and Maria. There had been a small party when she returned, one she had invited Kiff to. He and Andy seemed to bond quickly. Her days had been filled with several interrogation sessions with the prisoner that she had brought back and a lot of checking into his past.

"So that's it then?" he finally asked as Kiff finished his PowerPoint slides. "The Chinese and the Newmericans are financially and militarily propping up the Republic of Texas."

"Yes," Kiff said, leaning back in his chair and closing the laptop. "This guy in Michigan, Dr. Weber Liu, is the front man for the Chinese on this. He's even gone so far as to deliver them military hardware, apparently smuggled in from Canada."

Jack said nothing for the moment, then allowed a smile to form on his rigid face. "This will throw the Republic into chaos when we release it. Texans all secretly yearn for independence, but not by being propped up by our enemies. I almost feel sorry for Marshall and Hickox."

Kiff looked over at Caylee. "Did you show him the picture?"

She nodded a response.

"And what about your prisoner?" Jack asked.

"We were able to identify him as John Moshu Quang. First generation citizen; no doubt he's a Chinese operative from the digging we have done. His rap sheet is short—arrested a few times, but he's never gone to trial—the witnesses either withdraw the charges or disappear. His lifestyle seems to be above what he could earn, which is an indication of serious funding. He's not real talkative, but that is to be expected. What little I have gathered from my feelers is that he is some of this Liu's hired muscle."

"What were they doing there?" Jack asked.

"He won't say," she assured him. "The other one was not a pro though, at least not in my arena. The way they came in wasn't entirely well planned, which means it was impromptu and a little sloppy."

Jack paused for a moment in deep thought. "Kiff, I'm taking you to the President. He's going to want to see this and determine what parts, if any, we make public. My gut tells me that he'll want it out ASAP. If nothing else, it might help quell this whole Republic of Texas bullshit, at least for the time being."

Kiff nodded. "Sure. I've never presented to the President before." She could tell that he was nervous.

"You'll be fine," Jack assured him. He then turned to Caylee. "Was I right? Did he do good?"

She unleashed a rare smile, glancing over at Kiff who seemed to lean in to hear the answer she was going to give. "He's a lovable scamp," she said, which made Jack pause, then chuckle for a moment. "In a pinch, he's top notch. Truth be told, he saved my life back in Texas."

Jack turned to him. "You saved *her* life?"

Kiff shrugged, and his face reddened. "She may be exaggerating. Let's just say I had a good teacher and did what I had to do."

Jack shook his head. "Will wonders never cease? Alright Kiff, be reading in an hour. I'm going to walk you in. Come down to my office then." Jack Desmond walked out leaving Caylee alone with Kiff.

"'Loveable scamp?'" he asked with a smile.

"Everyone says I am too serious. Now and then I like to shake things up. You did real good out there," she said firmly. "I owe you one."

"Let's hope I don't ever have to collect," Kiff replied.

Caylee started for the door, then stopped, reaching into her bag. She pulled out the plastic package and tossed it over the conference table to

Kiff, who caught it. "Twizzlers!" he said, grinning broadly.

"Good luck with the President," she replied, walking out of the room. As she went down the hall, she marveled at how her world had changed. As an operative, she had been a loner—out of necessity. Now she had a place she could call home, at least for now. And her circle of colleagues ... no, *friends*, was growing.

As she entered the elevator, she drew a long breath. For the time being, she had time on her hands—and people to spend it with. It was a strange sense of family, one she openly embraced.

Nashville, Tennessee

General Trip Reager rose to his feet from behind his temporary desk as Captain Judy Mercury entered the room. She stood at attention, and he immediately told her, "At ease," gesturing to the chair opposite of him. Seeing Judy again was somehow assuring to Trip. The battle of wits with his enemy and the vicious fighting in Knoxville had made him weary. His first twenty-four hours back in Nashville had been a complete collapse. When he woke up, he was stunned to find out that an entire day passed. His sleep had been so deep that he hadn't moved. Just rolling over in the hotel bed made every joint protest and ache.

The mopping up of the Newmerican assault force had taken two days. Only when he was assured that the front had been stabilized did he dare risk leaving it to return to Nashville to report to the President in person. The result was he had been promoted again, up to O-8, Major General. Trip didn't protest this time when the President pinned the new star on his lapel. ... The fighting in Georgia and Knoxville made him feel as if he earned it.

"So," he said, settling down into his seat. "This is the officer that saved Davenport. I'm sure your former CO would be proud."

She cocked her head and grinned. "I hope you are sir. For the record, I didn't save Davenport. I simply gave the Illinois troops a good reason to leave."

"That was a brilliant bit of wild-ass cavalry soldiering you pulled off—sneaking through their lines, taking out their HQ, kidnapping the Governor. Nice touch by the way."

"My troops deserve the credit, along with a lot of others like

Lieutenant Colonel Mihalek. I was just the creative side of this equation."

"You're too modest Judy," he said, leaning back slightly. "They are prepping a bunch of interviews for you and your Grab Asses. You have a lot of the enemy wondering just how safe they really are. Even now, states are shifting their forces to reinforce their borders because they don't want the same thing that happened in Springfield to happen to them."

"From the sound of it, you had your hands full too sir," she said. "Word is that the fighting was pretty brutal."

Trip nodded. "It's going to be a long time before Knoxville is a tourist destination again." Memories of the destroyed convention center and the dead bodies on the World's Fair Park were going to haunt him for some time.

"So," she said with a sigh. "What's next for me?"

Trip admired that about Judy, her ability to constantly move forward. *That's why I chose her for her last operation—that determination.* "The President and I spoke about you and after your little media circus he's going to want to get a photo op with you. Should be in a week or two."

Her eyebrows went up a little at that news. "Look at me, rubbing elbows with the President," she said in a cocky tone.

"He'll be presenting the Medal of Honor to you Judy."

For a moment, her face fell, as if every muscle in it had suddenly disappeared. Judy's mouth was open. "You're kidding, right?"

"It's got to be approved by Congress, but he expects no issues. Despite having a common enemy, they are still doing what politicians do, squabbling with each other. This is probably one of the few things they can get onboard with."

"I'm—I don't know what to say." Trip looked at her and realized that it was a first, … the first time she was stunned into silence. He savored that moment.

"You have earned it," he replied, letting the moment hang between them for a few minutes. "After that—back to Texas to prepare for the next offensive."

"Am I going against the Republic of Texas folks?" she said with a hint of trepidation. Both of them were from Texas, and he understood her hesitancy about moving against fellow Texans, even rebellious ones.

"No," he said firmly. "The President and Chief of Staff both told me yesterday that they believe that can be resolved without the use of force. No, I need you in Texas because I have another mission in mind—something further west."

"So," she said with a grin. "Am I going to get some beach time on the West Coast?"

Trip returned the smile. "That might very well be the case. But, if I remember properly, you liked skiing more than the sun."

Ann Arbor, Michigan

Dr. Weber Liu watched the television screen in his house alone. His mouth was agape at what he heard and what images came on the screen as the American President spoke. Each word felt like a knife being plunged into his body. *How could this have happened?*

"As the emails and documentation that we are releasing to you now shows, the so-called Republic of Texas has been funded and armed by enemies of America abroad and domestic. Not only did the rebellious Newmericans provide them arms and funds, the Chinese government did the same. Their alleged bid for freedom was bought and paid for by our foes. They care nothing for Texas; this was just a bid to undermine America. We even managed to capture one of their agents who has been a wealth of information."

He now understood why he had not heard from Quang or Taylor. *One of them has been captured? Quang would never talk, but Taylor is untrained in such matters. There's still a chance for me to recover. We will refute these claims.* He was hot with nervousness, his usual shell of calm had been shattered by the news conference.

The President continued. "As a result of our investigation, we have learned that networks of Chinese agents are operating in Newmerica and our territory as well. The one responsible for this interference in our domestic affairs was run out of Michigan by one Dr. Weber Liu. While he resides in territory claimed by the Newmerican government, I have still issued arrest warrants for him. There will be no place where spies and saboteurs will be tolerated. If the Newmericans do not move to arrest him as well, we can only assume that they too were supportive of foreign interference and have allied with China in this effort. As such, our new ambassador to the People's Republic is delivering a list of sanctions for their interference in our internal affairs.

"To the good people of Texas, and those in this sham Republic, I call on you to put an end to this farce. I withheld the use of military force because we are all Americans. The people that seized these counties have done so under false pretenses. I look to you to end this and turn over Salem Marshall and Booker Hickox to the proper authorities on charges of sedition and treason."

Liu slumped in his seat as beads of sweat ran down his forehead. His hopes that this entire failure could be swept under the rug were over, washed away with his now public exposure. Panic, pure and sweet, devoured him, leaving him paralyzed as he watched the rest of the news broadcast.

There was a temptation to flee, to run and hide, but he knew that would be futile. Worse yet, it lacked honor. *My people would find me, and the punishment would be far worse for running.* He knew that the Newmericans would not respond quickly—their hands were caught in the cookie jar as well. America might send someone to try to apprehend him, but it was doubtful that would be swift.

Everything that I have built is now at risk. All of the people I have associated with are endangered because of me. Shutting off the television, he returned to his spot in his favorite chair. Liu balled his fists tightly, to the point that his arms were shaking. In that moment, he thought back to his youth, back to China ...

Twenty-two years earlier ...
Huangyan District, Taizhou, Zhejiang, China

As he sat in terror, looking at the People's Armed Police officers, looming over him, he knew they would not leave without the name of the person who had sold the illegal book. The problem was that Jianyu Liu truly did not know. He had assumed that the Hsiungs were honest people, running a tiny bookstore.

Fen, another student employee, glanced nervously down the line as the summoned the courage to protest his innocence. "I had nothing to do with any illicit book," he said. "Whoever did, you need to confess what you did!" he demanded of the other employees lined up in front of the PAP officers. His demand that the guilty party confess did not yield a response.

"That is enough," the PAP officer said. "Take them away. A few weeks of isolation will jar their memories. In the meantime, toss this place."

An officer grabbed him hard, yanking him hard. He felt panic, pure and simple. Stories of what happened in PAP custody were the stuff of legend in China. Torture, starvation, mutilation—all for something he had no involvement in. *My family will be shamed for this; they too could be targets ... all because someone here sold a book that was illegal. This isn't fair!*

His mind swung quickly to a way out of his predicament. *If they have a name, they may let the rest of us go!* "Wait!" he called. "If anyone here sold such a book, it would have been Fen! The Hsiungs are good people, but Fen is the only one that might have done so!" He chose his words carefully. He did not want to say that Fen did it because that would implicate him for not turning in his coworker. All he did was shine the light of the investigation on the most likely person.

Fen was shocked; betrayal washed over him, and he reeled, twisting hard to get away. His jerking bought him a few moments of freedom from the officer that was holding him, and he sprinted to the door. Two officers pounced on him; their clubs came out, beating him viciously. Fen dropped and tried to curl into a fetal position, but the blows rained down on him, along with some booted kicks. In a second, he seemed to collapse as blood splatter rose from his prostrate body. Ju Hsiung, wife of the owner, wept and averted her eyes.

For all Jianyu knew, Fen was dead on the floor; he could not see any sign of him breathing. *He should not have run. His attempt to flee only confirmed his guilt.*

"Take him away," the officer in charge said. Then he turned to Jianyu Liu. "You have behaved correctly, pointing out his potential disloyalty."

The words hit Jianyu hard. *Potential disloyalty? There never was a book sold illegally at the bookstore! They were simply looking for people that might not be loyal to the nation!* The officer patted him on the shoulder, almost father-like, giving him a nod of approval.

In that moment, he understood the nation he lived in better than he could ever hope. *I will find a way to rise high enough that I will not be a potential target ever again. It is better to be loyal than dead.*

Ann Arbor, Michigan

Weber Liu finally rose from the chair almost an hour after the broadcast. He put on his best suit coat, carefully dusting the hint of dandruff off of the dark gray coat. In silence, he assembled his computers and the encrypted CDs, putting them on a table near the door. Liu was filled with a deep resolve, one he could not shake. He did not fear the Americans. They had rules they played by, and their reach in Michigan was limited at best. Even the Newmericans, who were far closer to the practices of his own government, still had rules they followed. They would not move against him out of fear of what he might expose about their own activities.

I have only my honor.

There was a hard knock at the door. With grim resolve, he gathered himself, and opened it. Standing there were three individuals. Two large men and Lori Lemon—CNN commentator and long-time Chinese spy ring leader. *They have honored me by sending her to handle me.* Some of his other peers might savor the moment, rub his nose in his failure like some dog that had pissed on the floor. Lori would not do so, or so he hoped.

He bowed to them, and gestured for them to enter. "I have prepared all of my material. It is on that table."

Lori nodded and one of the men moved to scoop up everything in his massive muscular arms that were visible under the sleeves of his own suitcoat, bulges that betrayed his strength. She looked at him for a long moment, their eyes locking. "I thank you for not making this a confrontation," she said.

"I know my place and my duty," he replied. "I am a loyal son of China."

She gestured to the door, and he walked out in the cold night air, followed by one of the hulking men she had brought with her. He knew there would be a high price for such a public failure. His people did not tolerate the bright lights of public scrutiny well. At the same time, Weber Liu knew he would face whatever punishment awaited him with dignity. It was what was expected.

College Park, Maryland

David Steele, now David Adair, walked across the campus, drinking in every detail. Unlike the University of Virginia, the University of Maryland Campus had stronger security in place. Entrance to student buildings had been tricky at first. His father had stolen a student ID card to remove the magnetic strip and attach it to a fake card so that he could move about freely.

His father had gotten them an apartment about a mile from campus. It was a dump. They had already filled two roach traps, but it was perfect for their needs. It gave him a place to live that provided access to a new campus and fresh hunting grounds.

Some piles of snow were visible, but they were waning as the days got warmer. Winter was coming to an end. Situated just outside of The District, David found the campus to be smaller, more intimate than UVA. The signs of divisiveness were ever present. In the middle of campus, in front of Trigg Hall, a twisted and half-melted statue had been erected. At one point it had been a statue of Abraham Lincoln that had been taken from some other park and mutilated into the current monument. The brass plaque in front of it was labeled, "Death of the Great Lies."

As he crossed the campus that day, he stopped and looked at it. *How could they view Abraham Lincoln as an enemy ... a target? He freed the slaves.* David knew that he had to hide any expression of disgust as he looked at the visage of the former president.

A female voice spoke up at his side. "Pretty neat monument, right?"

David turned to her. "Yeah," he said looking at the shorter student. She had brilliant blue eyes and short blonde hair. "Where did they get it?"

"Someplace down south I heard," she said. "I heard they were going to send it to the Graveyard, but the students raised money to get it sent here. It's a monument to those that have died in the protests for our country."

"I'm new here," he said, extending his hand. "David—David Adair."

"Allie Nelson," she replied. "Where are you from?"

He shrugged. "My family moves around a lot. We've been all over."

"Well, if you need someone to show you around campus, let me know."

David smiled. "Allie, that would be great!"

As she took him on a tour of the campus, he knew that this place would be easier to operate in than the University of Virginia. The student banners calling for the death of the 'Pretender President' told him that these students were even more fanatical than the ones he had dealt with before. Everywhere he looked, he saw potential targets and opportunities.

It won't bring you back Maddie—but it will make your death stand for something ...

A SNEAK PEEK AT THE NEXT BLUE DAWN NOVEL— PATRONS OF TERROR

Five Years Earlier ...
San Francisco, California

Darius Thorne had come to California for the weather. After his three tours in the Army, serving in Iraq, all he wanted to do was kick back, find a good job, and enjoy life. He had earned it, at least in his mind.

At first it seemed like things were going his way. He and two veteran buddies opened a coffee shop in a good suburb of San Francisco called Hayes Valley. They could have opened a ritzy place, but they opted for something that the everyday worker could afford. All Jacked Up Coffee had an industrial feel to it, a lot of steel furniture and live edge wood tables ... classy, but utilitarian. The transition from a military mindset to that of a businessman was a struggle at first, but he managed to wrap his head around it. For the first few years, things had been working out well. Darius and his partners were making a good income. There was even talk of opening a second location. Like he told his sister, "This is what the American dream is all about."

The riots during the summer of 2020 had been a trying time for their startup. Several nights Darius had taken watch over his business in case things got out of hand. "Activists," or at least that was what they called themselves, were more prevalent in the neighborhood. They were peaceful, at first ... little protest marches on the streets with a myriad of signs for their various causes. It seemed innocent enough at first. Then their numbers grew, and the cries for social justice seemed to be louder.

Then they began to block the entrance to his business. His partner, John, asked them nicely to move on. He was greeted with the middle finger. John had been in the service two tours longer than Darius. The thought that some young punk kids would simply flip him off was unacceptable. They called the police, but when San Francisco's finest showed up, albeit two hours later, they proceeded to tell them they couldn't do anything about it. When they left, the protesters outside continued to mock them, throwing garbage at their front window and door, screaming obscenities. The fact that the police had walked away only seemed to embolden the protesters. They marched on, looting and damaging other businesses along the street.

Now, though, things were different. The news was flooded with images of what had gone down in Washington DC earlier in the night. Parts of the city were in flames ... federal buildings were 'occupied' by protestors. The images of the White House ablaze tore at him, as did the images of the American flag being stomped on by the armed insurrectionists, who the media were already referring to as, 'The Liberators.' *This is no damned liberation; it's an overthrow.* Darius had expected that kind of shit in Iraq, but never in his own country. *This is something far more sinister. There's an agenda at play here.*

Outside of his own business, he watched as the black bloc and masked children began to show up. Some carried clubs; others carried guns. Darius watched as one angry protester, twenty-something walked by, his finger on the trigger, waving his gun about. *No goddamn discipline,* ... Darius knew that this was going to lead to trouble.

There were a lot of problems in America. As a veteran, he had more than earned his right to have a list of bitchable items he wanted changed. *These punk ass white kids haven't suffered a day in their lives. They haven't put their lives on the line for anything of merit.* He didn't like the man in the White House, but to burn the building down, ... well, that was just damned un-American. The riots were unfolding in a number of cities now that Washington had been taken ... including San Francisco. In the pit of his stomach, he knew what was coming and dreaded it.

Darius shut off the television behind the counter of the closed coffee shop. Then he armed himself with a baseball bat. John, one of his partners, pulled his Glock G21 and chambered a round. Darius didn't protest. John had been an Army Ranger and had a knack for spotting trouble before it happened. His other partner, William, was a former gang-banger that joined the Army and straightened out his life. He held a shotgun at the ready. The three of them looked at each other and said nothing for a long moment. The commotion outside was growing, and all of them knew that there was a chance that things might go south. *I didn't fight in that forsaken hell-hole to come here and have a bunch of punk-ass kids trash my business.* To Darius and his partners, All Jacked Up was more than an investment—it was their lives. Their little coffee shop was a symbol of freedom, built by vets and supported by former brothers and sisters in arms.

The size of the crowd outside continued to grow, and their disorganized and often competing chants were demands that were simply the noise of a lot of people yelling seemingly random words and sounds. Darius took a position behind the bar, with his partners on each flank. They had moved the tables and chairs away from the windows out of fear they would be destroyed if the rioters rushed inside. Laying them on their sides formed a protective barrier that might slow anyone trying to get in to do further damage. As he looked at the barricade, he realized that he was still in the Army in his mind. *I'm still preparing for battle.*

For a few minutes, it looked like the crowd of angry rioters might thin—that they had lost steam or had moved up or down the block. *Maybe this will blow over.* His sense of relief was shattered at the same moment that a hurled brick slammed into the front window of All Jacked Up. The crack and cascade of the glass falling down like deadly guillotines, tinkled everywhere on the floor. It was followed by another object that broke the door window, and then the crowd surged in.

The black-clad rioters spilled in the holes, angry and vicious. They eyed the three veterans, guns in hand, and for a moment, there was a weird standoff of sorts. John, raised his gun toward the ceiling and fired, probably hoping that the shot would frighten off the vandals. The boom made Darius's ears ring with pain as a few of the rioters turned and ran out. Others looked at them as if they were a pack of hungry hyenas. There was a rush toward the overturned tables; then came the shots— fired wildly at the bar where the men stood their ground.

One woman stepped forward, waving a .357 revolver that was so big in her hands it wobbled in the air as she tried to aim at the rioters. Her face, what little he could see of it over her mask, was filled with rage. He could even see the outline of a big smile on her face as she fumbled with the weapon.

John leveled his aim slowly at her. Darius opened his mouth to call to him not to fire, but it was too late. His gun barked loudly, popping Darius's left ear. The woman was hit in the throat, thrown back, as the bullet sped through her soft tissue and into another rioter behind her. She dropped on her back, blood squirting in fast pulses upward as the crowd surged back through the opening of the window, their feet crunching and grinding the shattered glass as they fled. One young Asian kid bent down and scooped up her gun, fleeing with the others. Three of the protesters grabbed the young man that had been hit, pulling him into the street, leaving a smear of crimson on the black and white tiles of the floor.

Damn! He instantly wished that John hadn't fired that shot. The woman tremored on the floor as her life fled her. William vaulted over the counter, then the barricade of tables, kneeling in her blood and trying to treat her wound. Darius knew it was a lost cause.

After a few moments, William looked up; the ebony skin of his hands were slick with her blood. "She's dead," he announced.

Darius could see that the crowd was moving on outside, heading up Laguna Street. Even with his ears ringing and popping, he could hear the sounds of glass breaking at other businesses. He looked down at William, then the dead woman, then back to John. "Call the police. We need to report this."

John nodded, putting his weapon on the counter and pulling out his iPhone. Darius pinched his nose and blew, managing to pop his left ear, though the ringing was still persistent. *This is bad ... real bad. William and I are black, and John is white. That might be the only thing that helps him when the police arrive.* Glancing around the battered coffee shop, he wondered what would happen to it if they were arrested. *I put my whole life into this place, and because of some idiot woman waving a gun at us, we might lose it all.* Dread and the fear of the unknown chewed at his thoughts as he waited for the police to arrive.

www.ingramcontent.com/pod-product-compliance
Lightning Source LLC
Chambersburg PA
CBHW011341010726
47493CB00009B/2903